BEIGNETS, BRIDES AND BODIES

BEIGNETS, BRIDES AND BODIES

J.R. Ripley

This first world edition published 2016
in Great Britain and the USA by
SEVERN HOUSE PUBLISHERS LTD of
19 Cedar Road, Sutton, Surrey, England, SM2 5DA.
Trade paperback edition first published
in Great Britain and the USA 2016 by
SEVERN HOUSE PUBLISHERS LTD

Copyright © 2016 by J R Ripley.

British Library Cataloguing in Publication Data
A CIP catalogue record for this title is available from the British Library.

ISBN-13: 978-0-7278-8644-6 (cased)
ISBN-13: 978-1-84751-745-6 (trade paper)
ISBN-13: 978-1-78010-810-0 (e-book)

All Severn House titles are printed on acid-free paper.

Severn House Publishers support the Forest Stewardship Council™ [FSC™],
the leading international forest certification organisation.
All our titles that are printed on FSC certified paper carry the FSC logo.

MIX
Paper from
responsible sources
FSC FSC® C013056
www.fsc.org

Typeset by Palimpsest Book Production Ltd.,
Falkirk, Stirlingshire, Scotland.
Printed and bound in Great Britain by
TJ International, Padstow, Cornwall.

ONE

'Welcome to Maggie's Beignet Café.' I swiped back a strand of hair falling from the confines of my visor and smiled. 'What can I get you?' I recognized the athletic-looking young man as one of the paramedics who worked for the town. 'Keith, right?'

He beamed. 'Yep.' He had big teeth and broad shoulders.

Aubrey, my assistant, came through the swinging doors from the back storeroom lugging a ten-pound bag of barley flour. I make my beignets with a special blend of barley and all-purpose flour.

'Here you go, Maggie.' Aubrey and I wore identical periwinkle polo shirts and beechwood cargo shorts. We were practically twins, except she was younger and prettier, and blonder. I've never checked with a ruler but I was pretty sure her teeth were straighter, too.

Our uniforms had been her idea and her creation. She'd sketched out the logo and a local embroidery firm had made the patches that she'd then sewn onto our shirts and visors. She was pushing me to start selling Maggie's Beignet Café T-shirts to the customers but I was still concentrating on selling folks my own brand of New Orleans-style beignets.

I was experimenting in my free time on a chocolate dough beignet – so far I hadn't gotten the balance of cocoa powder to flour where I wanted it. But when I did, look out world.

Aubrey's a gem. I was recognizing more and more just how lucky I was to have her. 'Set it next to the fryer, would you?' I said.

Aubrey set down the big awkward bag and wiped her hands briskly together. She smiled expectantly at Keith. Her jade-green eyes sparkled. 'So, what'll it be?'

'Two coffees and two orders of beignets,' he replied. 'Make that to go.'

I smelled strawberry-scented shampoo. I smelled romance.

I had a feeling this young man might be smitten with my lovely young strawberry-blonde assistant. She gets a lot of that – not that I'm jealous. I'm just saying.

I've got enough going on in my life without needing a man and all the complications that come with consorting with one of the cute, cuddly yet difficult critters. Did I mention I have a cat? I sniffed a lock of my hair. Maybe I should get some of that shampoo Aubrey was using. My hair didn't smell like strawberry, it smelled like cat.

'You got it.' Aubrey's hands ran deftly over the keys on the register – something my hands never did. But at least I knew how to make a mean beignet. I got busy on Keith's order. All our produce is made fresh. There's no other good way to eat a beignet. Once the sweet treats cool, they toughen up and you may as well be chewing on a loofah. Maybe I could give the old ones a second life and sell them as bath scrubs.

'Maggie!'

I looked up. My dream bubble burst. 'Good morning, Clive. Come looking for a treat?'

'Actually,' Clive said, pulling up to the glass barrier in front of the fryer where I make my beignet magic, 'I've come looking for a ride.' He tugged at his blue polka-dot bowtie.

I scooped half-a-dozen beignets from the fryer and set them on the draining tray. In another few seconds I'd dust them with powdered sugar and presto! They'd be ready to serve. 'A ride?' Somehow the image of Clive struggling to balance his lanky frame astraddle the handlebars of my Schwinn dressed in that fancy dark suit of his refused to make sense. 'You know I drive a Schwinn, right?' I'd pedaled past his shop often enough.

Clive nodded. 'I know, but I'm desperate.'

I watched Keith walk out with his order. I watched Aubrey watch him walk out. Yes, romance was in the air – at least for some of us.

I smothered a sigh.

'Where's Johnny?' Johnny Wolfe was Clive's partner, business and otherwise. Johnny drives a flashy black BMW convertible. Clive and Johnny own The Hitching Post next door. This being the Old West, of sorts, you'd think The Hitching Post would be selling saddles, reins, braids and tack. But this was Table Rock. This was the New West. This was the New-Age West. This Hitching Post sold bridal gowns, sashes, garters and veils. Items of the 'I do and forever after' variety.

I've suggested to Johnny that he might want to change the name of his shop. In return, he's suggested to me that I might want to change the location of mine.

Johnny and I have a special relationship.

'Johnny's had to go to a client's house. He's making some last-minute alterations to a gown. Please, Maggie, I'm desperate. I've got to get to Markie's Masterpieces at Navajo Junction – pronto. The bride's mother insists that we make sure the dress and cake are properly coordinated.' He held up a square of lace and tulle.

'What about your shop?'

'I stuck a sign in the window: Closed, be back soon.' Clive ran a nervous hand through his hair. 'I don't have any appointments scheduled.'

'Well,' I said with hesitation. 'I might be able borrow a car . . .' I looked at Aubrey. 'But I've got a business to run.'

Navajo Junction was the moniker given to a once-abandoned industrial complex on the far edge of town. It had been a big commercial and warehouse center back in the day, built beside the railroad tracks. In the thirties I'm told it was a bustling center of business activity. That activity had wound down to nothing by the fifties and the buildings had been abandoned. In the sixties, a bunch of artists took over and Navajo Junction stuttered along for a couple of decades. Then one of those artists hit the bigtime with his red rock landscapes, bought Navajo Junction and gave it a makeover. Since then the area has experienced a revival as an arts and crafts community and tourist destination.

'You go ahead,' said Aubrey with a wave of her hand. 'I've got this totally, totally covered. Besides, Kelly is due in less than an hour.' When Aubrey totally did something, she did it times two.

I pursed my lips. Kelly Herman was a new hire, so I really had no idea what she could or couldn't handle. Kelly also worked for my sister, Donna, part-time over at the health-food grocery that she and my brother-in-law Andy own. Not that

they like it being labelled a health-food store. They consider
the food they sell to be the real thing and they consider super-
markets nothing more than food factory outlets. They also
believe we're all part of some giant earthly consciousness and
that everything we say, do and think has an effect on all of us.
They do their best to set a good example to others. Donna and
Andy: Guardians of the Noosphere.

Me? I consider food to be food. I'm OK with my food coming
from a factory, just so long as I don't find any stray factory
parts in it like cogs or gaskets. Such things are barely digestible
– like my sister's cooking.

Donna and Andy both spoke highly of Kelly. 'Fine,' I said,
seeing how desperate poor Clive looked, 'but you call me,' I
insisted, 'if anything comes up.'

Aubrey promised she would and Clive and I marched the
two blocks to Mother Earth/Father Sun Grocers. We went up
the alley. I spotted Andy's yellow Yukon mid-1955 Chevy pickup
tucked up close to the back wall. The vehicle was in impeccable
condition. Andy worked hard to keep it that way, too. I didn't
see Donna's Mini Cooper around anywhere. She was probably
home with the boys, fourteen-year-old Connor and twelve-year-
old Hunter.

I frowned and tapped the side panel of the truck.

'What's wrong?' worried Clive.

'Looks like Andy's here.' I'd been hoping for my sister. I'd
rather ask to borrow the Mini than my brother-in-law's truck.
It's not that he'd refuse, he's much too sweet for that, but I
knew how fretful he'd be the entire time I was driving it.

I really couldn't put him through that, could I?

I decided it was better not to ask. I'd be saving him from
undue stress. 'Give me a minute.' I pulled open the back door
to the grocery and quietly stepped inside. A blast of moist, chill
air hit me. Donna and Andy rarely lock the back door during the
day, what with deliveries coming in and going out all the time.
They also kept the lights to a minimum throughout the store to
save on energy. Everything ran on solar panels up on the roof.

There was a strong earthy smell back here – potatoes, onions,
leeks. I noticed Andy's truck key on a hook near the battered
oak desk that served as the store's office. I heard voices out

front but the backroom was deserted. I pocketed the key and hurried outside.

'Well?' Clive asked, his eyes filled with expectation.

I pulled the key from my pocket and dangled it in the sunlight. 'No problem.' With lady luck on my side I'd have the truck back before Andy was any the wiser.

Table Rock, Arizona is in the heart of Red Rock Country, about halfway between Sedona and nowhere. Though Sedona is a New-Age mecca in its own right, you'll not hear that from a Table Rocker. Table Rock is where folks move to who feel that Sedona is too 'mainstream.'

I'm a recent immigrant to Table Rock. With a population of approximately five thousand (and one) or so humans, and another twenty thousand or so extraterrestrials – according to the New-Age gurus living and operating from our odd little red-rocked corner of the world – Table Rock is a mite on the small side. According to the gurus, aliens outnumbered Arizonans four-to-one.

Gurus themselves are as ubiquitous as cacti around here – and equally as prickly if you question their belief systems. I'd gotten into conversations with more than a few of them in the café and things had gotten testy. But really? I'm supposed to believe that there are such things as alien-crafted crystal skulls lying around the desert through which those aliens are communicating with these New-Age gurus? And the gurus claim they understand what the aliens are saying?

Please, I can barely comprehend my mom half the time, let alone aliens. I can't even understand my cat and she only knows one word: mrowl. What's that supposed to mean? From what I've been able to deduce, the darn word has at least a dozen meanings, from 'feed me' to 'pet me' to 'clean my freaking litter box already!'

'It's really nice of you to give me a ride like this,' Clive said, turning to face me as we rumbled down the asphalt. Fifty-five Chevy pickups don't cruise silently, they rumble. Clive's thick red hair blew in the wind being drawn in through the open pickup windows. Though his hair was so closely cropped it couldn't blow far.

'No problem.' I squeezed my eyes together. 'We redheads have to stick together.' My long hair blew everywhere – mostly into my eyes at the moment – and it stung like the dickens. Dickens made out of barbwire. A bit annoying but I could still see the road, at least most of the time – not worth mentioning to Clive. He'd only worry about me crashing the truck and us into the orange-red rocks flanking the road.

I really shouldn't complain, because at least my bangs – not so much the result of a bad hairstyle choice as a bad hair stylist choice – had finally grown out enough to get in my eyes.

The Chevy had no AC, so that's why we drove with the windows down. This was a bit of a distraction in other ways, too, because Andy had transformed the engine to run on vegetable oil and I got a fierce craving for French fries whenever I was in the truck. Like I was getting now. My mouth was watering and my stomach grumbling. My eyes were watering up, too – like some sad character on a soap opera who's just learned she's the adopted daughter of an orphaned single mother who died tragically in a factory fire after her husband left her when he found out she had an inoperable brain tumor – but that wasn't the French fries, it was my hair pelting my eyeballs.

Maybe I could convince Clive to stop at Bell Rock Burgers for a quick bite on the way back. They've got the best fries. I could fill up the gas tank, too. Bell Rock Burgers ought to have gobs of old French fry grease I could get on the cheap, if not free.

My hands hugged the wheel. It had been months since I'd driven a car. The last time I was chasing down some New-Age lunatic who I thought was a murderer but was merely a lunatic. Things had been a lot calmer since then and I'd been relying on my Schwinn for wheeled transportation, but when Clive had come running into the shop desperate for a lift over to Markie's Masterpieces, I hadn't been able to resist helping him out.

He and Johnny had done me a favor or two themselves since I'd moved to Table Rock a few months back. Like buying my old wedding dress off me when the chips were down and I needed some quick cash.

'I just don't understand it,' said Clive, worrying the swatch of dress fabric in his hand. He fidgeted. There was a nasty spring on the bench seat on the passenger's side that always drove me crazy, too. 'Markie isn't answering his phone. Neither is his assistant, Lisa, nor anyone else for that matter. I don't know what to do, Maggie. Normally we wouldn't be having anything to do with the wedding cake at all.'

He levelled his green eyes at me. We matched up there, too. 'But the bride's mother,' he rolled his eyes, 'let me tell you, she is a force of nature.' He sighed. 'As if Johnny and I don't have enough to do for this wedding. Now we have to deal with the wedding cake, too.'

'Why the last-minute rush?'

'Johnny just finished altering the lace overlay because the bride-to-be had some last-minute requests. I'm supposed to take this sample to Markie as a go-by.'

I told him it looked good.

Clive nodded, his hands playing with the fabric. 'Johnny does excellent work.' That he did. For a former figure skater, Johnny was a formidable seamstress and dress designer.

With Clive's help, we found the Entronque building on the edge of the Navajo Junction Arts Center complex alongside the railroad tracks. The Entronque was the tallest building in sight. A scattering of vehicles lay about the adjacent blacktop lot.

'You can pull up by that awning,' pointed Clive. 'The freight elevator is right there.'

I noticed a late-model sapphire-black Markie's Masterpieces decaled Nissan Cube parked nearby. I slid up to the mauve overhang and stopped. A sign on the side of the wall beside the door read Employees and Deliveries Only. 'Are you sure you can get in this way?'

Clive nodded.

'Want me to come in with you?'

'No need. I should only be a minute,' Clive replied briskly, climbing out.

I found a spot to park, shut off the engine and cranked up the radio. I had to flip through several New-Age stations, a station giving the farm report and another station, on which a Dr Jane Denver was telling listeners about her latest trip to someplace called Gamma Orionis in the Orion Constellation before alighting on Patsy Cline. Patsy's a bit before my time – I'm thirty-nine and intend to be for many years to come – but I liked her style.

I laid my head against the seat and closed my eyes. I rarely got the chance to relax like this these days. Patsy had barely finished her second song on this two-fer Tuesday when Clive jumped in the pickup and slammed the door.

I bounced up and stared at him. 'What's wrong? Are you OK?' He was sweating – hard to do in Arizona where the moisture gets sucked off your skin almost as fast as you can shed it out. I noticed frosting on his pant cuffs and black dress shoes and my brow went up. Clive is a stickler for cleanliness and elegance. They could paste his picture up next to the definition of dapper on Wikipedia.

Clive looked almost giddy, but not in a good way – in a kind of Looney Tunes way. 'Do you remember that time I was in your café and we found—'

I swear, his eyes bugged out like something in a cartoon and his Adam's apple swelled up like a Damson plum. I held up my hand like a five-fingered stop sign. 'Don't say it!'

I paused and stared him down. 'I do not want to talk about it. Not now, not ever again.' My life was difficult enough, what with a 'dead' ex-husband who wouldn't stay away and the struggle of running my fledgling beignet business. And now a cat named after somebody else's dead wife. Who needs a cat? And who needs a cat named after somebody else's dead wife?

Mrowl.

'But Maggie—'

I shook my head. 'No, Clive.'

He sighed and pushed the door back open with his shaking knees. 'Fine.' He gestured with his finger. 'Follow me.'

I scratched my head and ran after Clive. What the devil was he up to?

We crossed the parking lot. I started to angle toward the covered entrance where I'd dropped him off. 'Not that way,' Clive corrected me. 'The elevator's broken.' He led the way to an unremarkable solid unmarked gray door closer to the corner of the four-story brick warehouse that was home to the renowned Markie's Masterpieces bakery.

Clive grabbed the brass handle and pulled. The door opened out with a pig-like squeal that sent chills up my arms. The body lying beneath that four-tiered masterpiece at the bottom of the narrow stairwell sent those chills coursing through the rest of me.

TWO

'Clive!' I spun around to face him. He was huddled near the door, looking scared. 'What happened? What did you do?'

'I didn't do anything, Maggie,' Clive replied rather shakily. He tugged worriedly at his polka-dot bowtie.

The cake, which smelled like lemon, with vanilla buttercream frosting, was mashed up on the ground. A trail of cake led up the stairs. The body beneath was mashed up under layers of cake, frosting and fondant, arms and legs akimbo. I couldn't see the face.

I couldn't even see the head. It was hidden somewhere under the bottom layer of cake. Definitely a woman, though, from what I could see of those black flared trousers and that lavender polo shirt with the Markie's Masterpieces logo emblazoned over the right breast, not to mention the upside down stone-gray high heels.

'What happened?' I repeated, struggling to steady my voice.

Clive was looking pastier by the moment. A few seconds more and his face would match the color of the powdered sugar I sprinkle on my beignets.

'I don't know,' he wept, wringing his hands. 'The freight elevator was out of order so I took the stairs up to Markies but no one answered. Then I heard noises – voices at the end of the corridor. They seemed to be coming from the stairs I'd just climbed.' His mouth formed a giant O. His gaze went up the stairwell. 'Oh, no. Maggie!'

'What is it, Clive?'

'Don't you see?' He pinched his cheeks together with his palms. 'When I was up there I pushed the stairwell door open.' He gulped. 'What if it's my fault? What if I knocked her down the stairs?' His eyes grew wide.

I considered Clive's statement. If she had been standing behind the door and, if Clive had pushed open the door . . . I had to admit, it was a definite possibility. 'No way,' I said. I had to reassure him, didn't I? Clive was my friend. I leaned closer. 'Maybe she lost her balance and fell all on her own.' Clive's cakey footprints were all over the place. 'Maybe,' I suggested, 'she isn't really dead?'

Clive started shaking his head up and down like a piston in a race car. His eyes were as big as the moons of Jupiter. 'Oh my gosh. You're right, Maggie!' His hands groped at his pockets. 'We've got to call an ambulance. She could be terribly injured. She could be suffocating,' he gasped, 'under all that cake!'

Clive threw his phone at me and dropped to his knees. 'Call the hospital!' he cried. 'I'll start digging her out!'

I watched as he desperately pulled away handfuls of cake, sending lumps flying in every direction. Most of it seemed to be landing on me. I wasn't sure Clive should be touching the cake like that – there could be a lawsuit in an accident case like this and it could be evidence – but then again, whoever was under all that lemon cake might really be suffocating.

I nodded and dialed 911. As I shouted at the emergency operator to fetch an ambulance and gave her our location, Clive cleared lemon cake away from the side of the young woman's face. She was very pretty – maybe a little too much blue eye shadow. But it did match the wickedly beautiful azure-blue eyes of hers. I guesstimated her age as somewhere in the mid-twenties. She had been banged up quite a bit on the way down. There were bruises on her face and hands and her fingernails were broken, like she'd tried to catch herself. Gravity had won the battle.

And the way she was looking up at me, it was pretty obvious that she was also dead. 'You can stop now, Clive.' I stuck his phone in my shorts and put my hand on his shoulder. 'Clive, you can stop.'

Clive looked up at me. 'Maggie, is she—?'

I nodded and helped Clive up from his knees. 'Let's go outside and wait for the ambulance. They should be here soon.'

I heard the sound of a door opening somewhere further up and a woman's voice called out, 'What's going on down there? Is everything OK?'

I cupped my hands around my mouth and shouted back,

'There's been an accident!' I listened to my voice echo through the shaft. 'The ambulance is on its way!' I heard the door creak shut and shrugged my shoulders. Some people don't like to get involved. 'Let's go, Clive.'

We tumbled out into the sunlight, rattled and out of breath. I swiveled my head, looking for signs of help arriving in the form of an ambulance, and spotted flashing lights across the parking lot. But it wasn't an ambulance. It was a Table Rock police cruiser. I saw a man in a blue uniform poking around on the driver's side of Andy's pickup.

Another officer, a sturdy woman about my age, stood next to the cruiser talking on a radio. If fireplugs and people could have offspring, she'd be the product. I was too far away to hear what she was saying. I waved. 'Hey!' I beat my arms. 'Over here! She's over here!'

The woman on the radio looked over at me, said something into her handset then approached. Her partner closed the door to the pickup and came toward us as well.

The man who'd stepped from the pickup slowly unsnapped his holster and drew his weapon. 'Stay where you are!' he ordered. 'Place your hands behind your heads.'

Clive and I looked at one another. I shrugged and took a step toward the officers. 'You don't understand,' I began. 'I'm the one who called nine-one-one to report—'

'Remain still!' he ordered. His partner now drew her weapon, too.

'Don't shoot!' cried Clive. He looked a little wobbly, standing with his fingers laced together behind his head. I decided to join him in the assumed position.

The woman frisked me first, then Clive. She nodded to her partner. 'All clear.'

Which was funny, because nothing was clear to me.

An ambulance siren grew louder and a moment later we all watched as the boxy red-and-white emergency vehicle zoomed into the lot. I bit my tongue, wanting to run to the EMTs and tell them where to find the dead woman, but was afraid one or both of these cops might shoot me before I could get a whole sentence out.

One dead woman was enough for the day.

The male officer slid his gun back into its holster and pointed a finger at me. 'What can you tell me about that pickup?'

I creased my forehead. 'Well,' I began, trying to remember what Andy had told me about the vehicle, 'it's a mid-fifty-five Chevy pickup. Originally it had a V8, but—'

The officer held up a hand and glared at me. He wasn't anyone I recognized from around town. I certainly didn't remember him ever being a customer of mine. 'You were driving the vehicle?'

I nodded. 'That's right, why?' My arms were aching from holding them behind my head. 'Can we put our hands down now?' Out of the corner of my eye I saw the female officer talking to the EMTs as they spilled out of their ambulance.

The officer nodded. 'We got a report that this vehicle,' he pointed at Andy's pickup as if I didn't already know what vehicle we were talking about, 'was stolen.'

I squeezed my eyes shut. Andy was going to kill me.

I heard Clive groan loudly. 'Why, why did I listen to you?'

Hey, was he talking about me? I screwed up my face and turned to Clive. 'What are you blaming me for? I didn't know, I couldn't know that Andy would report his pickup stolen. Besides,' I snarled, 'you asked me for a ride, remember?'

Clive was shaking his head and clutching his chest. There was buttercream all over the lapels and knees of his suit. Clive, as meticulous as he normally was, didn't seem to mind or even notice. He frowned at me. 'Johnny's always warning me about you. But I never listen.' He shook his head forlornly. 'This is what I get: a stolen truck, a dead woman.' He sighed deeply. Sweat dripped from the sides of his face. The Arizona sun showed no mercy on any of us.

The paramedics pushed closer. 'What dead woman?'

'That's what I was trying to explain earlier,' I began. 'There's a woman,' I pointed toward the Entronque building, 'inside, lying at the bottom of the stairwell. We think she's dead.'

The paramedics sprinted toward the door and disappeared inside.

'Keep an eye on these two, Ellen.' His badge identified him as Officer Ravi Singh. He ran his free hand through his cropped black hair.

The woman nodded. Her right hand rested lightly on the grip of the gun that was holstered at her side.

We stood sweating in the sun for a minute or two and then Officer Singh beckoned us over. He held the door open and we stepped into the stairwell. 'Don't touch anything,' he ordered.

Clive and I did as we were told. The paramedics were standing to one side.

'Is she definitely dead?' whispered Clive.

'Afraid so,' said the paramedic on the left. His partner nodded. 'Probably broke her neck.'

'Do you recognize this woman?' Officer Singh asked.

'Not me,' I answered. 'Never saw her before in my life.'

'I do.' Clive's voice was still nothing more than a whisper. 'It's one of Markie's assistants, Lisa.'

Officer Singh nodded curtly. He took a careful step closer to the body. There was cake scattered everywhere, but then part of that was Clive's doing. Her short mahogany brown locks, which had probably earlier been styled into an updo, were now more of an up-goo. Who knew hair could hold so much buttercream?

'What's this?' Officer Singh pulled a pair of latex gloves from his pocket, bent down and gingerly pulled out a scrap of fabric from under Lisa's left hip.

He straightened and held up the cake-smeared material. It dangled in the confined space between us like an accusation. 'Do either of you recognize this?'

Clive sucked air in between his teeth and blanched.

It was the swatch he'd been carrying.

THREE

I swiveled in Clive's direction. His mouth was hanging open. 'It's mine,' he finally croaked.

I cleared my throat. 'Well,' I began, turning to the paramedics, 'it's an awful, terrible *accident*.' And some bride was probably going to have to settle for a store-bought wedding cake. 'But shouldn't you guys be, you know,' I motioned with my head, 'removing the body? Notifying the next of kin?' It seemed wrong seeing the woman simply lying there amid all that cake. Disrespectful, even. Something told me nobody would be bringing cake to her wake.

I wished they would let us go. I'd been around enough death to last me a lifetime.

The two paramedics looked at Officer Singh who shook his head in the negative. 'I don't think so.'

'Why not?' I replied.

He looked first at me, then at Clive. His dark brown eyes were flat. 'Because first we must rule out foul play.'

Clive hiccoughed then covered his mouth with his hand. 'Sorry,' he said, looking awkwardly around the stairwell. His cheeks had flushed red. 'Just nerves, I guess.'

I took a step toward the victim and scrunched up my nose. 'What makes you think there might have been foul play?' The very suggestion sent goosebumps rising along my forearms. 'The woman slipped, probably on some buttercream, and fell down the stairs.'

'Please step back, ma'am.' Officer Ellen Collins gripped my upper arm firmly and pulled me away. 'Maybe you two should wait outside.' Her eyes connected with her partner's and he nodded his agreement.

We stepped back out into the sunlight. I used my hand for a visor and watched as an old but clearly well-maintained bright red Pontiac Firebird slowed off the main road then surged into the parking lot. I don't know much about cars but I knew this model with the flashy black decal of a Firebird on its broad hood was straight out of the eighties. Several of the boys at Camelback High School had driven similar cars, including my then boyfriend.

The Firebird roared to within inches of us and then came to a tire-squealing halt. Whoever sat behind the wheel of that tinted glass ode to testosterone was *so* high school.

I lowered my hands to my hips and watched as the driver-side door popped open.

I should have known.

I stared as Table Rock's one and only detective slowly unfolded himself from the Firebird and stepped toward Officer Collins. 'Morning, Ellen.'

The corner of her mouth inched up. 'Sorry to bother you on your day off, Mark.'

Wearing baggy cargo shorts and a sleeveless pale green shirt that showed off all his muscles, Detective Mark Highsmith glanced at Clive then loomed over me. He made a sour face. Even so, those chocolate M&M eyes of his still looked mighty appealing. I don't know what it is, but I practically got type-2 diabetes just looking at them. 'Ms Miller,' he sighed. He rubbed his temples. 'I should have known.'

What was that supposed to mean?

I pursed my lips but stayed mum. Officer Singh must have contacted the detective.

'Ravi thought you'd want to be in on this,' Ellen said. 'There's a dead woman inside. It might be an accident but Ravi says something doesn't seem right.'

'He thinks it might have been foul play,' I added.

'Maggie!' cried Clive.

Sorry, I mouthed, realizing I shouldn't have said that.

Clive shot a handful of green-eyed daggers at me.

Highsmith silently studied us for a moment then nodded. 'Where?'

Ellen jerked her thumb toward the side entrance.

'Fine.' He pointed a finger at Clive and me. 'Make sure these two stick around.' He disappeared inside.

Several minutes later the door squeaked open and Detective Highsmith beckoned us with his finger. That digit of his was a real multitasking tool.

'What does he want with us?' Clive whispered urgently.

I shrugged. 'I guess he just wants to hear what happened.' I started for the door.

'But I don't know what happened,' complained Clive.

'Tell him that.'

Highsmith held the door open. 'Tell me what?'

I answered for Clive. 'That we don't know what happened to her. This Lisa woman.' Except that she's wearing a lot of cake, that is.

'Lisa Willoughby, age twenty-seven,' said Highsmith, filling in the blanks. 'Single.'

I arched an eyebrow.

'We found her purse under the cake.' He pointed to a small bubblegum-colored clutch. Very nice. She'd been carrying a four-tiered cake down a narrow flight of stairs *and* a clutch? No wonder she'd lost her footing.

We all looked upward upon hearing the sound of light footsteps above. A woman turned the corner of the next landing up and cried out. 'Oh my gosh! What happened?' She was probably in her twenties. There was a streak of white in her hair. I couldn't tell if it was paint or early graying. She wore a loose pair of paint-and-varnish-stained overalls with a sleeveless cotton T-shirt underneath. Her light brown hair was knotted in back.

'Please,' said Highsmith, thrusting his hand up like a stop sign, 'don't come any further. There's been an accident.'

'An accident?' She looked downward. Her hand flew to her mouth.

'I'm Detective Highsmith. You are?'

She wiped her lips with her tongue. 'Blake Sherwood.' She gestured with her head. 'I have a studio on the second floor.'

Detective Highsmith patted his pockets and came up empty. 'Sherwood, right. Got it.' He nodded to Officer Singh. 'One of us will be up later to get your statement.'

'But I don't know anything, I just—'

The detective cut her off. He was good at that. 'Please wait for us upstairs, miss.'

She nodded and disappeared.

Several additional officers pushed through the side door and joined us. One of the cops opened a small soft-sided black case and pulled out a digital camera. He began snapping pictures while Officers Singh and Collins started stringing yellow crime-scene tape around the perimeter.

Clive and I just stood there looking stupid. And useless. Neither of which was much of a stretch. I smiled at Clive as if to say, 'Buck up, buddy. Everything is going to be OK!'

He glowered back at me, as if to say, 'I could kill you, Maggie Miller!'

Clive and I have a special relationship too.

Highsmith borrowed a notepad and pen from one of his colleagues. I noticed it was a Karma Koffee-logoed pen from the coffee-and-pastry shop across the street from my café. I gritted my teeth and bit my tongue. That place and its husband and wife owners, the Gregorys, were getting to be a thorn in my side. A six-inch prickly cactus thorn.

And to make matters worse, I was addicted to their muffins.

To make matters their very worst, I'd recently discovered they also own the fourplex where I rent my apartment. I was only a few months into a one-year lease and I wasn't sure I was going to make it – financially or mentally.

Come to think of it, if the Gregorys found out I now had Mom staying with me and a cat, what would they do? Evict me? I was going to have to tread carefully.

'You both found the body?' Highsmith asked, his pen hovering over the pad.

I turned to Clive.

'I – I found her,' he answered.

I nodded and Clive glowered in my direction. He had found her, hadn't he? It wasn't like I was throwing him under the bus or anything.

The detective closed in on Clive. 'Was she like this when you found her?' He waved his pen in the direction of the dead woman and cake catastrophe.

'Well—' Clive began. Sweat pooled at his hairline.

I interjected: 'We weren't sure if she was dead so,' I mimicked shoveling, 'we dug her out a little.' I smiled weakly.

Highsmith groaned loudly. 'Why don't the two of you wait for me in Ethiopia?'

'That sounds a little far away,' I replied, confused, 'but sure, we'll be glad to drive back downtown and get out of your hair.'

Clive tugged my sleeve. 'Ethiopia is the name of a restaurant here in the Entronque, Maggie.'

'Oh?' I flushed red. Thank goodness; I didn't think I could afford the price of any international airfare at the moment.

Clive nodded. 'It's on the first floor in the main entry. I'll show you, Maggie.'

After promising not to go far – at least no further than Ethiopia – Clive and I left the way we had come. Clive led me around to the building's main entrance. An art gallery was to the left of the double-door entry and Ethiopia filled the space on the right. Clive held the door to the lobby open for me. The first floor was an upscale arts and crafts mini-mall with shops leading back along either side. The floors were paved in old brick. A green, blue and yellow nine-foot-tall Spanish-tiled fountain in the center of the atrium held a larger-than-life bronze roadrunner. Water trickled from its beak.

Shoppers wandered in and out of the stores. If the cameras around their necks were any indication, the majority of them were tourists. Navajo Junction was a shopping destination for the locals as well, but during the busiest seasons of the year Navajo Junction, like Table Rock itself, swelled up with out-of-town visitors. Resorts in the area included Navajo Junction on their shuttle bus routes.

It was all very serene. I might have felt serene myself if it wasn't for the woman lying dead just yards away from where I stood. The only thing remaining to be seen was whether she'd died a violent death or a clumsy one.

A middle-aged woman in an orange, red and yellow caftan greeted us inside the door to Ethiopia – a cozy place, with teakwood paneling running halfway up the walls and apple-green paint from there to the ceiling. A full bar ran along the left side. An unattended creamy white baby grand piano sat in the corner near the bar. She guided us to a table for four next to the window and laid out two menus atop the thick gold tablecloth.

Clive sighed heavily. 'I don't think I can eat a thing.' He thumbed the small menu.

'Come on, Clive. It's important that you keep your strength up.' I read through the list of drinks. 'How about a nice glass of *tej*? It says here it's sort of like mead, made with honey and is a traditional Ethiopian beverage.' I unfolded my tented raspberry-colored linen napkin and draped it across my lap.

'It's a little early in the day for alcohol, don't you think?'

'Fine,' I said, 'but you've got to eat something.'

'I'm telling you, Maggie, I have no appetite.'

I leaned over the table and felt his forehead. 'You're not feeling lightheaded or anything, are you?' His temperature seemed OK to me, not that I knew what to expect. I fell back in my chair. 'Your blood pressure isn't acting up again, is it?' Clive had a bit of a BP issue.

Clive shook his head in the negative. 'No, really, I'm fine.' He fanned his face with his hand. 'Maybe I will have a drink.' He turned and looked for our server.

'That's the spirit.' I waved to a couple of servers hovering near the register at the bar.

One of the two waiters stepped over to take our drink orders. 'I'll have an iced tea,' Clive said.

I ordered the same because it's no fun drinking alone. 'So who is this Lisa Willoughby exactly?' I asked between sips of tea.

Clive had asked for an extra napkin and was fastidiously wiping cake and icing off his shoes with it. The hostess looked at him with open hostility. No doubt she wasn't used to her clientele using the restaurant's expensive linen as shoe rags. 'One of Markie's assistants. She is – was – a cake decorator.'

'Did you know her well?'

Clive hesitated a moment. 'No, not well at all.'

I nodded. 'Still, what a pity. And so young, too.' My appetizer arrived and I dug in. I'd ordered something called a *sambusa* – a pastry dough stuffed with beef, minced lentils, green chilies and herbs. Delectable. I wondered if I could make some version of it for the café. I'd been toying with the idea of expanding my menu, possibly including some savory beignets to attract a lunch crowd looking for something more than a sweet treat.

I offered a bite to Clive but he declined. Our main courses arrived and we ate in nervous silence. I figured Clive was worrying about what was going on back in the stairwell as much as I was. What was taking the police so long? Why hadn't Detective Highsmith or one of the other Table Rock officers come to tell us we could leave already?

For the main course, I'd ordered the *doro wet*, which the menu described as a traditional Ethiopian delicacy: a mixture of chicken simmered in onions and *berbere*, a blend of spices that I didn't recognize. Clive had recommended the dish. 'It's a delightful, spicy chicken stew,' he'd explained, urging me to try it.

Good call. The taste was like nothing I'd ever experienced. Ethiopia was definitely a restaurant worth coming back to. Though remembering the prices in the menu, it would have to be on somebody else's dime. I wondered, optimistically, if the police would be reimbursing us for the cost of lunch. Highsmith had practically ordered us to come here, after all.

I'd have to bring Donna, Andy and my nephews. There were several vegetarian options on the menu that I was sure they'd enjoy – like the *tikel gomen*, made with cabbage, carrots, green beans and potatoes sautéed with olive oil, garlic and ginger. Heck, that even sounded palatable to me, and I was no vegetarian.

Clive had ordered the *gomen besiga*, made with beef, boiled collard greens and Ethiopian spices, but left most of his food on the plate.

I took a sip of tea and sucked in a lungful of spice-scented air through my nostrils. Wow. Not only was the food spicy and delicious, it was good for the sinuses. I should tell Donna about it. She'd probably want to bottle the stuff and sell it in Mother Earth/Father Sun as an all-natural nasal decongestant.

A shadow fell over the table. I turned.

It was Detective Mark Highsmith and his M&Ms were looking C&C – cryptic and critical. He pulled out the empty chair beside me and relocated it to the end of the table. 'Mr Rothschild, right?' He focused in on poor Clive. I'd been the subject of that focus before. It wasn't pleasant.

Clive swallowed a lump of beef and nodded, then set down his fork.

'Let's go over your movements this morning, Mr Rothschild.' Highsmith rested his elbows on the table. I watched his biceps flex.

With occasional prompting, Clive carefully went over his entire day, what little of it there had been before arriving here at the Entronque. 'And then when I came back down the stairs,' Clive waved his hand helplessly, 'there she was.' He looked across the table at me. I patted his hand.

Detective Highsmith scribbled some notes on his borrowed pad and thumped the page with the back of the pen. 'Let me get this straight, Mr Rothschild. Ms Miller dropped you off at the freight entrance.'

Clive nodded.

'But because the elevator was broken, you went to the stair-well door?' Highsmith's eyes locked onto Clive's. Clive nodded once again. 'Why didn't you go around to the main entrance?'

Clive shrugged lightly. 'I knew the stairs entrance was closer. I didn't relish the idea of climbing up four flights but it seemed better than walking all the way around to the front of the building.' Clive glanced across the table to me. 'Besides, the public elevators may have been down as well.'

'And you didn't notice anything unusual on your way upstairs?' Clive shook his head. 'Not a thing.'

I nudged Clive. 'Tell him about the voices you heard.'

'Voices?' said Highsmith, coming to attention.

'Yeah, you know,' I encouraged Clive. 'The voices you said you heard in the stairwell.'

Clive licked his lips nervously. 'Well . . .' He tugged his bowtie for the umpteenth time then cleared his throat. 'I thought I heard voices. Arguing maybe. In the stairwell.' He gulped his tea.

'Were these voices male or female?' Highsmith inquired.

Clive frowned. 'I'm not certain. I couldn't tell.'

'And you didn't see anybody?'

'No,' Clive admitted after a moment.

Highsmith nodded thoughtfully while Clive and I shot each other questioning looks. 'There's only one thing I don't under-stand, Mr Rothschild . . .'

Clive chewed at his lower lip and rolled his neck nervously. 'What's that, Detective?'

Highsmith folded his hands on the tabletop. 'I tried the freight elevator.' His M&Ms bored into Clive. 'It works just fine.'

FOUR

'That's impossible!' Clive flew to his feet. His raspberry napkin fluttered in the air like a young purple finch on its maiden voyage and his largely untouched plate shot my way like an out-of-control flying saucer.

I put out a hand to prevent all that alien-looking *gomen besiga* from ending up in my lap. 'Whoa!' I cried. 'Are you sure, Detective? I mean, if Clive says the elevator was broken . . .'

Clive nodded rapidly. 'There's a sign and everything.'

Highsmith scooted back his chair. 'You want to show me?'

'Of course, Detective.' Clive squeezed past Detective Highsmith and started for the exit. I swallowed the rest of my tea, wiped my lips and hurried after them. 'Hey,' I shouted as they walked quickly past the hostess station, 'what about the bill?'

Clive turned and waved as he yelled over his shoulder, 'Thanks, Maggie!'

My jaw sagged. I blinked.

The hostess held out her palm and I handed over my plastic. At least Detective Highsmith hadn't ordered anything. He looked like he could shovel it away pretty good. What with all those muscles, he probably required a lot of protein. And protein's expensive.

The hostess called to the waiter who stuck the bill under my nose. I nodded then waited impatiently for the hostess to run my credit card.

I caught up with Clive and the detective at the delivery slash employee entrance. The two men were standing inside the small vestibule just outside the freight elevator doors. The doors were open and Detective Highsmith was playing with the buttons.

'I don't understand,' Clive said, turning to me. 'I promise,' he held up his right hand like he was going to say a pledge, 'the elevator was broken when we arrived.' He pointed as the stainless-steel doors closed together with a soft rumble. 'There was a sign and everything,' he said for the umpteenth time.

There was no sign now. I scratched my chin. 'Could the sign have fallen?'

'We looked inside the elevator. There's nothing on the floor.' That was the detective.

I peered at the crack between the floor and the elevator. 'Down the shaft?' It was a microscopic slit, barely a millimeter or two, but still . . .

Highsmith's lips quirked up. 'It seems pretty unlikely but we'll put in a call to maintenance and have the shaft checked out.'

'Maybe someone removed the sign?' Clive suggested. The elevator doors slid shut once again. Clive tapped the steel door. 'I'm telling you. It was taped right here.'

'Did you try pushing the button?' Highsmith asked, pointing to the elevator control panel.

'No. I mean, why would I?' Clive snapped. 'I simply assumed it was out of order and went around to the stairs.'

'Where you proceeded to climb four flights of steps without managing to see Lisa Willoughby lying at the bottom of the stairwell?' Highsmith sounded a wee bit skeptical.

'I'm telling you, Detective, she simply wasn't there. Not until I came back down. I saw cake all over the steps and Lisa at the bottom of them.'

'So, I'll ask you again: how did your swatch of dress fabric end up underneath the victim's body?'

Clive opened his mouth. 'I don't know. Maybe I—'

I cut my friend off. 'Wait a minute,' I said to the detective, 'why are you calling her a victim all of a sudden? So far, all we know for sure is that Lisa Willoughby is dead. The only thing she may be a victim of is clumsiness.'

Officer Singh stuck his head in the door. 'Detective, I think you're going to want to see this.'

'What is it?' Highsmith asked.

'I was upstairs canvassing the tenants to see if anyone saw or heard anything and I noticed something.'

'Well?'

You really should see it for yourself, sir. Make up your own mind,' Officer Singh replied rather sheepishly, dropping his gaze to the floor. 'It may be nothing.' He looked up at Clive and me. 'Or it may be something.'

'OK,' Highsmith said. 'Wait.' He pulled back Officer Singh's hand as the patrolman went to push the button for the freight elevator. 'Let's get this thing dusted for prints. Just in case.'

'Of course, sir.' Officer Singh's cheeks reddened. He called for Officer Collins on his radio and asked her to secure the vestibule.

'What about us?' I asked.

'Come with me,' ordered Detective Highsmith.

We dutifully followed the detective back around the

building to the main entrance. From there we rode the passenger elevator to the top floor. Stepping off, I spotted the sign for Markie's Masterpieces at the opposite end of the hall. The logo matched the one on the vehicle I'd seen parked out back. The freight elevator was on our left further down.

'Where to?' Highsmith said.

'This way.' Officer Singh waved us forward.

'Hang on!' Clive stopped beside the freight elevator. His index finger lightly touched the steel door.

'What is it?' demanded Highsmith.

'There was a sign here, too.' He turned to the detective. 'An out-of-order sign.' He looked nonplussed. 'It looked just like the one downstairs.'

'Well, it's not here now,' Detective Highsmith said.

A clatter at the end of the hall caught our collective attention. A stooped Hispanic man in his fifties wearing a navy-blue jumper pushed a mop bucket out of a door marked Restroom.

Highsmith waved him over.

The little man looked back at us curiously. He leaned one hand against his mop and ran his free hand through the other mop of long gray hair on his head.

'You work here?' Highsmith asked.

The little man nodded. 'Yes. I clean.' I caught a whiff of lemon and ammonia. The white patch over his heart bore the name Aronez in red block letters.

Highsmith pointed to the freight elevator. 'Was this thing out of order earlier? Broken?' He mimed snapping something with his hands.

Before Highsmith could stop him, the little man thumbed the controls and the door rattled open. 'No, is not broken. You see?' He motioned with his hand that we were free to enter.

Highsmith nodded. 'Yeah.' He scratched the underside of his chiseled chin thoughtfully. 'I see. Thanks. You can go now.'

The little man nodded and proceeded to enter the jeweler's shop on the right.

I tapped Highsmith on the shoulder. 'You forgot to ask him to look for the sign in the elevator shaft.'

The corner of the detective's mouth quirked up. 'You mean the out-of-order sign that wasn't there?'

'We don't know—'

He held up his hand. 'For the elevator that was never broken?'

I bit my lip. If Clive said there was a sign, there was a sign. 'Are you sure you saw an out-of-order sign, Clive?'

'Maggie!' Clive scolded me with his eyes.

'I mean,' I recovered quickly and turned to Officer Singh, then the detective, 'why would Clive lie about there being a sign?' I planted my hands on my hips. 'Maybe the janitor is lying about there not being a sign.' I stabbed the air with my chin to put an accent to my point.

Highsmith's eyes danced with amusement. 'So now you fry pastry and solve crimes?'

I felt my ears grow hot. 'We don't know there's been a crime, Detective.'

Officer Singh cleared his throat. 'If I may?' Detective Highsmith nodded and Officer Singh led our small group to a rather ordinary-looking brown door in the corner. Glancing at it, you'd never know the secret it concealed – a dead woman lying in a pile of cake. A fire-exit sign hung above the door.

The officer slipped a latex glove over his hand and held the door open for the detective.

Highsmith pointed to me and Clive. 'You two stay here.' I rolled my eyes. Detective Highsmith crept slowly down the stairs, careful to keep his feet near the inside edge. I guess he didn't want to destroy any evidence. Of what, I couldn't say.

He stopped just above the landing between the fourth floor and the third and stooped over. His right hand reached out and he nodded. He turned and looked back up the stairs. 'Let's make sure that no one uses these stairs.' He pulled himself up to his full height. 'And let's get the photographer up here, Ravi. I want shots of everything. Top to bottom.'

Clive and I raised our eyebrows at one another. 'You mind telling us what's going on?' I demanded as Detective Highsmith brushed past me.

His jaw tightened. 'What's going on is that it looks like Ms Willoughby had some help falling down those stairs.'

Clive gasped.

I frowned. 'What makes you think that?'

He laid his hand on my shoulder and pointed. 'Not that it's

any of your business, but do you see those marks near that far step? The one right before the landing?'

I nodded. The wood had been scarred and frosting and cake were scattered everywhere.

He turned to me. 'If the young lady had slipped, why are all these first steps up here near the top clean?'

'Because she only slipped when she got to that step?' I suggested.

Highsmith shook his head. 'If she'd slipped right there she'd only have ended up on the landing. A matter of inches. She might have dropped the cake she was carrying but she wouldn't have tumbled down the entire stairwell.'

He mumbled something about momentum and inertia. Was he a detective or a quantum physicist? I was neither, so I had no idea what he was going on about.

'No,' Highsmith said, leading me back into the hall, 'I'd say someone gave her a good solid push.' His eyes fell on Clive, who had his back pressed against the wall.

FIVE

'I've seen enough.' Detective Highsmith turned to Officer Singh, who'd snapped off his glove and thrust it in his back pocket. 'Escort Mr Rothschild downtown, would you, Ravi.'

Highsmith turned to Clive. 'You don't mind going down to the station and answering a few more questions, do you, sir?'

'No, I don't mind at all.' Clive's eyes said otherwise, but what choice did he have? Clive and Officer Singh headed for the passenger elevator at the opposite end of the hall.

'I'll see you back at the café!' I waved as the elevator door swung across Clive's troubled face. The poor guy. I knew how much he hated being around dead guys. And women. 'What about me?'

'What about you?' The detective folded his arms across his chest. Showing off his biceps, no doubt.

I tried not to look or act impressed. 'Am I free to go?' His arms were impressive. I imagined he could likely lift me one-handed.

'Yep.' He nodded and pulled at his watch.

'Great.'

'In fact, your ride ought to be here by now.'

'What ride?' I sniffed. 'I don't need a ride. I've got my pickup.' Well, it wasn't exactly *my* pickup. It wasn't even sort of or even remotely my pickup. But I had brought it here so in that sense the truck was mine. And I did feel a certain obligation to Andy to return it.

'Like I said, you're free to go.' Why was he smiling? 'But not in the pickup.'

'What? Why not?'

'We're impounding it. The tow truck is on its way as we speak.'

'But you can't do that!' I cried. 'It's not even mine; it belongs to my brother-in-law, Andy.' I grabbed Highsmith's wrist. 'You've met him. Tall, skinny guy. Ponytail. Loves his truck,' I said with emphasis.

'Sorry, nothing I can do.' Highsmith plucked my hand from his wrist like my vice-like grip had meant nothing to him. The show-off. 'At this point we're holding it as potential evidence.' Now he outright chuckled. 'Not to mention, I hear it was reported stolen.'

I groaned. Why the heck had Andy reported it stolen? 'Evidence of what? We didn't do anything. Clive is innocent.'

'Can he prove it?'

'Not yet.'

Highsmith shrugged. 'There you go.'

'So now what? Are *you* going to give me a ride home?' In that bright red testosterone-fueled Firebird?

'Don't worry.' Highsmith smiled, his M&Ms twinkling. 'Like I said, your ride ought to be here.' He laid his hand lightly on my shoulder. 'I'll call you later this afternoon. Will you be available?'

I said yes.

'Great. After I've interviewed Clive in detail I'll want to get your story.' Highsmith told me to see myself out. I guess he was staying to make sure nobody came in or out of the stairwell. Evidence and all that.

I rode the passenger elevator to the ground floor, crossed the lobby and stepped out into the midday sun. I saw a green-and-red tow truck turning out of the Entronque building's parking lot with Andy's precious Chevy pickup on its flatbed. No doubt it was on its way to the Table Rock Police Department's impound lot.

Then I saw Andy.

I flushed and came to a stop. 'Andy! Boy, am I surprised to see you!' I flashed a bright smile.

He scowled. That wasn't the way this body language stuff was supposed to work. 'That's funny, Maggie,' he said, 'because I'm not at all surprised to see you.'

I tried again. I'd read an article recently while waiting in my dentist's office. Body Language 101. 'What do you mean?' I fluttered my eyelashes and let my hands relax at my side. It's supposed to set the other person at ease.

'You stole my truck is what I mean.' Andy stepped toward me and stuck his chin out. There'd been an edge to his voice that belied his usual laconic nature. 'What on earth were you thinking?'

I stepped back, looking up at my brother-in-law who's as tall as a redwood, and blubbered, 'I can explain everything!' Besides, stole was such an ugly word. I mean, it was a completely appropriate and accurate word in this particular instance, but still . . . talk about ugly.

Andy swatted his ear and his ponytail danced like a snake. 'Forget it, Maggie. Let's get out of here.'

'How?' The Table Rock PD had impounded his Chevy pickup. 'I mean . . .' I stopped talking. He knew what I meant.

Andy pointed to Donna's blue-and-white Mini Cooper. Oh, great, Donna probably knew about the whole stolen vehicle thing now, too.

I took a heavy step toward the Mini, then came to an abrupt stop. To an outsider it might have looked like I'd hit a pocket of heavy gravity. But I knew better. I hadn't hit any anomalistic gravity pocket. I'd hit the realization that if Andy knew . . . and if Donna knew . . . I groaned.

Mom probably knew too.

I groaned some more and squeezed my eyes shut.

Andy chuckled as if reading my mind as he opened the car door and somehow folded his long frame into the short car. 'Mom and Donna are waiting at the store.'

'Blabbermouth,' I said sourly.

Andy started up the Mini and rolled into traffic. 'Hey, it wasn't exactly a secret. When I went out to the dumpster my truck was gone. I ran in and told Donna and Donna called the police.'

I frowned. 'So who told Mom?'

Andy smiled, his hands gripping the wheel in a proper ten and two position. Me, I was lucky if I had ten fingers anywhere on the steering wheel at the same time while I drove. Another reason I was better off with the bicycle rather than the old car I'd sold because I'd needed to raise funds to open the beignet café.

He shrugged his bony shoulders. 'That was a lucky coincidence. Your mom came in to do some shopping and overheard your sister talking to the police dispatcher. She felt real bad when she heard somebody had stolen my truck.' He turned his eyes from the road for a moment. 'When we got the call that the police had found my truck and that that somebody was you—' He chuckled some more. 'The look on your mom's face was precious.'

I'll bet. I folded my arms across my chest and sunk down in the car seat. Everybody always complains about Mondays but, so far, Tuesday wasn't exactly turning out to be the prize in a box of Cracker Jack.

We drove in awkward silence for several minutes. 'You can drop me off at the café,' I said stonily.

'OK,' Andy acceded, 'but you're going to have to face your mom sometime.'

'I know,' I replied glumly.

Andy shook his head and sighed loudly as he pulled to the curb outside Maggie's Beignet Café. 'Poor Mrs Malarkey.' That's Mom. 'The poor woman's devastated to learn that she's got a car thief in the family.' His eyes danced. 'She blames it on that videogame, Grand Theft Auto. I didn't know you were a gamer, Mag.'

'Very funny.' I slammed the car door harder than necessary

and took a step toward my café. I stopped on the sidewalk and turned back to the Mini. I gestured for Andy to roll down the window. I stuck my head in. 'I'm sorry I took your truck without asking, Andy. It's just that Clive came running into the shop all desperate and—'

Andy held up his hand like a stop sign. The tattered, spiral-patterned hemp bracelet that I'd never seen him without, even in his lawyer days, flopped around his slender wrist. His lips formed a smile. 'Next time, just ask.'

I nodded. Andy was OK.

I pushed through the door, listening to the tinkle of the leather string of bells. 'Hey, Aubrey! Did I miss anything?' About half the tables were occupied. That was a good sign. I'm a table is half full kind of person.

Aubrey pushed the register shut and adjusted her visor. 'Nope. Nothing special. There's been a steady stream of customers. Nothing Kelly and I couldn't handle.'

I nodded. The empty tables were spic and span and everything appeared in order. 'Where's Kelly?'

'I sent her to pick up some lunch. Did you want anything?'

'No, thanks.'

'Are you sure? I could call her on her cell.'

I shook my head. I'd had my fill at Ethiopia. And after seeing that woman, Lisa Willoughby, lying under a pile of lemon cake, dessert might be off my menu for a while. I stepped behind the counter and threw my white apron over my neck. I was reaching back to tie the apron strings when the door banged open.

'Miller!' screamed Johnny Wolfe. He aimed his finger at me like a scud missile. 'Clive's been arrested and it's all your fault!'

SIX

I was happy to be on the opposite side of the counter – something to protect me from the wrath of Johnny Wolfe. Johnny's a white-fleshed fellow no wider at the shoulders than he is at the hips, so you'd think it would be an even match.

But he's also a former pro skater, a former bronze medal-winning Olympic skater, too. He's got the ego to match.

Right now, his charcoal-blue eyes were flashing like a storm crossing the desert. And that storm was aiming straight for me. Yes, better to have a sturdy counter between the two of us.

'What do you mean, all my fault?'

Johnny's a real coxcomb and a pain in the patooty.

'He was with you, wasn't he?' Johnny jammed his fists against his hips. He wore an expensive tailored gray pinstriped suit with a solid black silk shirt underneath. Johnny's also a real clothes horse.

Aubrey swiveled her head back and forth, catching all the action while sucking lemonade through a skinny straw.

'Well,' I stammered, 'sure he was with me. But what's that got to do with anything?' Not that there wasn't a certain logic to his argument, borne out by history, but still, who did this guy think he was? An Olympic gold medalist? Heck, he'd come in third. There were days when I slipped in the shower reaching for the towel rack and twisted in ways that could have seen me take the silver if there'd been any judges there to score me.

'Don't play coy with me, Miller. I heard from the police. Clive has been charged with murder and they say you were with him.' His eyes blazed at me as he planted his hands on the counter and pushed. 'Why they haven't arrested you, too, I'll never know!'

'Uh,' Aubrey raised an index finger, 'would somebody mind telling me what's going on?' She raised a hopeful brow.

Kelly Herman came through from the storeroom. 'What's with all the shouting, peeps?'

'That's what I'm trying to find out,' replied Aubrey. 'Something about a murder?' She scrunched up her nose.

Kelly gaped. 'A murder? Where?' Kelly's a half-Havasupi, half-Jewish beauty about Aubrey's age – twenty-three. The color drained from her face like somebody'd just pulled her plug.

'That's right,' Johnny spat. 'Murder.' He glared my way. 'What are you going to do about it?'

I bit the inside of my cheek. 'Now, now,' I said, pushing my palms at him. Customers were getting up and leaving, their faces troubled. 'Let's all calm down.' I didn't want people thinking they weren't safe stepping inside Maggie's Beignet Café. I took a chance and leaned closer to Johnny, hoping he didn't punch me in the nose. 'Let's talk about this privately.'

He scrunched his brows together and pouted. 'Fine,' he huffed finally. Johnny pirouetted across the tiles and followed me into the storeroom. I gave him a six-point-five for execution and a perfect ten for obnoxiousness.

I pulled a stool over to my office desk. OK, so it was a cardboard box turned on its side, but it was a pretty sturdy one. Though I'd been a little annoyed with Aubrey when she'd drawn a couple of drawers on the face of it as a joke, I was over it now. 'Have a seat.'

I looked forlornly at the pile of invoices and receipts scattered across my cardboard box slash desk. Bookkeeping is miserable work. That's why I kept putting it off. Too bad my dead husband Brian wasn't still around. He used to work in a bank; he'd have been great at all this mindless paperwork.

Johnny remained standing, obviously preferring to loom over me – something he couldn't do if I was standing as well. After all, I was about five-seven and I figured he was about the same depending on how much gel he'd bathed his hair in that day. Today his unnaturally black locks were swept back across his swelled head like a wave of ego externalized. Perhaps he was trying to channel Elvis. Maybe I'd buy him some blue suede shoes for Xmas.

Johnny's right hand twisted the Rolex on his left wrist. 'You've gone too far this time, Miller.'

'Are you ever going to call me Maggie?' I smiled. Maybe I could counterbalance his strident attitude with a rident one.

His eyebrows formed a single line and he stared down his nose at me. 'When there are so many other things I'd like to call you first?'

I chewed my lip. Boy, I'd really thrown him a softball that time. 'OK, OK,' I said, waving my hands. 'I can see you're upset about this.' Lesson learned. Strident definitely tips the scales in a contest with rident.

'Of course I'm upset!'

'And you have every right to be.' I glanced at the café's electric bill lying open on my corrugated cardboard desk. Did electricity really cost that much? If I paid my Table Rock Electric Co. bill I might not be able to afford to eat for a month. I'd be reduced to mooching canned food from my mom's condo when she wasn't looking. Worse yet, I'd be taking potluck – and I do mean luck – at Donna and Andy's house. Trust me, there's no luck coming out of those pots. More like bulgur wheat, soggy tofu, beansprouts and broccoli. Stuff I wouldn't even force my cat to eat. And she enjoyed stuff like sardines and kidneys. 'I'm sure this is all a big misunderstanding.' I crossed and uncrossed my legs. 'Detective Highsmith told me he was only taking Clive down to the station to ask him some questions. You know, to try to figure out what happened to Lisa. Put all the pieces together.'

Though there was no way they'd ever put all the pieces of that cake together again. Lisa Willoughby and Markie's latest masterpiece had done a major Humpty Dumpty. And a unidirectional one at that. There was no way of putting either back together again.

I suddenly wondered who'd ordered that cake and if it might have something to do with the young woman's demise. An ex-lover, perhaps? Someone with a grudge who'd ordered the cake, intent all along on using that cake to send her to a messy death? Improbable? Maybe. But impossible? Who was to say?

Johnny shook his fist at me. His jacket popped open revealing a slash of bright pink silk lining. It looked every bit as garish as some of those costumes he used to wear out on the ice during his pro performances. Once a showman, always a showman, I suppose. 'Clive telephoned me and told me he'd been arrested!'

'Oh, please.' I sighed. 'You know Clive.' I tossed a hand in the air. 'Always so melodramatic. Overreacts to everything.' Like Johnny Wolfe was doing now. 'He's probably sitting in a cozy room down at the police station, sipping coffee, nibbling on a maple donut and having a grand old time.'

I glanced at the Boar's Head-branded clock on the wall, a remnant from the previous deli owner of my space. 'In fact, I wouldn't be surprised if he isn't done by now.' I leaned forward and placed my hands on my desk. It wobbled and caved. I hastily straightened. 'In fact, I'll bet he's next door at The Hitching Post wondering where you are.' I turned in the bridal shop's direction. 'Why don't you go check?' *Please.* I snapped my fingers. 'If he isn't there I'll bet he's resting at home, out on the veranda, watching the sun skate across the sky—' I threw the skate metaphor in there for Johnny's sake. 'A nice piña colada in hand.' *Go join him.*

Kelly Herman popped her head between the swinging doors. 'Ms Miller?' She tugged at the white headband on her forehead. She wore indigo jeans and a white shirt with Mother Earth/ Father Sun written over the chest in green script. I'd have to ask Aubrey to make Kelly an outfit to match ours. I love my sister but I needed my staff to promote beignets not vegetables.

'Yes?'

'There's a Detective Highsmith here to see you.' She looked uneasy. I guess it's always tough when there's talk of murder and police the first day on a new job.

'Perfect!' I jumped to my feet. 'Send him back here, would you?'

A moment later, Detective Highsmith pushed the swinging doors aside with all the swagger of a gunfighter in the Old West. He strode into the room like he owned the place. I checked his feet for spurs. Nope, not even cowboy boots. Adidas. That explained the lack of a jangle.

He'd added a brown sports coat to the cargo shorts and muscle shirt he'd been wearing that morning. It wasn't an improvement. In fact, it looked like a four-year-old's attempt at dressing up for church on Sunday.

'I'm so glad you're here, Detective.' I turned to Johnny, who stood glowering near the walk-in fridge. Maybe he wanted to keep his blood chilled. I'd read somewhere that vampires have lower core body temps than we humans – probably in a vampire mystery novel. So it had to be true. 'You remember Johnny Wolfe?'

'Of course,' replied Highsmith. 'Mr Wolfe.' He nodded toward Johnny. 'I'd like to get Ms Miller's statement now.' He pointed to the door. 'In private.'

'Fine,' I said rather snappishly. 'But first, would you please explain to Johnny that you only asked Clive to go down to the station to take his statement.' I forced a laugh. 'Johnny here is under the impression that Clive has been arrested. Can you believe it?' I shook my head and laughed some more. Nobody joined in. Party poopers.

Johnny glared at me. I pulled at my lower lip with my teeth.

'Yeah, I can believe it,' Highsmith said, his words falling like stones down a waterspout. He stuffed his hands in his jacket.

'You see!' Johnny shouted triumphantly. 'What did I tell you?'

I swiveled toward Johnny. 'Quiet,' I hissed.

He thrust his chin out at me.

I stepped toward Detective Highsmith and looked up into his M&M eyes. 'What's that supposed to mean?'

Highsmith shrugged. 'It means I didn't really have much choice in the matter.'

I creased my brow. Table Rock's lone detective could be annoyingly inscrutable.

'He confessed.'

SEVEN

That thump I heard wasn't my heart, which I feared for a second had burst – it was the sound of Johnny Wolfe fainting dead and hitting the tile floor.

What a drama queen.

I raced to the sink, filled a glass with ice-cold water from the tap and tossed it in Johnny's limp face. I wasn't sure if he needed it or not, but it sure made me feel better.

Johnny sputtered and sat up. Water dripped from his nose to his chin to my floor. I was going to have to mop that up before somebody slipped in it.

I ripped off several sheets from a roll of paper towels and handed them to Johnny. 'Why would Clive confess to pushing Lisa Willoughby down four flights of stairs?' Somehow that sounded better than calling it murder. Maybe it was simply horseplay gone awry. Boys will be boys, after all. Had playground antics turned fatal?

'Lisa Willoughby?' Johnny wadded up the damp towels and tossed them toward the sink. He missed and they skittered along the counter and hit the floor. 'That's the Lisa we're talking about?'

Highsmith shrugged. It was a move he used a lot.

'Yes, Johnny. I thought you knew?'

Johnny scrubbed his damp face with his hands. 'I only knew that Clive had been arrested,' he sniffed. 'That he'd confessed to killing some woman named Lisa.' He collapsed in on himself, his head hanging like it was only attached by the slenderest of spines.

Johnny glanced nervously at Highsmith. 'I didn't know it was *that* Lisa.'

'What do you mean, *that* Lisa?' I was getting a bad feeling about this. Was there something Johnny and Clive knew that I didn't? And whatever it was, did Detective Highsmith know it too?

Johnny stepped in front of the detective, his hands attached to his boyish hips. 'I want to see Clive right now.'

Highsmith appeared almost amused as he gazed down at the infinitely tinier and more slender man before him. The side of his face turned up in a wry rictus of a smile. 'I think that might be a good idea, Mr Wolfe. In fact,' he said, turning to me, 'I think it might be a good idea if we all went down to the station.'

I rode with Johnny Wolfe down to the Table Rock police station in his fancy BMW 335i convertible. Black on black, of course. What else? Perfect for those hot and sunny Arizona days when you felt like burning the flesh off your thighs. I rubbed mine as we drove. If I left a couple of pounds of skin and flesh behind on his seat I'd count the weight loss toward my eternal diet goals – the number one goal of which was to actually set some diet goals.

Detective Highsmith pulled up at the red light beside us on Laredo and Gibson and revved the engine of that puerile Firebird of his. Johnny's fingers tightened around the leather-wrapped steering wheel and I was sure I was about to see a drag race. 'I wouldn't if I were you,' I cautioned.

Johnny pouted. 'Why not?'

'Because you might end up sharing a cell with Clive.'

The light turned green and Highsmith zoomed ahead. I caught the glint of sunlight on his teeth as he smugly pushed ahead. A guttural growl emanated from Johnny's throat as he lifted his foot from the brake. Johnny looked a little green himself. I guess it was his competitive nature. That had probably served him well as a professional ice skater but it wasn't always a good thing when dealing with the real world, especially when that real world included real cops with real guns. And real attitudes.

Then again, boys will be boys. Even when they grow up to be men.

'I don't get it,' I said as Johnny tailed the detective at a more sedate speed. 'Why would Clive confess to murdering one of Markie's employees?' I shook my head, hoping to rearrange some brain cells into a picture that made sense. 'I mean, he didn't say anything even remotely resembling a confession when we were at the Entronque.'

'I don't know,' Johnny shot back, his jaw set, his fingers tight. I didn't know either so I remained mum the rest of the drive. Johnny and Clive had been married for over three years. I knew. I'd been a guest at their recent anniversary party. Markie's Masterpieces had supplied the cake, a replica of The Hitching Post.

Detective Highsmith was waiting for us inside the police station, which was located along the main highway that skirted the edge of Table Rock. I led the way inside. 'Let me do the talking, Johnny.'

'I can speak for myself,' retorted Johnny. 'I'm not about to be bullied by some small-town cops.'

'Oh, yeah,' I said under my breath, 'that's the kind of attitude that's going to get us far – like tossed in the slammer along with Clive.' Or buried in a shallow hole in the Painted Desert.

'Fine,' chuffed Johnny. He waved me forward.

'So, a Firebird, huh? Nice car,' I said to Detective Highsmith as he led us back into a restricted area of the building. 'High-school graduation present from mommy and daddy?'

'Very funny.' He punched some numbers on an electric lock and opened the solid door. 'And it's a Trans Am.'

'What's the difference?' I asked as I sidled past him.

The detective rolled his eyes and sighed heavily.

'Maggie!'

'Hello, Clive. How are you holding up?'

Clive's fingers were laced tightly around the thick steel bars. He looked an utter wreck. Clive pressed his pallid skull to the bars. He looked a little like a lost sheep. I half-expected him to 'baa' any minute. He glanced hopefully at me, then he spotted Johnny and his eyes fell. 'Oh, hello, Johnny.'

'Clive.' Johnny reached through the bars.

'Did you really have to lock him up like this?' Was I really looking at a cold-blooded killer? A cold-blooded pusher down the stairs? No, not Clive Rothschild. I may not have known him all that long but I did know that Clive was a pussycat. I meant that in the kindest fashion, despite the agony my recently adopted cat put me through on a daily basis. I mean, it's not that having a cat is so bad, but why can't they clean their own litter boxes? Surely, as advanced as science is these days, some biologist can come up with some genetically modified cats who can handle a pooper scooper? After all, there are dogs out there who can play Frisbee. How hard can it be to create a cat capable of cleaning his or her own litter box?

And why was it that Carole Two would gladly scarf down anything I laid in her bowl from kibble to probiotic yogurt but steadily ignored any food I dropped on the floor? Didn't cats believe in the five-second rule?

Detective Highsmith leaned against the wall and said nothing. We stood in a narrow hall along which were three modest jail cells. All very clean. All very scary.

The walls were painted yellow and drawings of Disney characters were scattered along the backs of the cells. See? Scary. I raised an eyebrow toward the detective. 'Disney?'

Highsmith grinned. 'Some shrink's idea. He said it would make the prisoners more docile.'

I shrugged. Images of Mickey Mouse, Donald Duck and Minnie didn't normally lead one to run amok, explode in rage or engage in murderous mayhem, so the shrink might have been onto something. Either that or he'd been having a laugh at the Table Rock Police Department's no doubt significant expense. 'Don't worry,' I promised. 'We'll get you out of here,

Clive.' I turned to Detective Highsmith. 'Have you got a hacksaw handy I can borrow?'

'Quiet, Maggie!' Johnny hissed between gritted teeth. 'Must you always make jokes?'

'Sorry.' Jokes were my defense mechanism. I was lousy at kung fu.

Johnny gripped Clive's hands through the bars. 'How are you, Clive? What on earth were you thinking?' He looked over his shoulder at me and the detective then turned back to his partner. 'And why on earth did you confess to killing Lisa?'

Clive's eyelids drooped as he jutted out his chin. 'I had to,' he said firmly. 'I did it.'

'Oh, please,' I whined while Johnny gasped and made rapid up and down motions with his right hand in the universal gesture of shut your freaking mouth before you dig yourself down a deeper hole. It was at that precise moment that Veronica Vargas made her grand entrance. Veronica Vargas knows how and when to make an entrance.

VV, as she's known to her friends and admirers – though I suspected she had more admirers than she had friends – is a real piece of work. She was rocking a pinstriped charcoal-gray jacket with peaked lapels and matching slacks. The detective's jaw went a little slack just looking at her. I suspected other parts may have gone less slack.

VV's elegant auburn tresses were pulled severely back behind her skull, no doubt held in place by sheer willpower alone. No hairpins or barrettes need apply. Her pumps rattled across the tiles like a burst from a Thompson submachine gun as she came toward us. I expected to see a sea of dead men strewn in her wake like empty shell casings.

Highsmith straightened. The big jerk.

'Sorry it took me so long to get here.' She dropped a hand lightly on Highsmith's arm, then pulled it quickly away. 'I had a hard time getting away.'

Sure, she'd probably been having tea at the country club with all her privileged friends and been forced to wait while a good-looking young valet in khaki shorts and a polo shirt ran to fetch her Mercedes.

I am not jealous. I just want what she's got. Like her car and her house and maybe those shoes she was wearing, though I doubted I could squeeze into them. VV must have had her feet bound as a child.

VV's sharp eyes scanned over our small group, mostly with disapproval. Her irises were the color of – and I suspected the hardness of – hazelnut shells. She brushed past me and stopped in front of Clive's cell. I smelled a subtle top note of orange blossom from her fancy perfume. 'This is the suspect in the death of Ms Lisa Willoughby?' Though VV's looks said all Latin, her lingo sounded all Manhattan snooty.

'That's the one,' Highsmith answered from behind her.

She nodded once. When you're a princess, once is enough.

'Clive didn't do anything,' I said. 'He was with me the whole time.' I crossed my arms over my chest. 'He couldn't have.' So there.

Ms Vargas looked down her aquiline nose at me. 'The beignet lady, right?'

Well, that seemed a bit, I don't know, denigrating? The way she'd said it, she might as well have said *bag lady*. 'That's right.' What else could I say? When you're right, you're right.

A hint of a smile passed her lips. 'Just checking. For a minute I thought perhaps you were Table Rock's prosecuting attorney and I a mere civilian.'

I pulled a face. Who did this woman think she was? I mean, she *was* Table Rock's prosecuting attorney, but still. It was only a part-time gig. And she'd only gotten the position because dear old Daddy was mayor. 'Listen,' I said sharply, 'Clive is innocent. I know he is.'

She paid me no mind. 'Take him to the interrogation room,' VV ordered Highsmith. 'I'll talk to him there.'

Highsmith popped the cell door and Clive limped out.

'I want to come too,' Johnny said. He placed himself between Clive and Veronica.

'Just a minute,' I said, squeezing between Johnny, Clive and Veronica. It was getting awfully tight in here. 'Nobody's going anywhere until Clive's had a chance to talk to his lawyer.' I took Clive's hand. Wow, cold. Had he died in that cell? Should we notify his next of kin? Was I holding hands with a walking corpse? Yuck. 'Have you talked to your attorney yet?'

Clive's shoulders rose and fell. 'I don't have an attorney.' He looked at Johnny.

Johnny draped his arm around Clive's waist. 'Don't worry, Clive. I'll call my attorney in New York.' He faced down VV. Not an easy thing to do. 'He's the best there is. He'll straighten this whole mess up in no time.' His hand ruffled Clive's hair. 'I'm sure it's all just a big mistake.'

'Fine.' Veronica turned to Detective Highsmith. 'After Mr Rothschild has spoken with his attorney, have him give me a call and we can arrange a proper interrogation.'

At the word 'interrogation' Clive and Johnny blanched. Johnny patted Clive's hand once again. 'Don't worry,' he cooed, 'I'll take care of everything.'

Highsmith locked Clive back in his cell and we all spilled back out into the world of the un-imprisoned.

Seated in the BMW, which I figured was now hot enough inside to bake a medium-sized pizza in under five minutes, I said to Johnny, 'Look, I sort of feel like somehow Clive being in jail might be my fault.'

Johnny sighed as he started the engine. 'It isn't Miller – forget it.'

'I can't forget it,' I replied. 'Clive is my friend. I want to help.' Had my ears heard correctly? Had Johnny actually absolved me of blame? Not accused me of being the source of all his troubles? Wow. Something was definitely wrong here.

Johnny turned to me. His face sagged and his eyes were rimmed in red. I'd never seen the guy look so down before. I'd seem him look angry plenty of times – like the time I'd plowed into him with my bicycle – but never depressed; certainly not this depressed. 'I'll call O'Neal and Partners as soon as I get back to The Hitching Post. I'm sure O'Neal will know what to do to extricate Clive from this mess.'

I nodded. But I didn't believe it. 'Forget about this big-shot lawyer of yours, Johnny. What's he going to do? He's thousands of miles away.'

'But—'

I cut him off. 'But nothing.' My hands slapped my knees. Partly to make my point, partly to see if they still had any feeling left in them. That black leather was tanning my hide.

'You leave this to me.' I beamed. 'You and Clive need a local attorney. Somebody who knows the town, the people. All the players. And I've got just the guy.'

Johnny pulled the BMW to the curb between my café and The Hitching Post. 'Who?' He eyed me skeptically. 'Your brother-in-law? The grocer?'

'Yep, my brother-in-law, Andy.'

Johnny's jaw dropped. 'He's a hippie.'

'He's not a hippie, he's a—' Well, he was a hippie but before that he was a darn fine lawyer too – when he wanted to be. I could only pray this was one of those times. 'Let me call him.' I escaped from the oven on wheels then checked the passenger seat to ascertain just how much skin I was leaving behind. Always good to know. 'I'm sure he'll be glad to help.'

EIGHT

Johnny grumbled, as was his way, but caved.

I ran inside and immediately called Andy. He wasn't answering. Either he was away from his phone or he was avoiding my call. I cursed the inventor of caller ID and dialed my sister. 'Where's Andy?' I blurted as she picked up. 'I need to speak to him right away.'

Donna made *tsk-tsk*ing noises on the other end of the line. 'I don't know,' she teased. 'I'm not sure I'd be going anywhere near him right now if I were you. Even on the phone.'

'C'mon, Sis,' I pleaded. 'Clive's in jail. He needs Andy's help.'

'Clive? Your friend from the bridal shop?'

'Yes. He's been arrested. Held on suspicion of murder!' I shouted into the phone. Several customers over at the tables were eyeing me. Aubrey and Kelly looked at me like I was nuts. I stuck my tongue out at the girls and they went back to work, or at least pretended to.

It seemed being a manager wasn't so tough after all.

I pleaded into the phone. 'So, can I talk to him?' There's not much worse than having to plead with one's kid sister.

After a long, pregnant pause, Donna said, 'He's unloading goods at the back of the store. He'll never agree to talk to you right now. Not after what you did to his precious truck.'

I stifled a groan. What was it about men and their cars? Or in this case, trucks? I mean, it's just four tires and a steering wheel. Why couldn't he get over it already? I had two tires and a pair of handlebars. You wouldn't see me getting all bent out of shape just because somebody borrowed it for an hour or two.

'Keep him there!' I cried. 'I'll be right over!'

'Wait!' shouted Donna. 'Do not tell Andy I told you where he was. Promise?'

'Promise,' I answered quickly. Whether I'd remember to keep my word or not was another story. I'd try, but still, Donna's my sister. She ought to know better than to trust me. Despite my best intentions.

I tossed off my apron and grabbed the Schwinn from the storeroom. 'I've got to leave,' I explained. 'I'll be back just as soon as I can.'

Aubrey rolled her eyes, more for Kelly's benefit, I suspected. 'There she goes again,' I heard her say as I struggled to get my bike out the door without too much bumping and scraping.

I pedaled up on my pink beauty in stealth mode, through the alley between the Mother Earth/Father Sun Grocers and Earl's Hardware. I came upon Andy out back, muscling some bushel baskets of produce from the back of Donna's Mini Cooper. My pink beauty being a Schwinn, stealth mode was pretty much the norm, unless the brakes started squealing like a piglet missing her mommy at feeding time.

'Hi-ya, Andy!' I called. I jumped down from the saddle and adjusted the kickstand.

He frowned. 'Hello, Maggie.' Andy jostled a bushel of corn from the open hatch and carried it through the rear of the grocery. I followed. 'Donna's up front. Your mom left when she saw you weren't with me. Chicken.'

'Bawk-bawk,' I replied. I'd rather be chicken than mom-pecked. 'It's you I wanted to talk to.' Andy laid the basket from Tinker Family Farms, a local grower, on the ground beside two others. I tailed him like a puppy dog as he went back for another.

Donna and Andy took pride in ordering as much of their produce locally as possible. Andy leaned in to grab another basket. 'Watch your—'

'What?' Andy turned and his head bounced off the car's headliner. 'Ouch.' Andy extracted his torso and simmered at me while rubbing the top of his skull.

'Sorry,' I mumbled. Not that it had been my fault. 'That's a lot of corn and cucumbers to pack into a little car. Wouldn't you be better off using your—'

Andy glared at me.

'Oh.' That's right, his truck had been impounded. Sort of my fault. At least I knew that was what he and everybody else was probably thinking. I'm no mind-reader but I was doing a good job reading the expression on my brother-in-law's face just then. I scuffed the ground with my toe.

'Look, if you've come to apologize, Maggie, forget it. What's done is done.' He took a breath and smiled. 'Next time, just ask, OK?'

I promised I would.

He smiled. For real this time. 'So what is it you wanted to talk to me about?'

I grabbed the last bushel of cukes and followed Andy back inside. 'It's about Clive. You know Clive.'

'Of course.' Andy set down his corn, then took the cukes from me and dropped them near the sink. 'What's up?' He wiped his hands down the front of his jeans.

'He's in a bit of trouble.'

'What sort of trouble?'

I twisted my jaw and talked to the cement floor. 'He's sort of been arrested for murder.'

'He what?'

I looked my brother-in-law in the eye. 'He's been arrested,' I blurted. 'And he needs your help.'

Andy waved his hand side to side. 'He doesn't need my help. He needs a lawyer.'

'You are a lawyer.'

'Not any more. I'm a farmer.' His arm arced around the storeroom. 'And a grocer.'

'You've still got your license. You're still a lawyer.'

'Is this about the accident involving that young woman this morning over at Navajo Junction?'

I nodded. 'Except the police don't seem to think it was an accident.' I chewed my lip nervously. 'They sort of think it was murder.'

Andy flopped onto a stool and sighed. 'So that's why they impounded the Chevy. I haven't been able to get a straight answer out of anybody.' I knew Andy had a friend or two on the force so I was surprised he hadn't heard all the details.

Andy scrubbed his face with his hands. 'So what makes them suspect Clive was involved?'

'Well,' I cleared my throat, 'he sort of confessed . . .'

Andy barked out a laugh. 'Then he's going to need a criminal defense attorney. I practiced corporate law.'

'Come on,' I pleaded. 'You've helped me before.'

He shrugged those skinny shoulders of his. 'That's different. You're family.'

'Clive is a close friend of mine. That's like family.'

'That's a stretch, even for you, Maggie.'

A produce clerk swung through the doors from the front of the store and glanced at the two of us. 'Am I interrupting something?'

'What do you need, Len?'

'Miss Donna asked me to restock the lettuce.' The gangly, freckle-faced kid in denim bib overalls and a white T-shirt had a soft style of speech, like he was in church. 'We're running low.' He scratched his chin. 'It's on sale today.'

Andy smiled at him. 'I know. Go ahead, Len.' Andy waved toward a pallet of food cartons near the far corner. We watched in silence as Len moved quickly to a large, waxy box of lettuce heads, hefted it and disappeared. Andy slapped his thighs and stood. 'Sorry, Maggie.' He rested a hand affectionately on my shoulder. 'I really don't think I'm the man for the job.'

'Of course, you are,' I retorted. 'Please?' I can whine like the best of them.

'I said no.'

I reached into my purse. It was time to pull out all the stops – bring out the big guns, go for the jugular, bring out my secret weapon. I extracted a four-inch long, two-inch-thick bar wrapped in clear plastic.

Andy's eyes lit up. 'What is that?' His tongue flickered along his upper lip. 'Is that what I think it is?'

I unwrapped the tip of the bar and waved it under his nose. 'Yep, a nanaimo bar.' I took a whiff myself. Heavenly. 'I made a fresh batch yesterday.' I cocked an eyebrow at him. 'I thought you might like one. In fact, I've got a whole batch of them back at the apartment.' These yummy confections were Andy's absolute favorite. There was no way he'd turn this down. I'd eaten his wife's cooking – the poor guy deserved a break.

Andy's hand reached for the bar and I snatched it back. I shook my head, holding it aloft. 'First Clive, then the bar.' Donna was always getting on Andy about eating too many sweets. She frowned on such things.

Andy looked at me for a moment. OK, he was looking mostly at the bar. Then he did the unexpected. He shook his head adamantly and locked his arms across his chest. 'No can do.'

'No can do what?' We both turned. I stuffed the bar back in my purse. Donna peered at us quizzically. 'What's going on?' She looked up at her husband. Donna's shorter than me and Andy is as tall as a skyscraper. 'What can't you do, Andy?'

Andy looked at me, opened his mouth, looked at his wife then snapped it shut again. He looked at me once again. We both knew he wouldn't turn me down in front of my sister.

'I was just telling your sister how I couldn't wait to go down to the police station to see what I can do to help out her friend,' Andy explained.

Donna turned to me, her eyebrows pushed together. 'What friend?'

'Clive's been accused of pushing Willoughby down the stairs at the Entronque building this morning,' I replied. 'Can you believe it?'

'That's ridiculous!' Donna replied.

'Worse,' said Andy, wrapping an arm around Donna's waist. 'He's confessed.'

'He what?' Donna's hand flew to her mouth. 'I don't believe it.'

'Neither do I,' I said.

Donna extricated herself from her husband's arms. 'Clive is such a gentleman. No wonder you can't wait to go down to the station and help him out, Andy.'

'Yeah,' I grinned. It was a sort of evil grin, but only Andy and I knew that. 'Andy's a sweetheart.'

Donna planted a kiss on Andy's cheek. 'Don't I know it.' She snatched the rag tucked into her belt and swatted it at Andy. 'You two go on ahead. We can manage here.'

I planted a kiss on him too before climbing into the Mini beside him. 'Thanks, Andy.'

Andy's sigh shook the car side to side. Or maybe it was a gust of wind. 'I needed to go down to the station to see about getting my pickup back anyway.' He shot me a look. 'I guess it couldn't hurt to talk to Clive.'

I grinned – a normal one, this time. 'That's the spirit.'

'And I want all the nanaimos.'

As we pulled out onto Laredo and waited for the light to change, Andy turned to me. 'Your mom is waiting for you at your apartment.' He smiled wickedly.

'What? Why?' My body tensed. I love my mom but she can be quite the handful. A handful that went better when I had another hand filled with a margarita glass.

'She's spending the week with you.'

'OK.' I was wondering how Clive was making out. He'd been in that jail cell for hours. Personally, I'd be going stir crazy. . . 'Wait.' My arms jerked forwards and my hands slapped the dashboard. 'What?' The glovebox popped open and slapped me across the knees. My eyes bugged out and I glowered at Andy as he laughed. 'Why is my mother staying at my apartment for a week?' I demanded between his irritating snorts of laughter.

I didn't think it was possible, but Andy's smile grew to twice the size of his face. 'Because they're replacing all the roofs over at her condo. She's got no place else to stay. You know we haven't got room, except on the sofa. Can't have Mom sleeping on the sofa for a week, can we?' Andy jostled my shoulder. 'She is family, after all.'

One week. One whole week living with my yoga enthusiast mother. How many poses would she urge me to try? How many awkward positions would I be forced to see her contort her frame into? 'You're a real rat.'

'Squeak,' Andy twittered.

NINE

'What are you dropping me off here now for?' The Mini rolled to a stop on the street outside my fourplex. 'I thought we were going to the police station first?'

'I work alone.'

'But you need me,' I protested.

'I need you to let me do my job.'

'But my bike's at the grocery.' I was grasping at straws.

'I'll drop it off later.'

'But—'

He pointed toward the apartment. 'Out you go. Your mother's waiting.' I pushed open the door and started to rise. Andy's hand clamped down on my knee. 'Leave the bar,' he ordered.

Mom's metallic-green Volkswagen Beetle was parked a couple spaces up under the shade of a juniper. Its Beetle eyes, lashes and all, seemed to wink at me as I turned the key in the lock and stepped into a frigid blast of air. Mom's going through one of those phases where even a week in the Antarctic would have required packing a bikini. 'Mom,' I called, 'I'm ho—' Yikes! Mom had moved the coffee table away from the couch and rolled out her yoga mat – a green mat with a cherry blossom pattern. She travels everywhere with it.

Mom looked at me from between her skinny legs. Her unitard was the color of a ripe peach. Her butt was in the air, facing the ceiling, and her legs extended like somebody should be pulling on them and making a Thanksgiving wish. The tops of her feet touched the ground behind, which I was pretty sure was impossible. A knee squeezed each ear. She'd somehow managed to tip so far over backwards that I thought she might be in danger of turning herself inside out.

'Hello, Maggie.' Her voice sounded a bit strangled but then she was upside down, backwards and, possibly, soon to be inside out. Everything about this situation was off. Her red locks dusted the floor. The floors did need dusting, but still.

'Mom,' I said, dropping my purse on the displaced coffee table and staring down between her legs, 'what are you doing?'

'It's the karnapidasana pose, darling. You should join me.'

'The karna-what?' I flopped onto the sofa. I'd seen enough. Things a daughter shouldn't have to see. 'No, thanks. I think that move is illegal in Arizona.' Besides, one pretzel was enough; two would be an obscene tangle.

Mother uncoiled herself easily and sat up, pulling one arm behind her head, then the other.

I don't know how she'd managed to unwind so facilely. It would have taken me hours to disentangle my arms and limbs from a position like that. I'd have been screaming like the maiden victim of Torquemada's rack the entire time, too.

'I hear we're going to be roommates.' A travel-weary red plaid canvas suitcase sat just inside my bedroom door. It looked like I'd be sharing a double bed or going solo on the lumpy green sofa that came with the apartment.

'And I hear you stole Andy's pickup truck.'

'I didn't steal it, Mom.' My voice instantly reverted to whiny teen mode. 'I borrowed it. Clive needed a ride. I couldn't say no, could I?' I rose and crossed to the tiny kitchen. 'I'm making a margarita. You want one?' *Please say yes.* Mom was better when she'd had a margarita. Mom was better still when I'd had a couple myself. I grabbed the tequila.

'No, thank you.' Mom followed me to the kitchen. Her snug peach unitard showed off her figure. For someone a generation older than me, she was in annoying good shape. 'And I don't think you should be drinking, Maggie. Not when you're going to be driving.'

No sign of a bulge around her middle at all. She definitely was not eating enough beignets for her own good, or mine.

I blinked at Mom, my eyes falling to the crystal hanging around her neck. I was beginning to think maybe aliens were controlling her mind via the rock thing. That was the only explanation I could come up with for the way she'd been thinking and acting since Dad died. 'Where exactly am I going to be driving?'

Mom pulled her lower lip with her teeth. 'Well, I suppose Navajo Junction might be the best place to start. That is the,' Mom drew a pair of quotation marks with her fingers, '"scene of the crime," as they say.'

My eyes lit on the tequila. One little drink, that's all I wanted.

'You are going to figure out what happened to that poor dead woman, aren't you, Maggie, dear?'

There was an empty margarita glass right there, next to the sink. And it was practically clean.

'Clive is one of your best friends.'

'Why don't we let the fuzz handle it, Mom?'

Mom frowned. 'Don't say fuzz, dear. Fuzz is what grows in your navel.' She waved her fingers. 'Now, off you go.'

'But Mom,' I persisted, 'are you forgetting? It's ninety-five degrees outside. And that's in the shade. I drive a Schwinn, for pity's sake.' I reached for my glass. 'And I left the bike at the grocery.' Not that I'd intended to.

'And,' I said rather smugly, 'you know Andy's not about to let me borrow the pickup again so soon. Fresh wounds and all that.' Not to mention, it was still in the police impound yard. I chuckled and grabbed the tequila bottle, its golden yellow insides beckoning.

Tinkle, tinkle.

I spun around. Mom's Beetle keys dangled from the tips of her fingers. 'Drive carefully, dear.'

'You do remember that the last time I stuck my nose into a murder, I almost got killed, right?'

Mom nodded. 'Be more careful this time, Maggie. Look before you leap. Remain open; let your spirit guide you.' Mom spread her hands and gazed upwards. I don't know what she saw. I saw cracked plaster. 'The answer is out there if you open yourself to it.'

Right, and measure twice, cut once. Mom's great at aphorisms. 'Thanks for the advice, Mom.' Apparently there'd be no margarita, no curling up on the sofa with a good book in my near future. 'Thanks a lot, spirits,' I muttered to the cracked ceiling and said a wistful goodbye to the eighty proof spirits I'd be leaving behind in the tequila bottle.

I plucked the car keys from her fingers. Mom was right. A drive was just what I needed. After phoning the café to tell the girls to hold down the fort, I headed out to the Entronque building for a look around. I figured Andy would call me if there was any news.

The parking lot was nearly full. A couple of Table Rock squad cars stood by the side entrance, as a warning no doubt to lookie-loos or anyone else thinking of pushing an unsuspecting soul down four flights of stairs. If indeed that was what had happened. Personally, I was still hoping Clive's confession and current incarceration had all been a silly mistake – maybe he had low blood sugar and had needed a cookie and it had addled his mind. Maybe Lisa Willoughby had unfortunately slipped and fallen to her death.

The entrance to the elevator that Clive had claimed was broken earlier today was marked off with yellow crime-scene tape so I headed for the front of the building. I rode the elevator to the fourth floor and knocked on the door to Markie's Masterpieces. The frosted glass held an etching of a classic wedding cake.

A fluty voice shouted, 'Come in!'

I pulled the handle and walked into a large kitchen with a lofted ceiling. Rough-hewn beams crossed the room lengthwise. A modestly rotund man in a tight black T-shirt and loose black jeans was skipping in the background. He waved and kept on flying. I say flying because he was wearing a purple cape. I suspected his feet, which I couldn't see because of the solid counter between us, were on the ground – at least half the time.

Plenty of Table Rockers believe people can fly. I'm just not one of them.

I'm funny that way.

I'm not sure what superhero he stole the billowing purple cape from – Captain Eggplant, maybe – but I was pretty sure, whoever it was, they were going to be wanting it back.

I approached the long worktable that ran parallel to the front and edged up to a man grimly working a clump of dense white dough while ignoring the commotion behind him.

'That's some pretty tough dough you've got going there.'

He wiped a small line of perspiration from the side of his chin and cracked a smile. 'It's fondant. For covering the cake.' He blinked at me through thick glasses and slammed the wad against the butcher block countertop so hard I felt it in my bones. 'This stuff can be a bear.' He set the fondant aside. 'Here to pick up a cake?' His brown close-cropped hair glistened with glitter dust. His nose was broad and his brows were bushy. All together he was quite an ordinary-looking specimen, though he came to life when he smiled. Most of us do. I pegged him to be about thirty.

'No, not exactly.' The man in the cape flew past once again then disappeared into another room. 'Aren't you at all concerned about him?'

The young man looked over his shoulder. 'You mean Markie?' We heard the sounds of yelling coming from the room into which Markie had disappeared. 'Nah.'

I nodded. So that was the famous Markie. From my first impression, Markie was a real piece of work, but I wouldn't have gone so far as to call him a masterpiece.

'If you're not here for a cake, what can I do for you?' Strong fingers dug back into the fondant.

I held out my hand. 'I'm Maggie Miller.'

'I'm Ben Baker.' He smirked as he took my hand. 'And yes, I'm aware of the humor in that. Believe me, I've heard all the jokes.' In a goofy tone, he said, 'So, how long have you been the baker, Ben the baker?' He rolled his eyes and dropped the fondant ball next to the large sheeter to his left. It looked like some school kid's science project clay model of the moon made out of sugar. 'What can I do for you, Ms Miller?' He wiped his hands across the white apron covering him from chest to knees.

'Actually, I was here this earlier morning.' I dropped my voice though I wasn't sure why. 'When your coworker, Ms Willoughby was found.'

Ben's eyes twitched and his teeth pulled at his lower lip. 'Oh?' He nodded. 'Poor Lisa. Such a tragedy.'

I agreed. 'Were you here working when the body was discovered?'

Ben nodded. 'Like I told the police, I was in early. But I didn't see or hear anything. It must have happened when I was up on the roof.'

My brow furrowed. 'The roof?'

He shrugged sheepishly. 'What can I say? I'm a smoker. That's the only place I'm allowed to light up around here.'

'So you didn't see or hear anything unusual?'

It was his time to look puzzled. 'No. Why do you ask?'

'Just curious, is all. I mean, my friend did find the body. Maybe you know him? Clive Rothschild?'

A young couple came through the door holding hands. The woman approached and announced they were here for a consultation. 'Hey, Reva!' Ben called. 'Your appointment's here!'

A short, rather plump woman with a mass of brown hair tangled like a honeysuckle thicket atop her head popped out of a room to our right. Streaks of flour dusted her brown Markie's Masterpieces T-shirt. She wore her apron folded at the waist and clutched a sketchpad.

A small mustard-yellow loveseat and two olive-colored chairs were arranged in the corner, anchored by a white wool rug. Reva led her clients to the sofa and dropped into the chair across from them. There was a tray of small square cake samples on the table between them.

'Sure, I know Clive. Not well. But we've worked with The Hitching Post a bit.' He dropped the fondant down the back of the sheet roller and ran the ball through. It came out in a clean flat sheet that he caught in his hands. 'Bridal stuff. He's gowns, we're cakes.'

That made sense. 'What about Ms Willoughby? Did you know her well?'

He repeated the procedure, running the sheet of fondant through the sheeter one more time. He carefully draped the fondant over the top of a fourteen-inch white cake. 'Well enough.'

Did I detect some hesitancy? Some guardedness? Some crazed killer-ness?

'Can you think of anyone who might have disliked her enough to push her down four flights of stairs?'

'Push? What are you talking about, lady? Lisa fell down the stairs. Broke her neck.'

'The police don't think it was an accident.'

'Police can be wrong.' Ben wiped his brow with the side of his arm. 'Usually are. Lisa's dead. It's a tragedy,' he huffed. 'And it's going to be another tragedy if I don't get my job done.' He slammed another slab of fondant down on the countertop. 'As you can see, we are really busy here this morning. And short-staffed. If there's nothing else?'

I was being given the out the door hustle. 'Maybe I could help? I'm a baker, you know.'

He appeared dubious. 'You are?'

Well, I sort of was. I had a copy of the *Joy of Cooking* in the apartment and Betty Crocker's *The Big Book of Cupcakes*. I'd practically memorized that one.

He shook his head. 'No, thanks.' His eyes jumped to the door.

I pretended not to notice. 'Do you think I might speak to Markie for a moment?'

'What about?' Ben seemed to be getting less friendly by the minute. Maybe it was nerves. Maybe he needed a cigarette break.

'My sister's getting married and while I'm here I thought I might discuss the cake. I hear you guys do the best work in all of Arizona.'

Ben's hands worked themselves around the cake, smoothing the fondant until not a crease showed. I wondered if he could work some of that magic on my face. I was at that age where wrinkles and lines were beginning to show like San Andreas fault stress lines no matter how much foundation I layered on.

'I'll ask him but no guarantees. We really are behind schedule.'

Ben disappeared. I heard whispered shouting and expected the boot as Ben reappeared. 'OK,' he said. 'You can go on back.'

'Thanks.'

Ben laid a light hand on my shoulder. 'But I warn you. Markie's in one of his moods.'

I nodded soberly. Was it a mood for murder?

Markie's desk was cluttered with more toys than I'd had growing up. In fact, the office was covered wall-to-wall-to-floor with playthings. Was this a cake shop or a toy store?

The desktop collection included a red rubber ball, an American Girl doll – Josefina, I think – a Barbie Malibu Ave. Bakery + Doll and an assortment of Lego. I won't bore you with the rest. But if Markie turned his back, even for a second, I had my eye on that vintage Slinky Dog next to his business card holder that looked fashioned from a Meccano Erector set and read: Markie Gravelle, Markie's Masterpieces, Proprietor.

'I'm Maggie Miller,' I said, stretching out my hand. 'Thank you for seeing me.' I sat down in the chair he gestured toward. 'I was afraid you might be closed today. You know, after what happened this morning.'

Markie set down the plastic replica pirate ship he'd been inspecting and pouted. Six cannons on each side. 'It's so sad,' he said with a shake of the head. His purple cape swirled behind him. 'Poor, dear Lisa.'

Markie had a ruddy complexion, as if he'd been spending too much time with his face too near the oven door. His flesh was sort of flaccid, as if his features had been crafted out of folds of fondant like I'd seen Ben kneading earlier. 'I wish we could have mourned for her, you know. Paid our respects by shutting down for the day.' Markie clasped his hands atop the desk. 'But we have so, so many orders to fill.' His dark brown eyes latched onto mine. 'Lisa would have wanted us to continue working. She lived for cake.'

And died for it, I thought.

A row of walnut plaques hung on the wall to my left. Each contained the bas relief of a cake done in gold leaf. Markie Gravelle had been named Cake Decorator of the Year five years running by *Baking Bridal* magazine. I was impressed.

'Who would do such a terrible thing?' Markie's fist banged the desk. The little pirate ship listed to port.

'Had Lisa worked for you long?'

Markie clamped his lips together and thought. 'Six months, maybe more. She was a jewel. And a wonderful cake decorator.' He kissed his fingertips. 'Such an artiste!'

I nodded. Such a ham.

'She was especially adept at working with fondant.' Markie wiggled his fingers. 'I'm a buttercream man, myself.'

I smiled and crossed my legs. 'I'm more a margarita girl.'

Markie returned my smile. His teeth were big and white. He pointed his thumb at me. 'I like you, Maggie.'

'Thanks.' I gazed out the wall of windows behind his desk at the red rock mountains in the distance. It was a view that Lisa Willoughby wouldn't be sharing any longer. Her last vision was of herself falling down a stairwell. I stifled a shiver. That wasn't the way I'd want to go. 'Did Lisa have family here?'

Markie shook his head in the negative. 'I believe she was from Santa Fe.' He looked out his office door. 'Ben might know. He and Lisa had a thing going for a while.'

'Oh?' Interesting. Ben hadn't mentioned that.

Markie shrugged then pushed his hands against his temples. 'What a morning. We lose Lisa. The Robinsons were forced to buy a store-bought cake.' Snatching the end of his cape, he dabbed his forehead with the satin cloth. 'I had nothing in the shop to give them and the event was today.' He lifted his sagging head. 'Can you believe it, Maggie?' He shook his fists overhead. 'A store-bought cake. For a vow renewal!' His voice rose to the ceiling. 'I'm humiliated.'

And one of his employees was dead. I sensed Markie's priorities were a bit warped.

'Plus I had to eat the cost of the cake we'd spent days designing and building.' His hands fished around a pile of papers on his desk and he pulled up an invoice. 'That was a thirty-five-hundred-dollar cake.'

Yikes! Thirty-five hundred dollars for cake? That was about a hundred supermarket cakes. Who spends that kind of money on cake?

Hang on, what was I thinking? I'd once spent a small fortune on a wedding dress. And what had it gotten me? A dead ex-husband who left me for another woman and wouldn't stay dead. I should have spent more money on the cake and less on my bridal gown. At least with cake, if I socked it away in the freezer and could control my sweet tooth, I could eat for a month. 'You must have been here when . . .' I hesitated, '. . . *it* happened.' I laced my fingers across my lap.

Markie shook his head. 'No, I came in late today. After the—'
He paused, a solemn look crossing his face. 'You know.' He
swallowed. 'I saw all the police cars. I wondered what the devil
was going on.' He reached into the drawer of his desk and
stuffed a stick of chewing gum in his mouth. 'Ben and Reva
would have been here.'

'Oh? I'm sure I saw the Markie's Masterpieces Nissan Cube
parked in the lot about that time.'

Markie shrugged; his hands fiddled with a red and green
Lego block. 'That's our delivery vehicle. I rode my bike in
today.'

I sat taller. 'You ride a bike? Whatcha got? I ride a twenty-
six-inch Schwinn.'

Markie's left brow arched up like it was modeling for the
Arc de Triomphe. 'I ride a Harley. Softail.'

I shrunk back down. Show-off.

'Now,' Markie said. Did I just imagine it or were his eyes
glittering with dollar signs? 'About that wedding cake for your
sister.' He rubbed his thick hands and grabbed a gnawed number
two pencil. 'How many guests will you be serving?'

I cleared my throat. 'I'm not sure.' I stood. 'Maybe I'd better
get back to you on that.'

'Wait,' said Markie, rising and following me out of his office.
'When is the wedding?'

'I'll have to get back to you on that, too!' I threw open the
door to make my escape before committing my already married
sister to a cake neither she nor I could afford. I slammed into
an elegant fiftyish woman with long, thick blonde hair – like
Goldilocks – and crystal-blue eyes. 'I beg your pardon,' she
said as she lightly brushed a perfectly manicured hand along
her shirt.

'You can beg,' I said, 'but you're not getting it.' OK, I didn't
really say it. But I thought it real hard. What I really said was,
'Hi, I'm Maggie Miller.'

She looked down at my hand. 'Samantha Higgins.'

I retracted my untouched hand and checked it carefully for
any fresh signs of leprosy. Nope. Good to go.

'Mrs Higgins!' Markie cried. 'Did you hear what happened?'

Samantha Higgins looked like a woman who always got what

she wanted. She wore a chic white tennis outfit – the kind women buy to look good in, not necessarily sweat in. A pumpkin-colored cashmere scarf was wrapped around her slender neck.

The woman nodded. 'Yes, I was working in the gallery when one of the other gallery owners broke the news to me. Such a terrible tragedy.' She turned to me. 'I'm sorry if I seemed brusque a moment ago.' She managed a smile. 'I think I'm in shock, is all. I've never been so close to something so . . . so . . .' Her voice faded away.

I nodded. 'I know. I was there when Ms Willoughby's body was found.'

Mrs Higgins sucked in a breath. 'How terrible for you!' She looked around the shop and lowered her voice. 'I heard the fellow from The Hitching Post was involved.'

Wow, news had travelled fast.

Markie nodded and folded his hands behind his back.

'Were you and Ms Willoughby close, Mrs Higgins?'

She shook her head. 'No, but she was supposed to be working on my wedding cake for this Sunday.' She bit at her lower lip. 'I don't know what we'll do now.' She gasped and her eyes grew wide. 'What about our Labor of Love?'

'Getting married?' Not for the first time, I suspected.

Mrs Higgins looked at me blankly before replying. 'No, my daughter, Sabrina.' Before I knew what was happening, she'd pulled out a wallet containing a picture of what looked remarkably like a younger version of herself.

'Don't worry,' Markie cut in, grabbing the woman's hand, 'we'll manage. Everything will be ready in time for your daughter's wedding.'

'Thank you, Markie, dear.' She worried her wedding ring. 'I've been a ball of nerves.' Mrs Higgins pulled a lacey handkerchief from her purse and daubed her eyes. 'What with Sabrina and Cody's wedding and the Labor of Love both coming up this weekend . . .'

That was the second time she'd used the expression 'labor of love.' I love weddings as much as the next gal, but still. Weddings are work, lots of work. The labor I got, the 'of love' was stretching it. I started to say my goodbyes. So far my search for answers had come up short. Far short.

'And to think,' I heard Mrs Higgins say, 'that Mr Wolfe might be a murderer.' She shuddered.

I shuddered too. Maybe it was contagious. 'No,' I said, clutching the door handle. 'You're mistaken. It isn't Johnny Wolfe that the police are interested in. It's Clive Rothschild.'

Mrs Higgins' brow curled up. 'Are you sure, dear?'

I nodded. 'Sure as can be. I should know. Like I said, I was here.'

A queer look passed over her face. 'That's funny.'

I was getting a bad feeling. A very bad feeling. In fact, I felt my blood chilling down. 'What's funny?' I asked, cocking my head to one side, pretty sure already that the next words out her mouth wouldn't be funny at all.

Mrs Higgins wrung her hands and deposited her handkerchief back in her oversized tan leather purse. 'It was Mr Wolfe that I saw speeding away from here this morning.' She shrugged. 'So I just assumed . . .'

TEN

'Do you mean to say you saw—'

The phone in Mrs Higgins' purse started ringing like an old-fashioned telephone. She reached in to answer it. 'Hello?' She smothered the phone with her palm. 'You'll have to excuse me,' she said. 'I really must take this.'

Mrs Higgins turned her back on me and settled down on the corner loveseat. Markie showed me the door.

The freight elevator was still marked off limits with crime-scene tape so I rode the passenger elevator down to the ground floor. Mrs Higgins had dropped a bombshell and, though I was properly shell-shocked, there was nothing I could do about it now.

I'd have to find Johnny and wring the truth out of him. Had he been at the Entronque building this morning? If so, why hadn't he said so? Maybe he saw something. Something that could help Clive.

Yikes. Maybe he *did* something! But why?

I spotted the woman Ben had identified as Reva sitting alone at a round pine table out front of a small café called Magic Beans beside the roadrunner fountain. The smell of coffee hung in the air. I angled over. 'Hi, I'm Maggie Miller. You're Reva, right? Work for Markie's Masterpieces?'

She snatched a tube of raspberry lip gloss from her open purse atop the small table and applied it generously to her full lips. 'That's right.' Reva seemed nervous as she looked me up and down. 'I saw you upstairs.' She popped the top back on her lip gloss and tossed it into the bowels of her purse. 'And earlier today, with the police.'

'I'm helping them with their investigation into Lisa Willoughby's death.'

Her brows shot up and her eyes twinkled with obvious amusement. 'In a Maggie's Beignet Café polo?'

I stopped a frown on its way to blossoming. The blush I couldn't hide. This woman was perceptive and smart. I hated her already. 'I'm sort of undercover.'

Her brown eyes flickered. She didn't look like she was buying what I was selling but she moved her purse aside and waved for me to take a seat. I sat quickly before she changed her mind. Her pale complexion highlighted a sprinkling of freckles across the bridge of her nose. Definitely not a sun worshipper. I pegged her as fortyish. I didn't see a wedding band. Not that that meant anything. Maybe working with cake all day she didn't want to take a chance on her ring ending up the prize in somebody's forkful.

'So what are you really doing here?'

I decided on the blunt approach – after all, she'd started it. 'A friend of mine has been accused of being involved in Lisa's death.'

Reva nodded. 'Clive.' She batted her empty coffee cup from hand to hand across the tabletop. 'Some cop was up earlier. He said they suspected foul play.'

'I don't think Clive did it,' I replied. Even less after that bombshell Mrs Higgins had dropped. I really needed to talk to Johnny. 'Did you see or hear anything unusual this morning?'

Reva shook her head and stole a look at her watch. 'Not really. Everybody was running around, trying to get the day's orders out. Ben was baking sheet cake. Markie was being Markie . . .'

'Markie?' I interrupted. 'Markie wasn't in the bakery this morning. He came in later. After Lisa's body was found.'

Reva was adamant. 'You must be mistaken. He was here.'

Was I mistaken or had Markie lied to me? If so, why? A woman had been murdered and she was one of his employees. That sounded like two very good reasons to lie.

'Can I join the party?'

I turned.

Brad Smith, looking relaxed and easy on the eyes in his usual blue jeans and plain white T-shirt stood behind my shoulder. Brad's a reporter for the *Table Rock Reader*, the town's local newspaper. 'Hi, Maggie.' His hand shot across my shoulder. 'Reva Reynolds of Markie's Masterpieces, correct?'

She smiled at him. She hadn't smiled at me once.

Brad looked a lot like my dead ex-husband. Maybe that's why I was so leery of him. He'd asked me out once or twice but so far I was keeping my distance.

'That's me,' she replied. Eyelashes went flutter-flutter.

Good grief.

'I'm Brad Smith, with the *Table Rock Reader*.'

Brad deftly snatched a chair from the empty table beside us. He twisted it around backwards and straddled it, leaning his arms across the arched chairback. A notebook hung open in his left hand. His right hand held a pencil.

'Do you mind?' I said.

Brad smiled broadly. 'Not at all.'

I glowered.

He scooted the chair up until it touched the table. 'I wanted to ask you some questions about the murder of Lisa Willoughby.' His electric-blue eyes cast their evil spell.

Reva came alive like somebody had thrown the switch to her central nervous system. I swear she grew two inches taller. 'Oh,' her hands flew to her cheeks, 'it was awful. One minute poor Lisa was alive . . .' She shook her head. 'The next thing I know the police are telling us she's been murdered!' Her eyes bugged

out like ping pong balls and she fanned herself with her right
hand.

'So you first heard about the murder from the police?'

Reva nodded quickly. 'That's right. I was upstairs in the cake
shop. Two officers came in and told us.'

Brad scratched something in his notebook. Probably remembered to add bananas to his grocery list. The big monkey. He
turned to me. 'Dinner later?'

'In your dreams.'

He grinned a big ape grin. 'How did you know?'

I blushed.

He turned his interrogation back to Reva. 'Did you know
Ms Willoughby well?'

Reva chewed at her lower lip. 'As well as anybody in the
shop, I suppose. Except for Ben.' She chuckled.

'Oh?' Brad scooched nearer.

Reva fluttered her eyelashes. 'Ben and Lisa went out a few
times. Nothing serious.' She paused before adding, 'Lisa was
like that.'

Scribble, scribble.

Had he forgotten he was out of tomatoes, too?

I felt like a proverbial third wheel. It wasn't a pleasant feeling.

'So Ben and Lisa were a couple?' I interjected. 'Did they
break up?' Did Ben not take the breakup well? I'd seen him
mangle that fondant upstairs. The guy had very strong hands.
He could easily have given Lisa a shove that would have sent
her soaring and then plunging to her death.

Before Reva could answer, Brad asked, 'What do you know
about the lawsuit between Ms Willoughby and The Hitching
Post?'

'What?' I spluttered. What on earth was the man babbling
about?

Brad twisted his head toward me. 'Didn't you know? Lisa
Willoughby was taking Johnny Wolfe and Clive Rothschild to
court. Something to do with her former employment at The
Hitching Post – unfair termination and slander.'

I pulled myself together. An unfair termination suit? Slander?
'Of course I knew. I'm no idiot.' What an idiot I was! Why
didn't I know this? Why hadn't I figured it out? Put two and

two together and come up with trouble times two: Clive and
Johnny. They'd been holding out on me, the weasels.

'Great, because I'd like to interview Johnny. I was hoping
you could set it up for me.'

'I'd love to,' I said through gritted teeth with a plastered-on
smile.

'I've got to cover a zoning commission meeting after we're
done here but I'd like to get his take on this story. Maybe later
this evening?'

'Wonderful,' I lied.

Brad turned to Reva. 'Think there's any way you can get me
an interview with Markie?' He gave her five dollars' worth of
charm. 'He shot me down on the phone.'

Reva's tongue made tsk-tsking noises even as she shook her
head. 'Sorry, Markie's in a mood, you know? Even for Markie.
What with the murder and the lost cake and all.'

Brad nodded. He patted Reva's hand. 'I understand.'

Reva smiled. 'How about tomorrow? I know I can get him
to talk to you then.' Yeah, right, I thought.

Brad agreed.

I fumed. I could feel my innards heating up like a steam
engine train firebox. I'd read somewhere that the flue gas temper-
atures in a firebox could reach as high as a thousand degrees
Fahrenheit. That's why they contained a safety valve called a
fusible plug, to prevent catastrophic firebox failure. I feared my
own fusible plug was in danger of being exceeded. I looked at
my tummy and considered the possible explosion and its ramifications. It wasn't a pretty thought. I'd eaten Ethiopian food.

Reva pulled out her cellphone and checked the time again.
'Sorry, break time's over. Markie's going to throw a hissy if I
don't get back to work.' She stood and grabbed her purse. Brad
stood too. Very gallant of him.

Rummaging around a moment, she came up with a pale blue
business card that she handed to Brad. 'Here's my number,' she
said with a smile, 'if you want to talk some more later.' Brad
took the card with thanks. Reva ran a hand through her locks
and headed for the elevator.

'If you want to talk some more later,' I mimicked wickedly
under my breath. The woman hadn't answered my question

about Ben and Lisa. My fingers thrummed the tabletop. Nor had she offered me a business card.

'What's that?' Brad loomed over me.

'Nothing,' I practically spat. 'I mean, about dinner. Later. That would be great.'

'It would?' Brad eyed me suspiciously.

'What?' I said. 'A girl's got to eat, doesn't she?'

'Yeah, it's just that I didn't really think you'd say yes.' Brad looked downright flustered. Good, it served the normally unflappable reporter right. I'd taken him by surprise. Like I said, he'd asked me out a time or two in the past and I'd always turned him down flat. I knew trouble when I saw it. And I was looking right at it.

I pushed back my chair. 'So, what do you say? Pick me up around seven?' I fluttered my eyelashes the way I'd seen Reva do it. I felt like an idiot. 'Why don't we meet at Hanging Louie's?'

'OK, see you then.' Brad shoved his notebook in his back pocket and walked off.

I noted the time spinning away on a stylized rust-colored coyote clock above the elevator. Perfect. Hanging Louie's is a bar slash restaurant located about midway between Sedona and Table Rock. Legend says the joint was erected on the spot where Louis 'Louie' Dumbrowski met the hangman's noose back in 1885 or so – at least, that's what the engraved wood sign at the entrance would have one believe. I believed. Hanging Louie's featured Southwest cuisine with an intergalactic flair, like the mesquite smoked UFO burger. This is Arizona. We Arizonans have a unique perspective on things.

I'd have just enough time to get back to the café to close it down for the day, head home, shower, change and then leave again. Plenty of time for me to be long gone before Brad got tired of waiting for me at Hanging Louie's and decided to come looking for me at home. And wait for me he would. I wanted Brad Smith the reporter out of the way while I went tracking down Johnny Wolfe. If I hadn't made the date with Brad to distract him he might have beaten me to the punch, with or without my help. As much as it pained me to say it, the guy was good at his job.

Maybe I was fighting dirty. But Brad was a news reporter. Fighting dirty was probably the only kind of fighting he knew and respected.

ELEVEN

'Where is he?' I demanded, storming into The Hitching Post like a gunslinger out of the Old West.

'Maggie.' Clive stood straightening a rack of Johnny Wolfe label bridal gowns in an alcove. Besides the popular high-end designer gowns they carried, the shop had a small section of Johnny Wolfe originals. No two were alike. There were no two quite like Johnny and Clive either. 'This is a surprise.' He stepped forward, tugging at his bowtie. 'Where's who?'

I pointed at Johnny's name on the sign above the rack. 'Him, that's who!'

Clive's green eyes followed the line of my finger. 'Johnny? He isn't here, I'm afraid.'

'Where is he then?' I pushed up on my tiptoes to see over Clive's shoulder. 'Is he in back?'

Clive shook his head. 'Johnny isn't here at all, Maggie.' He rested a paternal hand on my shoulder. 'Are you sure you're all right?' He quirked a smile. 'Can I get you a cup of tea?'

'Don't get all solicitous with me, Clive Rothschild. It's not me you should be worried about, it's Johnny who—' I screeched to a halt and took one giant step back. I took a deep breath, sucking in the odor of vanillin – no doubt emanating from the three vases of red-brown Chocolate Cosmos clustered on a glass table in the center of the store. Three-dozen Chocolate Cosmos. Those bundles much have cost a bundle. Chocolate Cosmos aren't cheap.

'Wait a minute.' I pointed at Clive's chest. 'What are you doing here?' I had so many questions that I wanted to ask Johnny building up inside me like a champagne bottle about to blow that I hadn't seen what was right in front of me.

Clive.

'We're closed for the day,' Clive said, working his way toward his desk on the opposite side of the store near the back. 'I was straightening up.'

'No,' I said, pushing my fists against my temples until it hurt. 'What are you doing *here*?' I waved my arms around. If I'd kept squeezing my skull like that I'd end up with a rectangular-shaped face or, worse yet, a burst cranium. 'Surrounded by poufy wedding gowns?'

He sat and elegantly folded his arms and legs.

'The last time I saw you, you were surrounded by crooks and drunks.' I shook my head and flopped into the chair opposite. 'Not sashes and garters.'

Clive smiled and offered me a pink sugar cookie on a silver platter. I declined. 'Your brother-in-law, Andy. He arranged bail.' He leaned on his elbows. 'It wasn't cheap, let me tell you.'

'Well,' I sighed, 'I'm glad you're out. But I'd really like to talk to Johnny.'

'What about?'

I frowned. Should I tell Clive that Johnny might be involved in Lisa Willoughby's death? That he might be so spineless as to be letting his partner, Clive, take the fall for him? No, better to talk to Johnny first and hear his side of the story.

I squirmed in my chair. 'I'd really just like to talk to Johnny, Clive.'

Clive tapped the desk for a minute and looked at me. He stood. 'Fine. Johnny's at the house. Let me lock up and we'll go.'

The café was already closed for the day. Aubrey and Kelly had locked up. I felt both a little guilty and a little uneasy about that – and about my lackadaisical management skills. But I had more important things to worry about right then, so I'd leave my uneasy guilt for another day.

I'd left Mom's Bug on the curb out front. I unlocked the door for Clive then hopped in the driver's seat. 'I don't get it. Why did they let you out? You confessed.' Like an idiot. Maybe that was it – he and Andy were opting for the insanity defense.

Clive shrugged as he clipped on his seat belt. 'I don't know, but after some discussion Ms Vargas and the judge agreed to my bail. Your brother-in-law is quite good.'

'Yeah, still . . . that's weird.'

Clive shot me a look. 'Turn left here.'

'I mean, I'm glad you're out but still . . .' I spun around the corner.

'Still what?' He sounded like he was getting annoyed. Or maybe offended.

'Why did they release you?' Did the police know something Clive and I didn't?

'Would you rather they hadn't?' He sounded offended.

'Of course not.' I followed Clive's instructions as we headed toward a gated community at the edge of town called Four Seasons. I'd passed it a couple of times. Very snooty. Very pricy. I wondered how many beignets I'd have to sell to be able to afford to live in one of these houses. Probably more than I could make in my lifetime. Too bad. I figured I could be a rich snob as well as the next gal. How hard can it be?

I pulled up to the guard house. Clive waved and the serious-looking guy at the gate let us pass after getting my name and license plate number. I was surprised he hadn't asked for a DNA sample. 'What's this business with you guys and Lisa Willoughby?'

Clive ignored my question and pointed to an immense hacienda-styled house on the right. 'That's the one.'

My jaw dropped. 'You guys live here?'

'You can pull in behind Johnny's BMW.'

Clive led the way through a double-door archway that took us into an expansive courtyard. 'Holy cow,' I breathed. The burnt sienna brick pavers that covered the drive extended throughout the courtyard. A ceramic-tiled fountain gurgled in the center. My heart went pit-a-pat.

Clive smiled. 'You like it?'

'I want it.' I think I was drooling. Clive fished in his trousers and pulled out his house key. I fished around in my handbag for a tissue to wipe my chin with.

We found Johnny in the kitchen. He wore a black sweater with the sleeves pulled up to the elbows and loose black trousers with matching house slippers. 'Clive,' Johnny said, tumbler in hand, 'what's she doing here?'

I answered for myself. 'I'm here to ask you about Lisa Willoughby.' I anchored my hands on my hips. 'And what you were doing at the Entronque building this morning.'

Clive and Johnny shared a look. Whatever they were thinking, they weren't sharing with me. Clive worried his hands. Johnny downed whatever was in that diamond and wedge-cut crystal tumbler.

I stared out the window. They had a pool – a freaking pool. With a diving board and an infinity edge! I forced myself to turn away. If I didn't, any second I'd probably rip my clothes off and jump in. 'Well?'

Johnny frowned. 'Have a seat, Miller.'

I dropped onto a cherry-wood barstool at the marble counter.

Clive poured us each a glass of whatever it was that Johnny was quaffing.

A tentative sip told me it was bourbon. A gulp that sizzled its way down my tongue told me it was the good stuff. From my vantage point, I spotted a quiche in the oven. My stomach began making 'feed me' sounds. I pushed my tumbler aside and rubbed my hands together. 'Talk to me, guys.'

Johnny flopped onto a buttery leather sofa in the great room and I was forced to turn. 'Lisa worked for us at The Hitching Post for a time.'

Johnny's eyes were glossy. I wondered if that drink in his hand was only his second.

I quirked my right eyebrow. 'And neither of you thought this worth mentioning earlier?' I glared at Clive, who'd taken up a position on the sofa as well.

Clive fidgeted and tugged at his bowtie. I felt like strangling him with it. Oh, not enough to kill him, just enough to get his attention. Get him to take this murder – and me – seriously. 'Like when you were showing me Lisa's body at the bottom of the stairwell?'

Clive cleared his throat. 'Well, you see, Maggie—'

The doorbell sounded, sending the peal of sweet chimes echoing across the Spanish-tiled floor. These tiles were the real deal, too. You could see the footprints of the coyotes in them from when the clay tiles were left out in the sun to dry.

I looked toward the door as the bell chimed a second time. 'Isn't anybody going to get that?

'Ignore it,' said Johnny with disdain. 'It's probably one of our neighbors.'

'Could be a salesman,' I said, 'or some little girl trying to sell her first box of Girl Scout cookies. You could be breaking her heart if you don't answer. She could be traumatized for life.'

'This is a gated community, Maggie,' replied Clive, dryly. 'Nobody just gets in.'

'Except for neighbors,' Johnny said with a scowl.

I got the impression that Johnny wasn't big on the whole 'let's be neighborly' deal. 'Fine,' I said, with my most put-upon sigh. 'I'll just take a peek.' The bell ringing for the third and now fourth time was getting to me. If it didn't stop soon I feared I'd be hearing bells in my sleep. I sauntered down the hall and peeped around the corner. The front doors were glass. I could see straight outside . . . into a pair of M&Ms. A pair of M&Ms I knew all too well.

I narrowed my eyes. 'It's Detective Highsmith,' I murmured over my shoulder.

'What's he doing here?' Clive said.

'How did he get past the guard gate?' demanded Johnny.

'I guess having a badge trumps having a security gate,' was my answer.

'Still,' hissed Johnny. 'The guard should have called and warned us.' He stood. 'I mean, told us. I'm going to have a word with his supervisor.'

I rolled my eyes. Those two worried about the strangest things. 'If neither of you are going to let him in, I will.' I turned back toward the foyer. 'Before he decides to break down the door.' I turned on my most welcoming smile as I twisted the doorknob. 'Detective Highsmith, what a surprise.'

He scratched his cheek. 'I'm a little surprised, too.' He looked beyond me. 'I was expecting Mr Rothschild and Mr Wolfe. Not you, Ms Miller.'

Well, gee. I'm glad to see you too. 'I stopped by for a visit,'

I explained. 'Come on in.' I led him down the foyer to the great room like I owned the place. Clive sat on the sofa leafing through a bridal magazine.

'Look who's here,' I said. 'You remember Detective Highsmith.' The man who'd questioned him for hours on end.

Clive stood. 'It's hard to forget the man who's put you behind bars.'

Good point.

'Just doing my job,' Highsmith was quick to reply. 'Speaking of which, where's Johnny? It's him I'm here to see.'

My eyes flitted around the room. 'Yeah, where is Johnny?'

Clive gave me a funny look and locked his eyes on mine. 'Why, he's not here. You know that, Maggie.'

I opened my mouth then shut it again. I may be slow but I'm not brain-dead. Highsmith had traded out his day-off clothes for a nice gray suit. Very becoming. The man looked good even when being a pain in the butt.

Highsmith slowly paraded around the room. His eyes fell on the tumbler on the coffee table. The third tumbler in the room. Mine was over on the kitchen counter. Would he notice? Had he already?

In case he had not, I positioned myself in front of the third glass. 'That's right,' I said, hoping my voice wasn't quivering as much as my stomach was on the inside. 'Clive and I were having a drink and some dinner.' I sniffed the air. 'Spinach and ham quiche. Care to join us, Detective?'

Highsmith looked at me so hard I thought my knees would crumble to dust and I'd collapse right there on the floor. Johnny would hate the mess that left on his fancy rug. Finally Highsmith shook his head. 'No, thanks.' He turned to Clive. 'When Mr Wolfe returns, please tell him I'd like to speak with him. Soon,' he added. 'Here's my number.' He handed Clive one of his business cards.

I watched Highsmith drive off, then checked my reflection in the gilt-edged mirror over the entry table in the foyer. I was sure I had to be blue in the face because I hadn't breathed the whole time the detective had been in the room.

I raced back to the great room. Clive stood. I noticed his glass was empty. 'Where is he?'

Clive shrugged.

'Johnny!' I hollered. 'Get out here now!' Not a sound, not a whisper, not a rustle. Not even the scurrying of little paws across the tiles. I frowned and marched over to Clive. 'Where did Johnny disappear to now?'

'He went out the back.' Clive pointed toward the French doors leading to the pool patio. 'He said he was in no mood to talk to the police.'

'Well,' I replied, in disbelief, 'can you imagine what kind of mood the police are going to be in if he keeps trying to avoid them?'

The oven timer beeped twice.

Clive headed for the kitchen. 'Care for some dinner, Maggie?'

'No, I wouldn't care for some dinner, Clive.' I stormed after him. 'What I'd care for is some answers.'

He opened the oven door, slipped on an oven mitt and pulled out the most heavenly scented quiche I had ever laid nostrils on. My stomach begged for attention. I ignored it. For once.

Clive set the quiche on a trivet and pulled off the black silicone mitt.

'I know that Lisa Willoughby was taking you and Johnny to court, Clive.' I stood between him and the quiche. 'What I don't know is why.'

'Lisa was a clerk in our shop,' Clive answered. 'She also did some alterations work.'

'And?'

'Johnny accused her of stealing from us.'

'Money?'

Clive nodded. 'Over twenty thousand dollars.'

I whistled.

'He also accused her of stealing clients from us.'

My brow wrinkled up. 'How? You mean she was selling gowns, too?'

'No,' answered Clive. 'But customers would come in for alterations and she would suggest doing them herself, out of her home. Johnny found out, fired her and told everybody why. Lisa learned he was badmouthing her and decided to take us to court. Hired a lawyer down in Flagstaff and everything.'

I took a deep breath and thought about the ramifications of

what Clive had told me. That sounded just like Johnny. The guy had a mouth. 'So both you and Johnny have what the police would consider strong motives for killing her.'

Clive nodded reluctantly. 'But I didn't! We didn't.' He raised his right hand. 'I swear, Maggie.'

'I know.' I ran a finger along my cheekbone and paced the kitchen. 'So, you knew that Johnny had been at the Entronque before we arrived. You were afraid he might have had something to do with Lisa ending up at the bottom of the stairs.' I shook my head. 'You confessed because you wanted to protect him.'

Clive nodded ever so slightly.

'But how did you know?'

'How did I know what?' Clive asked. The quiche sat on the counter, ignored and growing cold.

'How did you know, or why did you suspect that Johnny had been there before us?'

Clive managed a smile. 'It was his cologne. It's quite rare and expensive.'

'I'll bet,' I muttered.

'I don't know anyone else in the area who uses it,' Clive continued. 'So when I smelled it in the stairwell on my way up I immediately thought of Johnny.'

I was having some thoughts about Johnny myself. While I didn't like to think he was a murderer, he did have a quick and keen temper. 'So where is he now? Behind the sofa? Hiding under the bed?'

'I told you, Maggie. Johnny went out.'

I bit my lower lip. 'The BMW's still in the driveway. I saw it when Highsmith drove off.' Besides, I'd blocked the car in. There was no sign of Johnny in the yard.

'He probably went for a walk around the neighborhood.'

I rolled my eyes. I couldn't wrap my mind around Johnny taking a pleasant evening stroll around the neighborhood, waving to his neighbors as he passed and patting their little doggies on their little doggy heads. I could picture him pushing Lisa Willoughby down a stairwell. Maybe not in cold blood but in the heat of the moment? Definitely.

'One more thing,' I said. 'How do you explain how your dress swatch came to be lying beneath Lisa Willoughby's body at the bottom of the stairs?' That little but incriminating detail had been bothering me for a long time.

Clive gave a one-shouldered shrug. 'I must have dropped it climbing the stairs. I'd put it in my pocket. It must have fallen out of my pocket on my way up.' He shook his head and paced the kitchen floor. 'I didn't realize I'd lost it. Like I said, when I got to Markie's Masterpieces no one was around. At least, not that I could see. So the fabric was, or at least I thought it was, still in my pocket.'

He paused, his sad eyes falling on me. 'Then I heard the noises and . . .' He flapped his arms haplessly. 'Well, you know the rest.'

I did.

I grabbed my purse and left Clive with his quiche. Glancing at the clock on the VW's dashboard, I figured Brad Smith, ace reporter, was somewhere between Hanging Louie's and wanting to hang Maggie Miller about now. I couldn't help smiling over the thought.

As I backed down the drive, sharp, unseen bony fingers dug into my shoulder.

TWELVE

I screamed.

The tires screamed, too, as I slammed on the brakes. I screamed a second time as my head bounced off the roof. I twisted my neck around, unfortunately twisting the steering wheel in the same motion.

The VW dodged to the right and scraped a large chunk of sandstone at the edge of the drive. The car shuddered.

So did I. I mean, who places a freaking rock so close to their driveway?

'Careful!' hollered Johnny, his hands clutching the back of my seat. 'Have you lost your mind?'

'Me? Have you lost yours?' My eyes bugged out at him.

'Just keep driving,' Johnny hissed. 'I paid a fortune for that rock installation!' He drove his fist into the back of my seat while remaining hunched over in back.

I eased slowly down the drive. Very slowly. A glance at the boulder the right front bumper had connected with told me that I did not want to see the bumper itself. And when Mom saw it, she was going to kill me. Maybe I could blame it on an alien invasion.

For a brief moment, I considered running away. Unfortunately I'd already done that once. That's what I was doing in Table Rock, Arizona. I wasn't sure how much further there was to run. I'd previously considered Alaska, but trading a dry heat for a wet bitter cold was not an option. The only good iceberg was lettuce – with plenty of Thousand Island dressing.

'Any place in particular you'd like a lift to?' I asked, sitting outside the guard gate of the Four Seasons and waiting for a break in the traffic on the street. 'Like a loony bin?'

'Very funny, Miller.' He peeked over the seat. 'Any sign of that detective?'

'Not unless he's hiding behind a cactus.' Personally, I didn't think the detective could carry it off. Too much muscle.

Johnny sat up in the back and dusted himself off. He straightened his precious hair, looking at his reflection in the rearview mirror. I eased in line behind a couple of slow-moving pickup trucks. Pickups seemed to outnumber people in Table Rock at a ratio of about three to one, having replaced the horse ages ago. I supposed that was a good thing, at least from the horse's point of view. 'Where to, Johnny?'

He pushed out his lower lip. 'You can drop me off at your place.'

That suited me. I was exhausted. Drop Johnny off, take a long bath. Enjoy a relaxing meal in front of the TV watching one of my favorite home remodeling shows. The perfect end to a perfectly awful day.

I parked at the curb. Johnny extracted himself from the tiny backseat and followed me to the door. I quirked an eyebrow, the house key dangling in my hand. 'Did you want something?' Small flying insects buzzed around the porch light. Great, I'd probably end up having my arms chewed up by flesh-eating zombie no-see-ums. I'd seen it happen in a late-night horror film once. It wasn't a pretty sight.

Johnny shoved the sleeves of his sweater down to his wrists. 'No, thanks. Show me to the guestroom. A good night's rest is all I need.'

My hand froze, key in lock. 'The guestroom? This is a one-bedroom apartment and a tiny one at that. It isn't the Ritz.'

The door popped open. Mom stood in the doorway wearing her bathrobe and slippers. 'I thought I heard voices,' she said with a big grin on her face. A damp towel curled around her hair. 'Well, hello, Johnny.' She pulled the former pro skater inside. 'You didn't tell me you were bringing home company, Maggie. Have a seat, Johnny. What can I get you to drink?'

'I didn't know I was bringing home company,' I muttered under my breath. My mother and Johnny had met on several occasions. For some unfathomable reason, she adored the former Olympian. My cat, Carole Two, curled her tail around my left leg and mrowled. I headed to the kitchen to check the status of her food and water.

'I suppose I could settle for a dry martini,' Johnny called from the sofa.

I gritted my teeth and yanked open the refrigerator. Gee, no instant dry martinis. I grabbed a can of Bud Light. 'Could you settle for a beer?'

When Johnny declined, I popped the top anyway. Waste not, want not. I found a foil-covered pie tin in the fridge and extracted it. 'What's this?' I held it out.

Mom glanced my way. She'd made herself comfortable on the sofa beside Johnny. 'Shepherd's pie. Your sister brought it over. I helped myself but there's plenty left if you want to warm it up. How about you, Johnny?' my mother asked. 'Would you care for some?'

Johnny declined. Smart choice. He'd met my sister. I picked through the mashed potato top of the pie. There was no telling what was in this thing, but I could make a pretty good guess what wasn't in it – anything tasty or normal, like ground beef, instant mashed potato mix and whole-milk cheddar cheese. No, this devil-in-a-pie tin probably contained not-so-beef-flavored wheat gluten granules, quinoa and soy cheese. I tossed it back in the fridge.

I thought I recognized okra and banana peppers in the thing, for crying out loud.

I grabbed a store-bought frozen bagel to go with the beer and took the chair opposite the sofa.

'So, what brings you here this evening, Johnny?' Mother is ever so polite.

'He's on the lam from the police,' I said, somehow managing to speak with a mouthful of semi-thawed plain white bagel.

Mom looked from me to Johnny. Her hands gripped her knees. 'Is that true?'

Johnny scowled. 'No, your daughter's exaggerating.'

'Detective Highsmith showed up at Johnny's house wanting to talk to him.' I smiled malevolently at Johnny. 'Johnny preferred hiding in the backseat of your car to talking.'

Johnny's ears turned red. He folded his arms over his chest. 'I wasn't in the mood. I needed some alone time.'

I rolled my eyes and took a swig of beer. I was about to choke on the dry bagel lodged in my throat. 'Chicken.' I didn't bother to tell him that if convicted of murder he'd be getting his fill of alone time.

He pressed his hands to his temples. 'I need some time to think.'

'Of course, Johnny. You take all the time you need. You'll stay here tonight with me and Maggie.'

'I don't know,' Johnny said. He shot me a crafty look. 'I don't want to be any trouble.'

'It'll be no trouble at all, Johnny.' Mom made a face at me. I stuck my tongue out at her. 'Maggie and I will share the bed. Maggie will make up the couch for you.'

'I will?' No way I was spending the night with Johnny under the same roof. 'There are plenty of topnotch hotels in the area.' I could picture the two of them already, out on the patio doing sunrise yoga together. What next? Carole Two dropping into the downward droopy eared dog pose? Mom would probably expect me to join them, too. Yeah, right. I'd join them the day some yogi master invented exercises designed for actually humans, not circus contortionists.

Mom stared me down. I gave in first, pretending I needed a drink.

By the time I'd gotten the sofa made up with the spare sheets, it was quite late. Just my luck, there had been an old Sonja Henie movie playing on TCM called Thin Ice. Ms Henie had been a real-life, three-time Olympic gold medalist. We sat through the entire film, despite my yawning hints that it was past my bedtime – I did have to get up early to open the café.

But Johnny and Mom paid me no attention. Not even Carole Two took an interest in my welfare.

Johnny was quite smitten with Ms Henie's skating sequences in the film. I was about to turn off the kitchen light when somebody pounded on my front door. Carole Two shot to the bedroom where Mom was already in the middle of her pre-bed yoga routine.

Johnny, still wearing his day clothes minus the slippers, looked at me from the sofa. I shrugged and motioned for him to get in the bathroom.

I stepped to the door. 'Who is it?' I pressed my ear to the door. Getting a visitor at nearly midnight on a Tuesday night was a little bit unnerving and I wasn't about to open the door without knowing who I'd be facing.

'Maggie? Is that you? It's me, Brad Smith.'

I groaned. The jig was up. I smoothed down my shirt, taking a moment to compose myself and making sure that Johnny had shut the bathroom door.

I threw open the front door. 'Brad, what a surprise.'

The reporter took a step back and looked at me. He was dressed as he had been earlier in the afternoon, though he'd thrown a nice charcoal-colored sports jacket over his shirt. 'I'll bet.' He didn't look happy. 'So what happened?' He twisted and peeked through the door. 'I waited over an hour for you at Hanging Louie's. I tried to call you but kept getting your voicemail.'

He had phoned me several times. I had ignored each call. I stepped onto the porch, swatted a mosquito and pulled the door shut behind me. 'Low signal, I guess, or the phone's on the fritz.'

'Oh? While I was waiting, I ran into some friends, had dinner and drinks with them then came here. I saw the lights on.' He tilted his head to look through the window. 'You have company?'

'Yes,' I answered quickly. 'Sorry about tonight. Family emergency.'

'Emergency? Is everything all right?' Concern showed on his face.

'Don't worry. Everything's under control now.' Or so I hoped. 'I'd invite you in but it looks like my mother will be staying with me for a while.' I nervously cleared my throat. 'You know, what with the emergency and all . . .'

'Anything I can do?'

'No, thanks. That's sweet. I'm sorry,' I said, lowering my eyes, 'I should have called.'

A piercing scream filled the air. I spun around.

Brad's hand flew to the doorknob. 'What the heck was that? That sounded like a woman's scream. Your mom's in trouble!'

I grabbed Brad's arm and yanked him back across the threshold, slamming the door shut behind me. I was out of breath. 'Don't worry,' I said, patting the reporter's arm. 'I'm sure it's nothing.'

'Nothing?' Brad seemed uncertain. 'It sounded like she was in real pain. Don't you think we should go check on her?'

I shook my head. 'No, really. It – it's part of Mom's pre-bed ritual.' I rolled a finger round my ear. 'She's quirky that way. She's into primal scream therapy.' I was going to be needing some therapy myself what with my mom, Johnny Wolfe and a cat named Carole Two all occupying my personal space.

Brad's hand rested on the doorknob. 'I still think we should check.'

I took his hand. 'No, really, I—' I didn't know what to say. I already sounded like an idiot. So I did an idiotic thing. I kissed him. Right there on the porch. Right there on the lips.

The kiss lingered for several moments longer than I had planned. I wasn't sure whose fault that was. Finally I took a step back and said, 'It's getting late. I'm sorry but I have to be at work at six.' OK, so really it's supposed to be five-thirty. One of these days I'd make it on time.

Brad nodded. 'I understand.' His voice sounded husky.

We kissed briefly once again then I watched him head to his car. As he pulled away I noticed a man on the sidewalk across the street watching me. He held an Irish setter at the end of a leash. At first I thought it was some pervert stopping to get a look at two people kissing in public. Then I realized I recognized this particular pervert.

I stormed down the walkway to the street and planted my hands on my hips. 'So now you're spying on me, Detective?' I hollered. It might have been midnight but I didn't care who heard me.

I saw the glint of smiling teeth under the glow of the streetlamp. 'Merely walking my dog, Ms Miller.'

'Yeah, right,' I quipped. I shook my head to show my contempt. 'You happened to be walking your dog on a Tuesday night at midnight right in front of my apartment.' I snorted. 'Like I'm going to believe that.'

Highsmith tugged at the dog's leash. The dog was busy inspecting a mailbox post. 'I just got home. I live a block over.' He pointed with his free hand.

It was a good thing it was dark so he couldn't see the brilliant red my face had become. 'Yeah, well, then.' I toed the ground and bit my lip. 'Carry on. Goodnight, Detective.'

Highsmith looked at me a moment longer. 'Goodnight, Ms Miller.'

I watched him and the dog turn the corner. I had a Table Rock cop for a neighbor. Worse, I had Detective Highsmith for a neighbor. Don't get me wrong, I'm sure he's the best detective on the force. He ought to be. He is the only detective on the force.

He's also quite a handsome detective. When I'd first laid eyes on him I thought there might be a certain chemistry between us. I didn't know whether that chemistry would produce beautiful fireworks or deadly explosions, but still, chemistry. Then I'd learned that he was seeing one Veronica Vargas, town prosecuting attorney, daughter of town mayor and Princess of Prissytown.

And now he'd seen me making out on my front porch with Brad Smith.

THIRTEEN

Andy had made good on his word to return my Schwinn, so Wednesday morning I took off early by bike for the café. I'd desperately wanted to be out before either Johnny or my mother woke up. The scream Brad and I had heard the night before had not been Mom. It had been Johnny. Mom didn't realize Johnny was in the bathroom. Johnny didn't realize my mother was going to throw the door open with him sitting there on the toilet. With his trousers at half-mast.

I still couldn't get the awful image out of my head. And I'd had two cups of strong coffee and several beignets heaped with powdered sugar. I'd have thought that would have sizzled at least a layer or two of short-term memory brain cells.

What good were vices if they didn't help you forget stuff?

Laura Duval was my first customer of the day. Laura is a very attractive ash blonde with soft features and inquisitive blue eyes. She sported a classic A-line bob and wore a dusky blue peasant dress with elbow-length sleeves and a cinched waist. 'All alone today?' she asked.

I smiled. 'For the first couple of hours. I told Aubrey to come in at eight.' That's when business really picks up. I offered a senior discount before ten a.m. on Wednesdays. I also offered free coffee with every beignet order to extraterrestrials. But, so far, I'd had no takers.

'Coffee?' I was a frequent visitor to Laura's Lightly Used, the vintage shop she ran. It's where I'd bought my Schwinn among other things, including several items for the café – like a certain rolling pin that I'd rather not think about.

Laura nodded. 'And beignets. Can't have one without the other, right?'

'Hey, cornflakes aren't the only breakfast of champions.' I liked Laura and was sure that over time we'd become fast friends. I stripped off a row of dough and dropped her order in the deep fryer, enjoying the sound of the sizzle almost as much as the smell of the deep frying dough.

'I heard about Lisa Willoughby,' Laura said, her voice low despite the fact we were alone. 'I also heard you found her.'

'Sort of,' I said, pulling her beignets from the fryer and dropping them onto the draining tray, where I dusted them with powdered sugar. I plated the beignets and handed them across to Laura.

She took her beignets and coffee to the nearest table and sat down. I joined her with a cup of coffee of my own. It was my third in an hour, but who was counting? 'Did you know her?'

Laura nodded and fingered a beignet. 'We went to school together.'

'I didn't realize.'

'I lived in Santa Fe once.' Laura blew across the top of her cup and took a tentative first sip. I watched the steam rise like a wraith, or like the ghost of Lisa Willoughby materializing between us. Was she looking for her killer? Was she looking for some sort of spiritual release?

Had I been listening to Mom's hoodoo-voodoo mumbo-jumbo too long? If this was what I was like now what would I be like after living with her in my cramped apartment for a week?

Laura set down her cup. The steamy ghost disappeared. 'She wasn't perfect but neither did she deserve to die.'

'Is there anyone who might have thought otherwise?'

Laura canted her head to one side and smiled wanly. 'Old boyfriends she'd dumped and girlfriends whose boyfriends *and husbands* she'd stolen.'

'So it was like that?'

Laura nodded. 'She lived in the condo below mine. Let's just say there were plenty of comings and goings.'

'She owned a condo?' I'd seen Laura's place. It wasn't posh but it was decent. I couldn't afford a car, let alone a condo in that building. 'How could she afford to buy a condo? Was she renting?'

Laura shrugged. 'Maybe she was renting but if she was it was without the condo board's consent. They're pretty strict.'

I puzzled over this for a moment. 'Did she have a roommate?'

'No. I'm sure she didn't. I think I would have noticed if there'd been anyone else staying there on a regular basis.' Laura smirked. 'Not that I didn't see a man or two going in or out of the place.'

'Maybe cake decorators earn more than I thought.' More customers started filtering through the door. I rose. 'Be right with you!' I smiled at my new customers, a well-dressed man and woman.

'I heard the rumors about Clive Rothschild.' Laura swirled the dregs of her coffee around the cup.

I waved my hand. 'It's his partner, Johnny, I'm more worried about.'

Laura's brow rose. 'You think he had something to do with Lisa's death?'

'No, not really. But the way he's acting lately I'm not surprised the police are interested in talking to him, too.'

Laura also stood. 'Guess I'd better get to the shop.' She dropped her tray at the counter. 'If somebody did help Lisa down those stairs I'd look real hard at the people she worked with.' She crumpled her napkin and dropped it in the trash. 'And slept with.'

Good point. Maybe I'd share it with Detective Highsmith.

Laura tapped her cheek. 'You know, there was one guy. I don't know his name. But he wore a Markie's Masterpieces shirt. I caught him banging on Lisa's door, yelling, creating quite a racket.'

'But you have no idea who he was?'

'None. He had short brown hair and bushy eyebrows.' Laura smiled. 'I remember that.'

'That sounds like Ben Baker,' I said. 'He's got strong hands, too.' I flexed my fingers. 'Strong enough to give a person a solid push . . . or crush a windpipe.'

As Laura scooted out the door, the two strangers at the counter shot each other worried looks. 'How's everybody today?' I asked with a pasted-on smile. Our conversation might have been a tad graphic and uncomfortable for them and I wanted to make it all better. Kiss the boo-boo time. I made myself irresistible as I leaned my hands on the counter and said, 'Here for the senior discount?'

The woman gasped and shot a desperate – and offended – look at the man I took to be her husband. 'I'm not sure I want anything now,' she growled, 'under the circumstances.'

I felt my face redden. 'I'm terribly sorry,' I said. 'I certainly didn't mean to offend you in any way.' But she looked so *old*. Did she want me to think she wasn't on the downslope of sixty-two? I cleared my throat and looked imploringly at her husband, too. 'You look really young!'

The man half-smiled and gave me a shrug as his wife pulled him out the door. As I sadly watched a cash sale exit stage left, I had to give her credit: she may be old but she hadn't lost any muscle. Or speed.

'Please come again!' I really couldn't afford to lose any customers. 'My treat!' I yelled in desperation as they bustled away.

'Wow, what was that all about?'

I swung to my right. A man about my age wearing pleated khaki slacks and a yellow polo shirt was resting his elbow on the register. He'd come in just as the couple was going out. 'Sorry, can I help you?'

He ordered a plate of beignets and a cup of coffee. Aubrey came in as I was handing him his change. 'Hope you'll come again.'

He smiled. He had big teeth and big brown eyes with just a hint of green around the edges. His hair was swept back. 'Maybe. To tell you the truth, I was going to try that Karma Koffee place across the street.' He pointed with his thumb.

I cheered up. He'd chosen me over my erstwhile competition. I was winning.

'But the line was so long I decided to come over here.'

I cheered down. I was losing. 'Well,' I said, trying not to sound or look like a deflated day-old birthday balloon, 'I hope you'll stop in again.'

He offered me an encouraging smile. 'I'm only here to visit my sister. I have some sad news for her actually. I thought I'd tell her in person.'

Aubrey grabbed an apron and joined me. I asked her to run a quick inventory in back. Tomorrow was order day. 'Oh, sorry to hear that.' I wiped the counter with my towel. 'Anybody I know?'

'You tell me,' he said. 'Her name's Lisa.'

I blanched. 'Lisa?' I gulped.

He nodded. 'Yep. Lisa Willoughby.'

'Lisa Willoughby,' I said, my tongue thick, my blood draining to my toes. Whatever sad news it was he had to share with his sister, Lisa, couldn't be any sadder than Lisa's own news.

'That's right. I'm Houston.' His eyes looked troubled. 'Are you OK? Is something wrong?'

I twisted the rag in my hand. 'How long have you been in Table Rock?'

He cocked his head. 'Just got here. Drove in from Santa Fe. Got up early to beat the holiday traffic and it still took me five or six hours. I'm starving and in need of coffee.' He looked pointedly at the French coffee press.

'You're in luck,' I poured him a cup of coffee and set it on the counter. 'I've been told my coffee is strong enough to bench press two-fifty.'

He took a sip and sighed. 'Exactly what I needed.'

'So,' I said again, 'just got here, huh?'

'Yep.' He took a larger gulp. 'Why?'

What was I supposed to say? Houston, we have a problem? What was I supposed to do? Tell him his sister was dead?

Aubrey came around the corner. 'Hey, Maggie, I finished the inventory. I forgot to mention, I saw the paper this morning. You must be truly, truly relieved.'

'What?' I turned to face my young assistant. I was still feeling stunned and totally, totally awkward. 'Why?'

She chuckled. 'Because the police let Clive go, silly. Out on bail, anyway.' She checked the coins in the till. 'I don't think they really suspected that Clive pushed Lisa Willoughby down the stairs and murdered her.' She chuckled some more. 'I know I don't!'

Thud.

Houston, we have a problem.

FOURTEEN

I scraped Lisa's brother, Houston, off the floor and checked his head for goose eggs. It didn't appear that he had hurt himself too badly. Not even hummingbird egg-sized knot.

The shock of hearing about his sister's death was probably far worse than the blow he'd sustained when he'd fainted dead on the floor. I gave him a glass of water and directions to both the Mesa Verde Medical Center, should he want to get himself checked out, and the address of the Table Rock Police Department should he want to learn the details of his sister's demise.

'Sorry,' muttered Aubrey, laying a hand on my shoulder as we watched Houston Willoughby slink out the door, shoulders drooping, a man defeated.

'Not your fault.'

At around ten a.m., Mrs Higgins showed up at the café flaunting a form-fitting red dress, accessorized with a red silk scarf and black heels that slammed against the wood floor as she marched to the counter. What was it with women around here staying in shape well into their fifties? Was peer pressure going to force me to keep up? I hoped not. I was looking forward to letting go.

'Good morning, Mrs Higgins,' said Aubrey. 'Can I help you?' Samantha Higgins' blonde locks were in a loose ponytail that bobbed up in back like a gold-colored waterfall.

Mrs Higgins looked at the menu. 'I don't think so, Aubrey.' She studied Aubrey for a moment. 'I heard you'd left Karma Koffee but I simply did not believe it.'

Mrs Higgins turned to me. 'Ms Miller, may I have a word?' She had a folder in her free hand. The other hand clung to the strap of her black purse. Maybe she was afraid we had purse snatchers lurking about behind the soda fountain.

I crinkled my brow in surprise. 'Of course.' I wiped my hands on my apron and stepped out from behind the counter. Maybe she was going to place a huger order of beignets for the impending nuptials.

She withdrew a stiff poster from her folder and held it by her fingertips. It was a poster for an event called Labor of Love coming up this weekend. I realized now that I'd seen a few of the posters splattered around town but hadn't paid them much mind. 'It's the annual Labor of Love,' Mrs Higgins began. 'We have arts and crafts, face painting, live music, clowns and food vendors.'

'Sounds great.'

'You can place this in your window.'

'Be glad to.' So that was the labor of love she'd been talking about yesterday at the cake shop. I thought she'd been talking metaphorically about her daughter's upcoming nuptials. I came back to earth as I realized Mrs Higgins was still talking.

'. . . And I realized after you left yesterday that I had neglected to include you.'

I nodded. I guess she had.

'Fortunately there has been a cancellation. So.' She set the poster on the counter, removed a small, stapled packet and handed it to me.

I accepted. 'What's this?'

'The paperwork for your registration, of course. You'll have to take it to Cosmic Ray, of course, to make it official.'

'Uh, of course,' I said, suddenly mimicking her speech pattern. 'Cosmic Ray?' What was she trying to say? Somebody was going to shoot some cosmic ray at the thing and that was going to make it all official?

Mrs Higgins rolled her eyes. 'Oh, that's not his real name. It's really Ray Bentley. Everybody calls him Cosmic. Lord knows why a grown man would want to go by the name Cosmic Ray.' She thrust the empty folder in her purse. 'You'll accept?'

'Sure,' I said. I was going to say 'of course' but I'd had enough of that. I pinched my eyes together as I read the top sheet of paper. 'What exactly am I accepting?'

Her hands clutched the strap of her purse. 'You'll have a booth at the Labor of Love, of course.'

Of course.

She beamed. 'All the money goes to charity.'

I shrugged. I couldn't say no to a good cause. 'Count me in.'

'Wonderful.' She looked at her watch. Nice. Probably eighteen-carat gold. 'You'll have to hurry, though. Registration closes at noon tomorrow. We need to make sure we have a proper number of volunteer vendors and booths to go around.'

I nodded once more. I was beginning to feel like a bobble-head.

'You'll want to get that paperwork filled out and over to Cosmic Ray ASAP.'

I waved the papers between us. 'ASAP,' I agreed, giving her an energetic thumbs up. 'Where do I find this Cosmic Ray?' I looked around the café. I was beginning to wonder if good old Mrs Higgins had flipped her wig. Maybe Cosmic Ray was nothing more than an imaginary alien acquaintance of the woman's. Perhaps the pressure of this whole wedding thing had pushed her over the edge. I'd seen first-hand how upset she'd become at the mere hint that her daughter's wedding cake wouldn't get done in time.

'He works at the Table Rock Visitor Center. You'll find him there.' Mrs Higgins rat-a-tatted toward the door. With heels like those I could chisel another Mount Rushmore. She pushed the door open then turned. 'Oh, and don't forget your checkbook!'

'Checkbook?' I knew I had one around here someplace. Oh, yeah. My cardboard box desk in back. I was using my checkbook as a coaster. It had a genuine forest-green vinyl cover. Perfect for holding a sweaty glass and preventing condensation from soaking into the cardboard.

'Yes,' Mrs Higgins explained, 'the booth fee is four hundred dollars.'

'Four hundred—' I gulped.

Mrs Higgins cut me off. 'Don't worry, Ms Miller, we'll have a lovely ten-by-ten tent-topped booth for you all ready to go Saturday morning. With all the utilities you need.'

'Dollars?' I looked madly at the papers in my hand. Was there an escape clause?

'Would you like gas or electric?'

Well, electrocution might kill me quicker but I had a feeling the gas would be less painful.

Mrs Higgins waved her hand to cut me off before I could even formulate a request. 'Simply fill out the appropriate box on the form. A for electric, B for propane.'

'K for kill me?' I suggested. No response. Nothing. Not even from Aubrey, and I was paying the girl's salary.

Mrs Higgins blinked. 'Most of the vendors try to get there early. Six a.m. Since you are selling coffee and beignets you should probably get there a bit earlier than that. Yes,' she smiled, 'let's make it five-thirty.' My mouth would be sore if I smiled as big and long as Mrs Higgins. 'That way there will be coffee and beignets for our other volunteers. Tell me,' Mrs Higgins said, looking pointedly around the café, 'is there a Mr Miller?'

'He's dead.'

'I am sorry.'

Aubrey rolled her eyes and muttered. 'Here we go again.'

I ignored my annoying young assistant. 'Why?' I blinked at Samantha Higgins.

'Because of your loss, of course.'

'Don't be,' I said quickly. 'I'm not. Besides, you don't have to feel sorry for me. Feel sorry for his new wife.'

Impossible as I would have imagined it, Mrs Higgins' brow wrinkled up. 'Whose new wife?'

'My dead ex-husband's, of course.'

Mrs Higgins' troubled eyes turned to Aubrey. Aubrey smiled apologetically. Samantha Higgins departed without another word.

'What's her problem?' I frowned at the registration papers in my hand. 'Volunteers,' I groaned, 'or victims?'

Aubrey laughed. 'It's for charity, Maggie. You'll be helping the less fortunate.'

'Great,' I growled, 'where do I sign up?'

'I think you just did.' Aubrey was smiling – at me, not with me.

'Don't be a wise guy,' I said. 'She called you by name. You know that woman?'

Aubrey nodded. 'Sure, she runs an art gallery. The Higgins live down the street from me.' Aubrey still lived at home with her parents. 'Mrs Higgins' husband is my folks' accountant.'

'I wish you had warned me.'

'About what?' Aubrey quirked her brow in my direction.

I didn't know 'about what' so I let it slide. More for my benefit than hers. A tap on my shoulder set me off and I spun around. The registration papers went flying, scattering across the floor.

The young man in his twenties who'd tapped me on the shoulder scrambled to pick them up. 'Sorry about that,' he said, a sheepish smile on his gorgeous face. 'I didn't mean to startle you.' He handed me a crumpled fistful of papers.

I eyed them. Maybe I could tell Mrs Higgins I'd lost the registration forms or, better yet, that they'd been destroyed. I could 'accidently' drop them in the deep fryer. 'Can I help you?'

'You're Ms Miller, right?'

'That's right.' He was a really good-looking kid, with wavy brown hair, smoldering dark eyes and a killer smile with the dimples to match. Probably captain of the football team in high school. 'Do I know you?' Surely I didn't.

'Hi, Cody.' Aubrey wriggled her fingers at the boy.

'Hey, Aubrey. How are you?' He stepped aside and approached the counter.

The two youngsters exchanged pleasantries while I cleaned out the French coffee press. Apparently I'd been forgotten – the fate of us *old* people. If you were under thirty then being nearly forty was like being nearly a hundred, it seemed.

Cody ordered a dozen beignets and four coffees. I decided to forgive him for scaring me and for being so young and handsome. As I handed him his order, he said, 'So I hear you were one of the people who discovered Lisa Willoughby.'

My brow shot up. 'That's right,' I said. 'Did you know her?'

He shrugged lopsidedly. 'She was working on our cake for Sunday.'

'Your cake?'

'Cody and Mrs Higgins' daughter, Sabrina, are getting married this weekend.'

I smiled broadly. 'Congratulations!' First the mother of the bride enters my shop, then the groom. Was that a coincidence?

He nodded. 'Thanks. It's going to be awesome.' He turned to Aubrey and pointed. 'You'll be there, right?'

Aubrey's head bobbed up and down. 'Of course. I wouldn't miss it.'

'Sabrina's mother was here only a minute ago.'

'Really? How about that. What did she want?'

'To give me these.' I held up the twisted registration papers.

'You know,' Cody said, rolling the top of the bag of beignets closed in his fingers, 'I don't believe what happened to Lisa was murder. She probably slipped and fell.' Cody dropped his change in the tip jar. 'People around here can be a little goofy.'

I had to agree with him on that point.

'Folks jump to conclusions. Lisa probably had frosting on the bottom of her shoe or something. It seems to me like the police are making too much out of the whole thing. Freak accidents happen all the time.'

'You could be right,' I said. It was true – maybe she had managed to go flying and falling to her death. Who was to say? 'The police seem pretty certain, though.' Clive's confession, no doubt, hadn't hurt their case. If the police had had time to examine the crime scene more thoroughly as well as the body who knew what else they might know about the case?

'I heard they locked up some guy from next door then let him go,' Cody said.

'I'm sure it's nothing. Besides, I was with "the guy next door" that morning. We went to the Entronque together. I really don't see how Clive – that's my next-door neighbour – could have killed anybody.'

Actually, I supposed it could have been easy. Clive was no killer, though.

But if the stairwell had been empty of dead bodies on his way up and then contained a dead body after he came down, why hadn't he seen anyone else in the hall or on the stairs? Why hadn't he seen the killer? Or had he? Had it been Johnny? Was he covering for Johnny for real?

'Do the police have any other suspects?' he asked.

'If they do they're not telling me.'

'Well,' his fingers fidgeted with the bags, 'I've got to go.'

'Good luck with the wedding!' I called out. 'That was weird,' I said to Aubrey as Cody left.

'Cody Ryan is a little weird,' she replied. She rapped her knuckles against her skull. 'High-school football. Took a few too many hits to the head,' she eyed me, 'if you know what I mean?'

A jock; I knew it. I set down the pastry cutter and crossed the dining room. I poked my head out the door and watched Cody head up the street. He spoke on his phone for a moment, shook his head and dumped the bag of beignets in the nearest trash bin at the corner. He grabbed one cup of coffee from the tray then threw the rest of the coffees in with the discarded beignets.

What the heck was that all about?

FIFTEEN

An unmarked and unremarkable navy-blue sedan pulled up at the curb and the M&M man got out – Mark Highsmith, Table Rock's top detective. He must have been on duty because he was driving the Ford instead of the boy fantasymobile. He unwound from the vehicle and stepped up onto the sidewalk. 'No Firebird today?' I remarked.

'I told you before,' he said, sounding none too amused, 'it's a Trans Am.' He wore an equally unremarkable brown suit.

I held the door open as he entered the café. 'Trans Am, trans-fat,' I deadpanned. 'What's the difference?'

'About a hundred horsepower.'

I guessed to him there was a difference.

'Must come in handy when you're reenacting Smoky and the Bandit with your high-school buddies.'

He gave me a dirty look. 'I wonder how much fat is in these beignets you're serving here.'

It seemed the detective was pretty good at being snarky too when he'd a mind to. All the more reason to dislike the man. He had me there on the fat issue. I didn't know and I didn't want to know how much fat, let alone trans-fat, might be in a serving of beignets. I wasn't advertising them as healthy eating alternatives or diet donuts.

Besides, I'm all about indulging. If you can't indulge in this life what good is it to be alive? 'Less than you think. I use non-fat oil. How about a dozen? To go.'

He looked almost amused. I say almost because with Highsmith it's always hard to tell. 'Have you seen Johnny Wolfe today?'

'You must be confused, Detective. This is Maggie's Beignet Café.' I stabbed my chest with a finger. 'I work here. The Hitching Post is next door. Johnny works there.' I opened the front door and held it open. 'Nice seeing you again.'

He moved toward the counter instead of the door. 'I'll have a coffee,' he said to Aubrey. 'Two creams.'

'Sure thing.' Aubrey prepared the coffee. I sighed and retreated behind the counter. The further I was from the long arm of the law, the better.

He turned to me, coffee cup in hand, steam rising toward his nostrils. 'You didn't answer my question.'

Getting rid of him wasn't going to prove to be as simple as I'd hoped. 'No, I have not seen Johnny today, Detective.'

I wasn't lying. I hadn't seen him today. Well, he had been asleep on the sofa when I'd left. But that was a technicality and could be interpreted one of two ways. I'd barely given him a look. Johnny had not been awake, he'd been asleep, legs kicking like he was competing in Skate America. We hadn't spoken. And most of him had been covered by a blanket.

And a cat. Carole Two loves snoozing on a warm body.

'Why do you want to talk to Johnny so badly, anyway? I thought you had your killer – Clive Rothschild. Though you did let him go.'

'We released him on bail,' Highsmith corrected. 'Besides, Mr Rothschild recanted his confession.' The detective shook his head. 'He said he didn't know what he was thinking. Got confused.'

Confused was right. 'He has blood pressure issues,' I said in Clive's defense. 'It affects his mental acuity at times.'

'Let's just say Clive Rothschild and Johnny Wolfe are persons of interest.' Detective Highsmith took a tentative sip.

Those two guys were interesting all right. But I didn't believe either of them were killers.

'Besides, there are certain inconsistencies concerning the body and the crime scene. When it comes to naming a killer, I'm keeping my options open.' He looked me over and not in a good way. I hadn't killed anyone, yet he still managed to make me feel like I had.

'Inconsistencies? Care to share?'

'No,' he said happily.

I decided to throw him a curveball. 'I spoke with somebody earlier who wasn't so sure Lisa Willoughby was murdered.' I folded my arms over my chest.

He looked down his nose at me. 'Did this person have a name?'

I hesitated but only for a moment. The kid hadn't told me anything in confidence, after all. 'It was Cody Ryan.'

Said nose wrinkled. 'Cody Ryan?'

I explained how he was the groom concerning the cake that Markie's Masterpieces was preparing for an upcoming wedding and for which Clive had been carrying the now-infamous swatch of fabric from the bridal gown.

'Interesting.' Highsmith pulled his tiny notepad from his breast pocket and scratched something down on the paper.

'What about the cake that was found, you know,' I cleared my throat, 'at the scene of the murder? Anything special about it?'

'You mean besides the fact that it was lying atop the victim?'

I arched my brow and waited. It could very well be that the cake was connected to the murder. 'Who ordered that cake?'

'Not that it's any of your business, but Lisa Willoughby was delivering the cake to the reception hall at the Table Rock Community Church. A couple were renewing their vows yesterday afternoon.'

I wished I could have rescinded my own. 'Maybe she had some connection to the couple.'

'Yeah, she did.' The detective shot me a withering look. 'She *made* their vow-renewal cake.'

And I wished I'd locked the café door before Highsmith had gotten inside. 'Speaking of Willoughby,' I scratched a fingernail along my temple, 'did Houston Willoughby come to see you?'

Now he openly smirked. 'Yeah, he told the desk sergeant that you were kind enough to tell him that his sister had been murdered.'

Out of the corner of my eye I watched Aubrey disappear into the storeroom. The coward. 'It just sort of happened.' No point ratting the poor girl out.

'A lot of things just sort of happen to you,' he replied. 'Don't they?'

I shrugged. Sometimes the shrug defense is the best defense.

I helped a couple more customers and shouted for Aubrey to get back out front. Highsmith lingered at the counter. I was beginning to fear he'd spook the customers. At least he wasn't wearing a uniform of any sort.

He sipped his coffee loudly. As Aubrey and I filled orders, Highsmith said, 'I kind of feel bad for the guy.'

'What guy?'

'Houston Willoughby.'

I stopped what I was doing. It was hard to imagine Detective Highsmith feeling sorry for anyone, let alone a stranger. 'Why?'

Highsmith set down his near-empty coffee mug. 'He came to town to let his sister know that their aunt, Willow Willoughby, had passed away over the weekend.'

Willow Willoughby? What kind of a name was that? 'He drove all the way here for that?' I extracted a half-dozen beignets from the fryer and dumped them over the drip tray. 'Why didn't he simply call?'

Highsmith shrugged those broad shoulders of his. 'He said she'd changed cell phones and switched her number. So he decided to come tell her in person.' He dropped a dollar bill in the jelly slash tip jar. 'If you see Johnny Wolfe, tell him I'd still like a word.'

Highsmith hopped in his car and disappeared.

I couldn't believe I had that guy for a neighbor. Plus, he'd seen me kissing Brad Smith. It was bad enough I had the owners of Karma Koffee, my across-the-street competition, as my landlords. No doubt about it, I was definitely moving when the lease on the apartment was up. 'You could have said something,' I scolded Aubrey.

She stuck her head out from the storeroom, her fingers clutching the doorframe. 'Like what?'

'I don't know,' I admitted. 'Anything.'

There was a gleam in Aubrey's eyes as she skipped to the register, took the next customer's credit card and ran it through the scanner. 'I wouldn't want to interrupt you and the detective in your mating ritual.'

'Mating ritual?' I spluttered.

The customer picked up his order and barked out a laugh. I turned the color of a maraschino cherry and tugged off my apron. I snatched the papers that Mrs Higgins had unloaded on me from under the counter and headed for the door.

'Where are you going?' called Aubrey.

'If I'm not back in time,' I hollered through the glass, 'lock up!'

SIXTEEN

Where I was going was to see a guy named Cosmic Ray. And I found him. From behind a twelve-foot-long lacquered wood counter he was speaking softly to a couple of tourists – a blue-skirted woman with a clunky camera around her neck and a man in cargo shorts with a pair of binoculars dangling from a leather strap around his own thick, suntanned neck.

Ray Bentley, or Cosmic Ray as his nametag so proudly displayed, was a thin man in his fifties wearing a 'Vortexes Are A Man's Best Friend' emblazoned tie-dyed T-shirt. I didn't know what he had on down below. It might have been the bottom half of a shiny silver spacesuit. His thinning brown hair was done up in two tightly wound pigtails at the back of his head, held in place with two purple coyote pigtail ties.

For a moment, I questioned Cosmic Ray being the best person to represent Table Rock but I quickly realized he was just right, given the nature of our fair, if off-kilter, town. He had dark, close-set eyes and I wondered if those pigtails were really

antennae for receiving signals from Venus. A lidded paper Karma
Koffee cup sat on the counter within easy reach of his left hand.
Those Karma people were inescapable.

A few more tourists wandered in from the street, asking for
information. To pass the time, I casually examined a wooden
rack filled to the brim with brochures from every hotel, motel,
restaurant and tourist trap within a hundred miles of Table Rock.
Note to self: when I'd saved up a few bucks, get a brochure
made of my own special tourist trap, Maggie's Beignet Café,
and have Cosmic add it to the rack.

I read through a pamphlet on Table Rock's history then
plucked a brochure for one of those Jeep tours from the rack
and thumbed through it. There's a Jeep tour practically everywhere you go in Arizona.

'Can I help you, miss?' inquired Cosmic Ray.

I replaced the brochure, albeit slightly crooked and slightly
mangled, and turned around. 'I'm Maggie Miller,' I explained.
'From down the street.' I pulled the registration papers from
my purse as I approached the counter. 'I own Maggie's Beignet
Café on Laredo.' I peeked over the counter. Cosmic wore
nondescript khakis with a bundle of keys lashed to a belt loop
with a teal-colored carabiner. Nothing alien or even fashion
forward.

'A local, eh?'

'Recent transplant.'

Main and Laredo make up two sides of Table Rock Town
Square. The Table Rock Visitor Center was at the corner of
Main and Gurley. John A. Gurley was a former territorial
governor. The very first governor of the Arizona Territory, in
fact. The fact that he'd never actually been to Arizona and had
died before ever arriving to serve didn't stop the town from
naming one of its major streets after him, though the pamphlet
hadn't explained why.

'Tell me,' I said. 'how did Governor Gurley die? Was it
Indians? Marauders?'

Cosmic chuckled. 'Appendicitis.'

'Oh.' Hardly the stuff of folklore and legend.

The fourth street marking the boundary of the square was
named Smile. The original name had been Aubergine. It seems

a prominent local farmer had once grown eggplant. Eggplant does like the heat. Where else but Arizona can a vegetable grow and precook at the same time?

Apparently a bunch of hippies back in the sixties – who had arrived like an invading horde – had thought renaming the street Smile was a good thing. The mayor at the time was a bigtime Grateful Dead fan, a real Dead Head, from San Francisco. It seemed the hippies outnumbered the more reserved voters of Table Rock because Smile it became and has stayed ever since. Have I mentioned that Table Rockers are a quirky bunch?

Speaking of which . . . I could see the bronze statue on a marble plinth in the center of the square from where I stood. It was a life-sized rendition of our fair town's founder, Arthur B. Honicker. I'd heard he had founded Table Rock as a haven from religious and political persecution. The religion he founded, still operating out of an abandoned feed store just up the road, is something called The Universal Guiding Light. Sounded more like a soap opera to me with episodes running daily on public access cable TV. Local historians say the middle initial B in Honicker's name stood for Brigham. I think it stood for Bonkers.

I handed Cosmic Ray the sheaf of papers. 'Mrs Higgins told me I was supposed to turn these in to you.'

'Maggie's Beignet Café, huh? Sounds familiar.'

'We're right next door to The Hitching Post on one side and Caitie Conklin's Salon de Belezza on the other,' I explained. I gave his Karma Koffee-branded cup a dirty look.

'Karma Koffee is across the street.' Unfortunately.

'Oh, yeah.' He smiled a toothy smile, his fingers reaching for the cup. 'I've seen your place. Used to be a deli.' He had a gap between his two front teeth. 'Before that,' his eyes came unfocused, 'a head shop. Before that . . .' Long pause. 'A dress shop.' His eyes shot back into focus. 'I wonder what it will be next. Oops!' He looked embarrassed. Cosmic held up his palms. 'No offense, ma'am.'

'That's all right.' I'd go home and have a good cry later.

'I've been meaning to try some of your product.' He made up for his social clumsiness with a broad smile.

'Come by anytime,' I said, returning his smile. The tourism office occupied one smallish corner cut out of a souvenir shop

on the edge of the square. Besides the lovely statue of our dear
founder, Table Rock Town Square held a covered white bandstand, numerous park benches and plenty of shade trees,
including rows of ancient sycamores that lined the perimeter.
A cobbled red-brick walkway crisscrossed the square in a giant
X with a ring circumnavigating the bandstand.

Some long-ago architect had had the foresight to design a
large number of the buildings lining the public square with
belvederes. The large open galleries looked down on the square.
Perfect for dining, people watching and just plain relaxing. The
architectural style also served to keep the sidewalks below well-
shaded. Always a good thing in this part of the world.

Cosmic Ray wet his thumb a second and then a third time
as he riffled through my paperwork. He pulled all the pages
together and thumped them on the counter. 'Everything appears
to be in order.' He thumbed through the packet one more time.
His jaw twisted. 'I'm going to be needing your check for four
hundred dollars, Ms Miller.'

'Of course.' I rummaged through my handbag. 'Ugh,' I grunted.
'I forgot to bring my checkbook.' I'd left it in the storeroom.
That's what I got for letting my emotions get the best of me.
'Can I bring it by tomorrow?'

'Sure thing.'

'Great.' I promised to come back first thing the next morning.
I spotted a handful of uniformed city workers out on the square
with trailers filled with electrical cables, tables and tenting.
They were probably beginning preparations in the town square
for the weekend's Labor of Love festivities.

More of a Labor of Poverty, if you asked me.

'Don't you worry,' Cosmic Ray called as I departed. 'I'll see
you get a great spot!'

After that I got carried away window-shopping downtown
and the café was closed by the time I returned. I stuffed my
checkbook in my purse so I'd have it tomorrow then pedaled
home in time to find dinner and dessert waiting.

Mom had made apple turnovers. I could smell them a mile
away. Good old Mom, I thought, ready to forgive her trans-
gressing on me for a week as I inhaled the scent of apple and
cinnamon. Apple turnovers are one of my absolute favorites.

Besides, the way I see it, if a dessert contains chunks of fruit it must be good for you. I don't care how much butter Mom puts in that oh-so-flaky crust she handcrafts. Fruit *and* dairy. What could be healthier?

Everybody was sitting around the table when I arrived: Mom, Andy, the nephews, even Johnny. Donna was wrapped in my apron and hovering over the stove like a happy hen.

Oh, no. Donna. Has. Made. Dinner.

I rolled the Schwinn out the sliding glass door to the patio, careful to avoid hitting the wilted cactus struggling to stay alive in a small earthenware pot while surreptitiously trying to figure out what my sister was going to try to poison us with tonight.

The attempt was futile. Nothing smelled remotely familiar except the lure of Mom's apple turnovers. I could see them collectively cooling on a wire tray on the counter. One delicious corner of a golden brown turnover peeked out from beneath the paper towel she'd set atop them. I saw sparkles of sugar embedded in the crust and licked my lips.

Could I skip dinner and go straight to dessert?

I sighed as I leaned the bike on its kickstand. The idea would never fly. Mom and Donna would force me to eat a proper dinner first, no matter how much I argued that anything Donna came up couldn't possibly fit the definition of proper. I washed my hands at the kitchen sink. 'What's cooking?' I dried my hands on a plump navy dish towel before giving Donna a peck on the cheek, determined to make the best of a bad situation.

Donna stirred some giant gold-brown balls around in the skillet. 'Icli kofte.' She set down the spoon and grabbed a bowl from the fridge.

'Icky what?' I peered at the big brown balls, wondering nervously what they held.

'Bulgur balls with flam.'

'Flam?' I'd heard of flan, but flam?

Donna smiled. 'Faux lamb. My own invention.'

Oh, great. I was going to die. And there was so much I wanted to do yet. 'Sounds yummy!'

Donna nodded. Boy, was she dense or what? 'Grab that bowl and take it to the table, would you, Mag?'

I carried the big green bowl to the table. 'Let me guess,' I said, 'tabouli?'

'Right,' replied my mother. 'Donna thought it would go great with the bulgur balls.'

Sure, what wouldn't?

Mom and Johnny were drinking wine, something red. I chugged the remainder of Mom's glass before she could raise a protest.

Donna carried the skillet to the table and began doling out the balls of doom. 'Yes, I got the recipe from one of my customers. It's actually a hemp seed tabouli. She tells me it's delicious.'

In other words, my sister had never tried it. Great, we were going to be her guinea pigs. Donna's a bit of a – and I'm being politically correct here – nut. So is Andy.

Don't get me wrong, I love them dearly. It was just that right then I'd love them to be eating dinner at their own house while I pigged out on a Bell Rock Burgers quarter pounder with cheese. And I mean real cheese, not that fake soya stuff Donna touts as cheese and sells in Mother Earth/Father Sun.

How they stay in business I'll never know.

'Dig in, Aunt Maggie!'

I looked at Connor, the older of my two nephews. I didn't know if he meant those words as an invitation or a dare but by this point I was too hungry to care. Besides, the sooner I got this over with the sooner we got to the apple turnovers. Across from me I noticed Johnny had already devoured half an icky. He wore the same clothes he had on yesterday, so he must not have gone home at all. Ingesting the icky didn't appear to have killed him or even have slowed him down. How bad could it be?

I snatched my fork with confidence and cut into the first of the three balls staring me down. Gray juice squirted over the plate. I ignored the unpalatable color and hoisted a mouthful.

'Delicious,' Mom cooed. She scooped a pile of chilled hemp seed tabouli onto her plate.

'Yeah, really good, Donna,' added Andy. What else could he say? He was married to the woman, after all. Was it any wonder he was thin as a proverbial rail? What would he weigh if he'd been married to a real American? One who cooked meat and potatoes with biscuits and gravy on the side and served him a cold beer to wash it all down with?

I feared we'd never know. They were a happy couple. Marriage was something Donna had gotten right and me wrong.

I chewed some more and wiped my face with my napkin. Sweat trickled from my hairline. I let my hand fall to my side and fed Carole Two the flam that I'd spit out into my napkin. In retaliation, she bit me on the calf. 'Ouch!' I swatted blindly, catching nothing but air.

'Something wrong, dear?' Mom asked, turning to face me.

I rubbed my calf. 'No, just a cramp.' I glared at Carole Two. She sat on her haunches under the table, glaring back at me. The flam rested on the floor between her paws like a dead mouse. Tasted like one, too, I'm sure.

'I'm surprised to see you here, Johnny,' Andy said as he cleaned his plate and washed down his dinner with a glass of iced green tea that he poured from a glass pitcher. 'I didn't realize you and Maggie were,' he seemed to be word searching, 'so close.'

My brow shot up. Andy didn't seem to realize that Johnny had spent the night.

'Hadn't I mentioned?' Mom said. 'Johnny spent the night.' She folded her napkin and laid it on the tabletop.

Thanks, Mom.

Andy spluttered. 'He did?'

Donna gasped and looked at me, then the boys. 'Maybe you two want to go watch some TV now.'

'Now?' said Hunter. 'We haven't had dessert yet.'

'Johnny did stay the night,' I replied. I pointed. 'He slept on that couch.'

'Oh.' Donna released a sigh of relief.

I rolled my eyes. Did she really think I'd get involved with Johnny Wolfe? Not to mention the man was married to Clive Rothschild.

Johnny returned from the bathroom. 'Not a very comfortable couch either,' he complained, pointedly rubbing his lower back. 'I've slept on cozier airline seats.'

'Besides,' laughed Mom, 'it's that reporter Brad Smith that your sister was kissing last night. If you had any thoughts of your sister with anybody, that's who you should be suspecting.'

I slunk down in my chair, nose to bulgur ball. My cheeks flamed. I wanted to scream. I settled for whimpering. 'Dessert, anyone?'

Dear Lord. Mom had seen me making out with Brad Smith. How had she seen me making out with the reporter?

'I'll get them,' Mom said, rising quickly and moving to the rack where they sat cooling. She set the aluminum sheet on a couple of trivets between us after Donna and Andy cleared some space at the table. 'Johnny only spent the night to avoid talking to the police.'

'Excuse me?' Andy's voice carried over the cries of Hunter and Connor to be served first.

Uh oh.

SEVENTEEN

'**D**on't get excited.' I pumped my hands in Andy's direction. 'It's not what you think.'

Andy folded his arms across his chest. 'I think Johnny is avoiding talking to the police about an ongoing murder investigation. I think the police might not be taking too kindly to that. I think you're butting in where you don't belong.'

Johnny looked like he wanted to skate away as Andy continued, 'I think you could be making things worse for yourself.' Andy ripped off the corner of his apple turnover. Baked golden delicious apple in a buttery sauce oozed out. 'And making them worse for Clive, too.'

OK, so it was exactly what Andy was thinking. 'It's really not like that at all,' I said, despite knowing better.

'Miller's right.' Johnny came to my defense. He stuffed a mouthful of turnover down his gullet and chewing heavily. 'I have a reputation to protect.'

Andy glared at the both of us.

'Sorry?' I whimpered.

'I'm sure Maggie and Johnny didn't mean to cause any trouble,' Donna said in an obvious attempt to assuage her husband.

'Of course, not,' Mom said lightly. 'I'm sure Johnny will be happy to talk to the police tomorrow.' She smiled. 'Won't you, Johnny, dear?'

Johnny readily agreed.

Johnny, dear? I ripped my turnover in two. Hot apple, sugar and cinnamon spilled over my fingers. 'Ouch!' I hollered as my fingers turned pink.

Donna warned me to be more careful as Connor asked, 'Are you going to jail, Mr Wolfe?'

'Yeah,' added Hunter, 'did you kill somebody?' Hunter was practically drooling. 'With your bare hands?'

'Like on TV?' That was Connor again.

Both boys bobbed their heads excitedly.

'Nobody here killed anybody,' Donna said sternly. 'Eat your dessert.'

'Thanks,' I said to my sister, then poked my nose at the boys.

'No problem.' Donna laced her fingers together and rested her elbows on the table. 'Now, let's hear all about Brad Smith and that kiss.'

Mom and Andy snickered.

'What kiss?' enquired Johnny. 'Did I miss something? Has Miller actually found another man?'

I glared at Johnny. 'You may have been a little premature, Donna.'

Her brow shot up. 'About what?'

'About nobody here having murdered anyone.'

Johnny shot me a look that would have withered a tomato plant quicker than a hundred-and-twenty-degree day in the sun, then refilled his wine glass. 'Spill it, Miller.' He wiggled his fingers in a come-hither manner.

I would have liked to have spilled that liter of wine over his thick skull. 'There's nothing to spill.' I turned to my brother-in-law. He was the only reasonably normal person in sight, after all. 'Can we talk about Lisa Willoughby's murder instead? You won't believe the things I've heard.'

Andy leaned back in his chair. 'I'm listening.' He turned to

Connor and Hunter. 'You can finish your desserts on the sofa, boys. Watch TV if you want.'

'OK,' said Connor. 'But there's never anything good to watch at Aunt Maggie's.'

'Yeah,' Hunter chimed in. 'She hardly gets any stations at all.'

Could I help it if the cable company had found out the last tenant had left and then cut off the premium channels when they had realized I wasn't paying for the package?

'Watch PBS,' suggested Donna. 'That's free.'

Connor gave his mother a look that implied she was just this side of the loony bin. He grabbed Hunter by the shoulder. 'We'll watch Sports Center.'

'So,' I began, 'Lisa's brother, Houston Willoughby, arrived today.'

'How do you know that?' asked my mother.

'He came in the café this morning. He arrived from Santa Fe.'

'Santa Fe?' Johnny rubbed the bridge of his nose with the edge of his empty wine glass. 'Great little town,' he reminisced. 'I skated there once.' His eyes rolled back in his head, searching for memories, no doubt. 'For some charity or another.'

'Anyway,' I said firmly, 'he came to break the news to his sister that their aunt had passed.'

'He didn't know his sister was dead?'

I shook my head.

'You told him?' Johnny looked appalled.

I shrugged. 'Sort of.' I leaned toward my brother-in-law. 'I also heard that there was something fishy about Lisa's death.'

That seemed to get Andy's interest. 'Like what?'

I heaved my shoulders. 'I don't know. Detective Highsmith wouldn't tell me. He got all official. He only said there were circumstances about the scene that raised questions or something.'

Andy tapped his finger against his lips. 'Interesting.'

'Yeah,' I agreed. 'I don't think he believes Clive had anything to do with the murder at all.' I took a mouthful of turnover then said, 'Have you learned anything new from your sources, Andy?'

'Not a word. But then, I do have other things to do besides

play lawyer. I've got a farm and a store to help run.' Connor and Hunter broke out into an argument on the sofa. 'And boys to raise. Quiet down over there, you two!'

I tapped my empty glass. 'You know, from everybody I talk to, it seems like Lisa Willoughby was anything but a saint.'

'Rumors,' Andy said. 'And innuendo.'

Mom agreed. 'I don't think it is polite to speak poorly of the dead.'

'I agree with Miller here.' Johnny stabbed his fork against the table. 'Lisa was a horrible person. She lied, cheated and stole from me and Clive.' He lifted his chin. 'I don't care that she is dead.'

Andy looked surprised. Mom looked shocked. I was somewhere in the middle. Donna was staring at her empty dessert dish. 'I wouldn't go blabbing that opinion around,' Andy warned Johnny.

Johnny wagged his head.

'Lisa lived in a condo in the same complex as Laura Duval from Laura's Lightly Used.' I drummed my fingers against the tabletop. 'I sure would like to get a look inside.'

Andy's eyebrows turned into dark thunder clouds. 'Don't you dare go near that place,' he demanded. 'Either of you!' He pointed a threatening finger at both myself and Johnny.

Johnny pouted then rose and started opening and closing my cupboards like he owned the place. He didn't.

'Can I help you with something?'

'Where do you keep the wine?'

'I keep an extra box on the bottom shelf of the fridge,' I explained. 'For emergencies.' And having Johnny Wolfe, my mother and the whole clan in the house definitely qualified as an emergency.

Johnny cringed but with no other options dragged out the chunky three-liter box of chilled red. Donna, Andy and the kids left soon after. Probably headed home to nibble on some pine nuts and watch a documentary on butter churns on the local educational channel.

Mom was out on the patio running through a yoga routine.

Before leaving, Andy had made Johnny promise to go down to Table Rock Police Department tomorrow morning. He made me promise to keep my nose out of the whole Lisa Willoughby murder business. 'Don't do anything crazy or illegal,' he'd insisted.

Sure, tie my hands, why don't you?

Donna made me promise to eat the left over icky balls and hemp seed tabouli for dinner tomorrow.

Johnny lied once.

I lied twice.

Johnny jammed the plastic cap back on the wine. 'So, what time are we going to Lisa's condo?' He whispered across the kitchen table.

I shot a glance over my shoulder. The sliding door between my mother and us was shut. Mom was in the midst of some pose that would have sent me to the emergency room. I had planned on attacking Lisa's place solo but I didn't see any harm in Johnny tagging along. 'Mom should be asleep by eleven,' I said. 'We go then.'

I felt good. I felt confident. I was doing something. Besides, what could go wrong?

EIGHTEEN

The narrow bathroom window stood six or seven feet off the ground. No light showed from inside but then I hadn't expected to see any, what with Lisa being dead and all. And if she was a spirit, something told me she'd have excellent night vision.

'Up you go,' I whispered, slapping Johnny encouragingly on the shoulder. Wearing yesterday's black sweater and trousers, he was perfect for playing the part of a cat burglar.

Lisa Willoughby's condo was a ground-floor end unit located in one of several blocks making up the Meadow Reach Condominiums complex. We stood outside between an AC unit and some prickly shrub that seemed to have it in for me. Mom's VW Beetle was parked around the corner. I'd waited until I heard the sound of her sleeping to sneak into my bedroom and steal the keys from her purse. We'd be back soon and Mom would be none the wiser.

It was like being a teenager all over again. Not that I'm saying I ever stole my folks' keys and snuck out in the middle of the night.

Nope. Not me. No way.

Johnny's pasty white skin looked even pastier and whiter by the moonlight cast by the waxing gibbous moon above us. 'Me?' he griped. 'You go.'

'No, you go.' I gave him a little push.

'Ouch! Careful!' he hissed as he backed into the deadly bush. 'Why me?' He brushed himself off. 'This was your idea.' He folded his arms across his chest.

I bit my cheek. Talk about stubborn. 'You're skinnier,' I said, much as I hated to admit it. The phone went off like a sonic bomb in my purse.

Johnny hissed at me. 'Turn that thing off or answer it, Miller!'

I thrust my hand into my purse, dug around in the dark and grabbed the pulsing phone. It was Brad. 'Hello?'

I waved my hand at Johnny, trying to get him to scramble up the wall to the window. I'd been avoiding Brad all day. He'd called three times earlier and left two messages. I didn't know what to say and was a bit embarrassed about jumping him last night. I didn't know why I'd bothered to answer now – reflex, I guess – or that nasty warning look of Johnny's.

'Hi, Maggie. It's me, Brad.'

'Hi, Brad.' It was nearly midnight. What the heck was he doing calling so late? 'Kind of late to be calling, isn't it?'

'Sorry,' he replied. 'I didn't wake you, did I?'

'No, no. You didn't wake me.' I made a face at Johnny, who leaned against the wall staring stupidly at me. I held my hand over the speaker. 'Get going,' I whispered. 'You're the athlete.'

'Is everything all right?' Brad asked.

I removed my hand. 'Oh, sure. Fine.'

'Do you have company? Am I calling at a bad time?'

'Company? Oh, yeah. Right. Company. Johnny and Clive are here. We're playing canasta with my Mom. And,' I added, glaring at Johnny, 'it's Johnny's turn to *move*.' I put a lot of emphasis on the word move.

'Sounds fun,' Brad replied.

'Oh, it is,' I said quickly. Johnny reached a tentative hand up to the window ledge. His fingers barely even reached and he was on tiptoes.

'Yes, I'll bet playing cards is a lot more fun than standing around in the dark trying to break into a dead woman's condominium.'

My blood froze quicker than a teaspoon of water in a blast chiller. 'Ummm.' My eyes widened. My head darted in three hundred directions at once.

There was silence on the other end of the phone. I stepped away from the shielding bushes and peered toward the parking lot. A dark Honda was parked in one of the handicapped spots near the clubhouse. A soft glow came from within.

Brad Smith.

'Are you spying on me?' I shouted into the phone.

'Quiet, Miller!' admonished Johnny. 'You want someone to call the cops?'

I stabbed the phone to end the call and marched to the car. I grabbed the top of the window frame and thrust my head in the open passenger-side window. 'What are you doing here? Did you follow me?'

Brad put up his hands in surrender. 'Settle down, Maggie. I have a friend who lives in the complex. As I was leaving his place I noticed your mother's VW on the street.'

I groaned.

'It's kind of distinctive with those eyelashes over the head-lights and the *Aliens Onboard* bumper sticker.'

He was right. I should have brought the Schwinn. It was pink with pink streamers coming out the handlebars and *still* less conspicuous than Mom's Bug.

Johnny beckoned me from the distance. 'Hey, Miller! I found a trash can. Hurry up.' He waved. 'I think we can reach now.'

Mr Stealth he wasn't. If I wasn't careful he was going to get us both arrested.

Brad smiled wickedly. 'I think your date's calling you.'

'He's not my—' I stopped. He knew darn well Johnny was not my 'date.' The reporter was only goading me. 'Go home, Brad.'

'I'm going. I'm going.' He reached for my hand. I didn't pull it away. His fingers were warm and my palm tingled. It must have been the night air. 'Please be careful, Maggie. That's a murdered woman's home you're about to enter. Not only is that breaking and entering—'

'The window's half-open,' I interjected. 'Technically, it's only entering.' I had no idea of the legality of what I'd said but it sounded good to me. I could only hope it sounded good to the police if they caught us.

Brad began again, his voice firm. 'Not only is it breaking and entering, but it could be risky. Whoever killed Lisa might be lurking about. And that person may not take too kindly to seeing you poking around.'

'So, you know it's Lisa Willoughby's condo.'

He nodded. 'Of course.'

'I guess that means you've been poking around too.' Take that, wise guy.

He twisted his jaw. 'I'm a reporter, Maggie. It's what I do.' Touché. Brad turned the key in the ignition. The Honda started up quietly. 'Call me if you need me.' He squeezed my hand then released it.

I watched the red taillights disappear then hustled back to the side of the building.

'Hold the can for me,' Johnny said. He climbed up, shimmied his skinny hips through the open window, kicked his legs madly then dropped inside. The trash can fell over, spilling reeking trash all over the grass and my shoes. I smelled rotten eggs and spoiled cabbage.

'Ooof!'

Apparently he'd found the floor. It sounded loud. And hard.

I heard scrambling and not a small amount of cursing, then Johnny whispered from within. 'OK, Miller. You're next.'

I didn't see any reason for both of us to enter the hard way. I cupped my hands to my mouth and whispered, 'Go unlock the front door. I'll meet you there.'

Johnny cursed again. I worked my way around to the front of the building. The complex was quiet and the lights were out in most units. Small torchlights along the walkway lit my path.

The door to Lisa's condo squeaked open and a hand grabbed

my shoulder and yanked me inside. I stumbled across the foyer and caught myself on the edge of an armchair. 'What is your problem?' I swiped at my shirt.

'Sorry,' Johnny said. 'I'm nervous, that's all.' He paced the small living room. 'Help me find a light switch.'

I grabbed his arm. 'No, no lights.'

'Why not?' complained Johnny. 'We're supposed to be searching the place. How are we supposed to do that if we can't see?'

I held onto his arm. The place was a little spooky. Dark. Quiet. A murdered woman's home. I was beginning to wonder if this had been such a good idea after all. Maybe Brad was right. Maybe we should leave this to the police. 'What if somebody sees the light? What if they know Lisa Willoughby and that she's dead and can't possibly be turning on the lights?' I mean, was I wrong? Did ghosts need lights?

'So what do we do?' Johnny sounded on edge. 'I can barely see my fingers in front of my face.' He yanked his arm free of my grip and wriggled his fingers in front of his nose.

I thought for a moment then snapped my fingers. 'I know.' I fished my phone back from my purse. 'We'll use our phones.'

'Good idea, Miller.' Johnny dug his iPhone from his front pocket.

I hit my screen and let the dim glow from the phone play across the walls. Johnny fiddled for a minute with his own phone. The next thing I knew, a bright beam of white light shot from the back of it like a flashlight.

'How did you do that?' I gasped, looking lamely from my phone to his.

He smiled smugly. 'Got a flashlight app. Don't you?'

I scrunched up my lips. 'Just keep that lighthouse beacon of yours away from the windows,' I said stiffly. 'We don't want to be attracting the attention of anyone passing by.' I ran a hand along Lisa's sofa. Expensive fabric. Everything in the place looked high-end. 'How could she afford all this?'

Johnny sniffed. 'I told you, the woman was a thief. Yet she had the nerve to sue us!'

Johnny could have been right about Lisa. This girl had lived way better than I did.

'So what do we do now?' asked Johnny. The light from his phone lightly played across the beige carpet. 'Where do we start? What are we looking for?'

I stuck my phone back in my purse. Its dim glow paled in comparison to Johnny's flashlight app, so what was the point? 'I don't know,' I confessed. I never thought we'd get this far but I wasn't telling Johnny that. 'Let's look for a desk. Or a computer. Someplace she might keep her papers and other personal effects.'

'Good idea,' Johnny said again and shone his phone light around the living area. Two chairs, a sofa and a dark stained painter's easel in the corner with a table covered with paints, charcoal pencils and chalks. A pair of black-rimmed reading glasses sat in a white bowl.

Apparently Lisa was an artist. It wasn't surprising and explained her career choice as a cake decorator and a dress designer before that. The penciled outline of a man occupied the canvas on the easel. 'Hold it!' I whispered to Johnny as the light played over the canvas.

'What is it?'

'I'm not sure. He looked familiar for a second.'

Johnny twisted his lips. 'Could be anybody,' he said. 'The woman was a terrible artist.'

Sounded like sour grapes to me but I wasn't about to poke the bear. We moved on. The kitchen was in the rear on the left with a dining table and chairs against the wall to the right. A sliding glass door led out to a patio stuffed with expensive-looking rattan furniture and a stainless-steel barbecue grill that must have set her back a thousand bucks. I pointed toward the corner of the patio. 'Is that a pizza oven?' I gasped.

'Focus, Miller.' Johnny aimed the light directly at my eyes and everything went nova.

I shook my head, wiped the tears from the edges of my eyes and turned around. Moving slowly. On the prowl for clues.

On the lookout for ghosts.

The one thing I hadn't seen so far was a TV. Not even a little one. Weird. Practically inhuman. Who doesn't own a big-screen TV or three? This is America, after all.

A couple of empty takeout Chinese food containers sat atop

the table beside a wadded-up paper napkin. Probably the remains of Lisa Willoughby's last dinner. The two chopsticks rested across one another looking eerily, and prophetically, like a cross.

A frisson ran up my arms as light as the touch of a dancing hummingbird.

There was nothing else of interest in the living room so we headed down the hall toward Lisa's bedroom. I could only hope her ghost wasn't there waiting for us. Johnny went first, holding the light. We passed a bathroom and entered a bedroom that held the light scent of blackcurrant and iris.

Johnny's light explored the near wall across from the bed. There was a narrow desk with an open laptop and a collection of hats one atop the other – like something out of Dr Seuss' *The Five Hundred Hats of Bartholomew Cubbins* – to the right of it. The door to the walk-in closet stood open. 'I'll check in here.'

While Johnny checked out the closet, I moved to the desk. I touched the spacebar on the laptop and it sprang to life. The wallpaper she'd selected for her screen's laptop was the logo for the Detroit Tigers. So, Lisa was a baseball fan. My dead ex-husband Brian was a big baseball fan. I knew all the team names and logos. I knew more about baseball than I cared to.

I clicked the left-side button of the built-in mousepad and a small white arrow appeared on the screen. The computer wasn't password protected. I ran my finger along the touchpad and clicked on the My Files folder. If Lisa Willoughby had any secrets – secrets that might lead to her killer – this was the place to start, though I didn't have high hopes. If there was anything useful on the laptop, surely the police would have found it already.

Johnny tapped me on the shoulder.

'Hold on, Johnny,' I whispered. 'I want to look at this.'

He tapped me again. 'I think you'd better take a look at this first, Miller.'

I spun around. 'What? What is so interesting that I—'

Johnny had his light trained on the bed and an open brown suitcase. The contents of the suitcase were spilled out across the bedspread.

I crossed to the bed and fingered a pair of trousers. 'These are men's clothes.' I looked at Johnny. He nodded in agreement.

There were several papers tucked behind a mesh pouch on the right side of the suitcase. 'Shine the light over here,' I said, squinting to get a better look. There was a receipt of some sort on top. 'It looks like it's made out to' – I pushed Johnny's arm lower so I could read the bottom folded edge – 'Willoughby,' I said finally. 'Houston.' I straightened. 'Uh oh.'

'You mean Lisa's brother?' Johnny's eyes widened.

I nodded.

'Her brother is here? Staying here in her condo?'

I placed my hands on Johnny's shoulders. 'Calm down, Johnny.' If he got this nervous over a simple breaking and entering it was no wonder he'd never taken the gold medal – you need nerves of steel not marshmallow. 'It's no big deal. Nobody knows we're here,' I assured him. 'And nobody will ever know we've been here.' I returned to the desk and snapped the laptop shut.

'What are you doing?' I could hear the worry in his voice. This guy was more skittish than a racehorse. This was the last time I was going to take Johnny Wolfe along on a break-in. 'I'm taking the laptop.'

'Taking the laptop?' Johnny's hands flew to his face. 'Are you nuts, Miller? That's stealing!'

'From a dead woman,' I said. 'Mitigating circumstances.' I pushed Johnny toward the door. 'Besides,' I added, 'I'll bring it back after I've had a chance to go through her files.'

'But you can't—'

I clapped a hand over Johnny's mouth. 'Did you hear that?' I whispered.

Johnny pushed my hand from his lips and spat like I'd just forced him to drink a jigger of arsenic. He shone the light in my eyes. 'Hear what?'

I winced at the sharp light. 'I thought I heard steps. Voices.' I held up a finger. 'Listen.' We both strained to hear. 'It sounds like somebody's putting a key in the front lock.'

'A key in the—'

I clapped my hand over Johnny's lips once again.

He knocked my hand away. 'Must you keep doing that?'

'Sorry.' I pointed to the phone. 'Shut off that light,' I whispered.

Johnny nodded, did whatever he needed to do to turn off the flashlight and slid the phone into the pocket of his jeans.

I heard the door swing open. 'Uh oh,' I whispered.

'Funny,' I heard a voice that sounded like Houston's say, 'I thought I'd locked the door when I left. No wonder I had such a hard time getting the thing open; every time I thought I was unlocking it, I was locking it.'

A woman's gentle laugh.

'Come on in.'

Double uh oh.

NINETEEN

Clutching the laptop to my chest, I moved stealthily out of the bedroom and down the hall. Hopefully they weren't heading straight to the bedroom. What would Houston do if he caught us? I edged to the corner and slowly peeked around the wall. It was Houston all right. And the woman with him was Laura Duval! I almost shouted out her name but caught myself in the nick of time.

I tiptoed back to the bedroom and reported to Johnny who was crouched behind the far side of the king-sized bed. 'It's Houston and Laura from the thrift shop.'

Johnny bit his fingernails. 'You've really done it this time, Miller. What are we going to do if they come in here?'

'Hide under the bed?' I suggested.

He glowered. 'I already tried that. It's on a platform.'

Yikes. 'Closet?'

'Sure,' he said, way more snidely than he need have. 'Because nobody ever goes into a closet.'

'Do you have a better idea?' I demanded.

Johnny pouted. 'No.'

'We could go out the bedroom window.' I looked at the big window appraisingly. 'No problem.' One curtain was pulled open, the other shut. Moonlight gave us just enough light to stop us banging our shins into hard objects.

'Sure,' said Johnny. 'Only we have to open it *and* take the screen out first.' Johnny gave me a blistering look. 'All without making a sound and I don't think that's poss—'

'Shh!' I hissed, dropping to my knees. 'Someone's coming,' I whispered close to Johnny's ear. I settled in beside him. From this angle we could see down the hall a bit. There was plenty of light coming from the front room now. Laura was silhouetted against the wall.

'I'll only be a moment,' she called over her shoulder.

I pushed away from Johnny and raced to the bedroom door. 'Pssst!'

'Oh!' Laura gasped.

'Everything OK?' I heard Houston ask loudly.

'Fine, just fine,' Laura called back, though she sounded rattled.

I pumped my arms at her, hoping she'd understand that I wanted her to keep her voice down. 'It's me, Maggie. Maggie Miller,' I said as quietly as possible. Laura hung in the shadows near the powder room for a moment then came toward me.

I backed away from the bedroom door, pulled her inside and shut the door behind her.

'Maggie, what are you doing here?' Laura's hand went to her chest. 'You about scared me to death.'

'Me and Johnny were looking for clues as to Lisa Willoughby's killer.'

'Johnny?' Laura appeared confused.

Johnny popped up from behind the bed and I clapped my hand over Laura's hand to smother her scream. Laura stared at Johnny, then at my hand covering her mouth.

'Bufyoucamfbe,' she began. I lowered my hand. 'But you can't be here,' Laura said. 'Houston's staying here. He's in the other room right now.'

'We know,' replied Johnny. 'We're trapped.' He was looking at me when he said it.

'You've got to help us,' I said, grabbing Laura's hand.

'What do you want me to do?'

I thought for a moment. 'Distract him. Get him out on the patio. Better yet, take him up to your place.'

'My place?' Laura didn't appear to like the sound of that.

'That would be perfect,' Johnny piped in, his head bobbing.

'Fine,' Laura relented after a moment. She shook her head as she said, 'But I don't like this one bit.'

'Thanks.' I gave her a squeeze.

Laura headed for the door, resting her hand on the knob. 'Give me five minutes.'

We nodded agreement. I shot Johnny a thumbs up. He shot me something back. It wasn't a thumb. We waited in silence for five minutes to pass and it felt like five hours.

'Finally.' I pressed my ear to the door. 'Sounds like they're leaving.'

Johnny pirouetted to the door with all the grace of a doe. I had to admit, the guy had some moves. 'The coast is clear. Let's get out of here before Houston gets back.' I followed Johnny to the door. He stopped dead in his tracks. 'Leave it,' he insisted. He was pointing to the laptop.

'But it could be full of clues.' I clutched the laptop tighter to my chest. 'This computer could lead us straight to Lisa's killer.'

'And if we're caught with the thing it could lead both of us straight to jail.' Johnny blocked the front door. 'Leave it, Miller.'

'Fine,' I said, letting out a surrendering breath. 'I'm putting it back.'

A minute later, we were on the road. I looked around, half-expecting to see Brad Smith spying on us, but there was no sign of him or his car.

Ten minutes later I stopped at the gated entrance to Four Seasons.

'What are we doing here?' Johnny asked.

The guard asked my name and my business. I jerked a thumb toward Johnny in the passenger seat.

The guard nodded and let us in.

I eased up into Johnny's driveway. Outdoor lighting lit the palms, cacti and the front of the house, showcasing its magnificence. 'Goodnight, Johnny. I think it's time for you to sleep in your own bed, in your own house.'

One house guest at a time was enough – more than enough – for me.

'Fine.' Johnny kicked open the door. 'Your couch is terrible anyway.' One of his legs tangled in a purse strap. He snarled, unhooked his foot and thrust the purses at me. 'Why the devil do you carry two purses anyway?' He tossed them on the empty passenger seat. 'Goodnight, Miller.'

I wiggled my fingers. 'Give my love to Clive!'

He started up the driveway alongside his beloved BMW. I put the Bug in reverse. Johnny spun around. 'Wait a minute!'

'What now?' I sighed. 'I'm tired. I have to be up early in the morning.' Like every morning. It was one of the downsides to owning a beignet café.

Johnny thrust his head through the open passenger window, staring at the purses. One red, one black. 'Why do you have two purses, Miller? *How* do you have two purses?' His jaw tightened. 'You only had one when we left your house.'

Sure, suddenly he's Mr Observant. I pushed my tongue across my upper lip. 'Uh, the red one was in the car already. It's my mom's.'

He frowned. 'You left your apartment with the red one.'

'Oh, yeah. I meant the black one.'

Johnny slitted his eyes at me. 'You stole it, didn't you?'

My hands clutched the steering wheel and my foot held the brake pedal down. I stared straight ahead.

'You took a dead woman's purse.' He shook his head, admonishing me. I could see his look of disgust from the corner of my eye.

'Fine,' I admitted. 'You said to leave the laptop.' I turned and faced him down. 'You didn't say anything about purses. Or anything else, for that matter.'

'Miller,' Johnny drew the surname out so far I thought it would break. The fingers of his right hand played against the hard plastic dash.

'Fine.' He threw the door open, lifted the purses off the seat and sat back down. He set the purses between us.

'Listen, Johnny.' I put my foot down. 'I am not going back there. It's late and besides, Houston might be home by now and—'

'And nothing, Miller,' snapped Johnny. 'Stop talking and open Lisa's purse. Let's see what you've found.'

TWENTY

'You already owe me,' Laura said with an accompanying wave of her hand. 'What I went through last night.' She sounded tired. Looked tired. There were bags under her eyes and faint red lines crisscrossed her eyes like Martian canals. H.G. Wells could've written a book about them.

'I know,' I replied contritely.

Laura ran her fingers through her bob. 'I mean, that guy Houston is all arms. I'd have been safer with an octopus!'

'Sorry,' I said for the hundredth time. 'So are you going to do it or what?'

Laura pouted and stared at me for several moments before answering. She smoothed the skirt of her pale yellow sundress. 'Oh, brother,' she said, shaking her head and slapping her hands atop her knees, 'I can't believe I'm doing this.'

'Thanks.' I cracked a grin. 'Besides, what's the big deal? You're only inviting Houston for breakfast. It's not like I'm asking you to sleep with him or anything.' I narrowed my gaze. 'You haven't slept with him, have you?'

'Of course not!' Laura blurted. 'It was our first date.' She sat with her left leg crossed over her right and her left foot kicking up a storm. 'And I thought it was going to be our last date.'

'Is he really that bad?' Laura had never met my dead ex-husband, Brian, but he surely couldn't be any worse than him.

'No.' Laura sighed. 'Just not my type. And he moves too fast. I like to take things slow.'

'I don't know,' I said with a grin, 'nothing wrong with moving a little faster in the right situation.'

Laura arched her brow. 'Says the woman who's been divorced for nearly a year, has no boyfriend and tools around

Table Rock at the stately pace of five miles per hour on a pink Schwinn.'

I scowled. I'd been bested. And the best thing to do in that situation is to change directions. 'So, it's settled,' I said, lowering my voice conspiratorially. 'You call Houston. Invite him for breakfast at Odel's Diner.' I glanced up at the clock behind the counter. 'Let's say nine-thirty.'

'I suppose . . .'

'Great,' I replied. 'Get a booth if you can. At least a table for four, so I can join you. I'll just happen to come in. You see me, wave and invite me to sit with you. You hook him,' I jerked my hand upward, 'and I'll grill him.' I had a question or two for the late Lisa Willoughby's brother.

'What if Houston can't make it? What if he wants to sit at the bar?'

'Please,' I waved a hand at her. 'He's a male, you're a female.' I wiggled my eyebrow. 'Use your wiles.'

Laura looked skeptical. 'My wiles?'

'Yeah, your wiles. You've got wiles, haven't you?'

Laura rose. 'What I've got,' she said, looking down at me, 'are reservations.'

I stood, picked up our mugs with one hand and laid my other on her shoulder. 'Just make sure you get reservations for Odel's at nine-thirty.'

'Very funny.' Laura nodded and headed for the door. 'Wait.' She stood in the open doorway. The bells tingled. 'You never did tell me what you found in Lisa Willoughby's purse.'

'The usual girlie stuff. Makeup, checkbook, coin purse, tissues . . .'

'That's boring.'

'Follow me.' I led Laura to the storeroom and removed Lisa Willoughby's purse from the drawer where I'd hidden it from prying eyes. The small clutch that had been found with Lisa's body at the bottom of the stairwell had probably contained the essentials, like her driver's license, car and house keys and lipstick. The larger purse I'd found held something more.

'What's that?'

I smiled. 'A little red address book chockfull of names.'

'Not so boring.' Laura fingered the cover. 'So whose names are in it?'

I thumbed through the pages – not that I hadn't done so a couple of times already – and read aloud. Some entries were only a name or initials and a phone number; others included addresses, including one for Willow Willoughby, the recently deceased aunt in New Mexico. There were more men's names than women's, but I wasn't sure if that meant anything. Clive and Johnny were in her book, separately and as The Hitching Post. So was Markie Gravelle of Markie's Masterpieces along with the rest of the employees.

Some names I didn't recognize; others, like Cody Ryan, Samantha and Sabrina Higgins and the Robinsons (whose cake Lisa had been on her way to deliver when she'd been killed), I knew had been clients. The address book offered plenty of leads but I had no idea how I'd track all these people down, let alone get them to talk to me.

'Don't you think you should turn all this over to the police?'

'If they wanted it, why hadn't they taken it already?'

'I don't know . . .'

'Wait,' I said, not wanting to give her a chance to come up with a good answer. I needed some plausible deniability, after all. 'I was saving this for last.' I reached carefully into the reticule and withdrew my hand. 'A Smith and Wesson thirty-eight-caliber handgun.'

Laura gasped. 'That's scary.' She pushed my hand down. 'I wonder why she carried a handgun.'

I shrugged and put the little gun back in the purse. 'Who knows? This is Arizona. Lots of folks carry guns. It could mean nothing.'

'Or it could mean she was scared,' Laura said. 'Scared of somebody.'

I nodded. That's what I thought, too.

'So what do you intend to do with it?'

'I haven't decided.'

'You should turn it over to the police.'

I shrugged. 'It was in her apartment. Like I said, I'm guessing they'd have taken it if they wanted it.' I told Laura that I'd thought about maybe giving the address book to Brad and letting him dig around and see if he could make any interesting connections between the names and Lisa Willoughby's murderer. I turned the book over in my hand. 'Who knows? Her killer could be right here.'

'Yeah, but what about the gun?' Laura arched an eyebrow. 'That thing's dangerous.'

I stuffed the Smith & Wesson back in the purse. 'I'll hide everything in my apartment for now. Stick it under the sofa or something until I can figure out what to do with it all.' What harm could there be? Mom would never know it was there and the cat lacked an opposable thumb.

Laura left and promised to meet me at Odel's Diner at the appointed time. That left me just enough time to drop my four-hundred-dollar check off with Cosmic down at the Table Rock Visitor Center. What it didn't leave me was enough time to transfer some funds to my checking account to cover that check.

Oh well. I'd deal with that another time.

Cosmic smiled when he saw me. Sure I'd be smiling too if somebody was about to hand me a four-hundred-dollar check.

I waved the check in front of his face. 'Who do I make this out to?'

'Labor of Love Foundation.' He pulled out a ledger and laboriously wrote out my name and the amount as I scribbled in the name of the foundation. 'And don't you worry, Ms Miller.' He tapped his head with a long-nailed finger. 'I remembered what you told me.' He was smiling.

I like smiles. We should all smile more. 'What I told you?'

'Yep, about Maggie's Beignet Café.'

'OK.' I was glad he'd remembered. Now if he'd only remember to come and spend back some of that four hundred dollars there.

'Yep. About Karma Koffee and Salon de Belezza.'

'Right.' Two of my worst enemies. OK.

'Yep.' He unrolled a schematic.

I leaned over the counter and followed his finger. It was a drawing representing Table Rock Town Square. I noticed names and numbers scattered around the perimeter like spaces on a Monopoly board.

'Gotcha a nice spot right here.' His finger landed on A11.

'Nice.' I nodded. There was plenty of afternoon shade on that side of the square.

'Yep. Right between Salon de Belezza and Karma Koffee.'

Blood drained from my face. My mouth went dry. Yep, there was the Maggie's Beignet Café tent, right smack between Salon de Belezza A10 and Karma Koffee A12.

And I'd just shelled out four hundred bucks for the privilege.

TWENTY-ONE

I scraped my jaw up off the floor and hoofed it over to Odel's Diner on Smile Street just in time to see Laura walk in with Houston.

'Thank you, Laura,' I whispered from the sidewalk across the street as she glanced over. I gave them a few minutes to settle in so that my showing up wouldn't look too conspicuous, too much like a setup. Trina Odel met me at the door. She greeted the customers on their way in and rang the register on their way out. 'Table for one?'

I peered over her shoulder – pretty good crowd for a Thursday morning. I spied Laura and Houston at a four-top at the far side of the diner. 'I see my friends.' I waved. 'I think I'll join them.' Laura was facing the door and spotted me right away. Houston had his back to me.

Trina grabbed a menu from the stack at her station and led me to Laura and Houston's table. Trina is the Odels' daughter. Her mom runs the counter and her father runs the kitchen. Trina was a good decade older than me, which meant her folks were getting up there but they managed to stay active in the restaurant seven days a week.

I couldn't imagine how they kept up the pace. So far I'd been having a hard time sticking it out in the bakery seven hours a day, seven days a week. They probably put in ten hours a day each at the very least. I'd been in the diner several times. I waved to Mrs Odel who was waiting on customers at the long counter while Mr Odel manned the flat top fryer behind the window.

'Why, Houston,' said Laura, fluttering her eyelids, 'look who's here.' Laura was no actress. That line sounded as stiff as a starched pair of poplin shorts.

Houston turned.

I laid on a smile. 'Hi, mind if I join you?'

Houston half-rose but I waved him back down. I slid into the empty seat facing the street. I like to watch folks pass by. Houston squinted at me. He was dressed casually in jeans and a knit shirt. 'The beignet lady, right?'

I nodded and held out my hand. 'Maggie Miller.'

'Houston Willoughby.'

'I remember.'

A waitress came by to top off their coffee and asked if I wanted some too. I said yes and a full cup was quickly steaming under my nose.

'Who's minding the café?' Houston asked.

'Aubrey. She's great.' The way things were going I might have to give that girl a raise. As we waited for our orders I dove into the questioning. 'Any word on your sister's death?' There was no point beating around the bush.

'I heard they let that guy go that confessed.' Houston brushed the front of his grey shirt.

'Yes, I know.'

'Just a nut, I suppose,' quipped Houston. 'You get those. Nut jobs.'

'Yeah, you do.' Especially in Table Rock. And if he thought Clive was a nut what would he think of Johnny Wolfe if he met him? 'Did your sister have anyone special in her life? A boyfriend?' A boyfriend with anger issues?

The waitress dropped a three-egg omelet with whole-wheat toast in front of Houston, followed by two fresh strawberry-filled crepes for Laura and sourdough French toast for me. I poured a liberal dose of maple-flavored syrup over my toast from a plastic jug. I like my French toast to practically float in syrup – like a hovercraft over water.

Houston dumped ketchup over his eggs. 'Lisa had lots of boyfriends.' He smeared the ketchup around, shoveled the lot into his mouth then swallowed. 'No one special, though.' He shrugged. 'At least, not that I know of.'

I nodded slightly. That seemed to be the popular opinion of Lisa Willoughby. What about Houston? Like sister, like brother? I wished I could ask him about the gun in Lisa's purse but I'd have to explain how I knew about it.

'I'm sure going to miss her. First Aunt Willow dies, then Lisa.' His hand reached across the table and squeezed Laura's. 'It's a good thing I've got someone to help me through this.'

Laura looked ready to bolt.

'Laura's a real trooper.' I shot her a look that I hoped would keep her nailed to her seat.

Laura fought back. 'You'll never guess what happened, Maggie.' She smiled but I detected a touch of evil behind those glistening eyes.

'What's that?' I said, nonchalantly unrolling my napkin.

'Someone broke into Lisa's apartment last night.'

My elbow bumped the table sending coffee over the edge of my cup. I quickly dabbed at it with my napkin.

'Isn't that right, Houston?'

'Yeah.' Houston dropped his fork on his plate and folded his arms. 'It's the darnedest thing.'

'Oh?' I fiddled with my French toast, afraid to look him in the eye.

'Yeah. It doesn't appear that anything was taken.'

'Then how do you know anyone had been inside?' I swung my foot under the table, aiming for Laura's leg but caught the table leg instead. My big toe pulsed with pain and I cursed myself for choosing open-toed sandals that morning.

Houston leaned his elbows on the table. 'My laptop, for one thing.'

'I thought you said they didn't take anything?' Thank goodness I'd let Johnny talk me out of it. Apparently, it hadn't even been Lisa's laptop.

'I'd left it open when I went out to dinner. I was watching some baseball videos. When I went to bed later, I noticed the lid was closed and when I powered it back up it was on the desktop screen.'

'Let's think about this,' I said. 'Maybe there was some sort of a vibration, like an earthquake or something. The lid banged down and the computer rebooted itself.' I coughed. 'Or something . . .'

Houston seemed skeptical.

'Houston wanted to call the police.' Laura batted her eyes at me. 'I told him it probably wasn't worth the bother.'

I froze. Police? That would mean an investigation. That would mean fingerprints. 'I agree with Laura. Sounds like a whole lot of trouble for nothing, especially since nothing was taken.'

Houston nodded and attacked his eggs. 'I suppose I can afford to be generous.'

What did that mean?

Laura answered my unspoken question. 'Houston was telling me that Willow Willoughby, his aunt, passed last weekend and has left him with a significant inheritance.'

Houston nodded. 'It's gonna be easy street from here on out.'

'She left everything to you?' I said between bites of dripping French toast.

'Well, me and Lisa. But with Lisa gone . . .'

Houston Willoughby inherits everything. And he wasn't making a secret of it.

I'd seen the hotel receipt in his suitcase. I knew he'd been staying for two nights in Prescott. Two days before Lisa was killed. Prescott is not far from Table Rock. That meant Houston had plenty of time to stalk Lisa, waiting for the right opportunity to present itself and then . . .

How was I going to question him about it? I couldn't very well admit to snooping in his suitcase. While I gave the matter some thought, I continued the conversation. 'So what line of business are you in?'

He smiled. 'The restaurant business. I've got a two-hundred-and-fifty-seat place, plus bar.'

'Down in Santa Fe?'

'Yep. Right smack in the heart of downtown,' he boasted.

'That must be a lot of work. And quite an investment.' I'd had a hard time funding and was having a hard time managing my one tiny beignet café.

He nodded vigorously. 'I admit it was touch and go for a while. Only been open a year and a half.' He bit the unbuttered end of a triangle of wheat toast. 'But things are looking up.' Suddenly his face clouded over and he choked.

At first I thought it was the dry toast but then I saw what he was looking at with nervous dark eyes. A tall man with broad shoulders and arms like a pair of pythons had come through the dining room and stood half-a-dozen yards away. He filled out a pair of black jeans and his black T-shirt was having a hard time keeping all those muscles locked in.

He nodded our way and I saw Houston smile, but he didn't look happy.

'Irwin!' Houston didn't bother standing. 'What are you doing in Table Rock?'

Irwin? He looked more like a Butch. Or a Knuckles. The big guy loomed over the table like a total eclipse of the sun.

He rubbed one hand into the other. 'Keeping an eye on my investment.'

'Houston,' I said, 'aren't you going to introduce us to your friend?'

Houston sputtered an apology. 'This is Maggie Miller and Laura Duval. Ladies,' Houston waved toward the giant, 'meet Irwin Acheson.' Acheson's bristly black hair put the buzz in buzzcut. His large ears stuck out like they'd been haphazardly pinned on and his nose was broad and flat.

'A pleasure to meet you, Mr Acheson,' Laura said with a nod. Laura is ever so polite. Even in the face of deadly pythons.

'Ladies.' He cast a hard look at me, then Laura. His irises were silvery-gray, making him look more machine than man. He aimed his index finger at Houston. 'You and me gotta talk.'

Houston nodded quickly. 'Sure, Irwin.' He studied the expensive-looking watch wrapped round his wrist. 'Let's meet up at my sister's place around noon.' Houston extended his arm. 'It's over on—'

The big guy signaled for him not to bother. 'I know where it is.' He turned on his heel and strutted away and out the door. Once out on the sidewalk, I saw him look through the glass at our table for a minute or two, his fists clenched. Then he disappeared from sight. I was glad to see him go.

'That man is a friend of yours?' I asked. I was still waiting for my heart rate to come back down into the normal range.

'A business associate,' Houston replied glibly. 'I admit he's a little rough around the edges.'

'Rough around the edges?' Laura repeated. 'I'd say spooky.'

Houston pushed back his plate. 'Irwin wouldn't hurt a fly.'

Was that a fact or was Houston hoping that was true?

Houston rose and fished his wallet from his back pocket. 'I'm sorry, but if you girls will excuse me.' He threw a few bills on the table. 'I have an appointment with the solicitor handling Lisa's estate.'

'What possessed you to go out with Houston in the first place?' I asked Laura when the two of us were alone at the table.

Laura shrugged. 'I met him outside the condo building. I'd heard about Lisa, of course. I gave him my condolences and the next thing I knew he was asking me out.' She drank some ice water. 'I felt sorry for the guy.'

I looked around the crowded diner then leaned closer. 'Don't feel too sorry for him,' I said in my best conspiratorial tone. 'I think he might have killed his sister.'

Laura arched her back and pushed her hands against the table until it rocked. 'You think he murdered Lisa?'

I nodded solemnly.

She crossed her arms over her chest. 'Yet you asked me to invite the man up to my condo last night?'

'Yes, but—'

'And then you asked me to call him up the very next morning like some crushing schoolgirl and invite him to breakfast?' Laura's voice really crescendoed there.

'Well, yes, but—' I started again and got no further than I had the first time.

Laura pushed back from her chair. She grabbed her purse, anchored it by its leather strap over her right shoulder and glared at me appraisingly. 'You owe me,' she began.

'I know.' I nodded eagerly – anything to appease her.

She tilted her head. 'Free beignets.'

'Done.' I snapped my fingers.

'And free coffee.' She stared me down.

'And done,' I agreed readily.

She pressed her fists against her hips. 'For life.'

Ouch. That was going to hurt.

TWENTY-TWO

I tracked down the Robinsons next. My mother had informed me they ran a bird shop near the corner of Smile and Main. Mom keeps a birdfeeder outside her kitchen window and is always telling me about her latest visitors, creatures like Canyon Wrens, Yellow-Rumped Warblers and the Steller's jay.

To me, one bird looks pretty much like any other – a couple of wings and a beak. Set a plate of fried chicken in front of me and I could tell you if it was Kentucky Fried or Church's. But ask me to point out the difference between a Summer Tanager and a Western Tanager and I'd draw a blank. Stepping onto the Robinsons' Nest welcome mat set off a chirping that could have been a condor or a pterodactyl for all I knew.

Mrs Robinson was plumpish and pleasant and wore khaki-colored crops and a black polo shirt. Her husband, who looked pretty much like a bird himself with a hawkish nose, close-set eyes and a tuft of black hair sticking out in front, was similarly attired.

They turned out to be useless as far as my investigation went.

'We had a consultation with Reva,' Mrs Robinson explained while her husband chatted with a customer who'd stepped in from the street. 'She introduced us to Ms Willoughby who said she'd draw up some design ideas and email them to us.' She reached into a drawer and pulled out a printed sheet of paper. 'It was going to be covered with birds. See?'

'That's very nice,' I said. A bunch of birds for a vow-renewal cake? I shrugged. Why not? 'Perfect.' I'd have never guessed that the mess I'd seen splattered across the bottom of the stairs had been something so elegant looking.

I was surprised to see them in the shop what with the vow renewal and all. 'No honeymoon?'

Mrs Robinson smiled serenely. 'Every day is like a honeymoon with my John.'

'That's so nice,' I replied, feeling a tinge of jealousy. I thanked them both for their time, useless though it was, and started to leave.

'Oh, before you go.' Mrs Robinson pulled a brown paper bag from behind the counter. 'These just came in today. I told your mother I'd let her know when we got some more in.'

I took the bag and peered inside. 'What is it?' An unexpected odor of rotted corpses assaulted my nostrils.

'It's suet, dear.'

'Soot?' Was Mom planning on feeding the birds or poisoning them?

'Suet, for the birds. It's made from rendered fat, peanut butter, bird seeds . . .'

'There's bits of fruit in there, too,' chimed in Mr Robinson. 'And meal worms.' He went behind the counter and placed his arm around his wife's waist. A couple of real lovebirds.

Meal worms? Rendered fat? Whatever that was, it sounded disgusting. In fact, it sounded like something Donna would cook up to feed the family, minus the rendered fat, her being vegan and all. I wondered if they made a vegan version of suet. No, I didn't want to know. If Donna heard about it, she'd be serving it up to us at our next family gathering. Suet burgers. I could see it now. Worse, I could taste it. My tongue has a vivid imagination.

I thanked them once again and hurried back to Maggie's Beignet Café.

'Thank goodness,' Aubrey said, wiping her brow with the side of her arm. 'It's been truly, truly busy.'

'Sorry,' I said. I dropped the sack on the counter.

'What's that?' Aubrey fingered the bag.

'Some junk for my mom. Put it behind the counter, would you? I'll be right back.'

'Wait!' cried Aubrey. 'Where are you going? I could use some help here!' The poor girl looked a bit frazzled.

'I'll be right back. I promise,' I repeated. 'I'm going next door for a minute.' I found Clive and Johnny huddled around the big desk toward the rear of the showroom. There wasn't a customer in sight.

Clive was talking. 'I asked Mrs Higgins to be sure the band is finished by one to give us plenty of time to set up for the sho—' Both wore charcoal-gray pinstriped suits with white dress shirts. Johnny's tie was cranberry red; Clive's was ocean blue. I was surprised to see Clive in a necktie. He usually went in for the bowtie look. I thought he looked great, better really than with the bowtie. The bowtie always made him look a little geekish.

I felt like a bum in comparison to the guys. My shirt was covered in powdered sugar and grease stains and my khakis had more wrinkles than an elephant's behind. Johnny was nodding his head while looking over Clive's shoulder. Clive was seated behind the grand oak desk, hands holding down a chart of some kind.

'Hey, boys!' I hollered as I wound past miles of pricy wedding gowns. 'How are my two favorite criminals today?' I'd decided to make light of a rather dire situation. No point dwelling on the negative, I always say.

'Keep your voice down, Miller!' hissed Johnny, waving an angry hand in my direction.

'What?' I flopped into one of the two wingchairs facing the desk. 'There's nobody here to hear.'

Johnny frowned. 'What do you want?'

I scooted my chair forward. 'Hey, is that the layout for the Labor of Love?' I ignored Johnny's question.

Clive nodded. 'Yes. Johnny and I were just going over the weekend's activities.'

I leaned even closer and pressed my finger to the paper. 'Is that your booth?'

Clive nodded.

'That big one in the corner?' It sat far from the Salon de Belezza and Karma Koffee.

'That's right,' snapped Johnny. 'Is there a point to your question?'

I gulped. 'Wanna trade?'

'Excuse me?' Johnny's brow shot up.

'I've got this great booth right here.' I pointed to the spot

Cosmic had picked out for me. 'It would be perfect for The Hitching Post.'

'Forget it, Miller,' Johnny said, his arms folding across his chest like a drawbridge coming down. 'We've got a big corner booth.'

Clive nodded. 'We paid extra for it, too. Double what a normal booth costs.'

Double? Eight hundred dollars? My eyes doubled. 'Forget it,' I said, backpedaling quickly. I needed another option. Maybe I could get Aubrey and Kelly to take my place at the booth. 'What kind of show are you talking about?'

'A fashion show,' answered Johnny. 'Wedding fashions, of course.'

I cocked my head to one side. 'Sounds nice.'

'Speaking of which.' Clive elbowed Johnny.

Johnny swatted him away.

Clive looked beseechingly at his partner. 'Johnny,' he said, drawing out the former skater's name for all it was worth.

'Oh, fine,' sighed Johnny. He paced back and forth for a moment on the rug. 'We need a favor, Miller.' Johnny looked at Clive once more.

'A favor? From me?' I held back the grin that was about to erupt. There'd be nothing like having Johnny Wolfe owe me. He probably wanted me to model for them. What girl hasn't once dreamed she'd one day be a runway model? I guess it's true – you're never too old.

'We'd like to ask you to take this dress swatch over to Mr Gravelle.'

'Markie Gravelle?'

Both men nodded. Clive slid open the top middle drawer of the desk and removed a swatch of fabric identical to the one we'd taken to the Entronque building the other day.

'You want me to take that,' I said, pointing with my chin, 'back to Markie's Masterpieces for you? Why?' I pushed the swatch around on the desktop with my finger. 'Why doesn't one of you do it?'

Johnny pouted. 'Clive and I do not believe it would be in either of our best interests to be seen anywhere near the . . . you know' – he paused – 'scene of the crime.'

'Yes,' agreed Clive.

I agreed, too. In fact, this was perfect. I could use taking the swatch over to Navajo Junction as my excuse to snoop around a bit more and ask some questions. 'I don't know,' I whined. 'I'm not so sure I want to be seen there myself.' I was going to play these boys like a pair of fiddles.

'Please,' said Clive. 'We've told them we'd deliver the material to them. They really must get started on the cake if it is to be ready for Sunday.'

'Come on, Miller,' said Johnny. 'This business relationship with Markie is important to us. We do a lot of business together.'

'I don't know . . .' I let my voice trail off. I played with the swatch then laid it down on Clive's desk.

'What's it going to take?' demanded Johnny. 'I'll make it worth your while.'

'Oh, don't give it a second thought,' I said finally. 'I'd be happy to do you a favor.' And they could pay me back in spades one day when they least expected it.

'Thank you,' Clive said, rising from his chair.

'Yeah, thanks,' Johnny said grudgingly.

I folded the six-inch swatch and dropped it in my handbag. I raised my hands and jiggled my fingers at Johnny.

'Now what?' Johnny asked.

'The keys, of course.'

'Keys?' Johnny slatted his eyes at me.

'To the BMW.'

'The BMW? *My* BMW?'

Clive rose and laid a restraining hand on Johnny's forearm.

'Yes,' I replied glibly. 'You don't expect me to pedal my Schwinn all the way out to Navajo Junction, do you? It's miles from here.'

Johnny glared at Clive. His forehead had a swath of red across it. I thought he was going to burst.

'Now, Johnny.' Clive shrugged. 'What choice do we have?'

Johnny sighed and fished his keys from his pocket. 'Bring it back in one piece, Miller.'

'Of course, Johnny,' I said with a smile. 'Not to worry. I'm an excellent driver.'

'Yeah,' he quipped. 'You did an excellent job smashing your mother's Volkswagen into one of my landscape boulders.'

'A complete fluke,' I said. Johnny had me by the elbow and was leading me to the door. Before he had me all the way out, I asked, 'Have you spoken to Detective Highsmith yet? Is he still looking for you?'

Johnny pushed me outside. 'Your brother-in-law, Andy, called him. Clive and I are going down later to make our statements.' He pointed to his black BMW. 'Now, the Entronque, Miller.' He looked meaningfully at his watch. 'I expect you back here with my car within the hour.'

I raised my hand. The BMW key dangled like a prize. 'I promise.'

'And there'd better not be a scratch on it!' I heard him yell as I turned the key in the ignition and pulled away from the curb.

TWENTY-THREE

The BMW and I arrived at the Entronque building without a scratch and I went inside to quiz the shop owners. I'd deliver the fabric to Markie's Masterpieces after I had finished questioning the Entronque's tenants. I knew the cake decorators were anxious to get the fabric but another hour or so wouldn't hurt.

Besides, as long as I kept that piece of fabric in my purse and postponed delivery, I had an excuse for being in the building. If Detective Highsmith or one of his cohorts came around in the midst of their own investigation and caught me snooping, I didn't know how they'd react. Knowing Highsmith, he wouldn't take too kindly to my efforts to help him find Lisa Willoughby's killer.

Yep, as along as I had the swatch, I had plausible deniability. I'm big on plausible deniability. Just ask my mom. I'd spent my teen years perfecting it.

Unfortunately, my hunt for clues seemed doomed to failure. I reached a dead end everywhere I turned.

Until I knocked on the door of Blake Sherwood.

I recognized her right away. She was pretty in a soft not fulsome way, with long brown hair tied back in a loose red gingham ponytail tie, a strong nose and prominent cheekbones. Her eyes were gray-blue. The streak of white I'd spotted in her hair the other morning as she called down to us from the floor above must have been paint splatter because there was no sign of any graying of her hair now I had a chance to study her up close.

She looked at ease in a worn and baggy pair of stained lavender overalls with a pink sleeveless T-shirt beneath. A slender serpentine silver chain hung from her delicate neck. Her feet were bare. Simple gold bands adorned each of her middle toes.

This was the young woman from the stairwell who'd called down to ask what was going on the morning Lisa was killed. 'Blake Sherwood, right?'

Her golden toes wiggled against the pine floor like little dancers. 'That's right. Can I help you?' Her eyes search my face as if seeking recognition. Her arms were tanned and taut.

'I'm Maggie Miller. I was wondering if I might speak to you for a minute, Ms Sherwood?' Her right hand held a paintbrush, her left hand gripped the brass doorknob.

She considered for a moment, glanced over her shoulder then gestured with her paintbrush for me to enter. 'Call me Blake, please.'

I followed her inside.

'I'm afraid I don't have much time. I'm in the middle of a piece.'

There was wet brown paint on the tip of her brush. Blake Sherwood was obviously a painter and a talented one at that judging by the canvasses lining the walls and stacked on the floor.

Blank canvas, wood framing and paints lay scattered about. Two large, cluttered wood benches occupied the center of the high-ceiling space parallel to a row of windows. The distinct odors of oil paint, linseed oil and paint thinner filled the air. A tall easel in the center of the room held a half-finished painting. 'Town Square?'

Blake nodded. 'The tourists love things like that.' The young woman slid a stool toward me. 'Have a seat.' She removed a palette from a second stool and joined me beside the open window. Her hands gripped her knees. 'So, what is this about, Ms Miller? A commission?'

'No, and, please, call me Maggie. Everybody does.' Well, some people called me worse things, but there was no sense going down that road with a stranger. 'I wanted to ask you about Lisa Willoughby's murder.' Maybe she had seen or heard something helpful. Unlike everyone else I'd spent time with in the past hour.

Ms Sherwood brushed a strand of fine brown hair from her face, jumped off her stool and paced. Finally she turned toward me. 'You mean the woman who was found at the bottom of the stairwell.'

'Yes.'

Blake's puzzled eyes fixed on me. 'She was murdered?'

'That's right,' I said. 'Hadn't you heard?'

She shrugged. 'No. I don't mix much with the other tenants. And I don't watch the news or read the papers. Too much negativity.' She waved her arms around the space. 'It interferes with my creative process.'

I got that. I'm positive that my beignets taste twice as good when I make them with love and a smile on my face compared to when I'm in a foul mood and simply going through the motions. 'I understand.' It looked like this was going to be another dead end. I rose and crossed to a stack of finished canvases. 'May I?'

She nodded and I slowly flipped through the unframed canvases.

'These really are quite lovely.' Yep, another dead end, a waste of an hour. I might as well deliver the guys' swatch to Markie's Masterpieces and be on my way. 'Did you know Lisa well?'

Blake shook her head. 'I barely knew her at all. I'd seen her around. Knew she worked at Markie's. Knew she was also something of a painter. To be honest, I didn't think she was very talented from what little I'd seen. I was surprised to see her making some headway with the galleries.'

'Did you see or hear anything unusual the morning Lisa was killed?'

Blake shrugged. 'The police asked me the same thing.' She took her paintbrush and dipped it into a jar of murky fluid. She swished the brush around then pulled it out, dried it on a stained rag and left it on the workbench to dry. 'Not really. I mean, I heard the commotion downstairs but that was the police. They came and talked to me later. I told them everything I knew.'

'Did you see an out-of-order sign on the freight elevator?'

'No,' the young painter replied. 'But then I took the stairs. I take the stairs every day. It's good exercise and saves electricity.'

Another dead end.

'So you heard nothing?'

'I heard . . .' she hesitated, '. . . something. I'm not sure what. In looking back . . . it was probably the sound of that woman falling down the stairs . . .'

I nodded thoughtfully. 'So you were here when it happened.'

'I guess so.' A sadness seemed to sweep over the artist like a rogue wave. 'I got in a little before eight. I had an appointment with Mrs Higgins.'

'Samantha Higgins?'

'Yes, she displays quite a bit of my work in her gallery.'

'So you were with her when you heard this noise?'

Blake cocked her head and seemed to give my question some thought. Finally she shook her head. 'No. Mrs Higgins was only here twenty minutes or so. It was much later that I heard the noise. She was long gone by then.'

That added up. Clive and I had arrived well after nine and Lisa wasn't lying at the bottom of the stairs then. Blake grabbed a clean, dry brush and began mixing a couple of tubes of colors. One yellow, one green. 'The only other thing I heard out of the ordinary was the commotion downstairs later.' She pointed her brush at me. 'You were there, weren't you? I remember you now.'

'Yes.'

Blake shook her head again as if to clear all the negative images flying around the room that had sought refuge in her skull like bats seeking shelter before the coming dawn. I decided

I'd intruded enough and that it was time to let the woman get back to her work. She walked me to the door. 'It's funny,' she said, 'but if you'd told me Lisa Willoughby was murdered the other day I wouldn't have been half as surprised.'

I came to a stop in the open doorway. 'The other day?'

She appeared almost sheepish. 'Maybe I shouldn't say anything.'

'Please,' I gripped her hand, 'if there's anything you can say that might help, tell me. The police suspect my friends, Clive and Johnny, of being involved but they're completely innocent.'

'Well . . .'

I held my breath, imploring her with my eyes.

She looked up and down the empty hall before answering. 'I heard that girl and Markie Gravelle, from Markie's Masterpieces?' She looked at me.

'Yes.' I bobbed my chin. 'I know him. You heard them the other day?'

'It must have been a couple of days ago. They were arguing at the tops of their voices.'

'Where was this?'

'Outside.' She pointed a thumb over her shoulder. 'In the parking lot. As you can see, I keep the windows open. I like the natural light and air. It keeps the creative juices going.'

I joined her at the window. We poked our noses out. 'See?' she said. 'There are several picnic tables under the tree. People eat their lunch there or take a coffee break. That kind of thing. Mostly folks who work here but sometimes the tourists use them, too.'

'But the other day?'

'It was afternoon. I was working at the bench and suddenly I heard a man and woman yelling.' She glanced at her toes, then me. 'It's not like I was eavesdropping. I couldn't help hearing. Sound really carries. It bounces off the pavement and right up to my windows.'

'Of course.' My heart pounded against my chest. 'What did you hear?'

She collected her thoughts. 'All sorts of things. I don't remember everything. Yelling, you know?' I knew. 'Mr Gravelle threatened to fire her.'

My eyes grew. 'Markie was going to fire Lisa?'

Blake nodded.

'Did he say why?'

She frowned. 'He might have but I really wasn't listening – at least not trying to. She did laugh at him, though. I heard that all right. Her tone was quite mocking. Then she threatened to tell his wife about their affair.' She arched her brow slyly.

'Markie's married?'

Blake shrugged. 'Sounds like it.'

Who'd have thought? Not me, that's for sure. Another twist to the puzzle that was Lisa Willoughby's death. I thanked Blake Sherwood once again for her time. 'And if there's anything else that you remember about the day of the murder, anything at all, no matter how unimportant you think it is, please let me know.' I fished a business card from my handbag.

She turned the card over in her hand. 'Maggie's Beignet Café?'

'On Laredo. I've only been open a few months. Please, come by some time. Have you ever eaten a beignet?'

She shook her head in the negative. 'Never even heard of one.'

'Then you really must come by. I insist. You're in for a real treat. Deep-fried sweet pastry with powdered sugar on top. The first order's on me.'

Blake smiled and waved the card toward me as she said, 'I might take you up on that.' She thrust my card deep into the pouch of her overalls.

I punched the elevator button and headed for the fourth floor. Before going to the cake shop, I headed for the roof. I found the separate stairs located at the end of the hall. The door was unlocked so up I went. The roof is where Ben Baker claimed to be at the time of Lisa's murder and I wanted to check it out.

As I marched up the stairs I realized that while Ben had claimed to be on the roof, I had no idea where Reva Reynolds had been. The last time I'd spoken to her I'd gotten all excited and sidetracked when she'd told me about Ben and Lisa's affair and had claimed that Markie himself had been in the cake shop much earlier than he'd said.

I'd never even asked her to explain where she'd been the

whole time. Maybe she'd been trying to divert me from asking her.

That could make her a killer. Or an accomplice to a killer.

I vowed not to let her sidetrack me again.

The sun beat down on me as I stepped out onto the rooftop. I shaded my eyes with the flat of my hand. Tarpaper and gravel covered the large space. A two-foot pony wall ran the perimeter. AC units hummed.

A rickety and weathered outdoor table and chairs with a faded yellow umbrella stood in the far corner. A man sat there casually smoking a cigarette. I watched the clouds of vapor swirl over the edge of the building. His foot moved slowly, rhythmically.

It was Ben the baker.

At the sound of my feet crunching over the stony surface, Ben turned. He mashed the stub of his cigarette against the metal table. The side of his lip turned down in a half-frown. I guess he wasn't too happy to see me.

I smiled anyway. 'Break time?'

He rose. 'Just finishing.'

'Can I ask you a couple of questions?'

'Sorry.' He dusted his trousers. 'I've got to get back to work. Orders to fill.'

I kept smiling. 'That's OK. I'll walk with you while we talk. I'm heading to the bakery anyway.'

He sighed and walked toward the stairs. 'What do you want?'

I followed him down the steps. There was no way I was going first. What if Ben was the killer? I might just get a helpful push down those stairs. 'I want to know more about Lisa.'

He looked over his shoulder. 'I'm afraid I can't help you there. I barely knew the woman.'

'That's not what I heard.'

'Then you heard wrong.' His eyes hardened.

'I also heard you've been to her place.'

'So? Lots of people probably have, including Markie and Reva. I don't see you busting their chops.'

'Yes, but you're the only one who was seen banging on her condo door, demanding that she let you in.'

'That's bull.'

'I don't think so. I wonder what her neighbors might have to say if I flashed your picture around.'

Ben threw open the bakery door and slammed it in my face. But I didn't let that stop me. 'You can't hide whatever relationship you had with Lisa forever,' I said, scooting in after him. 'The police are bound to find out.'

Ben's hands clenched and I took a slow step backward. Finally he unfroze. 'Look,' he sighed, 'Lisa and I went out a couple of times. I admit, I liked her. But—'

'But?'

He shrugged. 'She said I wasn't really her type.' He washed his hands at a basin in the corner and slowly dried them with a paper towel. He picked up a very large, very sharp knife and began carving at a round vanilla cake at his workstation. 'She broke up with me. What a fool I'd been.' I swear I think I saw a tear forming in the corner of his left eye. 'There, are you happy?'

Not so much. 'I heard Lisa was a painter, too.' I thought about the unfinished piece in Lisa's living room. It could have been Ben. Hard to tell.

'So?'

'Did she ever paint or sketch you?'

He shook his head. His knife moved skillfully along the cake.

I looked around the bakery. 'Is Reva here?' I needed to talk to her, too. See where she fit in this puzzle.

Ben shook his head. 'No.' He slammed the knife down on the countertop. 'She's off sick.' He snorted. 'So she claims. That's why I've got twice as much work to get out. I mean, between her being out and Lisa being dead . . .' He let his sentence fall away like stones underfoot cascading into the Grand Canyon.

'Do you know where Reva was at the time that Lisa was murdered?'

He gave me a funny look. 'You leave Reva out of this. You don't think she had something to do with Lisa's death?'

'No, of course not.' I grabbed a bit of cake scrap with two fingers and popped it in my mouth. OMG, delicious. Was that a hint of almond I tasted? 'I'm curious, is all.'

He picked up his knife and started on a second cake. 'Then ask her yourself.'

I nodded thoughtfully. 'I just might. Do you have her address?'

He smiled and I don't think it was kindly as he jabbed the knife in the direction of Markie's office. 'You'd have to ask him for that.'

Markie's door was wide open so I entered without waiting for an answer. He was crouched over in his chair, a sketchpad in one hand and a charcoal pencil in the other. His tongue was pushed out between his lips. 'I hear you were here the morning Lisa was murdered.'

He jolted upright, hand clenching his sketchpad so fiercely he wrinkled the pages. 'Who told you that?'

I shrugged. 'Let's just say a little birdie.' OK, so it was a big birdie and her name was Reva Reynolds. No point throwing her under the bus. At least not yet and for no reason. I might need her cooperation later – if she didn't turn out to be the killer.

He carefully laid the charcoal pencil on his desk. 'Now that I think about it, I guess I did get here a little earlier. What does it matter?'

'It means you might have seen or heard something that might prove who killed Lisa.' I arched my brow. 'It could mean that you killed her.'

Markie leapt from his chair, his face dark red. 'Watch what you say, Miller. Nobody accuses Markie Gravelle of murder and gets away with it!' He waved a finger at me. 'My lawyers will ruin you.'

I swallowed hard. Markie had a violent streak I hadn't expected. I held out my hand. 'I'm not accusing you of murder.' At least not yet. 'I'm simply asking if you saw or heard anything. Did you tell the police that you were here?'

'I didn't see or hear anything,' Markie said coldly. 'I was in my office with the door closed.'

I glanced over my shoulder. Ben stood at his workstation and another couple of young fellows in bakery uniforms were working at the big ovens. I wanted to make sure I wasn't alone before I said what I was planning to say next. I chewed my lower lip for a moment before speaking. 'I hear you and Lisa were having an affair.'

Markie blinked and stuttered.

'I hear the two of you were arguing outside in the parking lot the other day. You threated to fire her. Lisa was threatening to tell your wife about the affair if you did, wasn't she?'

Markie suddenly broke down into sobs. He collapsed into his leather desk chair, his hands covering his face.

I watched helplessly.

He pulled his hands from his face and gestured for me to shut the door.

I did.

'Oh, Maggie,' he sobbed. 'I've been such a fool.' Talk about your bipolar personality types.

'What do you mean?' Was he about to confess to murder? I fished my phone from my purse. If so, I wanted to get this on tape. I wanted photos for my Facebook page. Heck, I wanted a Facebook page. And I wanted to invite that irritating Detective Highsmith to take a look at it when I revealed Lisa Willoughby's killer.

'It's true,' Markie sobbed, 'Lisa and I were having an affair. I didn't mean to.' He looked embarrassed. 'It was one of those workplace things that just happens.'

Yeah, I thought, to people who cheat on their spouses. I nodded like I understood. Like my dead ex-husband, Brian, had cheated on me. I didn't think I'd ever forgive him. 'What really happened here the morning Lisa was killed?'

Markie laid his hands on the desk and shrugged. Tears pooled under his eyes. 'I don't know. Like I said, I was in my office. On the phone with a client.'

'Any witnesses? Ben, Reva? One of the other assistants?'

'No. I didn't see anybody. When I came out of the office the workroom was empty.'

'And you didn't see or hear anything?'

He shook his head. 'Nothing. Until the police arrived.'

'What about Clive? You didn't see Clive?'

Markie shook his head again. 'I must have been on the phone when he showed up. I didn't see him. My door was closed.'

I leaned back in my seat. If what Markie said was true it bolstered what Clive had told me earlier. He said he came upstairs, found no one, heard loud voices coming from the stairs and headed that way. 'Who were you on the telephone with?'

'Samantha Higgins. We were talking about her cakes.'

'Cakes?'

He nodded. 'Wedding cake and groom's cake.'

'Speaking of cake . . .' I fished the bridal gown material from my purse and spread it flat on the desk. Markie's fingers were drawn to it. 'Johnny and Clive asked me to bring it by.'

'Thanks.' Markie wiped his eyes with his sleeves.

I headed for the door but Markie's hand on my elbow stopped me.

'You won't tell my wife, will you, Ms Miller?' His eyes pleaded with me.

I shook my head. 'I don't even know your wife.'

He beamed a thousand-watt smile. 'Oh, thank you, Ms Miller! You are wonderful!' He smacked me on the cheek with his damp lips. 'Just a sec—' Markie dashed to his desk and scooped up the Slinky Dog. He held it out to me, balanced in his cupped hands. 'I want you to have this.'

I narrowed my eyes. 'Your Slinky Dog?' My heart jumped. I'd always wanted a fifties-looking, tail-wagging Slinky Dog. The adorable dachshund had a metal slinky for a mid-section and a matching Slinky tail, too.

He nodded vigorously. 'I noticed you admiring it the other day.'

I wet my lips and felt my hands extending forward of their own volition. 'Are you sure?' I stroked its tail and got a child-like thrill watching it go *boing-boing*.

He pushed it toward me. 'Please.'

I was smiling all the way to the elevator, out the door and to the car.

OK, so I'm a kid at heart. Trust me, more people should be.

TWENTY-FOUR

I set Slinky Dog on the front seat of the BMW then crossed the parking lot connecting the Entronque building to the lower outdoor mall area that made up the rest of the sprawling Navajo Junction complex. I'd decided to go see Mrs Higgins before heading back to the café. I wanted to confirm what Blake Sherwood had said, and what Markie had said, too, while I was at it.

I checked the big map attached to a lamp post in the center of the parking lot while the September sun washed over me. The hand-carved and painted map – that's what you get when you order a map from a bunch of artist types – included a directory of every shop in Navajo Junction.

Her swanky gallery, Higgins Fine Art, was located in the old train station, redone now to house fine art galleries and high-end boutiques. You probably needed to be a millionaire just to get in the place. I hoped they didn't notice my lack of credentials. The vaulted ceilings of the grandiose station were accented with rows of stained-glass windows along the edges. Builders believed in making things look sharp back in the eighteen hundreds.

Mrs Higgins was posing near a large canvas hung on the wall in the middle of her gallery. The focal point of the painting was a bent and twisted ancient juniper that stood at the edge of a cliff as if struggling to maintain its balance, against a blazing red rock background. The artist's keen eye and a bold hand had captured every detail vividly.

I smelled perfume and money. The gallery itself oozed quiet luxury. So did the elderly couple she was speaking to – a silver-haired gentleman in light brown trousers and a tweed jacket, despite the heat, and a small woman with wispy blonde hair who lightly held his left arm. She wore a more appropriate sleeveless navy-blue linen-stripe shift with a thin red belt.

I nodded to Mrs Higgins who looked quite slinky herself in

a black A-line frock with a jewel neck. She returned my look with a blink, never losing step with her clients. I walked over to a fat leather-bound portfolio spread open on a pale gray marble plinth beside a pecan wood desk.

It was a catalog of the gallery's work. I began flipping through it. Not that I could afford to buy any art but it didn't hurt to look. The only original art I owned was taped up on my fridge and created by my two nephews when they were still in elementary school.

The portfolio was divided alphabetically by artist name. I spotted a number of photographs of pieces by Blake Sherwood. The woman was no slouch when it came to painting. Toward the back of the book I came to a section headed with Lisa Willoughby's name. She wasn't bad but she was no Rembrandt. Lisa Willoughby's subject matter included landscapes, cakes – no surprise, and men – again, no surprise. After that there was nothing but empty plastic sleeves.

I heard the sound of gentle chimes. Mrs Higgins came around to her desk. Her customers were gone.

'No sale?' I said. 'Too bad.'

'We'll see.' Samantha Higgins flashed a business card from her customers and placed it in a neat Rolodex atop her desk. 'Not everyone wants to spend twenty thousand dollars without thinking it over.' She smiled. 'It may take a day or two but I believe they'll be back.'

'Did you say twenty thousand?'

Mrs Higgins nodded. 'It's called *Among the Red Rocks*, by a local artist, naturally.'

'Naturally,' I repeated, my mouth drying up. Twenty thousand dollars. I could buy a ton of *real* red rocks for that amount of cash. A whole dump truck full, I'd bet. 'That's a lot of money.'

'They've got money.' She smiled knowingly.

My brow went up. 'How can you tell?' I mean, they didn't look like bums or anything but that didn't mean they had twenty grand to drop on a picture of a tree and some rocks.

'Oh, I can tell.' Her eyes sparkled with confidence. She settled into her chair and adjusted her scarf. 'So what can I do for you, Ms Miller?' She waved her arms around the store. 'I don't suppose you'd be interested in buying something? For your home or your place of business, perhaps?'

I shook my head. 'I don't suppose so, no.' Not without robbing a bank first.

She leaned in, folding her hands under her chin. 'Are you certain? I have a piece or two here that would look simply delightful in your café. Trust me, they could really add a certain ambience . . .' she waved her right hand in a circle, '. . . a charm, if you will, to your place.'

I shook my head again. 'Trust me, I couldn't begin to afford any of these pieces. Any one of them probably costs more than I spent building out my entire café.'

Mrs Higgins snickered with amusement. She motioned for me to sit and I did. 'So why are you here?'

I cleared my throat. 'I was speaking with Blake Sherwood this morning.'

Mrs Higgins smiled benevolently. 'I know Ms Sherwood.' She pointed to a large framed canvas on the wall over my shoulder. 'That's one of her pieces there.'

I nodded. I recognized the style instantly. It was a masterful rendition of Montezuma's Castle, one of the area's most famous Sinagua Indian ruins. The national monument is located in the Verde Valley about fifty miles south of Flagstaff. 'Nice.' I turned back to Mrs Higgins. 'She mentioned that you were at her studio the morning of Lisa's murder.'

Mrs Higgins sighed. 'Yes, earlier.' That jibed with what the artist had told me. 'Isn't it sad?' She shivered. 'And kind of spooky.'

Her hands clasped a gold ballpoint pen. 'I mean, one minute a person is alive and the next . . .' Her shoulders rose and fell. 'What if the killer had seen me? I could have been next.' Her hand went to her throat.

I agreed and said so. 'So you didn't see or hear anything unusual either?'

She appeared to give this some thought. 'Not a thing, I'm afraid. I wish I could help. I told the police the same thing.'

'I understand.' I nodded toward the portfolio. 'I see Lisa was a client of yours.'

Mrs Higgins nodded somberly. 'She was going to be. We

were just pulling together some pieces for an exhibition. Who knew she'd be lying dead beneath some frivolous bird cake a few days later.'

'Do you have any idea who might have wanted Lisa dead? Did she confide in you at all?'

'I'm afraid not.' Mrs Higgins stood as the chimes announced another visitor to the gallery. 'Be right with you!' she called, then turned to me. 'Is there anything else?'

'Was Lisa any good?'

'Excuse me?'

'Her paintings. Could she get twenty thousand dollars?'

Mrs Higgins chuckled softly. 'Oh, dear, no. A few thousand, perhaps. More once she became established – if she caught on.' Mrs Higgins patted me on the shoulder. 'The art-buying public is a fickle and undecipherable one.'

Tell me about it.

'One more thing!' I called, my feet already out the door.

'Yes?' Mrs Higgins stood beside a young man whose shirt bore the Ferrari logo. I feared he was about to part with some money. But that was his problem.

'Did you speak to Markie Gravelle the morning of—' I hesitated. No point wrecking a potential sale and a big one at that. 'You know.'

Mrs Higgins ran a finely sculpted fingernail along the underside of her chin. 'Yes, you were there, remember?'

I bobbed my head. 'I mean before.'

She thought another moment. Apparently Mrs Higgins' wheels didn't turn too quickly. 'We spoke on the phone earlier about Sabrina's cake.'

That was all I needed to know.

And I was back to square one.

TWENTY-FIVE

I was heading back to the café when I spotted Cody Ryan and a young lady friend as they passed me in a flashy yellow Corvette convertible that went zooming by like a bee late to a hive meeting. That reminded me – I still had a question or two for Cody. Like why had he ordered a bunch of my perfectly good beignets and dumped them in the trash just minutes later?

I pressed the gas pedal and fell into line a couple of cars behind them so they wouldn't get suspicious. His passenger was a real looker with long auburn hair. Definitely not Sabrina Higgins, who was a blonde, like her mother, I remembered from the photo she'd shown me.

Fifteen minutes later Cody pulled into a public parking lot a block from Table Rock Town Square. I sluiced into a slot located at a diagonal from his and watched. He opened the passenger-side door. Wow, this girl could have been a model. She wore a short fitted black leather skirt and simple scoop-neck white blouse. Her heels were dangerous red.

He said something and she laughed. It looked like trouble in nuptials land, if you asked me. They started walking. I locked up and hurried after them, not sure what I was going to do if I caught them.

Once at the town square, they headed across Smile to Main. The sidewalks were crowded so I wasn't worried about being noticed. The pair headed up a set of small, steep stairs and I followed. They climbed to the third floor, which was the top of the building. There was only one thing up there. High Steaks.

For more than forty years, High Steaks has been Table Rock's go-to steakhouse with a view of the square. I'd never eaten there – too pricy for my pockets – but it was a fave with residents and tourists alike. If you were foolhardy enough to wear a necktie to High Steaks, the reigning Mad Mary – as the locals had dubbed She Who Wields The Shears – would come running out of the kitchen with a big pair of scissors and clip you before you even knew you'd been clipped and nail your tie to the wall which, by this time, I guesstimated, held a couple thousand or so of all brands and colors.

I waited from my vantage point on the second-floor landing until the hostess had led Cody and his young lady friend away then climbed the last flight of stairs. The smell of rib-eye and mesquite wood coming from the ovens set my stomach to protesting.

'May I help you?' A pretty young Apache woman proffered me a folded menu.

I snatched it. 'I'd like to take a look at the menu first, if you don't mind.'

'Of course not.' She smiled and motioned for me to move to the side, toward the busy bar, as she greeted her next customers.

Under the guise of perusing the menu, I watched the happy couple. They were seated out on the belvedere. Their waiter brought a pitcher of water and bottle of wine. Cody's hand fell across hers and she smiled. A couple passed in front of me and I took a step back, jostling a waitress who'd been scurrying behind me. She dropped the glass she'd been carrying to the bar and shrieked. The glass shattered against the floor and wet drops hit the backs of my legs.

Cody and the woman turned toward the commotion.

'I'm terribly sorry,' said the young waitress who'd done nothing wrong. 'Let me help you.' She bent to wipe my dripping calves with a towel she'd snatched from her belt.

'No, really, it's OK.' I tried to shoo her away, afraid to draw attention to myself. But it didn't matter because it was too late. Cody and the woman had definitely seen me. It looked like he'd recognized me, too, because his eyes met mine and his face darkened.

I took a deep breath and decided to take the offense. I couldn't defend myself but I could attack. I marched to their table overlooking the busy square. 'Hi, Cody Ryan, right?'

He scooted back his chair and eyed me. His index finger toyed with the mole at the left corner of his lip. 'Ms Miller from the beignet place?'

'That's right. I hear you and Sabrina Higgins are getting married this weekend.' Or not.

He blushed and glanced at his companion. 'That's right.'

I turned to the young woman. Up close she was even more stunning. Her complexion was fair and unblemished. Her eyebrows looked like they'd been computer-designed, they were that perfect. I held out my hand. 'And who have we here?'

The young woman tossed her head and smiled as she shook my hand. 'Paula Aldiss.' Paula coolly pulled out a business card – thick oyster-colored vellum with platinum-embossed lettering. 'Wedding planner.'

My heart came to a stop, so I wasn't sure what was now pumping all that red blood to my cheeks.

Paula Aldiss held her smile, her eyes bouncing from Cody to me. 'Cody and I are planning a surprise for his fiancé.'

'A surprise?' My voice cracked. 'H-how nice.'

'A brand new convertible, a Corvette,' Cody boasted. 'Velocity yellow, like mine.'

Paula's brow rose. 'Are you all right, Ms Miller? Would you like some water?' Her fingers went to the water pitcher.

'No, thanks.' I ran my parched tongue over my dry lips. That tiny pitcher didn't hold enough water for me to go drown myself in. And drown myself was just what I felt like doing at that moment.

'Was there something you wanted?' Cody asked, his demeanor stiff.

'I just wanted to say hi,' I stammered, 'and congratulations.' I turned to leave, took two steps and stopped. No, I couldn't let the kid rattle me. I marched back to the table.

'Yes?' Cody said.

'When you came into the beignet café.'

He raised his eyebrows.

'You ordered a dozen beignets.'

'So?'

'So, a minute later I saw you walk out and watched you dump them all in the trash.'

He chuckled. 'Is that all?' He shook his head. 'My mom asked me to bring some to her weekly bridge game.' He glanced at

Paula. 'The minute I walk out of the bakery, Mom calls and tells me her friend, Shelley, is sick and the game is canceled. What was I going to do with a dozen beignets?'

Cody took a sip from his wine glass. 'I ate one and tossed the rest. Seemed like a waste, but, hey, it's Mom's money. Gotta stay in shape for the honeymoon.' His brow went up and down lasciviously as he patted his flat belly.

Paula laughed.

I headed for the stairwell. The stairs were narrow and boxed in on both sides. I thought I heard Cody calling my name and quickened my steps.

I felt his hand grab my elbow and spun around, halfway between the third and second landing. The stairs were deserted.

'Wait a sec,' Cody demanded.

'What do you want?' I felt vulnerable and alone on the otherwise empty stairwell. Was this what had happened to Lisa Willoughby? My eyes went to his fingers on my elbow.

'Oh, sorry.' He released his grip, looking abashed. 'You won't tell, will you? Please, promise me you won't, Ms Miller.'

'Tell what?' Was there something illicit going on between he and Paula, after all? Was he a killer?

'Sabrina.' He scratched his head. 'About the car.'

I breathed a sigh of relief. So that was what he'd chased me for. I patted his arm. 'Don't worry,' I promised. 'Your secret is safe with me.'

A noisy throng came bounding up the steps. By the sounds of it they'd had a few pre-meal drinks. Several were singing cowboy tunes. I pushed against the wall. A foot shot out and I tumbled into the crowd coming my way. I fell, hitting my tailbone and elbow, in that order. A strong hand plucked me upright. I looked over my throbbing shoulder.

'Are you OK, Ms Miller?'

I gulped and collected my wits, which seemed to have spilled across the steps along with my dignity. 'I think so.' I dusted myself off.

Cody pulled me closer as the crowd passed. 'You really should be more careful, Ms Miller.' His eyes dug into mine. Then he smiled. 'Well, gotta get back to Paula.'

I hobbled down the steps. I wasn't built for this detective

stuff. I stuck the key in the ignition and headed back to the café, glad that I had a motor vehicle rather than a Schwinn. Between having a drink splashed all over me and falling down half a flight of stairs, it had been one lousy afternoon.

One thought raced through my mind as I pulled into the slow-moving traffic as the light ahead turned yellow. Had Cody tripped me? Had he done so on purpose? Why would he want to hurt me? Certainly not because he was afraid I might spoil the surprise about his getting Sabrina a car as a wedding gift. If he had tripped me and it had been intentional, could it be about Lisa Willoughby? Was he a murderer?

Was that why he'd warned me to be careful? Or was my imagination getting the better of me? Note to self: check Cody Ryan's whereabouts at the time of the murder. Did he have an alibi or did I now have a new suspect?

The sun was in my eyes as I neared the intersection. I reached for the visor and felt a crash. The visor smacked me in the face as I slammed on the brakes and killed the engine. The traffic signal was red and so was the color of the car I had just knocked into. Oops.

The driver's-side door opened. The car bounced as a familiar shape stepped out into the road. Of all the cars I could collide with, I had to collide with Detective Highsmith's testosterone-fueled tribute to his youth, his Trans Am.

Oops again.

He folded his arms and motioned with his right hand for me to roll down my window. I obliged. 'What'd you do,' he scowled, 'steal another car?'

I groaned and waved him away from the car door so I could open it. I stood. My nose pulsed. I felt a drip of blood and squelched it with a crumpled tissue.

'You're a menace, Miller.'

'I know.' I felt woozy. I couldn't remember the last time I'd eaten or had a drink – besides the one that had splattered all over my legs. And while the thought of going on the offense had flashed through my brain, I wasn't fool enough to try it on a cop with a loaded gun. 'I am so sorry. I don't know what happened. One minute I was—' The hot afternoon sun seemed to slam into my face. I felt the world go sideways.

Highsmith's jaw slackened. Or maybe it had simply melted against the power of the sun. 'Are you OK?'

My knees crumpled. Highsmith caught me. I heard him holler for the traffic to go around. 'You'd better sit,' he said.

I nodded speechlessly. My hands were locked around his neck. I smelled leather and soap. His strong arms were under my knees. He eased me back behind the wheel of the BMW and his finger went to my cheek. My heart skipped a beat. Those big brown M&M eyes of his dug right into me. I squeezed my eyes shut before they sucked me in completely. I felt the warmth of his lips on my forehead.

He cleared his throat. 'I'd better check out the damage.'

I nodded, still unable to speak. Tears spilled from my eyes.

A moment later, he reappeared. 'Not too bad.' He smiled. 'Matching dents. Nothing major.'

'That's good,' I managed to say. *Nothing major.* Sure, try telling that to Johnny Wolfe. And what about that little kiss on the forehead? Was that nothing major, too?

'You've got some scrapes, though.'

I followed his eyes. 'Oh, I got them before.'

His brow shot up.

'I sort of fell down the stairs.'

His eyes narrowed.

'It was nothing. I'm fine. Really.'

He waved another car around us. 'I suggest we get these cars out of the middle of the road and swap insurance information. I'll come by your place later. I've got someplace to be now.'

'OK.' I spotted Brad Smith watching us from the sidewalk. I knew the *Table Rock Reader* offices were nearby. His arms were locked across his chest. Had he seen the accident? Had he seen the way Highsmith kissed me?

Highsmith's hand fell on my left shoulder. 'Are you sure you're OK to drive?'

I nodded curtly. 'Don't worry. I'll manage.'

He tapped his hand against the door. 'Good. Keep your eyes on the road. And if you're going to take them off the road,' he said with a gleam in his eye, 'don't do it when you're driving behind me.'

I watched the Trans Am speed off then slowly turned the key

in the ignition and pulled over to the side of the street. Brad was still there, waiting. Watching.

I knew I had to speak to him. I'd been avoiding him and his phone calls. A girl couldn't hide forever.

Could she?

I thought about it for a moment.

No, she couldn't. At least not in a town the size of Table Rock.

I waited for the traffic to clear then stepped onto the sidewalk.

'Are you OK?' Brad asked.

I nodded. 'More embarrassed than injured.'

He nodded once. 'I'm glad to hear it.'

'Listen, Brad,' my hand went to his arm, 'I've been really busy and I – we – haven't had a chance to talk—'

He cut me off with a wave of his hand. 'What's to talk about?'

What's to talk about? Was he kidding? Why are all men so difficult? 'For starters, we could talk about what happened the other night on my front porch.'

He forced a smile. 'Sorry, can't talk now. I've got a date.'

My stomach soured. 'A date?'

He shrugged. 'The editor wants me to interview Veronica Vargas about the Lisa Willoughby murder investigation.'

I flushed. 'VV?' Veronica 'VV' Vargas was Table Rock's very own femme fatale and pain in the buttocks. She was the doted on daughter of the mayor. And the girlfriend of one Detective Mark Highsmith.

Brad nodded. 'Shall I give her your regards?'

TWENTY-SIX

There were no parking spots out on the street so I parked Johnny's BMW behind our shops and went in the back way. I wasn't exactly sure what I was going to tell Johnny – or when. I had promised him there wouldn't be a scratch on his precious BMW – but I hadn't said anything about dents.

Mom was inside.

'Mom! What are you doing here?'

'I called her,' Aubrey answered.

Mom nodded. 'That's right.' She held up the bag from Robinsons' Nest. 'I came to get these. What happened to your face, Maggie? Have you been bleeding?'

'It's nothing, Mom. I must have bumped into something. Enjoy your suet.'

'No offense,' said Aubrey with a smile, 'but that stuff was truly, truly stinking up the place.'

Mom set the bag on the nearest table and looked down her nose at me. 'Is there something you want to tell me, Maggie?'

I twisted my jaw. 'I don't think so.' I glanced at Aubrey, who had suddenly frozen behind the register.

'Nothing at all?' There was an ominous undertone to Mom's voice. I hadn't seen her looking this upset since the night she'd caught me sneaking out of my room to meet up with my boyfriend, Artie Culpepper, the night of my sixteenth birthday.

'Well—' I angled my eyes up at Aubrey. She was mouthing something over and over but I couldn't make out what. I stood there helplessly, my mouth half-open.

Mom looked down her nose at me. 'What Aubrey's trying to say is "she knows."'

Aubrey blushed. 'Sorry.'

'Knows what?'

Mom pointed outside. 'About my car. Tell me, Maggie, when were you planning on telling me that you'd smashed my car?'

It was my turn to blush. 'Oh, I, uh . . .' I grabbed my apron and tied it round my waist as some customers came bustling in. 'Can't talk now, Mom. Gotta work. Besides,' I said nervously, 'it's only a scratch.'

'Only a scratch!' gasped my mother. 'Maggie Miller, I've been to the body shop.' She fished in her handbook and pulled out a printed sheet. 'I received a quote for nearly two thousand dollars.'

My eyes darted up and down the paper. 'Surely there must be some mistake.' A decimal point in the wrong place. Too many zeroes. 'I barely touched that boulder.'

'Boulder!' There went another gasp.

'Well,' I molded a small shape with my hands, 'it was really more of a tiny rock.' I smiled weakly. 'Just a pebble, really.' I pressed my thumb and index finger close together.

Mom frowned. 'Some pebble, young lady. I don't understand, Maggie, dear. When you had your own car there was never a scratch on it.'

I opened my mouth but nothing came out. She was right.

Mom wrung her hands. 'It's going to cost a bundle to fix it. You know I'm on a limited income. Not to mention the car will need to be in the shop for days. I'll have to have a rental. I can't exactly walk everywhere.'

I was going to suggest she ride a Schwinn like me but didn't have the nerve. Something told me Mom wasn't going to take that suggestion well. Maybe when she calmed down. Hey, we could rent a bicycle built for two. I'd seen some cute ones parked outside the bike shop on Main.

'Be right with you,' I said to Aubrey, who'd just taken five orders for beignets and needed me to get frying. I slid behind the counter. 'And I'm sorry, Mom.' I grabbed some pre-prepped dough and began rolling it out.

'How am I going to pay for this?' Mom waved the quote in front of my nose.

'Insurance?' I took the thin sheet of dough and began cutting strips.

'There's still a deductible, Maggie Miller. Five hundred dollars. And if I report the accident my insurance rates will go up. You know they always do.'

Man, she really wasn't letting go of this. 'Sorry,' I said again. 'I – I'll make it up to you.'

Mom squinted suspiciously at me. 'How?'

I smiled weakly. 'Free beignets?'

Mom didn't look convinced.

'For life?' Hey, why not sweeten the pot. Laura had gone for it. And unless business picked up life may not be all that long. I could have to shut the place in a year.

Mom only scowled. 'You aren't charging me now.'

I chewed on my lower lip. That was true. I could start. Maybe earn back enough money to pay her deductible. Nah, she'd probably never go for it.

'Don't worry,' said Mom. Was that an evil gleam I spotted in her eyes? She carefully folded up the quote from Carl's Paint & Body and placed it back in her purse. 'I've given this a lot of thought.'

'You have?' My toes tingled a warning. I didn't like where this conversation was going. I hadn't even liked where it had started. But I didn't see any way off this particular trail now.

She nodded. 'I have the solution.'

I dropped in the first batch of beignets and listened to the pleasant sizzle. I daren't look up. 'You do?'

Mom nodded. 'I'm going to work here.'

'Here?' I looked up. 'At the café?'

Mom nodded again. 'And you're going to pay me.'

'Isn't it wonderful, Maggie?' Aubrey's smile melted off her face as I lasered her with my eyes.

I pulled the beignets from the fryer, placed them on the drip tray then dropped in another load. 'Mom,' I said, shaking my head, 'I'd love to have you work here, believe me, just love to,' I said, adding a few ounces of sadness to the mix, 'but I am in no position to hire you.'

Mom grinned – it was practically a smirk. 'You can't afford not to, Maggie. This poor girl,' she pointed to Aubrey, 'is working herself to death ten to twelve hours a day—'

Ten to twelve hours a day? Was she really putting in those kinds of hours?

'Kelly Herman works twenty hours a week for your sister and twenty for you. So she can't help out any more than she is now.' Mom folded her arms smugly across her chest. 'You need me, Maggie. Let's face it, you're gone half the time.'

My face went deep red, and it wasn't because I was standing over the hot fryer and taking all the heat. Well, I was taking all the heat but most of it was coming from my mom.

I love my mom, but working with her side by side? That couldn't be a good thing. She'd drive me crazy. 'What about your yoga classes?'

Mom tsk-tsked. 'You know I only teach at the spa part-time.' She planted her hands on her hips. 'I can handle both.'

Yeah, but could I handle Mom working in the café? I slowly lifted the last batch of beignets from the fryer and laid them on the drip tray. I picked up the powdered sugar container and sprinkled it liberally over the warm beignets. I placed three on each plate and handed them one by one to Aubrey, who passed them to our customers.

The woman at the register lifted a plate up to her nose and inhaled. She sneezed and a cloud of sugar filled the air between her and Aubrey. Powdered sugar has a way of finding its way into places you'd rather it didn't. 'Smells wonderful,' the customer said between sniffs. 'And you really should give your mother a job. After all,' she patted the arm of the stodgy man beside her while looking at me, 'that's what family is all about, isn't it?'

I looked hard at my mom for a moment. 'OK,' I said, waving my finger at her. 'But I don't want you doing any of that yoga stuff in front of the customers.' What would passers-by think if they caught Mom stretched out in a leotard in the window with her butt in the air and her ankles wrapped behind her neck? Probably that I was running a circus school, not a beignet café.

Mom smiled. 'I wouldn't dream of it, dear.'

Wiped out, I returned home. Mom and I were too tired to cook so we ordered a large pizza. Mom tipped the delivery man and I ran the pizza box to the table and popped the lid. 'What did you order?'

'Large cheese with all the works.' Mom pulled up a chair across from me at the kitchen table.

I studied the pizza. It certainly looked good. A pizza of many colors: yellows, greens, reds, purples. I picked up my fork and stabbed at some yellow chunks. 'What's this?'

'Mango,' Mom replied.

'Ooo-kay . . .'

She ran the spatula under a large slice and dropped it onto her plate.

'And this?' The tines of my fork prodded something that looked sort of like pepperoni but not quite.

'Ostrich.'

'Ostrich.' I glanced across the table at my mother. My fork hung in the air. 'Did you say ostrich? Like the bird?'

'Yes, dear.'

I lifted my hand overhead. 'Big guy, likes to stick his head in the sand kind of bird?' Would I be coughing up feathers later?

Mom nodded. 'It's quite good.' She scooped up another slice, dropped it onto a plate and slid it toward me. Two pieces of sliced ostrich pepperoni stared up at me. It was like looking into dead ostrich eyes. 'Better start eating before your dinner gets cold.'

My mouth hung open. I slowly lowered my arm. The thick slices of ostrich pepperoni were a hideous reddish-purple, looking more like the fresh hematomas lining my right leg and elbow from the tumble I'd taken earlier than something I'd want to stick in my mouth.

I pushed back my chair and rose. This meal called for reinforcements. 'Can I get you something to drink, Mom?'

'Water for me, please.'

I ignored her and brought two filled drink glasses to the table.

Mom turned the glass around in her hand. 'I asked for water.'

I sat and took a swig from my wide-rimmed glass. 'Margaritas are the new water,' I quipped. 'Bottoms up!' I downed another swig. Delicious. My drink could have used ice but Mom, against my protests, had placed her suet packets in the freezer – to keep them fresh, she said. At least the apartment didn't stink now. Only my freezer did. I vowed to stay clear of it until Mom and her suet returned to her own place.

I could only pray I didn't wake in the middle of the night – due to coughing up those full-bodied ostrich feathers – with a craving for chocolate mocha-mint ice cream and discover I was spooning lard-laced bird suet instead.

Sated on ostrich pizza and soothed on margaritas, I rested my chin on my elbows. 'This whole murder thing is making me crazy, Mom,' I confessed.

Mom took a dainty sip of her second margarita. 'I know. Are the police any closer to finding Ms Willoughby's killer?'

'I ran into Detective Highsmith earlier today' – literally – 'and he didn't mention anything. I'm pretty sure he still figures that Johnny's his man and that Clive was trying to cover up for him.'

Mom nodded. 'I don't believe that for a second.'

'And then there's Houston Willoughby.'

'Who's he?'

'Lisa's brother.' I yawned. 'He says he got into town the day of the murder. He came into the café that morning saying he had just arrived to see her. He acted like he didn't know she was dead.'

Mom's brow arched. 'What makes you think it was merely an act?'

I hesitated. Mom didn't know Johnny and I had broken into Lisa's condo. I couldn't tell her. That would make her an accessory after the fact. Not to mention she'd kill me. Worse, she'd ground me for life. She'd probably force me to eat ostrich and mango pizza seven days a week. And do yoga with her. 'I happen to know he was staying in Prescott for two days prior to her murder.'

'That doesn't make him a killer,' Mom countered.

'No, but the fact that he was nearby gives him means. And,' I added, 'the fact that he and his sister's Aunt Willow Willoughby recently passed away and left the two of them her entire estate is certainly motive.'

Mom whistled softly. 'I'll say.' Mom stroked the cat. 'Have you confronted Houston about his story yet?'

'No, I keep meaning to.' I yawned again. 'I'll try tomorrow. That reminds me,' I glanced morosely at my empty glass, 'I still need to talk to Reva Reynolds from Markie's Masterpieces. I get the feeling she's holding something back. I mean, it's odd. Markie, this guy Ben and Reva were all in the bakery the morning Lisa was killed.'

'So?' My yawning must have been contagious because Mom was yawning now, too.

'So, nobody claims to have seen or heard anything. They all claim to not have been anywhere around. Ben says he was on the roof smoking. Markie initially lied about being in at all.' I grunted. 'And I don't know where Reva was.'

Mom stood, grabbed our plates and headed to the kitchen sink. She turned on the spigot and rinsed our plates.

I joined her, bringing the glasses and flatware. 'The only person who claims to have heard anything at all is some painter on the second floor.'

Mom turned off the water and wiped her hands on the kitchen towel. 'Oh? I've been thinking of having my condo repainted.'

'She's not that kind of painter, Mom. She's an artist. You know, landscapes and fruit.'

Mom ran our glasses under the water and sponged them out. 'What did she hear?'

'She says all she heard was what could have been the sound of Lisa falling down the stairs.' I grabbed the leftover pizza and Mom covered it in plastic wrap. The way that ostrich was tossing around in my stomach, I'd let Mom enjoy it.

'She did hear Markie and Lisa arguing, though. A day or two day before, outside her studio. Apparently they were really going at it.' I shared what Blake Sherwood had told me.

Mom shook her head. 'Sounds like this Markie person may have had a reason or two to want Ms Willoughby dead himself.'

I agreed. I definitely needed to dig a little deeper into Markie's life and whereabouts.

TWENTY-SEVEN

Friday morning at the café did not start well. Mom came in early to open the shop with me and learn the routine. Clive came banging on the door before we were open for business, bags under his eyes, hair tussled and face unshaven. He was in indigo jeans and a white shirt. No bowtie.

I turned the key in the lock and let him in. 'You look terrible, Clive.' I laid a hand on his shoulder. 'Come on in. I was about to start the coffee.'

'Oh, Maggie,' lamented Clive. 'It's simply awful.'

I spun on my heels. 'My coffee?'

He shook his head. 'No, what's happened to Johnny.'

Mom stepped in from the storeroom. 'What's happened to Johnny?'

'The police took him,' Clive gulped.

'Oh, dear!' cried my mom.

I hustled Clive to a table. 'Have a seat.' I held out a chair. 'Mom, would you start the coffee, please?' I sat in the chair opposite Clive at the table in front of the window. The orange sun was just coming over the horizon. It was beautiful in Table Rock this time of day – if you didn't have things like murder and trips to the electric chairs on your mind.

Mom brought three cups of coffee to the table and joined us. 'Drink up,' she urged Clive. She dumped a handful of creamers and sugar packets onto the table.

Two joggers trotted along the brick-lined sidewalk. An elderly man walking his collie stopped to read the headlines of the *Table Rock Reader* in the kiosk at the corner.

'Talk to me, Clive.' I set my cup down and glanced across the street at Karma Koffee. They already had a good crowd. I toyed with the idea of sending Mom over for a few of their muffins but pride got the better of me. They had one muffin in particular, aptly named Heaven's Building Blocks, that was to die for – to die and go to heaven for, to be precise. My stomach grumbled like a grouchy old man. Maybe if I wore some sort of disguise, a hat and some dark glasses . . .

Clive poured a creamer into his cup then added two sugars. 'It's because of that man at the Entronque.'

I scratched my nose. 'What man?'

'That janitor fellow,' Clive answered. 'You remember; he was there when we found the body. Detective Highsmith was talking to him about the elevators and whether they were broken or not.'

'That reminds me,' I interjected, 'did the police ever find those out-of-order signs you'd seen?'

Clive shrugged. 'Not that I know of.'

'Tell us about this man,' Mom said sternly, putting us back on course.

Clive took a sip of coffee then continued. 'The police showed pictures of me and Johnny to the janitor.'

'And?' I stifled a yawn. I really needed some sugar. Foregoing the muffin, I poured three packets into my coffee though I usually drink it black and unsweetened.

'He recognized Johnny. He claimed to have seen him there earlier.' Clive's jaw tightened. 'Arguing with Lisa Willoughby.'

Oh, that was so not good. 'What did Johnny have to say? There must be some explanation.'

Clive ran a hand along his forehead. 'He said he wanted to

talk to her again about this lawsuit business. He was afraid that it would reflect badly on The Hitching Post. He told her it would reflect poorly on her as well.' Clive frowned. 'Table Rock is a small town. Things have a way of spreading.'

'Tell me about it,' I quipped. 'Where's Johnny now?'

'Still at the police station.'

'I'll call Andy.'

'I already did,' replied Clive. 'He should be there now.'

Mom and I told Clive not to worry. Though I was worried about the guys, I figured that if Johnny was innocent there was no real harm in letting him stew down at the police station for a while.

Clive rose. 'I'd better get back to the store. Besides handling everything there I've got to deal with all the last-minute preparations for Labor of Love. Thank goodness Johnny had finished the late alterations to Sabrina Higgins' gown yesterday.'

'I'll bet it's a killer.' I smiled weakly. 'Sorry, poor choice of words.'

Clive laid his hand on his chest. 'I do hope Johnny is out in time to help me.'

'With Andy handling things you've got nothing to worry about.'

'No, perhaps not, but Maggie,' Clive draped his hand over mine, 'I'd be careful with Johnny.'

A furrow creased my brow. 'Why?'

'Because when he does get out,' Clive locked his eyes on mine, 'the first thing he said he's going to do . . .'

'Yes?'

'Is kill you.' Clive lowered his eyes and gave my hand a squeeze.

'Kill me?' I blustered. 'Whatever for? For helping him? For getting him out of jail? From saving him from a life in prison or, worse yet, the death penalty?' My voice rose shrilly. 'They don't have ice-skating rinks in prison, you know!'

Clive shook his head. 'For what you did to his car.'

I froze then suddenly melted in my chair. I was a dead woman.

TWENTY-EIGHT

'd asked Aubrey to run Johnny's key fob back to him last evening and to say nothing about the little dent in his front bumper, figuring I'd deal with the fallout from that minor disaster later. I'd been hoping Johnny wouldn't see the dent until I'd come up with a plan to fix it.

Since there was nothing I could do about it now, I turned to preparing for the Labor of Love myself. The logistics of participating in the charity event were daunting. Why had I let Mrs Higgins cajole me into taking part?

I drew up a list of things I was going to need and telephoned Laura Duval. She had some things in her store – tables, tablecloths, an extra coffee urn and even a used fryer that she said she could rent me for the weekend. She was giving me a rock-bottom price on everything, but this weekend's charity event was still going to set me back plenty.

Aubrey showed up around noon and I left her and Mom in charge of the café while I headed for Laura's Lightly Used. I was pleased to see that she'd laid the whole lot out in a corner of her store, arranging everything the way it might look under the tent. 'This is perfect.' I gave her a hug.

'Thanks. I tried to think of every item you'd need.'

I nodded effusively. 'Like I said, perfect.' She'd even remembered to include a couple of folding chairs and a napkin dispenser. 'How'd you happen to have all this stuff?'

'Restaurants open and close all the time. You know how it is.'

I got a sinking feeling in the pit of my stomach. I knew exactly how it was.

'Then the owners come in here trying to get a few bucks for their equipment.' Laura fingered a tabletop deep fryer that was going to be perfect for cooking up beignets. 'You'd be amazed how cheaply I'm able to get used restaurant supplies. The failure rate on restaurants is—' She stopped suddenly. 'Sorry.'

I managed a smile. 'It's OK. I'll cry later.' I clapped my hands together. 'Change of subject. Tell me about Houston. Have you seen him again?'

Laura invited me to sit on a second-hand white daybed with a flowery quilt top. 'Not since the other night. And breakfast.' She grinned sheepishly. 'He did ask me out. Tonight, in fact.'

I gazed at her. 'Did you accept?'

She shook her head no. 'He's not my type. And I don't care much for that weird business associate of his.'

'Irwin Acheson?'

She nodded. 'He scares me.'

He scared me too. 'He's still around?'

'I've seen him walking around in town and also at Lisa's condo.' She gave me a meaningful look. 'Or should I say Houston's condo. I suppose it belongs to him now.'

'Yeah, like everything else that had once been hers.' I filled Laura in on the latest news about a witness having seen Johnny down at the Entronque the morning of her death. Laura didn't believe Johnny was guilty of murder any more than I did. I wrote Lisa a check for the supplies and she agreed to drive the whole lot over to Table Rock Town Square early the next morning. That was nice of her. It meant I wasn't going to have to ask Andy to haul it over for me in his pickup.

I was pedaling back to the café when I glanced in the window of Hopping Mad, the Hopi-Irish pub run by Johnny Honanie. Irwin Acheson stood at the bar, all six foot forever of him, dressed in black jeans and a black T-shirt that hugged his pectorals and highlighted his biceps. A sports show played on the three flat-screen TVs behind the bar. He caught me looking at him and waved. 'Come on in.' There was a gleam in his eye.

I parked the Schwinn against the fire hydrant and went inside.

He draped a python over my shoulder and I drew back. 'Hey, Red. Let me buy you a drink.' He scratched the underside of his chin. 'What was your name again?'

Despite his sexy Irish accent, I suppressed a shudder. 'Maggie Miller.'

Irwin flashed a set of white teeth. 'That's right.' He pulled tighter and I felt the python squeezing the life out of me. 'Aren't you going to ask me my name?'

I extricated myself from his grip and took the empty stool at his side. 'Irwin Acheson.'

'Yep.' Irwin puffed out his chest, looking satisfied. 'What'll it be?'

'Coffee,' I replied, looking at the bartender. I didn't get it; what business did Houston Willoughby have with this lout?

Irwin laughed. 'Give her one of these.' He pinged a tall damp beer mug with his fingertip. 'In fact, get me another while you're at it.' He turned to me. 'It's the house beer. Pretty good stuff, too. I'm thinking of trying it out at one of my establishments back home.' He fiddled with his mug. 'Goes great with their beer-glazed bacon. Want some?'

'No, thanks.' I'd rather eat ostrich. My lips brushed my glass, catching mostly foam. I wanted to keep my wits about me. I feared Irwin's wits were long gone, and I wasn't sure that could be blamed on the beer he'd consumed. 'So, you and Houston go way back?'

His big shoulders heaved up then fell. 'A few years. We've done some business.'

'You're in the restaurant business, too?'

Irwin nodded. 'A sushi bar, an Italian fine-dining restaurant and a stake in Houston's Mexican joint.'

'Covering all your culinary bases, aren't you? No casual American?'

He smiled lasciviously. 'Not yet.' He practically purred. 'But I'm game if you are.'

A frisson of dread ran up my arms. I'd have to be careful around this guy. I cleared my throat and took a sip of beer. The brew was tangy and cold. 'What brings you to Table Rock? Looking for another investment?'

Irwin shook his head. 'I heard how nice it is this time of year. I had some time on my hands; I thought I'd see for myself.'

'Quite a coincidence that Houston Willoughby happened to be here at the same time.'

A smile crept across his chiseled face. 'A happy coincidence.'

'Did you know his sister, Lisa?'

'We'd met.'

'Maybe you visited her here before? In Table Rock?'

Irwin stared at me. I thought I saw something in his eyes that hadn't been there a moment ago.

'You mentioned at the diner that you knew where she lived.'

He downed half his beer and wiped his lips with a finger. His eyes fell to my glass. 'When you're finished with that how about showing me the sights?'

'Sorry, I've got to get back to the café.' I left before the Irish python could coil himself around me, constricting my chest until my heart stopped. Something told me that the only sight he was interested in seeing was the inside of my bedroom. That was definitely not part of the Table Rock tour.

I found Detective Highsmith at his desk and slapped my insurance card and a copy of my driver's license on his blotter. His brows edged up. 'What's this?' He was wearing the same brown cotton suit he'd worn the first time we'd met. The same milk-stained tie, too.

'My insurance information.' Of course, it was void. I had no insurance – I had no car.

The detective leaned back and stretched his arms overhead. The chair creaked loudly. I didn't blame it. 'Oh, man,' he said, 'you should have seen Johnny Wolfe when I told him about that.'

I fell into the chair opposite his desk. '*You* told him?'

He nodded curtly.

'You – you blabbed?' How could he do that? He'd been so kind, so gentle yesterday. He'd kissed me! On the forehead, but still . . . The big jerk. 'Do you have any idea how much trouble you've caused?' I could feel the heat rising in my face and my heart pounding against my chest.

'Trouble *I've* caused?' He leaned toward me. 'It seems to me that you cause trouble wherever you go.'

'Why, you—' I held my tongue and chuffed. 'Where's Johnny? I want to see him.' I scrambled to retrieve my license and insurance card off the desk. Let him pay for his own damages. Besides, I didn't see any good reason for him to see my biological age right there in black and white.

Highsmith shook his head. 'No can do. He's with his attorney. You know, the one whose pickup you recently stole.'

'I'm not going to dignify that with a response.' I folded my arms across my chest. 'Take me to Johnny and Andy. I'm sure they'll be glad to see me.'

Detective Highsmith rose from his desk and matched my pose. 'Maybe so, but I don't expect Veronica will be nearly as glad.'

I gulped. VV Vargas. Had Brad mentioned my little get-together with the detective to VV? 'Veronica's here?' I shivered. It was an involuntary response every time I laid eyes on the woman or heard her name mentioned. I'd rather face Medusa, snakes and all.

Highsmith nodded and gestured toward his door. 'Now, if you don't mind.'

I grunted. 'Fine, but you're wasting your time. If you ask me the real killer is still out there, at large, at loose, ready to kill again.'

Highsmith smiled. 'And who might that be?'

I smiled back. Two could play that game. 'One,' I said, counting off on my fingers, 'Markie Gravelle. Two, Ben Baker. Three, Houston Willoughby. He's going to inherit everything from that aunt now.'

Highsmith shrugged my words off like so much fluff.

I'd lost count. I mouthed the numbers as I counted my fingers again. 'Four, Cody Ryan.' Highsmith snorted and I ignored him. 'Five, Irwin Acheson.'

Highsmith wrinkled his nose. 'Who?'

'Some business associate of Lisa's brother, Houston. He and Houston are partners in a Mexican restaurant over in Santa Fe.'

'So why would this Acheson fellow want Houston's sister dead?'

'I don't know,' I snapped. 'You tell me. If you'd spend less time harassing Johnny and Clive and more time looking for the real killer, you might have the answer already.'

It was the detective's turn to count. This guy was a real copycat. 'Number one,' he began, pulling on an index finger, 'your friend, Clive Rothschild, was found at the scene, and that piece of fabric beneath the victim's body. Number two,' his eyes drilled into mine. '*He confessed.*'

I jerked my head. 'Big deal. He took it back.' Could you

recant a murder confession? I was a little fuzzy on the legalities of takesy-backsies when used as a legal defense in such cases as cold-blooded murder.

Highsmith looked down his nose at me. 'Number—' He hesitated, looking confused. Huh, not so smart after all, was he? 'Number whatever,' he said sternly, 'Mr Wolfe was seen arguing with the deceased within an hour of her death.'

I started for the door. Nothing he'd said was worthy of a reply.

'Oh, and Miller?'

I froze in the doorway. 'Yes?'

'I'm glad you're OK.' He cracked a little smile. 'How's the nose?' His fingers went to his own finely hewn smell detector and jiggled it.

I couldn't help chuckling. My collision with Highsmith's Pontiac had been just strong enough for me to strike my nose against the steering wheel but not severe enough to have set off the airbag. 'Still sore.' I sighed, my hand clutching the doorjamb. 'But thanks for asking.'

TWENTY-NINE

I held my hand against the sun, waiting for the bus. The police station was a bit far out of my comfort zone when it came to biking so I'd taken public transport to the station. I hoped a bus would be along soon. It was hot. I was tired and thirsty. Three sips of beer does not a luncheon make.

The toot of a car horn caused me to turn. It was Brad. I was happy, unhappy and embarrassed to see him, all at the same time. Most of all, I was glad to get out of the sun. He leaned across the seat and threw open the passenger-side door. 'Hop in.'

I did.

'Where to?' He wore denim jeans and a forest-green polo shirt. He looked adorable. I tugged at my unkempt red hair, conscious of my own slovenliness. Why is it that I'm always a mess, no makeup, tousled hair and wearing my 'beignet lady' clothes when a handsome man shows up?

'I could use a ride back to the café if it's not too much trouble.' I snapped into my seatbelt and explored my handbag for my sunglasses, at the very least hoping to mask the bags under my eyes.

'No trouble at all.' We waited for a break in the long line of traffic snaking by us. His hands fell over the steering wheel.

'Thanks. What are you doing out here?' Had he been coming down to the police station to see if there was anything new about the murder? I suddenly felt uncomfortable. Was it our kiss the other night? Was it that he'd seen me with Mark Highsmith yesterday?

'I'm on my way to Prescott.'

A bell went off in my head. 'Oh?'

Brad nodded. 'I had a tip that Houston Willoughby was seen hanging around Prescott several days before his sister's murder. That makes me curious. Very curious.' That made two of us. It must have shown on my face because he said, 'Want to tag along?' He rubbed his unshaven cheek with his knuckles.

I said sure.

'Great.' Brad pulled behind a mail truck. Trouble is,' he said, 'I don't know where to look exactly. Prescott's not big but it's big enough.'

I smiled as the miles ticked off. 'Try the Hotel St Michael,' I suggested.

'Oh? Any particular reason why? There are plenty of hotels, motels, resorts, B and Bs . . .'

'Let's just say I've got a hunch about that place.'

Brad found a parking space opposite the Hotel St Michael on the Courthouse Plaza. The Yavapai Courthouse Plaza, as it's officially known, but just 'the Plaza' to the locals, has been recognized as one of the first ten 'Great Public Places' in America by the American Planning Association. I know because I've seen the Prescott Office of Tourism ads running on TV. A couple hundred trees or so, the majority of which appeared to be American elms, covered the plaza. The broad lawns were crossed by interlocking paver walkways. There was also a bandstand, not unlike ours back in Table Rock. The four-story courthouse that sat in the plaza was built of granite and looked as solid as the surrounding mountains.

We went across the plaza to the hotel. Built in 1901, the Hotel St Michael was reported to be haunted. Maybe that's why they had all those gargoyles around the outside to protect the guests within. Personally, I wasn't so sure gargoyles trumped ghosts. Then again, I wasn't planning on spending the night and finding out. The gargoyles looked menacing enough but the idea of the ghost of Wyatt Earp or Billy the Kid haunting me in a hundred-year-old bed, protected by nothing more than my skimpy lingerie was twice as scary.

Brad paused on the steps and fished around in his back pocket. He unfolded a sheet of copy paper. I looked over his arm. He held a color headshot of Houston Willoughby. Houston looked rather stiff in a button-down pink shirt.

I was impressed. 'Where'd you get that?'

Brad shrugged like it was nothing. 'I downloaded it from the management page of his restaurant's website.'

I pursed my lips. I should've thought of that.

A large chandelier hung from the coffered tin ceiling. Brass bankers' lamps with glass Catalina green shades cast even more light over the counter. Maybe it kept the ghosts at bay. The scent of aged wood, leather and, incongruously, corned beef hash filled the air. There was no one at the reception desk in the lobby so we headed to where we heard voices – the bar slash restaurant.

The bartender nodded our way, taking his eye off the two patrons at the bar only briefly. A young waitress hollered nicely for us to take a seat wherever we'd like and that she'd be with us in a moment.

Brad shrugged and pulled out a chair for me. 'Hungry?'

I was and said so. 'I haven't had a thing all day.'

Brad laid the photo of Houston Willoughby very conspicuously atop our dark table. The waitress brought us a couple of menus. She was dressed in a tight-fitting pair of jeans and a short-sleeve red gingham blouse tied off at the waist.

'Hey, I know him.' She rested a finger on the edge of the sheet.

'You do?' Brad and I said as one.

She bobbed her head up and down. 'Sure, he stayed here a few days. Good tipper.' She tilted her head back and laughed, exposing her belly button. 'I always remember a good tipper.' Her hand rested on Brad's shoulder.

'Was he alone?' I asked. Was she flirting with Brad? And with me a foot away?

She scrunched up her nose. 'You mean, like did he have a wife or something?'

I nodded. Her hand finally left Brad. About time. Not that I cared. It's not appropriate, that's all.

'Nah. He was alone. Not that he wanted to be, if you get my drift.'

I smiled. 'He asked you out?'

'Yep. I turned him down. A little too old for me.' She waved her hands. 'No offense. I mean, it's not like you two are *old* or anything.'

'No, of course not,' I mumbled, feeling suddenly quite ancient.

Brad shot me a look like he wanted to get a word in edgewise. Who was stopping him? I made a face. 'So this guy.' He twisted the picture so it faced directly at our waitress. 'His name is Houston Willoughby, by the way.'

'Yeah, that's right. Houston. Funny name, right?' She giggled. Her long brown locks shook. Big gold hoops hung from her earlobes. They matched the tiny gold navel ring.

Brad continued, 'Do you remember anything else in particular about him?'

She tapped her foot against the floor and thought for a moment. 'Not really. Your typical tourist. Wanted directions to stuff like Sedona, Table Rock, places like that.'

I stiffened. 'Table Rock?'

She nodded briskly. 'Yeah.' She scratched her scalp with her pen. 'Said he was going there.'

Brad cut in: 'What about this person?' He dug into his jeans pocket and unfolded yet another sheet of paper. This one showed Lisa Willoughby in a crisp black chef's jacket with a Markie's Masterpieces name patch. 'Did you ever see her here at the hotel?'

'Together with Houston?'

'Well . . .' She leaned closer. 'Looks sort of like him.'

'It's his sister.'

Her teeth dug into her lower lip. 'No, sorry. Can't say that I did. So,' she tapped her order pad with her pen, 'you guys ready to order?'

'Give us a minute, please.' Brad pulled a pair of readers out of his pocket and slid them over his nose.

'I've never noticed you wear those before.'

'I try not to wear them any more than I have to.' He shrugged. 'Self-conscious, I guess.'

'Don't worry,' I quipped, 'old age becomes you.'

He looked through his glasses at me for a moment then returned to his menu.

After I'd had my fill of pasta and Brad had polished off a cheeseburger, we headed back to the car, taking South Montezuma Street, better known as Whiskey Row – and that wasn't because it was populated with flower shops and Christian bookstores.

I was doing some window-shopping when I thought I spotted a familiar face. I grabbed Brad's shoulder.

'Ouch!'

'Sorry,' I said, letting go. 'Look, isn't that Houston Willoughby right over there?'

Brad turned. 'Where?'

'Getting into that white four-door.' I pointed. Houston, if that's who it was, had his back to us.

Brad shrugged. 'Who knows?' He said it as if what he really meant was 'who cares?' 'Do you even know what kind of car he drives?'

'No,' I admitted. My mind jumped ahead. 'But if it is him, what's he doing here? Do you suppose he was following you? Maybe,' I said, taking a leap, 'he knows we're on to him and wanted to keep tabs on us – see what we're up to. See how close we're getting to naming him as his sister's killer.'

Brad didn't look impressed with my logic. 'Maybe he wanted to do some shopping or some sightseeing. People do that around here, you know.'

I pointed again, then pulled Brad across the street. 'Look, a New Mexico license plate – yellow with red lettering.' The state plate was quite distinctive.

'OK.' Brad slowed his pace.

'Don't drag your feet.'

'Huh?'

'We've got to follow him.'

'What for?' Brad pulled free from my grip.

'To see where he's going, what he's up to.'

Brad groaned but let himself be pulled to the car. 'Quick,' I said. 'Drive.' I stuck my arm out the window. 'That's his car over there near the intersection. Behind that motorcycle.'

Brad grumbled but complied. 'I don't know why we're bothering,' he said as we pulled away from town and hit the state highway. 'He's probably going back to Table Rock.' He swiveled his head in my direction. 'Same as us.'

'Then you've got nothing to gripe about,' I quipped. 'And keep your eyes on the road.' I pointed ahead. 'And on him.'

Brad shook his head and drove in silence. The distance between us and Houston's car kept growing. Every time we hit a dip in the road we lost sight of him. I gnashed my teeth in frustration. It was making me crazy. Of all my possible suspects, Houston Willoughby had the most to gain. 'You know his aunt died, leaving him and his sister her entire estate.'

'I know.' His hands tightened around the steering wheel.

'You know that he could be meeting some accomplice, like Irwin Acheson.'

'Who?'

I smiled smugly. The white sedan had become a mere dot on the road. 'Catch up with Houston and I'll tell you.'

Brad scowled my way. 'I'm going the speed limit already.'

'So go faster. He is.' I lowered my voice and looked gloomily out the windshield. 'Heck, practically everybody is.' A Toyota Prius passed us as if sent from above to prove my point.

'What'd you say?'

'I said, so go faster. There's nothing out here. You could do seventy-five easy.' Nothing but some dirt, rock, a cactus or two and maybe a roadrunner or a rattlesnake for color.

Brad's eyes widened. 'Are you nuts?' he bridled. 'That's twenty miles over the limit!'

'Please,' I explained. Sheesh, it was like talking to a child. 'Everybody just naturally goes nine or ten miles over the speed limit, right?'

'Well, I suppose . . .'

'So,' I said, 'going twenty miles an hour over the posted limit is really no more than going ten miles over the actual de facto limit.' I crossed my arms over my chest. 'And going ten miles over the actual de facto limit is just normal.'

'I don't know . . .' His face wrinkled up like a month-old prune. 'There's something about your logic that doesn't sound right . . .'

'Trust me, you'll only be going with the flow of traffic. And that's simply the normal rate of speed if you factor in the posted limit weighed against the de factor limit and don't go more than ten miles an hour over that. So,' I concluded, wagging my finger toward his nose, 'keep the speedometer at seventy-five and no more. We'll be fine.' And, just maybe, we wouldn't lose Houston Willoughby. I was certain it was him and I wanted to know what he was up to.

Brad didn't look convinced but he nervously pressed his foot down further on the gas pedal.

We were making good time, too – I was really proud of Brad – until I heard him groan, swear and ease up on the gas.

'Hey,' I began, 'what are you doing?' Was there a problem? Had we run out of gas? Got a flat tire?

He jerked a thumb over his shoulder. I caught sight of a large white SUV with a gold-and-blue insignia and flashing red, white and blue lights closing in on us.

Very patriotic, really.

THIRTY

I reached into the basket of lemon and pepper seasoned buffalo wings. 'You're not still mad, are you?'

Brad scowled and dug his elbows into the table. 'Two hundred and fifty dollars,' he said morosely.

I took a bite. Delicious. 'I said I was sorry.' Who knew a speeding ticket could be so expensive? There's no way I was going to go twenty miles over the limit if it was going to cost that much.

'I know,' he sighed, running his hands through the corners of his scalp. He looked over his shoulder toward the long bar. 'So this is where you saw that partner of Houston's, eh?' We had retired to Hopping Mad for a drink and to talk over what we knew. And what we didn't know.

I nodded and took another greasy bite. 'Irwin,' I said, filling in the name. Grease. What's not to like? I licked my fingers and took a swig from a bottle of orange cream soda. I loved the stuff. Sweet, creamy and tart. And plenty of sugar to keep the heart pumping and the synapses firing.

Brad hoisted his bottle of beer and took a weary swig. 'You know, it could have been a stranger in that car, an innocent tourist.' He took a second swig. 'Though I suppose it might have been Houston or even that partner of his you mentioned, whathisname?'

'Irwin,' I repeated. 'Irwin Acheson.' It *was* Houston, I just knew it.

'Right.' He rubbed his nose. 'I keep forgetting.'

'Believe me,' I said, 'once you've seen him you won't soon forget him.'

Brad pulled a face. 'You said he's from New Mexico, too. What's he drive?'

I had no idea and said so. 'I'm guessing some big black muscle car.'

'I can understand why you think Houston might want his sister dead – that's easy, the money.' He grabbed a wing as he said, 'But why Acheson?'

'Because Houston himself admitted that the restaurant was having money problems. Irwin Acheson seems to have made a big investment in the place. Maybe the two of them saw Lisa's death as a convenient solution.' I tapped the tip of my soda bottle. 'Maybe,' I said, 'they even killed Houston's aunt, Willow Willoughby.' I nodded, allowing myself to go with the thought. 'First kill the aunt then kill the sister. Neat.'

'Sure,' agreed Brad, some life finally coming back into his

eyes. It was about time he got over this whole speeding ticket melodrama. 'It makes sense, doesn't it?'

I nodded.

'Murder the aunt then the sister and all the money flows to Houston.'

'And our Mr Acheson.'

'And our Mr Acheson,' Brad said, appearing thoughtful. 'I wonder how this Willow Willoughby died . . .'

I grinned. I'd been hoping he'd finally come around to that thought. 'You're a reporter,' I replied. I fluttered my eyelashes. Scarlet O'Hara, eat your heart out. 'I bet you could find out.'

'Absolutely,' he said self-assuredly.

I took a pull on my orange soda. 'Tell me, what did VV have to say?'

'Veronica Vargas?' Brad smirked. 'Don't worry, I left out the part about her boyfriend ministering to you on the streets of Table Rock.'

The corner of my mouth moved down in displeasure. 'I wasn't worried about that.' Actually, I was quite worried about that. In a town the size of Table Rock one had to worry about the gossipmongers. Who else besides him had seen our little . . . what? Kiss? Rescue? Special moment?

No. Car accident. That's all it was.

If VV found out I'd been in the arms of her boyfriend, albeit all completely harmless, mind you – though people might exaggerate what they'd seen, people *always* exaggerate, especially in such circumstances – what evil might she be tempted to deliver my way? With her clout, she could she have the café shut down for some sort of health-code violation.

I vowed to get in early one day soon and give the place a good cleaning.

'You know what she's like. She likes to play things close to the vest.' He jiggled his brow. 'She did say the police had more evidence than what had been released to the public.'

I leaned forward. 'Really, like what?'

Brad shrugged. 'She wouldn't say. Believe me, I tried to get more out of her but it was hopeless. I can tell you this, though—' He stopped and took a swig of beer. I suppressed the urge to scream.

'What?' I got ready to throw a buffalo wing at him.

He held up a palm in surrender. 'She thinks Johnny Wolfe did it.'

I snorted. 'That's ridiculous.'

'I'm just telling you what she told me. And she said she's convinced that Johnny killed Lisa Willoughby. Well, Johnny and Clive.'

'She thinks they did it together?'

Brad snatched the wing from my fingers. 'Yep. She figures Johnny did the deed and Clive helped cover it up. She thinks he got you to go out to Navajo Junction as part of their murder plot.'

'Preposterous,' I spat. 'The guys wouldn't do that.'

Brad chomped into the wing as he spoke. 'Ms Vargas thinks they would. She told me she was going to see that attorney Lisa had hired to sue Johnny and Clive and The Hitching Post. Today, in fact.' He glanced at his watch. It was after nine in the evening. 'This afternoon.'

'I wonder what she learned.' My fingers drummed the oak tabletop.

Brad smiled. 'You could ask her.'

'Very funny. What should I do, go knock on her door later tonight like I wanted to borrow a cup of sugar and say, "Oh, by the way, what did Lisa Willoughby's attorney tell you about her case against Johnny Wolfe and Clive Rothschild?"'

'Yeah,' Brad nodded, fingering his beer, 'you could do that. Or,' he flashed his teeth, 'you could just walk over to her table and ask her now.'

I blanched. 'What?'

He jabbed his chin to the right. 'I said you could go ask her right now.' He aimed his eyes across the room. 'She's sitting right over there in that booth in the corner with her boyfriend.'

My head shot around and color rose to my cheeks. VV and Detective Highsmith were canoodling side by side on a bench in the corner all right. I slid down in my seat. 'Why didn't you say something earlier?'

He shrugged. 'They only walked in a few minutes ago.'

I ordered Brad to take me home.

'So soon?'

'Yes,' I said, snatching up my purse. 'I don't think Acheson is going to show.' It was why we'd gone to Hopping Mad in the first place. 'Besides, I have to be up early tomorrow for the Labor of Love.'

'You're participating? Good for you.'

'It wasn't my idea. I was sort of talked into it.' Talked into, coerced . . . put on the spot. All I knew was that it was costing me a bundle. On the plus side, all the money raised was going to some very worthy charities around town. 'I'm supposed to be there practically before dawn to set up.'

Brad threw some money on the tabletop. 'I'll be covering the event for the paper. Maybe we can hook up afterward?'

I stepped out onto the sidewalk. I hadn't realized how stifling the air inside the pub had become. 'Sure,' I said without thinking. 'Sounds good.'

Brad dropped me off at my door. Carole Two mrowled and wrapped herself around my legs. To settle her down I tossed her a treat from a bag on the counter. It was some sort of vegan cat treat called VegOut Cat that my sister, Donna, had brought over for her.

Incredibly – though the treats were made from such disparate and distasteful-sounding ingredients that included brown rice, corn protein, extruded soybeans, peas, flax seed, molasses and clay – she seemed to love the stuff. I gave her a couple more, rubbed her tummy, brushed my teeth, put on my PJs and headed off to bed with the cat one step ahead.

It was only a double-sized bed and Mom was already sprawled across more than half of it. I made do, too tired to care. It had been a long day.

Who knew it was going to be an even longer night?

THIRTY-ONE

I fell out of bed and scratched around on the chair by the door for my phone. A glance at the clock told me it was one a.m. Who freaking texts at one a.m.? I mean, besides the Grim

Reaper. I quickly looked over my shoulder. Nope, no Grim Reaper. I breathed a sigh of relief and got a mouthful of cat tail. I stuck my finger over my nose to stop me from sneezing. I shooed Carole Two away and wiped cat hair off my tongue.

The phone bleeped again to announce the incoming text. In this case, the alert also worked double-duty as a homing device. Following the electric bleep, I grabbed the phone from between my pile of dirty clothes and crawled to the living room, listening to Mom grunt and toss in her sleep.

Carole Two stuck her butt in my face once more and I scooped her up to prevent her doing it yet again. I pushed the hair from my face and looked at the text message. It was from Laura. All it read was: Maggie r u up? Something strange going here.

I rubbed my face. Something strange? What the devil did that mean? I composed a reply: It's middle of night – what r u talking about?

I about had a heart attack when the phone suddenly rang loudly and vibrated in my hand. I dropped the cat and answered it quickly so I wouldn't wake Mom. I wasn't in the mood to start making explanations. Especially when I didn't know what was going on.

'Oh, good, you're awake,' Laura said.

'I am now,' I grunted. 'What's up?'

'I don't know. I've been hearing lots of noises downstairs, though, coming from Lisa's condo. Sounds like fighting. I thought you'd want to know.'

I gulped in dry air, my heart pounding and my head aching. I was exhausted but curious. I glanced toward the bedroom. Mom was still asleep. I could borrow her car and be back before she ever knew I'd been gone. 'Be right there.'

I ended the call and, moving stealthily, pulled on an old pair of cotton candy-colored pink sweats. I stole Mom's VW key from her purse. Carole Two gave me the evil eye. 'Whose side are you on?' I whispered. 'Mom's? I took you in.'

I gave her a couple of treats – a bribe to keep her mouth shut – and was on my way.

There was a light on in Lisa Willoughby's condo when I arrived at Meadow Reach Condominiums. The light upstairs at Laura's place was on, too. I went there first and rapped gently on her door. Laura answered in a vintage pair of blue jeans that hung on her hips and a long-sleeved blue flannel shirt with the sleeves pushed up to her elbows. 'I'm glad you came.' She pulled me inside.

'So what's the deal?' I felt a little out of my league what with her managing to look so svelte and me so . . . svelteless in my wrinkled and coffee-stained sweatsuit.

'I'm not sure,' Laura replied. Her cornflower-blue eyes were stretched with worry. She held a coffee mug in her hand and pushed it toward me. 'Coffee?'

'Why not?' I reached for the mug. 'It doesn't look like I'm going to be getting any sleep tonight, anyway.'

Laura chuckled. 'That makes two of us.' Her eyes looked a little puffy but otherwise she seemed to be holding up way better than I was. Maybe she was used to these late hours. I wasn't.

I followed her to the kitchen where she poured herself a cup of coffee from a sleek machine resting on a gray granite countertop. 'I know it's quiet now,' Laura began as she fell into the chair beside me at the small dinette, 'but you should have heard the racket a little while ago.'

'What do you think it was?' I helped myself to an Oreo.

'I'm not sure but I definitely heard arguing. I recognized Houston's voice. But the other fellow . . .' She shook her head. 'I'm not sure who that was. He had a foreign accent.'

I sat straighter. 'A bit of an Irish lilt, perhaps?'

Laura nodded. 'Yeah, maybe. You think it was Mr Acheson?'

Sounded like a falling out among thieves. 'Houston Willoughby and Irwin Acheson had probably been fighting over the murder and the loot. Dissention among crooks and all that. You know how it is.'

Laura smiled. 'Like in the movies?'

'Exactly.' I banged the table. 'The lights are still on downstairs.' I set down my mug. 'I say we go bust up their little murderfest.'

'We?' Laura looked rather dubious.

'Sure, we. Why not, we?'

'Why not?' Laura's eyes widened. 'Because they're two big angry men. Because if you're right, they murdered Houston's sister in cold blood—'

'Maybe her aunt, too.'

Laura's brow furrowed. 'Really?'

'Yep – at least it's one theory. I haven't confirmed it yet.' I was waiting to see what Brad Smith dug up before making up my mind. 'But I'd say it's a definite possibility.'

Laura grunted and refilled our mugs. 'All the more reason to stay where we are.'

'Are you kidding? What did you call me for?'

'Well . . .'

'You want to know what's going on, don't you?' I zeroed in on her eyes. 'You don't want to be sleeping with a murderer or two right downstairs from you, do you?'

'I – I suppose not.'

'Come on.' I shoved back my chair. 'We can handle a couple of restaurateurs. We are women; we are strong.' I flexed my bicep. It was a good thing I was wearing a baggy sweatshirt: it hid the fact that I had no biceps to speak of. Certainly nothing like those guns Irwin Acheson was packing. I was definitely outgunned.

Laura slowly rose, grabbing an Oreo for courage. 'Actually . . .'

'Actually what?' I grabbed another cookie and popped it in my mouth.

'There was a third voice. A man, for sure. He sounded Spanish.'

I stopped mid-chew. 'Shpanishh?' I swallowed. 'Spanish?'

'Yes.'

This was a new piece to the puzzle. Who was this mysterious Spanish partner of theirs? More than ever, I wanted to bust up the party downstairs. As if to taunt us, the sounds of shouting started up again. I looked at the floor. 'Come on!' I raced downstairs with Laura at my heels. Through the half-open curtains I saw Houston and Irwin standing nose-to-nose arguing in the living room. Fists were balled.

I grabbed the front door handle.

'Don't you think you should—'

I threw open the door and listened to the hinges protest as wood cracked against stucco.

'Knock first,' panted Lisa at my back.

Houston and Irwin froze mid-macho poses.

'Mind if we join the party, boys?' I smiled.

The two men stepped apart, their eyes blinking. From the blood vessels snaking red along their eyeballs I'd say they'd each had a beer – or six.

Irwin looked at Houston. 'What's she doing here?'

Houston shrugged. He looked haggard. I noticed dark sweat stains running along his armpits, staining his shirt.

Irwin turned his eyes to me. 'Come to see me?' He winked my way.

Yuck.

Laura spoke up. 'You're creating quite a disturbance. You woke me.'

'Yeah,' I said. 'What's with all the shouting?' I waved my arms about. 'You're keeping the neighbors up.'

'Big deal,' snorted Houston. He waved his hand back at me. 'A bunch of old fuddy-duddies.'

I saw Laura bristle out of the corner of my eye. I guess she didn't like the *old* crack. I didn't blame her. I cast a chiseled look at Houston. 'What if one of them decides to call the police?'

Houston scowled. 'Shut the door, will you.'

Laura was closest to the door. She looked at me. I shrugged and told her to go ahead. I didn't think we were in any real danger – at least, not any real immediate danger. 'So you want to tell us what's going on?'

'Our business,' quipped Irwin, 'is none of your business.' He pointed his finger at me.

'Why don't you shut up?' Houston said wearily to Irwin. He fell into an armchair and sighed. 'This is all your fault anyway. You let him get away.'

I scratched my head. 'Let *who* get away?'

'The guy who broke in here, of course. Who did you think?'

They guy who broke in here? I thought I'd caught two murderers arguing over their spoils. What the heck was going on? I paced up and down the carpet. 'Are you trying to tell us that someone broke into Lisa's condo?'

Houston nodded. 'That's right. I thought you knew. You said you heard the shouting.' He looked at Laura. 'Sorry about the noise, Laura.'

Laura frowned. 'A burglary?'

'Yeah, we came home and there he was,' Houston said. 'I figure it was the same guy that broke in the other night. I can't tell you how mad it made me.'

The same guy as the other night? Oh, he meant me and Johnny. Far be it for me to correct his misconception.

'I'll say,' chuckled Irwin. He'd grabbed a six-pack from the fridge and waved it around the room. 'Anybody care to join me?'

Houston peeled off a can and popped it open. 'I caught him in the bedroom red-handed. I asked him what he was doing. He had one of the dresser drawers open. He looked surprised.'

'I'll bet,' I said. 'What did he do then?'

Houston shrugged a shoulder. 'Got all hostile. Started yelling. Opening and slamming the drawers.'

'Weird,' said Laura.

Houston continued, 'Yeah, said he was looking for something. But he wouldn't say what.'

'Looking for something?' I repeated.

Houston nodded. 'I tried to stop him but he wasn't quitting. And babbling in Spanish the whole time. Sounded angry.' Houston wet his lips. 'I was pretty angry too. I mean, some stranger rummaging around in my sister's stuff. I could see the busted screen on the floor. He'd climbed in through the window.' Houston spat. 'Gutsy.'

'I was out here,' Irwin explained, 'in front of the TV. I heard Houston yelling and caught him wrestling with the little guy in the bedroom.'

Little guy? What did that mean? Practically every guy was little compared to Irwin Acheson.

Houston's face soured. 'Yeah, well, little or not, that guy put up a fight.'

Irwin ground his fist into his opposite hand. 'He stopped fighting when I showed up.'

Houston laughed but it wasn't a pleasant laugh. 'Yeah, he stopped all right. And then when I told you to keep an eye on him until we could figure out what he was doing in here and maybe call the police, you let him get away.'

Maybe call the police? I'd definitely be calling the cops if I caught an intruder in my bedroom. If I didn't die of fright first.

'You let him get away?' I said incredulously, looking at all those muscles on Irwin.

Acheson blushed and looked at his feet. 'I only turned my head for a second—'

'Yeah,' quipped Houston, waving toward the entryway, 'and one second was all it took for that old guy to run out the door.' He shook his head and took a swig of Miller. No relation. 'Now we may never find out who he is or what he wanted.'

'Believe you me,' Irwin said, 'if I ever see that scrawny Mexican again he won't get away from me a second time.'

'Mexican?' I said. So Laura was right. She had heard someone yelling in Spanish too.

'Yeah,' Irwin answered. 'I don't know what he was saying but he was sure saying a lot of it.'

'No kidding,' mumbled Houston.

Laura toyed with a dry paintbrush near the easel in the front corner. 'Who's the guy on the canvas?' She ran the brush along the edges of the unfinished chin.

'Who cares? It's all trash now.' Houston rose. He draped his arm over Laura's shoulder. 'I really am sorry about all this. Let me make it up to you. Tomorrow.'

Laura shook her head. 'Sorry, tomorrow's a really busy day.'

Not to mention, tomorrow *was* today.

'OK, Sunday then.'

Laura set down the brush. 'I don't think so.'

'Are you sure? We could—'

Irwin laughed loudly. 'Give it up, man,' he chided. 'Can't you see you've been shot down?'

Houston shot his business partner a look that would have withered a lesser man. Not Irwin Acheson, though. He remained unbent, guzzling beer.

Laura's hand went to her mouth and smothered a yawn. 'I think we should be going. Tomorrow is going to be a long day, Maggie.'

I nodded. 'A very long day.' In fact, it was nearly time to get up. Ugh.

'Next time we get together in the middle of the night,' Irwin hollered, 'let's make it just you and me, Maggie!'

I stiffened and walked faster.

Houston held Laura back at the door. 'About tonight: it won't happen again.'

Laura nodded. 'I hope they catch whoever it was. You really should report the break-in to the police.'

'What would I tell them? That some unidentified Hispanic male broke in then took off when I caught him?' Houston chewed his lip. 'At least he didn't get anything.' He massaged the back of his neck. 'I sure would like to know what he was after, though.'

Me, too.

'Next time I see him,' bellowed Irwin, 'I'll hold him by his skanky ponytail until the fuzz show up!'

I paused on the front step. 'Did you say ponytail?'

Houston and Irwin nodded. 'Why does that mean something to you, Maggie?' Houston asked. 'Do you know this guy?'

I wasn't sure but somewhere, in the deep recesses of my mind, I had a hunch that I did.

THIRTY-TWO

C arole Two mrowled for her breakfast. I shook my head and yawned. 'OK, OK.' Mom was already out. I fed the cat, dressed and got moving. I felt like I'd been hit by a truck and the sandman. In that order. It was going to be one long day. My body was bruised and scraped from what might or might not have been an accidental fall on a hard flight of steps. I hadn't had three hours' sleep.

I still hadn't figured out whether Cody was clumsy or dangerous – or both. And I didn't know where he'd been at the time of Lisa Willoughby's murder. I was keeping him near the top of my list of suspects. I admittedly had absolutely no motive I could attach to him but I was putting him there anyway. Besides, he was younger than me and drove a snazzy new Corvette. He deserved to be on the list.

The only good news was that I had borrowed Mom's Bug and returned it unscathed with her none the wiser. I guess all that yoga made her a good sleeper. I rode my bike through the quiet predawn streets, nothing but the hum of my Schwinn's tires rolling along the pavement. I parked the bike in the café storeroom, grabbed an apron and the few supplies I could carry and started over to Table Rock Town Square on foot.

The lights were on across the street at Karma Koffee. That meant I'd probably be having predawn company – Trish and Rob Gregory. I'd have preferred Vampira and the Wolf Man. Heck, I'd have preferred my dead ex-husband, Brian.

Laura was waiting for me when I arrived. The whole square was buzzing with early birds setting up their tents for the weekend event. Strings of soft white lights were strung along the rooflines of each tent, giving the square a festive, holiday appearance. Samantha Higgins, the Labor of Love chairperson was conspicuously absent. Next year maybe I could chair the event and sleep in late too.

Laura smiled and lofted a steaming paper cup of coffee as I approached.

'Merry Labor of Love,' I said, stuffing a frown away. Laura's cup was a medium-sized Karma Koffee to-go cup. To make matters worse she had one of their muffins on a Karma Koffee-branded paper tray in her left hand. Crumbs clung to her glossy lower lip. Moist, delicious, succulent, flaky crumbs . . . I steeled myself.

Laura ran her tongue along her lips. 'You made it.'

I yawned and set my supplies on the tabletop. 'I see you've been busy.' I hugged her. 'Thanks for coming.' I waved my hand over the table. 'And for bringing all this.'

Laura nodded. 'I didn't sleep much after—' She cast a glance toward Rob and Trish Gregory lingering nearby. 'You know, last night.'

'Same here,' I admitted. I had a feeling I should know who'd broken into Lisa's condo, but the answer wasn't coming to me. Somebody with a ponytail. Helpful, but not very. That could mean anybody from a six-year-old in pigtails to half the hippies in Table Rock.

Houston and Irwin both agreed that this guy said he was looking for something. The big question was what? Was there something Lisa had that was worth stealing? TV, jewelry? If I could figure out what I might figure out who.

'Did anything happen after I left your place?'

'No.' Laura set down her coffee and muffin. My fingers twitched toward it. 'It was quiet downstairs the rest of the night.' She yawned. 'Thankfully. You know,' Laura said, arranging items on the tabletop, 'I can't help wondering if those two didn't make up the whole burglar thing.'

'I doubt it.'

'Why do you say that?'

I pulled a face. 'You've seen those two.' I sidled over to the table, my back to Laura's coffee and muffin. What was that? Pumpkin-maple? With a drizzle of icing on top? I love pumpkin-maple.

Laura's brow arched.

'You think they're smart enough to invent a story like that and,' I said, holding up my hand to stop her retort, 'keep their stories straight the whole time?' My hand snaked behind my back like it had a mind of its own.

Laura grinned. 'I guess not.'

'I know not. And I keep wondering what this mystery man that Houston and Irwin saw was up to. Maybe Lisa kept a secret journal.' I could feel the half-devoured muffin now; my fingertips crawled along its crumbling side.

'Maybe,' Laura agreed. Her hand suddenly shot behind me and snatched up the muffin. I watched it go down her throat in two bites. She held out the remaining sliver in her fingertips. 'Did you want some?'

'No,' I sighed. 'You finish it.'

Laura nodded, swallowed and licked her fingers. 'Where would you like the fryer?'

We adjusted the deep fryer on the center of the table and I laid the drip tray to the right. 'Who knew what secrets it might hold?' I added a jug of oil to the well of the twin fryer basket appliance.

'What might hold?'

'Lisa Willoughby's secret journal. Like maybe the key to her killer. Did Houston say anything about Lisa keeping a diary?'

Laura shook her head. 'Not that he mentioned to me.'

'Could you ask him?' I snatched some paper cups from a box on the grass and set them near the three coffee urns.

Laura groaned. 'I'd rather not.'

I turned to grab an electric cord off the lawn and bumped

into Rob Gregory, who had his hand on the same cord. Rob and Trish, in matching khaki trousers and green polo shirts, snarled and said, 'You're late with the rent on your apartment again, Miller!' In unison, no less.

'I know, I know.' I tugged at the cord. 'Do you mind?' Rob and his wife, Trish, are a discouragingly handsome couple who act like a couple of love-struck teenagers around one another. They were young, tan, fit and prosperous.

The Gregorys weren't keen on having my beignet café across the street from their own established coffee and bakery. Then again, it hadn't seemed to be putting a dent in their business. Rob has short, wavy brown hair with sun-bleached streaks at the temples that fall casually around his rectangular face. His hairline seems to be slowly receding, but other days I feel like it's halfway down his forehead, moving in and out like the tide.

Trish's hair is two shades darker and much longer, hanging down to her shoulders. Light freckles dusted the bridge of her nose. Karma Koffee-branded visors completed their look. I'd forgotten my visor at the café. Maybe I'd send Aubrey back for it later.

Aubrey had been working for the Gregorys when I'd met her. She'd asked me for a job. I couldn't afford to hire her but neither could I afford to say no and miss out on a chance to stick it to my competition slash landlords.

'This one's ours,' Rob replied, pulling back on the electric cable. 'That's yours.' He pointed his free hand toward an orange coiled cord under my table.

'Fine.' I had one more day before the late fee kicked in on the apartment rent – let them wait. Caitie Conklin's Salon de Belezza booth on the opposite side was still dark and empty. I guess she figured nobody wanted a trim at six a.m.

She was right.

And maybe I'd picked the wrong business to go into. Maybe I should have opened a salon. I'd worked in one for years, after all.

The big corner tent occupied by The Hitching Post, on the other hand, was abuzz with activity. Bright spotlights burned holes in the darkness and a half-dozen workers were bustling to the orders of Clive and Johnny. Looked like it was going to be a busy day for the guys.

I'd left instructions for Mom and Kelly. They'd be operating the café while Aubrey and I ran things at the tent. Out of the corner of my eye I caught sight of a lumbering figure in a loose white shirt and baggy jeans heading my way. My heart jumped. 'Oh, no,' I moaned as the shadowy figure took shape, looking more like a zombie straight out of the Living Dead. 'Brian,' I sighed, 'what are you doing here?'

My dead ex-husband's face lit up in a hundred-watt smile. He thrust his hands in his back pockets. 'I had a delivery.' He jerked his thumb toward the truck at the curb: Miller Transport. I should have spotted it earlier. Oh, well.

'Dry goods and soda for this Labor of Love thing. Plus I got a monthly contract with MacHobb's Aerospace Manufacturing over in Prescott. Pickup at Phoenix International Airport and drop off at their facility.' He spun his head around. 'Looks like it's going to be quite a shindig.'

'It's not a shindig,' I replied. 'It's a charity event.' And it looked like Brian would be in the vicinity monthly. Wonderful. Not.

'What-ev.' Brian smiled at Laura. 'Who's this?'

I scowled. 'This is my friend, Laura Duval.'

Laura held out her hand.

I saw him glance at her ring finger. 'Unmarried, I see.'

'Yeah, but you aren't,' I interjected. 'How's the new wife?'

Laura and I exchanged a look. 'Pleased to meet you, Brian,' she said.

'Wait till you get to know him better,' I mumbled.

Brian shook his head. 'Aren't you ever going to let go, Mags?'

I hate it when anybody calls me Mags. And only Brian does it. 'Aren't you ever going to go home?' I retorted. 'To your wife and stepkids?'

Brian dropped Laura's hand. 'Don't mind her. She's always cranky in the morning. Speaking of which,' his eyes bounced along the table, 'got any coffee ready? Maybe a beignet or three?' he asked hopefully, patting his stomach.

'Sorry,' I said. 'We won't be ready for at least half an hour. I expect you'll be halfway home to Phoenix by then.'

Brian shook his head. 'I'm staying the day. The wife's busy with the kids at her folks' house in Scottsdale so I thought I'd hang out.' He sidled between Laura and me. 'If you have some free time later maybe we can hang out together.'

'Sure,' I said, giving Brian a shove in the opposite direction, 'why don't you go wait for me? Like at the bottom of the Grand Canyon.'

THIRTY-THREE

'**S**o that's the ex, huh?' Laura said as we watched the big dope shuffle off, hands in his pockets.

'Yep. Sorry you had to see that.'

Laura took my elbow. 'So,' she wriggled her eyebrows, 'anybody new on the horizon? Like Brad Smith, maybe?' She filled the napkin dispenser. 'What's with the two of you, anyway?'

'Nothing,' I said. At least, I thought it was nothing. 'I mean, we're sort of friends, is all. Not even that really.'

'If you say so.'

'I don't have time for romance right now.' I filled the second napkin dispenser a little more ruthlessly than she had the other.

Laura wasn't letting up. 'No? That's not what folks are saying who saw that big strong detective carrying you in his arms and making out with you in the middle of the street.'

The heat rose in a whoosh to my face. My cheeks were redder than a couple of sunburned red beets. Thank goodness the sun was barely up. If folks noticed, they would think I'd developed some hideous disease.

'But-but . . .' I spluttered. Talk about exaggeration! What had people been saying? And how long would it be before VV Vargas found out and sought revenge on me? My pulse quickened. 'Making out with me? Is that really what you heard?' I dropped my voice as I glanced furtively around.

Laura nodded. 'Afraid so.' She squeezed my wrist. 'You mean it's true?'

'What's true?' Aubrey stood on the other side of the folding table. She tossed my visor at my chest. It thunked and fell to the ground. Laura picked it up and handed it back to me. 'What's true?' Aubrey repeated, looking from me to Laura and back again.

My mouth was too dry for words.

'About that detective and Maggie,' Laura answered. 'Making out in the street.'

'Oh, yeah,' Aubrey waved her hand, 'that. No wonder they call it Smile Street.'

'You knew?' I blushed all over again.

'Sure, everybody's talking about it.'

I pushed my hands against my hips. 'Well, it's not what any of you think!' Everybody. That meant Mom. That meant Donna and Andy. Did it mean my nephews too?

'If you say so,' Aubrey said, tying on her apron. 'Oh, hey, good morning, Mr and Mrs Gregory!' She gave a princess-like turn of the hand.

The Gregorys barely acknowledged her. If looks could kill, poor, sweet Aubrey would be a smudge on the ground right about now. It seemed the Gregorys held a grudge.

'What about Brad?' Aubrey asked, batting her lashes all innocent-like.

I narrowed my eyes at her. 'What about Brad?'

'What does he think about you and the detective smooching in the street?' Aubrey's hand flew to her lips as she suppressed a giggle.

'Oh, there's absolutely nothing going on between Brad and our Maggie,' Laura said. 'So I'm sure he didn't mind at all.'

How I wished to be an ostrich and bury my head in the ground.

'That's funny,' Aubrey replied. 'I thought he was sort of sweet on you.'

'Well,' I said out of the side of my mouth as I kicked the dirt, 'Brad did say he was going to be here today.' I ran my fingers through my hair. 'We sort of agreed to meet up.'

'Ooh,' chorused Laura and Aubrey.

I tossed a beignet at them. They dodged left and right and the beignet hit Trish Gregory on the bridge of her nose. 'Sorry!' I cried, trying hard not to laugh. 'Should have ducked,' I muttered under my breath as I averted my eyes.

'How's it going, ladies?' Cosmic Ray, Table Rock's own

visitor center greeter – and possible visitor from another planet – appeared before my eyes. 'Beautiful day for a little love, isn't it?'

I agreed. Cosmic was dressed *conservatively* in a tie-dye Woodstock Summer Of Love T-shirt and baggy, olive-green cargo shorts. Birkenstocks kept his feet from touching the ground. A raspberry beret sat atop his domed skull. If this was San Francisco and the Summer of '69, he'd blend in perfectly. Heck, he'd probably be taken for a member of the Grateful Dead. In fact, some Table Rockers swear Jerry Garcia is hanging out here in Table Rock in his Eternal Afterlife. And I'm not talking about inside pint ice-cream containers.

Laura bade hello to Cosmic and goodbye to us. 'Time to get to the store.'

Cosmic Ray turned his head toward the center of the square for a moment. Just long enough for me to notice his pigtails wrapped in raspberry-colored scrunchies. Now pigtails are not ponytails, but would Houston Willoughby and Irwin Acheson know the difference? Possibly not. They were men, after all. Probably didn't know a beehive from a blowout.

Could what Irwin described as a ponytail have been Cosmic and his tight pigtails? And just because I'd only seen him in pigtails didn't mean he sometimes might not sport a solitary ponytail instead.

'I'll take an order of beignets and a large coffee.' He whipped out a worn brown leather wallet, wet his thumb and plucked out a few bills.

'Coming right up, sir.' Aubrey set the money in the cashbox and counted out his change.

I got busy on the beignets, keeping one eye on the pastry, the other on Cosmic. 'Say,' I began, turning the dough over in the oil as they reached the golden brown I was looking for, 'you've lived here a long time, right?'

'Yep.' He nodded.

'Did you grow up in this area?' Or on Venus, maybe?

'Casa Grande, down near Phoenix. I moved up here after I graduated. Went to college a couple of years in Flagstaff and sort of drifted this way.'

I nodded. I knew Casa Grande; it lies east of the Sonoran Desert and I'd been there on a couple of occasions. Maybe that was where his flying saucer had landed. There's not a lot of folks out in the Sonoran Desert. Flying saucer pilots must love it.

He certainly didn't look Hispanic, but still . . . 'Your folks grow up in the Southwest?'

Aubrey shot me a look. I shot her one back that said to mind her own business as I tossed Cosmic Ray's beignets onto a paper plate.

'Mom and Pop were from Illinois. Mom's health was poor so they moved out to the desert when I was but a young 'un.'

'Probably learned to speak Spanish then.'

He chuckled. 'Enough to order a *cerveza*.'

I smiled back to set him at ease and keep his guard down. I was slick. 'I suppose you knew Lisa Willoughby?'

He hesitated for a moment before replying. 'You mean the young girl who was murdered?' Cosmic blinked and rubbed his wrist. 'Can't say that I did.' He blinked once more. 'Well, you ladies enjoy your day. I hope you like the tent I picked specially for you.'

I glanced at the Gregorys' tent. They seemed to be raking in the orders with a line twice as long as ours. Who was I kidding? They had a line. Maggie's Beignet Café's temporary stand had none.

On the other side, the Salon de Belezza was pulling in a steady stream of customers, too. Caitie'd pulled down a canvas divider between our tents. I wasn't sure if it was because she didn't want to see me or if she simply felt her clients expected a certain amount of privacy while getting clipped.

And getting clipped was exactly what they were getting at the prices Caitie Conklin charges. I'd let her cut my hair once and was still digging myself out of debt. I blew a strand of hair from my face. Maybe I'd give myself a trim later. I was pretty sure I hadn't lost my touch. Of course, I could always practice on the cat first, or Mom.

Fortunately, once the day warmed up and the crowds filled the square, we managed to hold our own in the beignet versus pastry and muffin wars. I'd even managed to snatch one of those

Heaven's Building Block muffins off the Karma Koffee table when the Gregorys weren't looking.

A girl can't live on beignets alone.

Aubrey elbowed me and I placed several dollar bills under their cream pitcher to cover the cost. I told her I was going to do it anyway.

During a late-afternoon break in the action, Aubrey pulled me aside. 'What was that all about before?' she demanded.

'What was what all about?'

'Why were you grilling Cosmic Ray earlier?'

'Grilling?'

'Yeah, like he was a criminal or an illegal alien or something.'

I took a seat in one of the folding chairs and motioned for Aubrey to do the same. It had been a long day and my feet were practically screaming to be let out of their misery. I explained how some Hispanic male had purportedly broken into Lisa Willoughby's condo looking for something the night before and been caught in the act by her brother, Houston. 'From what Houston and Irwin said, the guy was about Cosmic Ray's age too.' I pulled off my sandals and rubbed my aching feet.

'Sounds to me like there's a lot of dangerous activity going on around town, Maggie.' Aubrey dropped her voice. 'If you don't mind me saying so, I think you should truly, truly stay out of it. Let the police do their job.'

'I'm not sure they're all that competent, to tell you the truth.' I gestured with my head toward the bandstand. Detective Highsmith had his arms wrapped around VV Vargas. A group of teenagers and several adults were setting up on the stage. The Hitching Post's bridal fashion show had run there earlier. 'Look at him,' I complained. 'Instead of out trying to solve a murder, Table Rock's lone detective is playing lovey-dovey with the prosecuting attorney.'

'Yeah, there's some serious PDA going on there.'

I watched them move slowly hip to hip as the Table Rock High School band started banging out a Broadway show tune. 'What?'

'PDA – public display of affection,' Aubrey explained.

I didn't mind the explanation but did she have to make me

sound so ancient? 'I see.' I slapped the lid of the cashbox down. There was definitely too much PDA going on.

'Not jealous, are you?' Aubrey teased. The red sun set off the highlights in her strawberry-blonde hair.

'Of course not.' I snatched a towel and viciously wiped the tabletop. 'I just don't want to see innocent people get hurt.' I huffed. 'Or killers go free.'

Mom pedaled up on my pink beauty and parked it behind the tent. 'The café is closed for the day so I thought I'd come and help out here.' She planted her hands on her hips. 'It was slow over there anyway. This seems to be where all the action is today.'

I pecked her on the cheek. 'Thanks, Mom.'

Keith showed up next with a keyboard under his arm. I knew he was there to see Aubrey but I got to him first. 'Hi, Keith,' I said, gifting him my biggest smile.

'Hello, Ms Miller.' He looked around me to Aubrey.

'In the band, eh?'

He nodded and shifted the keyboard from one arm to the other. 'That's right. We're on later. You're going to be there, right?' He was looking at Aubrey again.

'I wouldn't miss it,' she said.

'What do you know about Cody Ryan? He's in the band with you, right?'

'Yep.' Keith leaned the keyboard against the table. 'Cody's a good guy. Comes from money but acts like a regular guy, you know?'

Aubrey pulled Keith out of my grasp before I could ask any more questions. She loaded him up with beignets and coffee and sent him on his way. 'Why were you giving Keith the third degree?'

'I was not giving the young man the third degree. I was simply trying to find out what insight he might have into Cody Ryan. I don't know why you're being so protective of him,' I said. 'Just because you're smitten with the boy.'

Aubrey pulled a face. 'Smitten? Who says that?' She grinned wickedly. 'How old did you say you were, Maggie?'

I growled and turned to our next customer, saving Aubrey from what would, no doubt, have been my barbed and witty reply. And dealing with the customer would give me time to compose one.

A little later, I was coming back from the portable restrooms the town had set up on the edge of the square when I caught the sound of furtive voices, one of which I recognized. I froze in my tracks. The voice belonged to Cody Ryan. But who was the other guy? The voices were coming from the other side of a pickup with a faded yellow camper shell. I tried peering at them through the windows but dirty beige curtains blocked the view. I crept around the side, stooped over and peeked around the rust-pitted chrome front bumper.

It was Cody Ryan all right and I still hadn't forgotten how he might or might not have accidently on purpose tried to push me down a flight of stairs. 'Don't worry,' he was saying. 'My band gets off around ten-thirty. I'll take care of things then. You'll get your money.'

'I'd better,' snarled the other man. He was short, squat and hairy. I suspected he contained an orangutan gene or two. 'What about Miller?'

Cody smiled, a determined look on his face. 'Don't worry.' His hand landed on the other man's shoulder. 'After tonight, Miller is not going to be a problem.'

A chill ran up my spine. Jiminy freaking cricket! Cody Ryan was seriously going to try to kill me!

The two men shook hands and I tiptoed away before I was discovered. No point getting killed now and putting him off his timetable. And mine!

I had a long life planned. I had to do something. I had to tell somebody!

THIRTY-FOUR

I spotted Andy traipsing along the line of booths, pausing to inspect a blue-green glass globe at an artist's display table. 'Andy,' I said between quick breaths, 'quick, you've got to help me.'

He pulled me between two tents. 'What's wrong, Maggie?' He was smiling but I saw concern in his eyes.

I pointed. 'It's Cody Ryan. I saw . . . I heard,' I gulped, 'him talking to some strange man, a dangerous-looking man.'

'Yeah?' he drawled 'So?'

'So, he – Cody, that is, threatened to kill me!'

Andy cocked his head to one side. 'Because he caught you spying on him? I can get why he'd be mad, but still—'

'No,' I whispered. 'That's just it. He didn't catch me listening in. I overheard the two men talking.'

'What exactly did Cody Ryan say, Maggie?' He was beginning to sound skeptical.

'He said he was going to kill me.' I crossed my arms over my chest.

'No, Maggie.' Andy shook his head. 'Tell me *exactly* what he said.'

I frowned and blew out a breath. I thought carefully for a moment before replying. 'He said he was going to kill me. He said after tonight I wouldn't be a problem.'

'He said *you*?'

I nodded.

'Maggie Miller?'

I nodded once more.

'Why would he want to kill you? Did you steal and/or smash his car, too?'

'Very funny,' I snapped. 'Because he killed Lisa Willoughby and he knows I'm on to him and now he wants me dead, too.'

Andy's nose wrinkled. 'I thought you figured the brother did it?'

I pouted. Andy was right. I had figured that. But maybe I was wrong. 'Maybe they were in it together.'

'I don't know.' Andy rubbed his chin. 'Did Cody and Houston Willoughby even know one another?'

I chewed my lip in silence.

'It does seem to me that the brother had the most to gain,' Andy said. 'Looking past the fact that Lisa Willoughby had filed a million-dollar defamation suit against Johnny and Clive.'

I whistled. Wow, I hadn't realized it had been that much. That was a motive with a lot of zeroes after it.

'Listen, if this is true you need to be careful.' He jerked his head toward the bandstand. 'I see Detective Highsmith over there. Tell him what you told me.'

'OK, I will.'

Andy grabbed my hand as I started to leave. 'And don't go anywhere alone. Donna and I will see you get home safe tonight.' He looked over the crowd. 'She and the boys are around here somewhere. Plus, you've got Mom staying with you.'

I agreed to be careful and not leave without him, then pushed my way through the milling crowd trying to get closer to the detective. Besides, if Cody did manage to break into the apartment, Mom could incapacitate him by tricking him into performing some deep-dish-dog-praying-cat-scratching-Buddha-bending yoga position with her. That'd have him tied up in knots in no time.

By the time I'd managed to climb past the close-packed bodies to the spot I'd last spied the detective with VV, both were gone. I arched up on my tiptoes and saw no sign of them, though I did spot Cody again, this time in conversation with his future mother-in-law, Samantha Higgins.

'Everything all right, dear?' Mom asked as I returned to our stand.

'Sure, everything's fine, Mom.' No point worrying her. I wasn't due to be dead for hours yet. 'Just talking to Andy.'

'Oh, I thought maybe you were spending some time with that nice young reporter.'

'Brad?'

Mom nodded.

'We were going to hang out today but I called and told him tomorrow would be better.' The event ran late today but ended early tomorrow. Plus, Brad hadn't had time to dig up anything on the cause of Willow Willoughby's death yet. I told him he should make time. It could be important.

Mom grunted. 'You know, I was talking to Donna earlier at the café.'

'I didn't know she'd stopped by.'

'We're both wondering when you're going to settle down.'

'I am settled down, Mom.'

'Not settled down and married,' Mom pointedly replied.

'You mean like with kids.'

'I think having kids would be wonderful.' Aubrey clapped her hands together. 'I can't wait.'

Mom smiled. 'Like with Keith, maybe?'

Aubrey blushed. 'Maybe. I mean, not yet, but I don't want to wait until I'm too old.' She waved her arms at me. 'Not that I'm saying you're old, Maggie!'

She was all of twenty-three. I was most of thirty-nine. It wasn't like we were eons apart. 'This entire conversation is getting old,' I quipped, tossing some empty cups in the trash can under the table. 'Can we please change the subject?'

Mom nodded. 'The biological clock is ticking, dear. I mean, no offense, but you're not getting any younger.'

'And getting older by the minute,' I grumbled.

'Look at me,' Mom continued. 'I had you when I was about your age. Tick-tock.' Her finger swung side to side like the pendulum of a clock.

I'd been married. That's not to say I wasn't open to the idea of marriage again but, sheesh, what was the hurry? Couldn't I hit the snooze button on my biological clock just a few more times? 'Look, ladies,' I said, 'to tell you the truth I'm not so sure I'm ever going to find my HEAP.'

'Heap?' Aubrey asked.

Mom rolled her eyes. She'd heard this before.

'Yes, you know. My happily ever after person. HEAP.'

'That's ridiculous,' replied Mom, ever so sensitive of my feelings.

I was saved from having my biological clock counting down to zero and me going off like a two-ton bunker-busting bomb by the arrival of some customers. Not that these customers were much of an improvement because it was Houston and Irwin who approached the tent.

'Hey, hey,' said Irwin. 'What have we here?'

The two men looked two sheets – or six packs – to the wind. Why were these two men, whom I had originally thought enemies – or unfriendly business partners at best – suddenly so chummy?

'Can I get you anything?' I inquired. Like a couple of gallons of my special coffee?'

Irwin's bloodshot eyes sparkled. 'What's so special about it?'

'For one thing,' I said, folding my arms over my chest – I didn't like the way his eyes kept landing on my breasts, 'there's not a drop of alcohol in it.' I looked the two men up and down. 'I'd say it's been a while since either of you boys had a drink that could make that claim.'

Irwin cuffed Houston on the back. 'This lady's a hoot, isn't she?'

'A real hoot,' Houston said morosely.

'What's eating you?' I asked. Was he one of those guys who gets sullen when he drinks?

'I guess it's sinking in that Lisa is gone.' Houston rubbed a knuckle under his eye. 'I'm sure going to miss her.' He shook his head. 'First Aunt Willow, now Lisa.'

Yeah, quite a tragic coincidence that. He could go lie in his bed, resting his head on a pillow stuffed with hundred-dollar bills and wallow in his misfortune.

Irwin ordered two plates of beignets and coffees from Aubrey. She got the coffees. I prepped the beignets. 'When's the funeral?' I asked.

Houston replied, 'Next week, down in Santa Fe. I know she'd like that.'

Sure, and he'd like all that money he'd suddenly come into sole possession of. I decided to go for broke. 'Funny,' I said, tapping my fingers against the side of the deep fryer.

'What's that?' Houston's brow dropped lower.

'The morning I first met you, you said you'd just gotten into town.'

'What's your point?'

'You were in Prescott for a couple of days or more before coming here.'

Houston bit down on his lip. 'That's ridiculous. Where'd you hear a thing like that?'

Irwin looked amused.

There was no reason to get the waitress over at the Hotel St Michael in any trouble. I picked up a rag and wiped the folding table slowly. 'Let's just say a little birdie told me.' There was also no point in telling him I'd been snooping around in Lisa's condo and riffled through his suitcase and found a hotel receipt.

Houston was silent for a moment. 'No big deal.' He shrugged. 'I wanted a couple of days by myself. Some personal time.'

'Houston is a very sensitive man.' Irwin clamped his hand down on Houston Willoughby's shoulder and I saw the other man wince. 'He was grieving for his little sister.'

My brow shot up. 'You mean his aunt.'

Irwin looked confused. 'Oh, yeah,' he said, rubbing his hand along the back of his neck. 'His aunt.' The men shared a nervous look.

'What about you?' I asked Irwin. 'Were you in the area prior to Lisa's death as well? And how did you know where she lived?'

'Who said I did?' he demanded.

'You did.' He took a step back. 'At the diner the morning I met you.'

The two men exchanged looks again.

Irwin's eyes darkened and he kicked the ground with his boots. 'I think you ask too many questions, Maggie.' He turned on a smile. This man ran hot and cold on the turn of a dime. A man like that could be dangerous. Deadly. 'You should learn to relax, have more fun.'

'Like with you, I suppose?'

He leered. 'You suppose right. How about if we—' Irwin's eyes widened and he tapped Houston on the shoulder. 'Hey, isn't that the guy?'

Houston stuffed a hot beignet in his mouth and bit down. 'What guy?'

'Look.' Excitement rose in Irwin's voice; he swung Houston around. 'That guy.' He pointed a finger. 'Right there.'

Houston scarfed down the rest of his beignet and hoisted his coffee cup. 'What guy,' he grumbled again, 'I don't see any—' Houston halted. 'Hey!' He pointed now too. 'That's the guy,' he said, swinging back around to make sure I understood.

I didn't.

'You two keep saying that,' I said, looking at the literally hundreds of men and women in the general vicinity, 'but I have no idea who or what you're talking about.'

'The guy that broke into the condo the other night.' Houston dropped his coffee on the ground. 'Come on!' He surged forward and Irwin lurched behind.

I still had no idea who they were talking about until I saw a little man in the crowd suddenly tense up then whirl around and take off in the opposite direction, wading deeper into the crowd.

I gasped. He had a ponytail and looked Hispanic.

I didn't bother to chase Houston and Irwin. They may or may not catch the man. But I knew exactly where to find him.

THIRTY-FIVE

I checked my phone again. It was past ten-thirty and Cody's band was breaking down their gear and packing up. I was restless. I was nervous. Our stand was closed for the day, the equipment turned off and the tent sealed.

Mom had taken off earlier to listen to the band with Donna, Andy and my nephews. Aubrey had sat at the corner of the stage the entire time, casting admiring looks at Keith as he played the keyboard. Cody was the bassist and he wasn't half-bad. Not that I know anything about music. I barely recognized the tunes they played. We're from different generations.

'Maggie?'

I turned. It was Brad.

'Is everything OK?' He asked. 'You look upset.'

'No.' I smiled and ran a hand through my hair. 'Did you find out anything about Willow Willoughby or anything new on Lisa's murder?'

He shook his head. 'I've been tied up most of the day.' Brad checked his watch. 'I'm heading back to the paper now. We're running a special edition tomorrow. Lots of human interest stories, stories on the vendors, plenty of pics. It's good for business.' He waved his hand around the square. 'Most of these vendors are *Table Rock Reader* advertisers.'

'I get it.'

He grabbed my hand. 'I'm sorry we didn't get a chance to hook up today.'

His electric-blue eyes buzzed their way under my skin and I gulped. 'Yeah,' I said. 'Sorry about that.'

'We still on for tomorrow? We could catch a bite to eat.'

I told him that would be nice and he left to file his stories. Maybe I should have told him about Cody Ryan and his threat to kill me but part of me was still feeling very competitive with Brad Smith the reporter. I wanted to be the one to solve this crime, not him or the police.

I checked my phone display once more: ten forty-five. If Cody was planning to kill me he was already behind schedule.

Not that I was complaining.

I edged up closer to the stage and settled against a sycamore. Cody was joking with his bandmates. He clapped a buddy on the back then hoisted his amp and guitar. The bass was in a gig bag that he strung over his shoulder. He headed toward the public parking lot.

I glanced around. There was no sign of Andy, Mom or any of my friends. Where had Aubrey disappeared to? Had she left with Keith? And where the devil was Detective Highsmith? Probably making out somewhere with VV.

Didn't anybody care what Cody Ryan was up to? Didn't anybody care that he had his sights set on me? That I was going to be his next victim? I ran back to my tent and retrieved my Schwinn. The Hitching Post's tent was dark and quiet. Apparently Clive and Johnny hadn't stuck around for the music.

I should have left early too. If I'd been smart I'd have gone home before dark, when there were still plenty of people around. And I should have insisted on a police escort. I walked the bike to the curb. I watched Cody as he lowered his equipment into the back of his Corvette. He gazed toward the town square. I dropped my head so he wouldn't see me looking at him. A moment later, I glanced up and saw the sports car's brake lights throb red. He was leaving.

I hopped on my bike, determined to see where he was going and what he was up to. The Miller Transport truck had finally gone and I hoped that meant Brian had finally headed back home to Phoenix. I didn't need my dead ex-husband hanging around mucking up my life. I seemed to have enough mucker-uppers around here.

The car turned the corner and I redoubled my efforts. What if I lost him? I took the corner at speed and shook my fist at a honking car that blazed past me. I wondered again where Cody was heading. Maybe he was going to my apartment. Maybe he was going to surprise me. Maybe he was hoping to murder me in my sleep!

In that case, there was no real hurry.

Several cars ran up and down the street. Cody turned right. I hugged the curb and followed. But when I turned the corner it was to discover that the Corvette had disappeared. I cursed my luck and banged my hands on the handlebars. Pain was my reward.

I took a couple of minutes to catch my breath and let my quivering thighs recover, then turned around and pedaled back the way I'd come. I wanted to stop back at the café before heading home to be sure Mom had locked up the cash drawer and added the money from the tent's cash box to the floor safe.

A big truck came lurching out of a dark alleyway and I veered out of its path. I cursed as it roared ahead in a puffy cloud of smelly diesel fuel. The side of the truck read Miller Transport.

Of course. It was my idiot dead ex-husband.

I shot across the street to cut Brian off and give him a piece of my mind when a second car rocketed around the corner. It was a yellow Corvette and it was heading straight for me!

A Buick coming the opposite way honked, slammed on its brakes and bounced to a stop. I drove the Schwinn toward the sidewalk, trying to avoid being run over by the sports car or squeezed between oncoming cars. The tire bounced sharply against the curb. The bike wobbled madly despite my best efforts and I came to a stop in the alcove of a small shop. I fell over, landing on my hip, and winced in pain.

I heard steps running toward me and struggled to right myself, but between the pain and the fact that one of my legs had gone through the spokes of the front tire, I wasn't moving fast enough.

Cody could finish me off right here. Right in front of Iggy's Aquarium and Reptile Emporium, I noted through my pain-induced tears.

'Are you all right?'

I threw my hands over my head to ward off blows.

'Ms Miller? Are you all right?'

I slowly lowered my arms and squinted up. My head was pressed against the brick. 'D-Detective Highsmith?'

He held out his hand.

I rubbed the back of my head. It hurt like the dickens but at least I didn't spot any blood on my hands. 'What are you doing here? How did you get here?'

Detective Highsmith deftly extracted my leg from my wheel. 'We'd left the square and were heading back to Veronica's place,' he nodded toward the Trans Am, 'when we saw you lose control of your bike.'

I noticed Veronica sitting placidly inside powdering her nose. I guess she wasn't in a hurry to rush out and make sure I was unharmed. I allowed Highsmith to help me to me feet. Thankfully, I could still stand. I wasn't dead and nothing appeared to be broken.

He peered into my eyes. 'Have you been drinking, Ms Miller?'

I swatted his hand away. 'No, I have not been drinking!'

'Is everything OK here?' Cody popped up beside Highsmith, panting.

'Yeah. Ms Miller took a spill, is all.' Highsmith propped up my bike and gave it a shake. 'The bike looks OK.' He looked at me more closely.

Was he going to kiss me again?

A chill raced up my arms and tingled my lips.

'You look OK, too,' Highsmith said, his M&Ms running up and down my body. 'You think you need a doctor?'

'No,' I said, finally coming to my senses and glaring at Cody. 'What I need is a policeman.' I pointed my finger at the young man. 'I want you to arrest this punk for trying to murder me!'

'Murder you?' Cody's eyes flew wide open and he ran his fingers through the sides of his scalp. 'Are you crazy?' He turned to Highsmith. 'Is she crazy?'

'I'll show you who's crazy.' I grabbed Detective Highsmith's arm. 'I overheard Cody Ryan talking, no, *plotting*,' I said, 'to murder me tonight.'

Highsmith plucked my fingers from his arm. 'Please, Ms Miller.

It's been a long day. I'd like to enjoy the rest of the night, if you don't mind.'

'I do mind, Detective. This punk specifically said he was going to take care of me,' I thumped my chest, 'Maggie Miller. Tonight.'

Cody stuffed his hands in his front pockets and squinted his eyes at me. 'When exactly did I say this?'

'This afternoon at the edge of the town square. I saw you,' I answered smugly, 'talking to some orangutan-looking man. Saying how he'd get his money and you'd take care,' I said, throwing a pair of air quotes around my words, 'of Miller tonight.' I nodded sharply to put an exclamation point to my news. 'Detective,' I commanded, feeling quite good despite the fact that I'd recently gone flying up a cement curb and crashed into a brick wall with my Schwinn, 'arrest this man!'

Cody scratched beside his ear. 'Oh,' he said finally. 'Miller.'

'That's right. What are you waiting for?' I said to Detective Highsmith.

'Hank Miller.' Cody smiled. 'What made you think I was going to murder him?'

'Not him,' I said, testily. 'Me. Wait, him?' I glared suspiciously at Cody. Was he trying to rattle me? Confuse me? Because if he was, it was working.

Cody nodded. 'Yeah, we'd hired his jazz band to play at our wedding reception but Sabrina changed her mind at the last minute.' The kid shrugged Detective Highsmith's way. 'Said she wanted an oldies band. You know.' He turned to me. What? Did he think I was ancient? 'Sixties pop music. So I hired Morris and the Moonglows.'

My mouth went dry.

Highsmith cracked a smile. 'Hey, yeah. Morris McNulty and his band. I've heard those guys. They're good.'

Cody glanced at me, then at his vehicle, which rested sideways in the street. 'Can I go now?'

Highsmith nodded.

'Thanks.' Cody stepped off the curb.

'No, wait!' I cried. 'What about what just happened? He tried to kill me. Practically ran me over!' I pulled Highsmith's sleeve. 'You saw him!'

Highsmith shook his head. 'You were driving on the wrong side of the road, Ms Miller. I saw you, remember? In fact, you were jaybiking.'

Jaybiking? Was that even a thing? 'And that's the second time he's tried to kill me.'

'What?' Cody's eyes widened. 'Come on, that's crazy. Do I have to listen to this?' His eyes pleaded with the detective. 'Why would I do that?'

'You were aiming that flashy yellow sports car right at me!' I argued.

'My foot got stuck on the gas pedal, Mark,' Cody said looking rather sheepish, 'between the pedal and the mat. Besides,' he added, 'you saw her, she was driving like a manic – jaybiking!' He folded his arms across his chest. 'She doesn't even have a headlight on that thing. I'll bet that's illegal.'

I took a step back. Jaybiking wasn't even a real thing and already I'd heard it twice and used against me in the space of minutes. My world was being rocked. I was certain that Cody had tried to run me down. 'Please, I know you tried to kill me. What a good plan too, right in the middle of the street. Everybody would think it had been an accident.' I pointed at Highsmith. 'Even the police would be your witness. The perfect crime!'

'Why?' Cody demanded.

'Because,' I explained for the detective's benefit, 'you killed Lisa Willoughby—'

'The cake lady?'

'And you figured out that I was on to you.' I nodded sharply. Huh. So there. 'Go ahead, Detective,' I pointed at Cody, 'ask him where he was on the morning that Lisa was murdered.'

Highsmith looked amused. 'I don't have to.'

I slatted my eyes at him. 'Why not?'

VV yelled from the car, demanding to know if Highsmith was going to be much longer. He looked back and held up a finger, signaling he'd be a minute longer. I didn't take that as a good sign. At least, not for me. Highsmith turned my way. 'Because I know where Cody was.'

'You do?' My voice trembled.

The detective nodded. 'I do.' He glanced at the young man. 'Cody was with me, playing football.'

'Football?' I squeaked. I think it was me. Could've been a mouse.
The detective bobbed his chin. 'Football. Every Tuesday morning we play touch football over at Honicker Park.'

My hands and my heart clenched up. 'How do you know he was there the whole time?' I gave Cody a dirty look. 'He could have sneaked away. Murdered Lisa. Then come back again.'

Highsmith sighed. 'Because he's the quarterback on my team, Ms Miller.'

Cody shot me a smug look. I guess I couldn't blame him. I could've slugged him but I couldn't blame him. 'But, still, don't you think—'

Highsmith held up a palm and cut me off. 'I think I'd notice if my quarterback was missing.'

I chewed on my lip. The man had a good point. He might not be the world's greatest detective but I had to agree that there wasn't much chance of him not noticing that his quarterback had gone missing.

'Look,' said Highsmith, 'tomorrow is his wedding. Give the kid a break, Ms Miller.'

I reached for my bicycle. 'Fine,' I said. 'But if he murders me in my sleep I'm coming back to haunt you.' I climbed on the saddle. 'And VV Vargas.' Especially VV Vargas, I thought as I pedaled slowly away.

OK, I was back to square one. And square one contained Houston Willoughby and Irwin Acheson. One or both of them had to be the killer.

THIRTY-SIX

I woke up with a raging headache. Solving crimes was a pain. Not solving crimes and being made to look a fool in the process was twice the pain. I'd promised the staff that I'd open the café so I dressed quickly and headed to work. By the time Kelly and Mom came in I was itching to leave. There was a man I needed to see.

It was too far a distance to cover comfortably on the Schwinn.

Besides, my pink beauty had a fresh ding or two as a result of the previous night. One of the tires was flat now, too. I'd have to haul it over to Laura's Lightly Used or the bike shop one of these days and get it fixed. But not today.

The festival wasn't opening till noon and would be over by four so I had a lot on my plate. Thank goodness tomorrow was Labor Day. One more day of the Labor of Love and I'd be done for the year. Next year, assuming there was a next year for Maggie's Beignet Café, I'd insist on a better tent location.

I caught a bus to Navajo Junction and hoped that luck was on my side. It was. I spotted the man I was looking for running a mop along the floors outside the first-floor restrooms. Didn't he ever take a day off? His hair had not been in a ponytail the first time I'd laid eyes on him and it wasn't now, but it was certainly long enough for one.

'Excuse me,' I began. 'May I speak with you a moment, Mr Aronez?'

He nodded but said nothing. I noticed his hands tighten around the wooden mop handle.

'I'm Maggie Miller. Do you remember me?'

'Yes. Last week. You were here with the police.' His eyes danced around.

I held out my hand. 'Don't worry,' I assured him, 'you aren't in any trouble. I only wanted to speak with you.'

Well, he'd be in trouble if it turned out he was a killer. Heck, I could be in trouble if he turned out to be the killer. He was the janitor working in the Entronque building. If anybody had the opportunity, it was this guy. I suddenly wondered what I might be getting myself into.

'What about?'

'Lisa Willoughby.'

His face darkened. Why?

If the mop handle had been a neck he'd have squeezed the life out of it by now. 'She was a bad woman,' Mr Aronez said. 'I am sorry she is dead. But she was a bad woman.' He made the sign of the cross.

My nerves pulsed and I felt the air grow still. 'Did you kill her?' Maybe get into an argument, accidently push her down four flights of stairs?

'No!' The mop fell from his hand. 'No, I did not kill this woman.'

'Why don't we sit down?' I suggested. We walked in silence to the Magic Beans Coffee Shop and took an empty table near the fountain. 'Tell me about Lisa. Why was she a bad person?'

He played with his black coffee for a moment then added three sugar packets and one artificial sweetener. 'Because Ms Willoughby said bad things about Maria.' He had a small mole on the side of his nose that bounced as he repeatedly flared his nostrils.

My brow went up. 'Maria?'

He bobbed his head. 'My Maria. Maria is my daughter. She cleaned here.'

'I see.'

'Ms Willoughby accused Maria of theft, of stealing things from the stores and shops.' He spat. 'Maria would never do such a thing.'

His hand thumped the table and coffee flew from the mug. He pulled a handkerchief from his pocket and wiped the table. 'She got my daughter fired. But I believe it was Ms Willoughby herself who was stealing things.' He looked at me slyly. 'People, they do not notice me. I am only the janitor. But I notice them.' He tapped the corner of his eye. 'I am here every day but Monday. I see things.'

'Like?'

'Like Lisa Willoughby, how do you say? Stealing from shops?'

'Shoplifting?' My eyebrows flew up. 'Are you sure?'

'I am sure. Sometimes even money. I found her address online and I went to her condo. I wanted to see what I could find. Prove that Maria did not steal these things.'

'And you thought that if you could find some of the items she stole and return them that Maria could get her job back?'

He nodded sadly. 'But those men were there.'

I smiled. 'They chased you yesterday. I saw you at the festival.'

'I ran.'

There were no signs of bruising so I expected they hadn't caught him. Thank goodness for that. Who knows what those two louts might have done.

He looked across the table at me. There was sadness in his eyes. 'What will you do now? Will you tell the police I broke into Ms Willoughby's home?'

'No.' I draped my hand over his. 'I won't tell.' Besides, I'd done the same thing myself. We drank in silence for a moment. 'Did you see anything at all the morning Ms Willoughby was killed? Anything unusual?'

He shook his head slowly. 'Nothing, miss.' He drained his sweet coffee and looked at me over the rim of his cup. 'I did see Ms Willoughby arguing with one of those men that were chasing me in the square.'

I bristled. 'About six foot?' I held up my hand. 'Big teeth and big eyes? Swept-back dark hair?'

Mr Aronez nodded.

'That's her brother, Houston,' I explained.

'Yes, the brother. I know that now.'

'Did you hear what they were arguing about?'

'No.' He shook his head. 'But I could tell by their gestures that they were both quite upset.'

'I'll bet.' More confirmation that not only had Houston been in the area, he'd been in Table Rock. Had he committed murder too? 'What about the other man?' I flexed my arms. 'The one with all the muscles. Did you see him too?'

'No, only the brother.'

'And only the day before the murder.'

'Yes.'

'Monday.' I silently ran through scenarios until something Aronez had said earlier hit me. 'Wait,' I said, my fingers fiddling with my spoon while my eyes watched him intently, 'I thought you said you were off on Mondays?'

The janitor rose slowly. 'Normally, I am. But I was ill on Sunday and could not come in to work. I came in early on Monday to make up the time.' He stuffed his dirty handkerchief into the pocket of his navy jumpsuit and shuffled away.

I swore under my breath. I didn't know who or what to believe any more.

THIRTY-SEVEN

I rode the bus to the town square and got things up and running for the afternoon. When I spotted Reva across the way at the kettle-corn stand I asked Kelly to hold down the fort and hurried over 'Hello, Reva. Have you got a minute?'

She plucked a couple of fingers' worth of kettle corn from her bag and popped them in her mouth. 'What for?' She wore a loose pink frock and a matching kerchief knotted in her hair. I couldn't see her eyes because of the dark sunglasses.

'I wanted to ask you about Lisa Willoughby.'

Reva's nose wrinkled up. 'What's with you anyway? I told you everything I know.' She shoved a fistful of kettle corn into her mouth. 'Which is nothing. How about letting the police handle things? That's what they get paid to do.' She pointed to my shirt. 'You get paid to deep fry beignets, as I recall.'

My face heated up. 'Don't you care what happened to your colleague? Your friend?'

Reva formed a smile. 'Lisa was no friend of mine.'

'Mind telling me why?'

'Because I left Reva for Lisa,' interjected Ben, coming up behind Reva and wrapping an arm around her waist.

Reva smiled up at him.

'You mean you two—'

Ben nodded. 'We are now. We were before, too.' Ben dropped his head. 'Until I got stupid.'

'That's OK, sugar bear.' Reva pecked his cheek. 'I forgive you.' She gave his cheek a pinch with kettle corn sticky fingers. 'Only don't let it happen again.'

Ben blushed. 'No way. I've learned my lesson.'

I studied them both for a second, my mind racing. If they were a couple and Lisa had broken them up, wouldn't that have given Reva a reason to want something bad to happen to Lisa? Like death, perhaps?

I bit my cheek. The problem wasn't trying to figure out who might want Lisa Willoughby dead, the problem was trying to whittle down the vast list of people who might have wanted her dead. That list now included Reva, Ben, the janitor and his daughter, and, of course, Houston and Irwin. The only one I could definitely cross off my list was Cody Ryan, which was no big loss since he'd had no motive in the first place.

'When was the last time you each saw Lisa?'

Ben shrugged. 'When I got to the bakery. She was there before me.'

'Who else was there?'

'Markie and a couple of the assistant bakers in back. They usually come in around five or six a.m. depending on the orders going out for the day. I got in at eight.' Ben snatched a handful of kettle corn from Reva's bag.

'Figures,' Reva said. Clearly there had been no love lost between her and the dead woman.

Ben nodded. 'Yeah, Lisa was supposed to finish the cake yesterday but she only got around to painting on those birds that morning. Typical of her to put things off to the end.'

'Same here, timewise,' coughed Reva, choking on a kernel of kettle corn. Ben handed her an open bottle of water and she sipped. 'Thanks.' She wiped her lips. 'I got in just after eight and got to work. Like Ben said, Lisa was there then putting the finishing touches on that bird cake that had to go out first thing. The one that,' she hesitated, 'well, you know . . .'

I knew. 'What about Mr Aronez?'

'Who?' They asked in unison.

'Mr Aronez,' I repeated. 'He's the daytime maintenance man at the Entronque.'

Both shrugged. 'Never heard of him,' answered Reva.

'Never noticed him,' said Ben.

Apparently Mr Aronez was right – he went about his job relatively unseen by many of the building's occupants. There was a good chance he could have noticed Lisa Willoughby filching goods and money from shop owners without her ever paying him any attention.

'Mr Aronez claims his daughter, Maria, was a cleaner there.

He says Lisa got her fired. Claimed she was stealing things from the offices and shops.'

Reva sucked on a kernel of corn then popped it in her mouth. Her head bobbed up and down. 'I remember that.'

'Me, too,' said Ben. 'Markie had several toys stolen.'

'Collectibles,' corrected Reva.

Ben rolled his eyes. 'Yeah, collectibles.'

'Do you think she was stealing?'

'Who?' Reva asked.

'Maria Aronez.'

The cake artist shrugged. 'I have no idea. If she wasn't and got fired for it I am sorry, though.'

'Yeah,' added Ben. 'Not to speak ill of the dead, but what you say doesn't surprise me. Lisa always seemed to be getting in trouble. She couldn't help herself.'

And maybe one time she went too far or crossed the wrong person. But who?

Ben hugged Reva. 'If a cake ever falls on me and kills me, I hope it's something manly, like a giant grizzly bear cake or a giant boulder. Preferably chocolate with chocolate ganache filling.'

Reva giggled.

'Anything but a cake covered with tropical birds and flowers,' he quipped. 'I mean, that's just *flighty*.'

Reva groaned at the horrible pun.

I didn't. Alarms went off in my head. 'Say that again.'

'Huh?' Ben scratched the side of his face.

'About the birds.' Birds, there was something about birds.

'I said if I ever got killed I wouldn't want—'

I waved impatiently. 'Never mind.'

I went in search of Detective Highsmith but there was no sign of him. I dug my phone from my purse and dialed Aubrey's number. 'Answer, please, answer,' I muttered with each ring. She did. 'Aubrey!' I cried. 'Where are you? You're at the wedding, right?'

'I'm at the reception,' she replied. 'Why? What's wrong, Maggie?'

'I know who killed Lisa Willoughby and I have to get in that reception.'

There was a pregnant pause. 'Wow, that's great but, I mean, this is invitation only and I didn't issue the invitations.'

I sighed into the phone. 'Fine, tell me where it is. I'll figure out the rest.' Aubrey gave me the name of the hotel and told me the reception was being held out-of-doors in the hotel garden. I fished Highsmith's card out of my wallet and dialed. It went straight to voicemail. I cursed the man telepathically. Probably out canoodling with darling VV.

That was OK. I'd solve this crime myself. I grabbed the Schwinn and pedaled as if my life depended on it. The wedding reception was being held at the Table Rock Hotel and Convention Center, not surprising as it was probably the biggest, flashiest and priciest place around. Aubrey had told me Cody's family was rolling in money and Sabrina's parents appeared to be well-heeled, too. Must be nice to be young and in love. And rich.

I handed the pink bike off to the burgundy-and-gold-liveried valet who looked at me like I was crazy. What? He'd never seen a Schwinn before? I found Detective Highsmith manning the entrance to the garden. He looked mighty fine in a black suit with a crisp white shirt and black tie. 'Detective!' I shouted. 'How come you aren't answering your phone?'

His lips barely moved. 'I didn't think it was important.'

'It was me.'

He blinked once. 'I know.'

Did this guy wake up dreaming of ways to be annoying or did it come naturally to him? 'You're here for the wedding?' I inquired. It even looked like he'd put some sort of gel in his hair, giving it a wet look. Not bad. I could get used to it.

Highsmith nodded. 'They hired me to work security.'

I rolled my eyes. 'Security? At a wedding? They're afraid of party crashers?' I stepped past him. 'This is Table Rock. What kind of wedding crashers could they get? An alien or two?' Heck, aliens could well be on the guest list.

He blocked my way. 'Sorry, invitation only.'

'You have to let me in,' I said. 'I know who killed Lisa Willoughby and I can prove it.'

Highsmith sighed. 'Come on, Ms Miller. You always think you know who did it. You're not Miss Marple and this is no story book crime. Go home. Leave finding Lisa Willoughby's killer to me.'

'But I'm telling you—'

He pressed closer and looked down his nose at me. 'No,' he said sternly. 'I'm telling you. Go home.'

I opened my mouth to protest and he stuck out his hand. 'This is a wedding, for crying out loud. A joyous occasion.' He gave me a gentle shove toward the exit. 'Let's let the happy young couple enjoy the evening.'

I fumed as he guided me out of the hotel entrance. There was no sign of the Schwinn. I guess my bike wasn't high class enough to be seen directly in front of the hotel with the Cadillacs and Mercedes. No matter. I was getting into that wedding reception and nothing was going to stop me.

There was a flagstone path along the right side of the hotel that ran beside an eight-foot-tall adobe wall. The gardens were on the opposite side. Lights spilled over and the sounds of sixties bubblegum music, laughter and conversation filled the night air. I followed the path as it wound around the corner and came to a wrought-iron door cut into the side of the wall. Bushes flanked either side of the entrance.

There was no sign of any security. I stepped toward the entrance. Ellen Collins, the officer I'd met at the Entronque the morning of Lisa's murder was pacing back and forth on the inside. She was wearing a simple navy pantsuit, but nonetheless looked all business. I moved back into the shrubs.

I pressed my back to the wall, wondering how would I get past her. Then it came to me. I picked up a small rock and heaved it gently over the wall. A little noise would distract Collins long enough for me to get inside. After that, if anybody spotted me I'd claim I was working for the caterers. Dressed in my work clothes, no one would ever believe I was a guest of the reception.

A moment later, I heard a small crash. It sounded like the rock had hit some dinnerware. I peeked around the wall. My rock rested atop one of the banquet tables among some broken dishes. Voices were chattering and pointing in all directions. Officer Collins was surveying the damage. Maybe they'd take it for a meteorite and let it go at that.

This was my chance. I pushed open the gate and closed it

silently behind me. The band hadn't stopped playing. I recognized the orangutan-looking man – no offense to orangutans everywhere – behind the mike. It was Morris McNulty. He was belting out a tune and had an electric red guitar strapped around his neck. The big bass drum was emblazoned with silver letters bearing the name of the band, Morris and the Moonglows. So Cody had been telling the truth. I was embarrassed to think I had once thought he was a murderer.

I hated being proven wrong and it was happening all too much lately. I was determined not to let it happen again. I slinked past the table holding the wedding cake. I counted seven immaculate snow-white fondant-covered tiers. Was this Ben's work? A spiral column of perfect pink sugar flowers gently climbed its side. I resisted the urge to pluck a petal for myself though I had skipped dinner.

There was no sign of Samantha Higgins. Sabrina Higgins, her daughter, was out on the dance floor with an older gentleman I imagined to be her father. She'd chosen a princess gown and it suited her – in more ways than one. I also saw Aubrey and Keith and only stopped myself from waving in the nick of time. I didn't want to draw attention to myself.

I continued the search for Mrs Higgins among the dozens of tables in the garden. Highsmith spotted me across the sea of people and I saw his jaw tense. He quickly stepped toward me. I dodged down a side path and suddenly found myself hopelessly lost.

A strong hand grabbed my shoulder from behind. 'Come on, Ms Miller.' I recognized the detective's voice before I saw him. 'It's time to go home.'

I leapt from his grip. 'No! I can't.' I heard his steps behind me as I ran. 'Samantha Higgins is the killer.'

Highsmith laughed as he loped after me and pulled me to a stop. He folded his arms across his chest and curled his fingers in a gesture for me to speak. 'OK, spill it.'

I caught my breath then said, 'It's the cake.'

'The cake?'

I nodded. 'The wedding cake that Lisa Willoughby was taking to the vow renewal on the morning she was killed,' I explained. 'It was the birds.'

Highsmith frowned. 'First you tell me it's the cake and now you tell me it's the birds. Which is it, Ms Miller?'

'Both,' I said. 'It's the birds and it's the cake. 'The cake the Robinsons ordered for their vow renewal had birds on it.'

'Who?'

'The Robinsons,' I said with growing exasperation. 'They own the bird supply store on Smile and Main – Robinsons' Nest.'

He looked at me blankly.

'It was their cake that Lisa was supposed to be delivering when she was killed.'

'Yeah,' Highsmith answered. 'I interviewed them myself. They were surrounded by guests and family. There's no way they had anything to do with Lisa Willoughby's death.'

'I know that.' I waved my hand at him, unable to hide my annoyance. 'But their cake held the key to the murder. The identity of the murderer.'

'I'm listening,' Highsmith replied. He rubbed the band of his watch. 'Though why I don't know.'

I chose to ignore that remark. 'The Robinsons' cake was decorated with birds.'

'You're repeating yourself, Ms Miller.'

'Well, I wouldn't have to if you'd just—' I stopped myself before I said something I might come to regret. Like a night behind bars for insulting an officer of the law. I took a breath and started slowly. 'Reva and Ben from the bakery told me that Lisa only added the birds at the last minute the morning she was killed.'

'So?' Highsmith looked bored.

'So,' I answered smugly, 'Mrs Higgins told me that Lisa was found under a bird cake.' I waited for the detective to congratulate me but it looked like it was going to be a long wait. 'How did she know?' I cocked my brows at him. 'It wasn't in the newspaper. And the cake was such a mess that you could hardly tell by looking at the cake anyway. I know, I was there. That cake was a trail of cake and frosting and one big pile of mush on the bottom of the stairwell.'

'You forget – I saw it too.'

'OK, then. How did she know?'

Highsmith pulled at his chin. 'I don't know, Ms Miller. Your theory's got a lot of holes in it.'

'Like what?'

'Like lack of motive for one. Like maybe she heard from someone at the bakery what the cake was going to look like. Like maybe she knows the Robinsons and they told her.'

I had no answer to any of that so I asked him a question. 'Where is Mrs Higgins? Have you seen her tonight?'

'Of course I've seen her. She and her husband toasted the bride not half an hour ago.' The detective sighed. 'Why don't you head home? Get some rest. I'll talk to Mrs Higgins again if it makes you feel better.'

If he wasn't bigger, stronger and an officer of the law I'd have kicked him in the shin for his patronizing tone. But since he was all of the above . . . I ran down a small path.

'Hey!' Highsmith shouted and chased.

I dodged through a thorny hedge, wincing in pain as the sharp sticks scratched my arms and legs. I stumbled out the other side into a modest clearing, lit by nothing but the stars and the moon. A small adobe brick wishing well sat in the center of a circle of small black stones.

And a figure in a slinky white gown and red heels lay face down beside the wishing well.

THIRTY-EIGHT

Mrs Higgins' lifeless eyes looked toward me. I sucked in a breath and took a step forward.

'Stop!' Detective Highsmith tumbled into the clearing and pulled me back. 'Don't touch anything!' I nodded. He pushed me behind him and knelt down, placing his hand on the side of her neck. 'She's dead,' he said, coming up slowly.

I forced myself to breathe slowly, deeply. I felt like I was going to pass out. 'What do you suppose happened?' I wasn't sure why I was whispering but I was.

Highsmith's voice was firm and in control. 'Her neck's been broken by the looks of it.'

I whimpered, my hands flying to my neck.

'Still think she's your killer?' Highsmith's hands searched his coat.

I shook my head in the negative. How could I have been so wrong? And so often!

Footsteps pounded up the pebble path. Cody burst around the corner opposite the wishing well, which blocked his view of Mrs Higgins corpse. 'What's going on? Ms Miller? Mark? What are you two doing out here? I heard shouting. Is everything—'

Highsmith motioned for him to come around to our side of the wishing well. 'Take a look. But don't get close.'

Cody swallowed and edged around to our side. He gasped. 'It's Sabrina's mom!' He blanched and pulled at his shirt collar. 'What happened to her?' His eyes went to the detective. 'Heart attack, maybe? Why did she come out here?'

Highsmith shook his head no. 'Looks like somebody crushed her trachea is my guess.' His hands patted his pants' pockets. 'But we'll let the ME decide that.'

The detective's eyes scanned the ground for clues. I heard a song in the distant background. It was hard to imagine a party going on while a woman lay here dead. 'I'm afraid this might put a damper on your celebration.'

Cody shrugged. 'It can't be helped.'

I watched mutely. I was confused. If she was dead, who killed her? And who killed Lisa Willoughby? And why?

'You two keep an eye on the body,' ordered Highsmith, patting his jacket one last time. 'I must have dropped my cell phone back there.' He looked at me like it was my fault. What? Did I tell him to chase me? 'I'm gonna go pick it up and call this in. Stay together. The killer could still be out there,' he said firmly, pointing a finger at me. 'Don't touch anything.'

I nodded and promised I wouldn't. Cody shot me a nervous look and promised the same.

'What do you suppose happened to her?' I whispered as Highsmith disappeared. It was cold and I couldn't stop shivering. 'I mean, how was she killed?'

Cody's face was half-hidden in shadows as we crouched on

either side of the now-deceased Samantha Higgins. 'Strangled,' he replied. 'For sure.' He turned his face toward me. 'Like Mark said.'

I gazed at Mrs Higgins' neck but in the darkness it was impossible to discern any signs of strangulation – only a few scratches. 'How can you tell?'

Cody pushed himself off the ground. 'Easy,' he said, pulling a long black tie from his tuxedo coat. 'I used this.' The tie dangled from his fingers, its end lightly dancing along the ground.

'What?' What was Cody talking about? Had he lost his mind? Was he blathering? Too much stress what with the wedding and now a dead mother-in-law?

'I said it was easy,' Cody smiled. He jerked the tie up and down. 'I used this on Mrs Higgins. In fact,' he said coolly, stepping around the corpse, 'let me show you.'

It was only then that I noticed his bare neck and his unbuttoned shirt collar. Cody hadn't been wearing his tie when he stumbled into the clearing.

I opened my mouth and my scream died in my throat. I tumbled backward as I tried to rise. Cody grabbed me by both arms and yanked me upright. I felt his breath against my ear as he pressed me against him.

'And I'd have dumped her body in the well and been done with her if you hadn't stuck your nose in and showed up.' He gave my arms a vicious pull and pain shot across my back, bringing tears to my eyes. 'Always showing up where you're not wanted, aren't you, Ms Miller?' His breath was hot and moist.

'Why?' I cried. 'Why would you murder your mother-in-law?' I mean, he'd been married less than a couple of hours. How bad could she be?

His hand slapped over my mouth. 'Quiet!' He shoved me toward bushes. 'I had to kill her. She wouldn't quit. She killed Lisa and was blackmailing me.'

I bit down on his fingers. He cursed me out but removed his hand. 'I was right? Samantha Higgins murdered Lisa Willoughby?'

Cody pulled back to a corner of the walled-in garden. Between the darkness and the thick vegetation there was no chance that anyone in the wedding party would see us here. 'That's right. Then she tried to blackmail me.'

'Blackmail?' Nothing Cody said was making any sense.

'Yeah,' spat Cody.

'What is this all about?' And how was I going to get out of this alive? Where was Detective Highsmith?

Cody blew out a breath and pulled my arms together behind my back. I winced as pain shot up my arms and back. 'Mrs Higgins killed Lisa because she found out that Lisa and I were fooling around.'

'Fooling around?' My eyebrow rose. 'Like having an affair?'

He shrugged. 'It was just for kicks, you know.'

I didn't.

'I mean, it didn't mean anything. I still planned to marry Sabrina. We were only fooling around.'

'And Mrs Higgins didn't like it?' Can't say I blamed her for that. But murder?

'Mrs Higgins confronted Lisa about our affair. I guess she was afraid I might not marry Sabrina and leave her for Lisa. Lisa and Mrs Higgins argued in the stairwell and Mrs Higgins flipped out and gave her a shove. Believe me, you do not want to make that woman mad.'

'She must have been mad at you too.'

'Yeah, but she still wanted me to marry her daughter. I think part of that was to get her hands on my family's money.' Cody's family were old money rich. 'Sabrina confided in me that her family is having financial problems. Their house is in foreclosure.'

Samantha Higgins didn't strike me as the kind of woman who'd enjoy seeing her financial and social status decline. If she thought Cody and Lisa were getting serious she might have figured her last chance at saving the Higgins' fortunes was to break them up for good. Lisa's death had certainly accomplished that.

'Mrs Higgins told me what she'd done and said that if I didn't pay her half a million bucks she'd tell Sabrina about my affair with Lisa next.' He pushed me to the ground. 'I couldn't let that happen. I love Sabrina, so I strung her along until after the wedding.'

'Why not simply pay her?'

'Are you kidding? How would I explain that to my dad?'
Cody chuckled. 'She met me out here in the garden thinking
I'd hand over a pile of my dad's money. But I couldn't live
with her blackmailing me for the rest of my life.'

'Please,' I said, 'let me go. Turn yourself in. I'm sure
everybody will understand.'

He snorted. 'Yeah, right.'

True, I didn't believe it either. 'So now what? Are you going
to kill me, too?'

'Of course,' Cody said glibly. He wiped his hand on his shirt.
'But I'll tell Mark you attacked me and ran away.' He chuckled.
'Thanks for biting me. Gives my story some meat.'

'Glad to oblige,' I said dryly.

'It would have been simpler and less complicated if I'd
been able to go with my original plan. But I'll tell him you
must have murdered Mrs Higgins and then disappeared after
attacking me.'

'Why am I supposed to have done that?' Not that I much
cared what his crazy reasoning was but anything to keep him
talking and me breathing.

He smiled devilishly. 'Because you're crazy. You killed Lisa
then Mrs Higgins.'

'No one will ever believe that.'

'No,' he said, a twinkle in his eyes, 'not even when they
search your apartment and find Lisa's purse – a purse that also
contains her gun – under your sofa?'

My eyes widened. 'How – how did you know that?'

'I watched you break into her place and leave with it.'

I frowned with disgust. 'Then you must have been spying
on me when I hid it under the sofa. Pervert.'

'Hey,' he replied with a slight shrug, 'if you don't want people
peeping in, close your curtains.'

'Why would I kill Lisa?'

'That will have to remain one of life's great mysteries. I
mean, with you being dead, the answer dies with you.'

'You'll never get away with it, Cody.' I sounded like a bad
movie. And my life was about to end like one.

'I don't know.' Cody's fingers felt like icicles on my shoulder.

'It's a big desert. I don't think anyone is going to find you very soon. At least not before the coyotes do.'

I shivered. Would coyotes and javelinas soon be picking my bones?

'And when they do find you, they'll think you tried to escape and died of exposure.' He leaned toward me. 'There won't be enough of you left for them to know that I've strangled you.'

The band had stopped playing. I took the opportunity to scream. 'Help! He—'

Cody caught me unawares, backhanding me across the mouth. I tasted blood and dug my nails into his arm before he struck again. Cody clamped his hand over mine. I grunted and slammed my heel on the top of his foot. He cursed and his hand relaxed.

I twisted free and ran, not knowing where I was or where I was running to. I tore through bushes and splashed through a koi pond working my way toward the lights and the sounds of the wedding party. The lights were getting closer. So were the sounds of Cody's steps.

'Stop her!' Cody shouted as he appeared suddenly to my left mere feet away.

'Stop him!' I yelled at Highsmith. 'He killed Samantha Higgins!'

Cody bolted through the crowd. I veered right, dodging between tables of startled wedding guests.

The band held still. Aubrey covered her face in embarrassment.

Cody ran past the stage. Detective Highsmith jumped over a crowded table, landing on his feet in front of him. The detective had some moves.

Cody took a swing at the detective. Highsmith slammed his fist into his nose. Cody eyes crossed over and he looked startled as he landed on his butt in front of the table bearing the wedding cake. But a moment later he was on his feet once again, a sharp knife in his hand. Probably the one meant to cut the cake, but now he was intending to use it to take a slice out of Detective Highsmith.

I gripped the edge of the table with all my strength and lifted. I'm not normally one to waste a good dessert, let alone a seven-tier beauty like this one, but I was about to make an exception. The table teetered for a moment, then gravity took over. The tall cake toppled, smacking Cody in the head. Seven tiers of fondant-covered cake are heavier than you might think. He crumbled to the ground. The knife slid across the flagstones. Officer Ellen Collins scooped it up.

Highsmith bent and picked up the trash. That being Cody Ryan.

THIRTY-NINE

J ohnny and Clive waved briskly from across the square. From the smiles on their faces I could tell they were relieved that Lisa Willoughby's murder had been solved and they had been cleared of any involvement.

I waved back and caught a yawn in my hand. Now if I could just get through Labor Day, life could get back to normal. Instead of my typical khaki shorts and Maggie's Beignet Café-logoed polo shirt, I'd selected a black skirt and frilly white blouse.

'Woo-hoo, look at you,' Aubrey cooed. 'Fan-cy.'

The corner of my mouth turned down. 'Hey, it's a holiday,' I said brusquely. 'A girl can get dressed up if she wants to.' I smoothed down my skirt. 'In fact, it would be unpatriotic not to.' Or so I claimed.

The fact that Brad and I had arranged to hook up later had absolutely nothing to do with my choice of outfits. Neither did the perfume I'd tossed behind my ears and along the hollow of my neck with its fragrant hints of vetiver and patchouli.

Clive hurried over sporting a coat and bowtie, of course. The coat was unbuttoned. Guess he was going casual. He latched his arms around me in a bear hug and squeezed.

'Ouch!' I chuckled. 'Let go!' It hadn't hurt a bit – Clive's more teddy bear than grizzly – but I thought it important to keep his confidence up.

'Sorry.' Clive allowed my feet to touch the ground.

'That's OK, Clive.' I checked my shirt for wrinkles.

'Thank you, thank you, thank you,' Clive said, gripping my right hand in his. 'I can't tell you how relieved we are that Lisa's killer has been caught. And you!' he cried. 'We heard you were almost killed yourself.' He traced his finger along my arm. 'We wouldn't want to lose you, dear.'

I shrugged sheepishly. 'Well, I don't know about that.'

Clive shook his head. 'Who knew Cody Ryan would turn out to be such a cold-blooded killer?' He fluttered a hand in front of his chest. 'Samantha Higgins, too! To think,' Clive said as he shot a look over his shoulder, 'we designed Sabrina and Samantha's dresses!'

'Is it true that Mrs Higgins was trying to blackmail Cody?' Aubrey asked. 'I always thought the Higgins had plenty of money. She had that gallery. Mr Higgins is a CPA.'

'Bad investments? Gambling?' I speculated. 'We may never know exactly.' So far, Mr Higgins had lawyered up and refused to talk. I told them how Andy's source down at the police station had told me that the DNA report on some skin samples under Lisa Willoughby's fingernails had finally come in from Phoenix. The sample pointed to Samantha Higgins. That explained the scratches on Mrs Higgins' neck and why she'd been wearing a scarf every time I saw her.

Clive wagged his head. 'Johnny heard from your brother-in-law Andy who heard from his friend from the Table Rock Police Department that the gallery had been losing oodles of money. She was in danger of losing it.' And apparently would do anything, including murder and blackmail, to keep it. She was probably thrilled when Sabrina and Cody got engaged and furious when she discovered Cody and Lisa's affair. There'd been an extremely volatile personality lurking beneath that cool exterior.

'I never would have believed it,' Aubrey said.

If I hadn't lived through it I might not have believed it myself. I took some satisfaction in knowing that I hadn't been completely wrong about Cody even if I had missed the mark on Samantha Higgins. The police had found a folder on the gallery owner's computer that contained an elevator out-of-order sign file that they think she printed out and used to get Lisa to go up the stairs. Despite Mrs Higgins telling Cody that it was an argument that got out of hand, the police speculated that she had been waiting there at the top of the steps for her chance to get rid of Lisa once and for all.

'And to think,' Aubrey went on, 'that Cody actually thought he could try to blame you for Mrs Higgins' murder.'

'I don't think that was his original plan. He only intended to dump her body in the well and let everyone think she had simply disappeared. But when I stumbled on him,' I paused for a moment, unable to erase the fresh memory of last night, 'he was desperate. He had to improvise.'

'What a hideous fellow,' Clive remarked.

I agreed.

'Cody must be crazy,' Aubrey remarked.

'I hear that's the way his family's high-priced lawyers are planning to go. With a plea of insanity.' I could only hope that justice prevailed.

'What about Houston and Irwin?' That was Aubrey again.

'I hear they've both left town, probably gone back to Santa Fe.' I hoped we'd seen the last of those two.

'Johnny is very, very grateful to you, Maggie.' Clive glanced toward The Hitching Post's tent. 'You and your brother-in-law. He'd come and thank you himself, but . . .'

I nodded. 'I know.' He was Johnny Wolfe. Not a man big on apologies. To know him was to love him, or at least tolerate him.

In small doses.

Small, distant doses. I caught Johnny looking our way and waved. He scowled.

Yep, that's Johnny. 'I think he wants you, Clive.'

Clive kissed us each on the cheek. 'Come by our tent later,' he said. 'We're giving away our door prize this afternoon.'

'Door prize?' I said.

'What is it?' Aubrey asked.

'A free design consultation with Johnny, along with a free veil.' Clive replied. 'Didn't you enter?'

I shook my head in the negative.

Aubrey bit her lip. What? Was she hearing the peal of distant wedding bells?

'Go ahead,' I said. 'I can hold down the fort long enough for you to go fill out an entry form.'

I couldn't help smiling as Aubrey and Clive exited the rear of the booth and headed toward The Hitching Post's tent, deep in animated conversation.

Yep, today was going to be a good day, labor or not. The coast was clear and my stomach was in the throes of hunger. I grabbed a cranberry-orange muffin from an open cardboard box on Karma Koffee's side and shoved it in my mouth.

'Did you just steal a muffin?' a steely voice demanded. Trish Gregory's matching steely eyes glared at me.

My face must have been strawberry red. 'Nomph,' I managed to say, crumbs spilling out of my mouth and clinging to my wet lips like witnesses for the prosecution. I forced a swallow. 'Just eating my sandwich.' I grinned feebly. Both Gregorys were looking at me now. I pulled a five-dollar bill from my cashbox and placed it in Trish's outstretched hand. 'I was going to pay for it.'

Trish stared at me a moment longer, made humphing noises that sounded something like a whale who'd swallowed a walrus that had gone sour, then turned away, back to her long line of customers.

I loathed that woman.

I mean, I was going to pay for it. I didn't mind paying for it. I just minded the Gregorys knowing that I was willing to pay for one of their muffins.

'I saw that,' said my mom, joining me inside the tent.

'Hi, Mom. Thanks for coming.'

'Glad to help. Look, here comes a customer.'

I spun around. It was Brad. He'd shown up with a stunning young brunette on his arm. She wore black leggings that showed off a pair of svelte legs and a white shirt that stretched tightly across her chest.

'Hey, Maggie.' Brad smiled. 'This is Sophie. Sophie, this is my friend, Maggie, the woman I was telling you about. Congratulations,' he said. 'I hear you helped solve another murder.'

Friend? That's all I was? His friend? I bit down on my lower lip. I mean, I didn't know if Brad and I were more than that or even if I wanted us to be . . . but friend?

'A pleasure,' Sophie said, extending her hand. She wore a shiny diamond on her right hand. Her left arm was locked through Brad's.

'What can I get you two?' I asked rather stonily.

'Nothing for me,' Brad replied. He hadn't lost his smile. 'Sophie?'

She shook those lustrous locks of hers in the negative. No doubt fearful of adding an ounce of fat to her fat-free figure.

'I came to see if you were free to join us later?' Brad explained. 'Share a dance?'

Was this guy out of his mind?

The band was working its way through an eighties ballad.

'You can tell us all about last night.'

So that was his angle. Brad the snake slash womanizer slash reporter wanted the inside scoop on Cody Ryan, Samantha Higgins and the whole Lisa Willoughby murder investigation. He'd probably take credit for solving the entire thing, too. 'Well . . .'

'Ah, Maggie Miller!'

I looked over Brad's shoulder. 'Doctor Vargas!' I smiled so big my face hurt. Doctor Vargas worked at the local medical center and we'd met on a couple of occasions. 'How are you?' My pulse quickened. What was it about this doctor that made my heart race? Certainly not the fact that he was Veronica Vargas' brother. I still couldn't figure that out – they were like two different species.

'Please, call me Daniel.'

I nodded. 'Daniel it is.' Brad and Sophie exchanged looks. 'What can I get you, Daniel?'

'How about the next dance?'

'Love to,' I said. I shot Brad and his girl toy a triumphant look. 'Take over for me, Mom?'

'Of course, dear,' Mom replied. 'Don't worry about a thing. I can handle the booth.'

Daniel cradled me in his arms and danced me slowly across the lawn. It was a good thing he knew what he was doing because I sure didn't. I'm a lousy dancer.

I bumped into Aubrey and Keith at the end of the dance. Daniel had to leave.

'What did you say to Brad and his sister to get him so upset?' Aubrey asked.

'Sister?'

'Yeah, Sophie,' replied Aubrey. 'He was truly, truly upset. I ran into Sophie at the refreshment stand and she told me that you and Brad had plans to meet up and that you dumped him for Doctor Vargas.'

'Oh, brother,' I moaned. Or should I say, oh, sister. 'You mean Sophie is Brad's sister?'

Aubrey nodded. 'His younger sister. I went to school with her.'

I was going to owe Brad an apology. I hate apologies, especially when I'm on the giving end rather than the receiving.

'Last call, Ms Miller!' Caitie Conklin announced, lifting up the tent flap and hollering my name.

'Last call for what?'

'It's Sunday afternoon – Labor of Love closes in an hour. It's time for my annual Charity Cut Extreme Event,' the salon owner explained, fashioning quotation marks with her fingers. 'What do you say? Only ten bucks a cut. All the money and hair goes to charity.'

My brows formed a V. 'The hair too?' I pulled at my split ends. I still hadn't gotten around to giving myself a trim.

'Yes.'

I shrugged. The woman had practically butchered me the last time I'd let her cut my hair and left me with bangs that were only now a fading memory. 'I suppose so,' I said cautiously. It was hard to pass up a ten-dollar haircut. 'But no bangs.' I waved my finger at her.

'No bangs?' Conklin snapped her fingers. 'No problem. So are you in or not?'

'I'm in,' I answered. The canvas fell to the ground. I swung around to Aubrey. 'How about you?'

Aubrey thrust her arms out. 'No way,' she said quickly. 'Not me.' She shook her head. 'I like my hair just the way it is.'

'That makes two of us,' Keith added with an enigmatic grin.

'Suit yourself. But the money does go to charity.' Hey, a little guilt never hurt anyone. Just ask my mom. And the hair went to charity too? I edged around my folding table and squeezed past the support post and rope to enter the Salon de Belezza's tent. Who wants buckets full of hair clippings? What on earth could they use them for?

'Have a seat, Ms Miller.' Caitie snapped a gown in the air. Bits of floating hair tickled my nostrils as she fastened the ties around my neck.

I twisted my head around and gave the stylist my sternest look. 'Remember, no bangs.'

Caitie smiled. It was only later that I realized there had been a touch of evil in that smile. Sort of like Dracula before he bites down on that poor girl in the skimpy nightie lying in bed when he promises he only wants a drop and that it won't hurt a bit. 'Not a problem,' she quickly replied. 'You worry too much. Relax.'

I tilted my head back and felt the warm water wash over my scalp. It had been a long weekend. Skilled hands massaged gardenia-scented shampoo through my follicles. I sighed. This was heaven. I shut my eyes and enjoyed the sensation. Sleep threatened to overtake me.

A few moments later, Caitie was swabbing me with a damp towel. Her hand touched down on my forehead. 'Now, relax, Ms Miller. Lean back and close your eyes.'

She didn't have to ask me twice. I closed my eyes and listened to the sound of her shears snipping quietly away. After this, I'd pack up the tent, maybe grab a bite to eat then go home and sleep for a week. Maybe soak in the tub . . .

I half-dozed and only came to my senses when Conklin unwound the paper towelette from my neck and untied my bib. I opened my eyes. The world was all blurry.

The stylist held out a hand mirror. 'Well, what do you think?'

I leaned forward. My heart stopped. I pounded my chest with my palm to get it started again. It did no good. It was like my heart was frozen solid. I rolled my tongue over my lips. I ground my fists against my eyes, pulled the hand mirror from Caitie Conklin's hand and looked at the image reflected back at me. 'I'M A BILLIARD BALL!' I swung madly around. 'A RED ONE!' I twisted the mirror left. I twisted the mirror right. I was an odd-shaped billiard ball from any and all angles. My hair, what was left of it, lay like a finely manicured lawn along my skull. I was hideous. 'You – you scalped me!'

Caitie looked confused. 'Of course. That's what this is all about.'

'Scalping people?' I hissed, rising from the salon chair before she could take what was left.

'Yeah. Why are you getting so excited? It's the Charity Cut Extreme Event. I cut off all your hair for ten bucks.' She folded the gown and tossed it atop a nylon gym bag on the grass. 'The money and the hair goes to charity.' She scooped my hair off the edge of the basin and placed it carefully in a big Ziploc bag, which she added to a pile in an open cardboard box.

'I look like a bald circus clown.'

She fingered what little length of hair I had across my fore-head. 'I don't know,' she said, scrunching her lips, 'I don't think it looks so bad.'

'It. Looks. Hideous,' I said through gritted teeth.

Caitie shrugged. 'Guess you can't please everyone.' She held out her hand. 'That'll be ten dollars, please.'

I grabbed my purse and yanked out two fives that I'd taken from the cashbox. 'I don't know why I'm paying you. You should be paying me for what you've done.'

Caitie looked down her considerable nose at me. 'This money and that hair go to cancer patients.'

My heart stopped once again. If this kept happening I could be in serious trouble. 'Oh,' I said, my voice soft. 'I didn't know.' I handed her another twenty.

'Why didn't you warn me?' I cried, ducking back to my tent where Keith and Aubrey were busy tearing everything down.

'Excuse me, ma'am?' Aubrey smirked. 'But do I know you?'

I snarled. 'Aubrey.' I shook my fist at her.

'Sorry,' she giggled. 'I truly, truly thought you knew. I mean, everybody knows. It's like a Table Rock tradition.'

I huffed. 'It's a catastrophe.'

'You look fine,' Laura assured me, having come to pick up her things. She hoisted the empty deep fryer. 'I'll take this to my car.' She took three steps then stopped. 'After we're finished here, what do you all say we hit Hanging Louie's for dinner?'

Aubrey looked at Keith, who nodded. She took his hand. 'Sounds good to us.'

'Me, too,' I said grudgingly. I spotted some smart-alec kid

taking a picture of me on his phone, snicker and nudge his girlfriend who snickered too. He'd no doubt be posting it online for the world to see. I was doomed.

Maybe I'd stop and purchase a new hat on the way to the restaurant. And a new pair of giant sunglasses. Go in disguise.

'Wonderful,' deadpanned Laura. 'You know, they have a couple of pool tables in back. Suddenly I'm in the mood for a game.' She looked at me and winked, then took off running.

I narrowed my eyes and gave her a couple of seconds' head start. Laura might be fast but I knew I was going to be faster. She was lugging that deep fryer, after all.